ALSO BY ELON DANN

Clockwise to Titan (prequel to *Awe of Mercury*)

AWE OF MERCURY

ELON DANN

HOT
KEY
BOOKS

First published in Great Britain in 2014 by Hot Key Books
Northburgh House, 10 Northburgh Street, London EC1V 0AT

A CIP catalogue record for this book is available from the British Library.

ISBN: 978-1-4714-0119-0

1

This book is typeset in 10.5 Berling LT Std using Atomik ePublisher

Printed and bound by Clays Ltd, St Ives Plc

Hot Key Books supports the Forest Stewardship Council (FSC),
the leading international forest certification organisation, and is
committed to printing only on Greenpeace-approved FSC-certified paper.

www.hotkeybooks.com

Hot Key Books is part of the Bonnier Publishing Group
www.bonnierpublishing.com

A neveryday story of:
seeking and never finding; of things, and things inside
things; of opposites and the opposites of opposites; of
never fully understanding or being complete.

(And cheese.)

For Louise
And all big sisters, everywhere.

Whoso beset him round
With dismal stories,
Do but themselves confound;
His strength the more is.
No lion can him fright,
He'll with a giant fight,
But he will have a right
To be a pilgrim.

Hobgoblin nor foul fiend
Can daunt his spirit;
He knows he at the end
Shall life inherit.
Then fancies fly away,
He'll fear not what men say,
He'll labour night and day
To be a pilgrim.

From 'To Be a Pilgrim' by John Bunyan

Contents

Prependix

Mo and his fellow inmates make use of a clandestine communications method known to prisoners all over the world, a technique that goes by many names and accommodates many variations.

Imagine the alphabet of your language – if it has one – arranged in a grid, perhaps like so. The same grid must be used by all people and learned off by heart.

	1	2	3	4	5
1	A	B	C	D	E
2	F	G	H	I	J
3	K	L	M	N	O
4	P	Q	R	S	T
5	U	V	W	X	Y

To pass on a message, transmit the coordinates of each letter. Everyone must agree if the order is columns then rows, or vice versa.

'HARETE' would be sent (in column-row style) as 3-2, 1-1, 3-4, 5-1, 5-4, 5-1.

If the two people are within sight of one another, they can

send the coordinates by holding up the corresponding number of fingers on one hand.

Alternatively, they may do such things as stamp their foot or flash a torch the correct number of times, with a short pause between the column and row values and a longer pause between each letter.

Sightless communication can be made by, for example, tapping on someone's leg, thumping on a wall, or rapping on a water pipe. Depending on the details of the building's plumbing, this last method may allow messages to be sent over long distances.

Most people find it easier to learn 'the grid' than to memorize the Morse code.

2-2, 5-3, 5-3, 4-1, 2-3, 1-5, 3-1, 1-3, 5-1, 4-4, 3-1, 1-1, 1-4, 4-2, 4-3, 2-2

Part 1:

Breakout

Chapter 1

The light was already on when I woke up, air was filtering down through the vents, the Spiral was chuntering and clicking and humming to itself as it booted up for another day.

I rolled off the ledge I'd been perched on during the night and planted my bare feet on the dusty cement floor, a taste like hot turpentine swirling in my mouth, baubles of sweat as big as a bus's wheel nuts dripping from me. Rush hour would not happen for another thirty minutes or so, I had time to myself. I flushed the reverberating debris of the night's dreams from my mind and reoriented myself. Where had I got to?

Painted on the wall facing me were the letters IV. After the chaos of the morning commute, when every penitent had shifted through his right-hand door into the vacant pen there, the characters would read III.

I breathed out, long and loud. Still on four! That wasn't so bad. Plenty of time. I'd dreamed . . . no, the nocturnal apparitions had already boiled away.

There hadn't been a window since pen fifty-eight. After that first twelve, the Spiral had screwed the wedge-shaped cells underground, sinking each one deeper into the earth than

13

the last. Even so, I could tell what the weather was like up on the distant surface. The air streaming in through the grille in the pen's ceiling was obscenely hot and dry. Up above me, the summer sun would already be flogging the life from the crumbling concrete of the Establishment, bombarding it with heat and light like a drunk hurling billiard balls in a barroom barney. There would be a cloud too, a wispy low-altitude haze banded and stranded with streaks of brown and orange and gently scintillating. I knew that because I could smell it; even over the twin reeks of sweat and the pen's uncovered slop bucket, I could smell the pungent, pugnacious, catch-and-scratch the back of your throat tincture of burning oil and wood and plastic that made up the cloud.

A war cloud. A *civil* war cloud, to be precise.

I made that cloud, and all the others like it.

Me.

I tried to feel something, to make the new day bite me. I ached to conjure up pumping torrents of blue-hot anger or even just an invigorating dram of panic. But I couldn't. The moment had no moment, the day was simply another day, and it would pass exactly as all others had before it. Any efforts to wring from it some additional drama or emotion were bound to flop.

Ho-hum. I scratched myself all over – the Spiral suffered from an infestation of spiders the size of kittens, they came up through the outlet under the spigot and shed hairs that made you itch – and wondered what there would be to eat that day.

Spiders aside, life on the Spiral was pretty cushy if you chose to look at things from a certain perspective. The boiling hot pens were small, true – hardly taller or wider or longer than I was – but that's always the way with solitary units. Comparing the place to the Institute, the dire, dismal dump I'd bolted from many months before, would be like comparing a five-star hotel to a radioactive cesspit. Well, maybe not five stars. Maybe one. Maybe a tatty boarding house. A tatty boarding house that was ever so slightly on fire. But think of it this way: we never felt cold; the other penitents couldn't bully us; the guards didn't beat us; we were not compelled to do any exercise or work; we were almost completely unaffected by the calamitous mayhem of the war outside; and the food – oh, the food was lush, top-notch nosh!

Best of all, you could truly *relax* on the Spiral, unbend your soul and chill out like nowhere else on earth; we were completely free from all the silly doubts that burdened other people. For instance, you wouldn't catch me getting my knackers in a knot over the spots on my nose, or having a paddy about exam results or what I was going to do for a job or how I stood with my mates, or any jack like that.

No, on the Spiral, we had a stupendous advantage over everyone mouldering away in more conventional prisons – indeed over everyone, anywhere.

We knew exactly when we were going to die.

In three days, in my case. Give or take an hour or two.

And we knew where, and at whose hands. After twenty-four hours spent in pen one, everyone wound up their stay on the Spiral with an appointment with Dexter Manus, death's right-hand man, the full stop at the end of every death sentence. Life's equation was solved for us, there were no worrisome uncertainties. We could really hang loose.

I'd stayed in quite a few of the Fartherland's gaols in my seventeen unfortunate years by that date, but on Mo's scale of hardness, the Death Spiral ranked a *ten*, my top mark, a thoroughly deserving winner of the platinum manacles award.

I was about to begin packing for rush hour when the phone rang.

Chapter 2*

The cell phone was ringing. I bent down and rested the back
of my hand against the clanking water pipe under the spigot,
the best way to sense the vibrations. They were strong, so the
sender must have been operating from a nearby pen.

Donk . . . donk . . . pause . . . donk, donk, donk, donk, donk . . .
donk, donk, donk, donk . . . pause . . . donk, donk . . . donk,
donk, donk . . .

A . . . T . . . L . . . A . . . S . . .

At last? No, wait. In sixty seconds I had the complete
message:

ATLASISCOMING

Atlas is coming. That was good news! Atlas was everyone's
favourite manciple, one of the trusted penitents who worked
delivering meals and collecting slops. He wasn't on the Spiral,
the prison within the prison, he was from some other part of
the Establishment, the great penal complex above us. He lived
and slept on the permanently dark gantry outside the Spiral's
coiled line of pens.

I recognised the crisp, confident pattern of knocks as coming
from Lew Slips, six days back in pen ten. I knew Lew well,

17

had spent a lot of time with him in the Establishment before we were both put on the Spiral. Lew was right la-di-da, an authentic aristo, probably had a hallmark instead of a belly button. All the same, being a sailor, his perfectly enunciated words were so salty you could have pickled a bison in them. Saying he could recognise a lad with brine in his spine, he'd taken me for a shipmate and protected me as best he could from the gangs and the clans and the crims and the 'verts.

Like me, Lew had been sentenced to death for low treason. He'd been a naval officer who'd trashed his own gunboat rather than open fire on people trying to swim away from the Fartherland to a neutral vessel. That had happened right at the start of the Lapse, when the country began to unravel like a snagged pullover. Lew Slips sinks ships . . . so in a way, it was my fault he was there. If he knew that, he never held it against me.

Donk, donk, donk . . . donk, donk, donk . . .

The next message took longer to receive and transcribe.

MOD RAW US AS KETCHUP TOY OUR AGE FORTH EDAM NED BEG INDEX TERM ANUS

Edam? A cheese that was made backwards. Lieutenant Lew was a lovely tapper, but like most people he suffered from poor timing of the letter and word gaps. You always had to think for a while about cell phone messages, slide the letters between adjacent words before the meaning dropped out. I had that one solved in a jiffy: 'Mo, draw us a sketch. Up to you! Rage for the damned. Begin Dexter Manus?'

I understood. He wanted me to do a painting on the pen wall, a picture of Dexter Manus. Not that I, or anyone else, knew what Manus looked like, but I could guess as well as the next man.

Making any sort of graffiti was arduous work on the Spiral; no penitent owned a pencil or chalk, and we had no metal to scratch the walls, no coins or spoons, even the zips on our bright orange tracksuits were plastic. The best we could manage was to improvise something from our food and use pieces of broken-off meal boxes as crude brushes. Having the best food, I had the best paintbox. Juice or gravy could stain the concrete, and if I was willing to spare it, bread could be chewed up and stuck on in thin ridges. The alternative was to use something solid from the slop bucket, dried out under the air vent. In any medium, the images lasted barely a day before crumbling to dust or being scraped off by the pen's next inhabitants. The Spiral abhorred permanence, it was the enemy of memory.

Yes, I thought, I would paint today. It was essential to plan your days, slice them into manageable chunks and arrange an activity for each one; my to-do list for the day would run like so, I decided:

TO DO:
Pack
Rush hour
Unpack
Wash
Eat
Paint
Use the cell phone
Sleep

19

What to paint? Manus, as requested? That would be problematic. I'd heard plenty of other people's ideas of what the Establishment's executioner might look like: a chain-smoking hunchback with two hearing aids and borrowed teeth; a curly horned giant, with slimy blue skin and a tattoo of your face on his genitals; an army type, with a neck like an elephant's leg. But I had no notions of my own. For me, Dexter Manus was less than a vacuum. He was a name, a sound divorced from all concepts.

A self-portrait, then? A scene from my life, perhaps. Escaping from the Institute . . . my months spent living with the Numbers, the wild, maths-mad gypsies who'd inhabited the marshes and the marches that bordered the Fartherland to the east. Or their massacre by men in hovercraft, men armed with submachine guns and flamethrowers . . . my fault, of course . . . no Numbers left now, except those we had to label our pens and count our days with. How did that nursery rhyme they taught me go, the one about pyramids?

One, five, fourteen, thirty . . .

I was still number-drunk when the spy slot in the front wall grated open. Atlas? I jumped up and peered through the slot into the oppressive, impenetrable gloom of the Spiral's hollow core. Nope, no sign of the friendly manciple. Must have been a draught rattling the cover plate.

And relax. Ho . . . hum.

Out of the darkness sprang a hyena, ramming its bare-fanged muzzle at my face.

I freaked, but only for the second it took to jumpstart my heart; a painted rubber gas mask, all the screws wore them. It was their habit to decorate the masks to resemble jackals or wolves, hyenas or dingoes, pit bulls or tosas. Even the teeth were painted on.

Hyena-head said nothing. The screws, the Spiral's guards, never did. They weren't allowed to, and weren't able to; the masks' snouts were formed from a chunky respirator that obscured the wearer's mouth. All I could hear was a strangulated panting and the sounds of his gloved hands clawing at the wall between us. He'd have a companion with him, lurking in the mascara-dark shadows; screws always worked in tandem.

Through the helmet's lenses the screw's eyes beamed out: two penetrating, phosphorescent-yellow almond shapes. The eyes locked onto me like gun sights, then began to blink dementedly. The guard leaned far forwards and squeezed his mask right up against the spy slot, determined I should notice his frenzied arousal.

'Scab off, you mutant mutt, you foul hound!' I shouted, cowering away from him. 'Leave me to die in peace. Go chase a postman, go lick your privates!'

Perhaps he'd heard about me, the boy who welcomed death, the one prisoner on the Spiral who believed he actually belonged there. No, death row, Death Spiral . . . those sorts of places always attract ghouls, there was no reason to assume the guards didn't have their share. We penitents were the blessed, we possessed a knowledge that set us apart from the rest of humankind, our cell-by dates, and we were but days away from possessing the ultimate wisdom; only natural we attracted the attention of the morbid and the disturbed. The spy slot banged shut, warped hyena-head padded silently away.

We hated the screws. We were on the Death Spiral, they were on death's payroll.

I was shaking, shivering, despite the skin-crisping heat, perturbed and unnerved.

More sounds came from the gantry, the *squeak-squeak* of trolley wheels. This time the small panel at the base of the wall rattled: the crap flap. I pushed the slop bucket through then lay down on the floor and spoke.

'Atlas! Who was that screw, the hyena-head?'

Atlas wriggled himself flat onto the metal gantry and stuck his head opposite mine; he didn't have a key for the spy slot. 'New one, yuk-yuk, trainee. Novice Ethereal . . . no . . . Ethera, summat like that, yuk-yuk,' he replied.

'What sort of a name is *that*?'

Atlas shrugged. 'Dunno. A mixed-up name for a mixed-up world, Mo.'

Atlas looked to be in his forties, his flesh had the pallor of fly ash and was as scarred and pitted as the surface of an asteroid, but I doubt he was much older than me; life in the Establishment could be much tougher than death on the Spiral.

'What's up with him?'

'Just new, I guess. Nosey hound. Keeps looking at the scran, especially yours, yuk-yuk. Sniffin' it and proddin' and pokin' it.'

Damn. That was a bother. My food was indeed special, better than anyone else's. Atlas saw to that. Before I'd even walked through the left-hand door of pen seventy and entered the Spiral, I'd bribed Atlas with the only thing I had ever owned worth more than a diseased flea's knees: a glitzy ring, a present from a one-time friend of mine, The Moth. *Rubies in platinum*, I'd told him. *Glass in tin*, he'd countered, but we'd compromised on garnets in silver, and that was more than enough for Atlas. When he held it in his hand and scrutinised the scarlet gemstones, he'd whistled and cried out, 'Ring a scabbin' ring o' scabbin' roses!'

With the Fartherland breaking up faster than a sponge cake in a dishwasher, jewels were much more desirable than money. He'd sold the ring on, bought himself the post of head manciple, and in return he ensured I ate well. Looked at objectively, I was probably one of the best fed people in the Fartherland. No sculpted giblets and injection-moulded grease for me!

I couldn't imagine what this unwarranted surveillance by the screws might signify. With only three and a bit days to go, small luxuries became not less important but ever more so. And much more than that, it was of the utmost importance to everyone on the Spiral that nothing changed; routine was everything. *Keep everything calm, keep everything regular*, that had been the advice from pen seventy onwards. Good, sound advice. Never think about . . . well, never think about *that*.

'Atlas, are our names written outside the pens? Do the screws know who we are?' I asked him.

'Yuk, nope, Mo. Only if they speak to the manciples, and we tell them nothing.'

I wasn't naive, and Atlas possessed more gorm than many supposed. 'Unless they pay you.'

'Oh, that one's got nothing, yuk-yuk. Who has, these days? You're the lucky ones in there, I tell you.'

I trundled the event from my mind and changed the subject. 'Didn't hear a peep from you last night, Atlas. Where was it?'

23

'Poly-scabbing-nesia, Mo! Couldn't have been easier. Like passing peas, it was.'

At nights, Atlas suffered from a recurring delusion that he was giving birth to different countries of the world, hence his pen name. As each emerged – don't ask – he would describe in horrible detail every wiggle and incision of its outline. Italy was a cinch, as long as it wasn't a breech birth; China, an hour and a half of hysterical agony.

'Good luck for tonight then,' I said. 'Bring me loads of chillies today and maybe it'll be stringy Chile for you tonight!'

Atlas grinned back. 'Yuk, will do, Mo. Rush hour in five minutes, then I'll do the grub round,' he announced, easing himself upright.

Through the flap I took a clean slop bucket (a plastic pale a quarter filled with neat disinfectant) and listened to the squeak of trolley wheels as Atlas pushed on towards pen three.

Time to pack, get ready for the commute. I made a bundle from my tracksuit top, wrapping up my possessions, the trappings of the trapped. A handheld soap dispenser, another ring-purchased luxury, along with the spigot the only way to stay vaguely clean; some plastic bags, useful if the slop bucket began to overflow; a cup. I was already missing Atlas. He was the sole person I could speak to directly without using the cell phone. But he wasn't on duty every morning, and none of the other manciples were prepared to stoop down and chat through the crap flap. That meant his was the only face I ever saw, the only voice I ever heard. There was no one else who would oblige me with a smidgen of human contact like Atlas could, no one at all.

From under the sleeping ledge something darted forwards, a disgusting thing with many hairy, articulated limbs and a flat, round body. It scuttled towards me from the shadows, hesitated, staying its progress as it sensed my burning hostility, then slowly withdrew.

A hand.

'Mo . . . Mo . . . be a pal, sit me on the bucket,' came a bleating, whining voice from under the ledge, a voice that pained me as much as tearing off a toenail with a pair of pliers. 'I'm busting to go, grievous!'

Yeah, well. There was always *him*, I supposed.

Chapter 3*

There were dire shortages of everything now that the Fartherland was disintegrating. Food, clothes, medicines, decency – there had never been a surfeit of any of them, war or no war, but now even space was in short order. The pens of the Spiral were intended for single occupancy, but we all had to share. Only condemned men (and women, although we did not know where they waited out their days) were in abundant supply, as the discredited leadership buzzed around like a hornet doused with insecticide, stinging as many enemies as possible before succumbing to the poison and giving a twitchy demonstration of the backstroke. The rump government itself was low on room; they were bunked up in the Establishment, our knackered nation's premiere prison, home of the Spiral. That wasn't altogether as much of a comedown as it might first appear; super-crooks who ran the crime clans and ministers who ran the country were like black and white chess pieces, notionally on opposite sides but in practice all from the same box and all gliding over the same chequered board, tattooed cheek by flabby jowl. The move of the surviving cabinet to the Establishment was less of an evacuation, more of a homecoming.

So we had to share. But still I didn't talk to *him*. We had a pact, agreed on the threshold of pen seventy, that we wouldn't talk. Well, *I'd* agreed. At my insistence he spent most of the day slotted under the sleeping ledge, snivelling and muttering to himself. That wasn't me being a bully, it was a good place to be; for sixteen hours a day the cell light burned bright enough to fry your eyes, the tortured air that dribbled through the ceiling vent was like the output of a hairdryer, a blow lamp by midday. He was weak and damaged, stowing him in the bitumen-black shadows was rank generosity on my part.

Lately, he'd started to violate the terms of the agreement.

'In a minute,' I growled back, reluctant to acknowledge that I'd heard him. 'Wait until after rush hour. We don't have enough time before then.'

Him. To say his name was to pollute my larynx, blight my lips.

They must have used a computer. I don't know much about those machines, no one in the Fartherland had one at home any more than they had an electron microscope or a radar set, but I know they can sift through teeming reams of information, digest spanking great scads of data faster than a heron can gulp down a duckling.

They *must* have used a computer. There's simply no way otherwise they could have catalogued the millions in our country, the entire planet, across all of history, then identified and arranged for me to share my pen with The Most Irritating Human Being Who Ever Lived:

Nonstop.

'Urchhhhhyyeah! Urchhhhhyyeah!' hacked Nonstop, clearing his throat explosively. The morning throat-scrape was only the least part of an arsenal of bodily noises he would deploy during his waking hours. Come night-time, entirely different armies equipped with novel sonic weapons took up the fight in the commodious battleground of his dilapidated body.

'Oh, that's done it! Blood. I knew it – bronchitis. Or pulmonary embolism. Or TB. And I'm *really* loose now. Please, Mo, help me onto the bucket. I wouldn't ask, but it's my knees. You know how bad my knees are, my cartilage is torn something rotten. And my back. *Terrible* this morning, worst it's ever been – sleeping on the concrete floor does me no good at all. Fused vertebrae, that's what I've got. And scoliosis. Slipped discs too, and . . .'

Nonstop flolloped part way out from under the ledge. When he had first entered pen seventy, minutes after me, it had taken the dog-headed determination of three heaving, blowing screws to compel his bulk through the entry turnstile. After that, it had been up to me to do all the work come rush hour, often needing to use margarine put aside from the previous day's meal to lube Nonstop through when his ample flesh became wedged against the door frame. He was a well-rounded character, to be sure.

During those early days, he did not so much *sit* in our tiny pens as wear them like concrete anoraks. I was reduced to human wallpaper. The situation improved drastically over the first two weeks as his virtually food-free diet caused him to rapidly deflate. By pen four, he was merely enormous, tall and podgy with rolls of pallid flesh that dripped from his bones like batter.

His thinning, ragged black hair was long and beetle-back

28

shiny with grease, his weak eyes were two pink pinpricks that squinted from the backs of deep depressions either side of a minuscule, upturned nose, a thing so small and dainty it seemed to have been parachuted into its doughy surroundings by error, like a misdirected interplanetary space probe. Straggly clumps of hair as thick as curtain tassels branched from his ears, but his beard was minimal, hardly more substantial than the teenage fuzz I sported. The contradictory patterns of hair made him difficult to age; I suspected he was the opposite of Atlas, much older than he looked. Nonstop had perfected a means of leeching the life out of all those around him, preserving his own relative youth at the expense of everyone he met.

'Oh, yeah. It's gonna be a biggie, Mo. Been brewing up for a while. Can't help it, my insides are shot. Shot! Stress, that's what it is of course, the stress of waiting for my appeal to come through. There's nothing worse for the digestion than stress, let me tell you that. Unless it's worms. Or cancer. Or lack of stress, taking things too easily, not enough exercise. Yeah, lack of stress can be as bad as stress. It's a sort of stress in itself when you think about it. Lack of stress stress, that's what they should call it. Mind you . . .' Nonstop's voice was a high, nasal drawl that had the same soothing effect on the ear as a dentist's drill.

'You can hold it in for five minutes!' I snapped back. 'Surely, even you can hold it in for that long?' He was disabled, that was no lie, a wreck of a man, hardly able to raise himself from the floor unaided. My own smarting back and torn muscles bore testament to his invalid condition.

Nonstop caught sight of the numerals painted on the front

wall. 'Three more days. *Three days*,' he wailed, choked up. 'I . . . I can't believe we're going to die in three days, Mo. Over. Finished. Dead!'

The snivelling snot-chomper had broken rule zero. To talk to me was bad enough, but to brazenly discuss *that* was a scabbing outrage.

My fragile equilibrium disassembled. 'Shut your slit, you suppurating pustule!' I screamed. 'Never, ever, mention that again!' I stamped at the hand that had furtively crept forwards again, but it dodged and my bare foot crunched into the floor, landing on sharp grit. I hadn't put my scuzzy trainers on yet and the chip speared my heel. Enraged, I reached under the ledge and proceeded to dish out a thumping.

Nonstop fought back. With one flabby, flappy arm, he batted at my head; the snatched blows were cumbrous and poorly aimed, but potent for all that, dumb momentum compensated for lack of skill. Shielded as he was by the ledge, I managed to score no more than a few strikes, each one eliciting a harrowing yowl. I jabbed a finger into an eye, he punched my nose, I caught him a hard blow on the chin with the heel of my hand, he pulled my hair; a real fight, cheap and crummy, not like in films where every manly fist impacts with the sound of a car boot slamming. Finally, still defending himself with one arm, Nonstop swung his free hand up to his mouth and bit into his thumb, chewing viciously on the shaft between the two knuckles. The babyish stunt was disgraceful, pitiful, but effective.

'Gah! Don't *do* that!' I shouted, leaping away from him. 'You *always* do that, it's so . . . so . . .'

Dizzy, fizzing, I rested my young, brown torso against the wall and closed my eyes. The pen's sizzling bulb was so bright I could perceive it searing through my screwed-up eyelids, the white light reddened by layers of thin skin and thick hate. Spiral fever; the place could really wind you up, send you right round the twist.

'I'm sorry,' I groaned. 'Lost control.'

'Same as yesterday, Mo, and the day before that and the day before that and the –'

Talk had to cease. Banging from the right-hand door and a shout of 'Move through!' heralded rush hour.

An hour for the whole spiral, but less than a minute for each pen. The Spiral's small cells were not like those of other prisons. The front and rear walls were subtly curved, convex and concave respectively, and the two side walls were flat but not parallel, nosing towards each other at the shorter front wall. The front wall would normally be where the door was, but in the Spiral it bore only the crap flap and spy slot. Our pens had two doors, one on the left wall and one on the right wall, connecting each pen to its neighbours. Once you entered into pen seventy, there was no way out of the Spiral before pen one.

With a clunk-clunk sound, our right-hand door unlocked. I hauled Nonstop up, propped him against the wall, slid open the steel door. Beyond it was a turnstile, a set of floor-to-ceiling bars that could be pushed but not pulled. I barged through, carrying the bucket and the bundles made from our tracksuit tops. The turnstile ticked and clicked as it revolved. I had to jump down into pen three; every pen was slightly lower than its predecessor. Nonstop followed, rasping and wheezing. I slid shut the door, our new left-hand door. I couldn't see it, but I knew the right-hand door in our old pen would automatically close at that point, and the left-hand one open. Five-a-Day and Kel Surprise would walk through it into pen four, just as Noah Fence and Nun Taken had shuffled into pen two the minute previous to our move. Pen names – no one used their real ones.

'Move through, plenty of room!' we both called together, and we banged on the door to signal our followers to begin their daily migration.

Nothing forced you to move. But if you didn't, you'd be four to a one-man cell, and that was not pleasant. We knew. We'd tried, once Nonstop's Spiral diet had reduced his circumference. Everyone tried once. Standing room only. And if no one moved, if the Spiral went on strike, the screws opened up hatches in the pens' ceilings and lobbed in gas tablets that dissolved slowly, emitting a lung-corroding gas. That always chivvied things along a bit.

Pen three was identical to pen four, an airless concrete kiln topped by a juddering ventilator. Only the fading graffiti made from dried food or faeces was different, and the fact that painted on the front wall was the number III.

Three days, seventy-two hours to live. *No! Don't think, don't count! Keep calm, keep the routine going.*

Not far away, Round Robin and Hans Free would have just walked from pen one into . . . only, we didn't know how it happened exactly, just when and who. No one had ever transmitted any news on the cell phone about what lay behind the final turnstile, what Dexter Manus looked like or how the Spiral's infamous decommissionaire operated. Sometimes you'd hear cell phone conversations where people speculated about the means and the manner, for not everyone shared my opinion that it was a subject best avoided. *They say he uses his bare hands . . . poison, that's what it'll be, they'll adulterate the final meal . . . no, no, firing squad, nice and quick, five rounds rapid. Ready, aim . . . wait for it, wait for it . . . Fire! Hanging's good enough for us, the long drop . . . reckon it's a lethal infection, they use us to test diabolical new microbes for biological warfare . . . Off with our heads! I read a severed head lives on for several seconds afterwards, and only a spurt of blood gushes from the neck, no more fluid than from a spilled glass of claret . . .*

The most persistent whisper put about by the rumour-tologists was this: the death that awaited us was the worst possible, the worst imaginable, an end beyond words.

No matter how hard we nagged them, the manciples wouldn't impart a single hint. They knew, they must have known, but they kept the knowledge to themselves, a kind of kindness I supposed, the expedient kinship that existed between cattle and slaughtermen. The screws knew even more, knew who Dexter Manus was. That's why they were muzzled and why they had to work in pairs, each guaranteeing the other's silence.

Life in pen three did not get off to a good start. It borrowed the same crummy opening it had used for pen four and pen five and . . . for weeks, I'd been meaning to devote some time to *preparing* myself for the end, although I had not the outline of a shadow of an inkling of an idea how I might go about that. Every day's intentions were rudely thwarted, however, by the need to assist Nonstop with his 'morning obligatory'.

'It's a mistake you know, Mo, me being here, an administrative oversight,' Nonstop groused, poised in my arms over the slop bucket. 'They'll spot the boo-boo before soon, let old Nonstop go free. I'll sue for compensation, be awarded damages. I'll put in a word for you too, of course, but I doubt it'll do much . . . urrrggghhh . . . oh! Something ruptured then, didn't you hear it? You're not holding me properly, lift me higher!'

'Yeah, yeah. You done?' I was staggering under his weight, wary of kicking the bucket, so to speak.

He turned purple in the face, tensed. I had to hold my breath and look away. Life inside is designed to put you on intimate terms with the mechanics of the organism, to rub your nose in the sticky stuffs. Food and farts and fights are the axioms of imprisonment, the thread of the Spiral.

'Dedicated my life and my health to science in the service of the Fartherland!' he blurted, relaxing and shifting his weight. 'You deserve to be here, Mo, if you don't mind my saying so – you've a criminal mindset – but I don't. It's grievous unfair. Not that I've ever been one to make a fuss, as you know, stoic is my middle –'

'You're slipping! Hurry up!' I broke in, beginning to feel faint. On days like this, I had to seriously downgrade my score for the Spiral. A four, no higher. Maybe even a two.

Days like this . . . *every* day was like this. The closer we got to pen one, the looser Nonstop became, loose in the lips and in the bowels. I was exactly the opposite, tightening up, closing down.

Oh, we had no bog roll. Nonstop was clumsy, but it was me who ended up cack-handed.

It wasn't Nonstop's size I objected to, nor his lamentably false conviction that every part of his body was about to pack up. I could have even tolerated needing to assist him with the gruesome business of emptying his bowels.

What made Nonstop unbearable was the noise.

Nonstop *never* stopped talking. And if not actually talking, Nonstop eradicated the peace with every form of non-verbal auditory assault that could be imagined. He clicked the bones in his fingers; he made involuntary ticking and snuffling noises; his swallows were louder than most men's shouts; his internal and external organs were permanently occupied in a fluidic game of puss-the-parcel, every transference of spit or bile being accompanied by exaggerated groans and bandsaw coughs; he snored, needless to say, plutonic rumblings that could have triggered earthquakes in distant nations; he talked in his sleep – and therefore in mine – and ground his teeth; and his nose whistled like a kettle when he breathed through it, which wasn't often, for Nonstop preferred to take whale-sized, throat-wobbling gulps of air in through his mouth at the same time as he talked, leading to hour-long bouts of belching and hiccups.

When we were finally done, I recuperated on the bed ledge, smell-shocked, blocking out Nonstop and waiting for the food to arrive, the high point of any day. And that particular day did not disappoint: gruntled I was, positively crest-risen! Two boxes heaped high with mashed potato, chicken cubes, slices of fluffy white bread that didn't look like they'd been used as the insoles of a boxer's boots. And my chillies! A brittle plastic spoon was supplied. *His* meal was one carton of plaster-dry crackers and a translucent slab of something that should have been arrested for impersonating cheese. Doom chow, felon fodder.

Ha, ha!

'Hey, Nonstop. You'll never guess what you've got today,' I teased him as I took the boxes from Atlas. 'Rare steak!'

'Wow! Oh boy!'

I showed him the real contents of his carton. 'So rare, it's missing. Tuck in!'

Don't feel sorry for him; Nonstop's titchy schnozzle operated as a double-barrelled, round-the-clock snack dispenser. Most people grew out of thinking there was a monster under their beds. Mine still existed, my personal bogeyman.

Atlas had done me proud, a be-scabbing-you-tiful assortment of chilli peppers, red and green and orange and yellow. I asked him for chillies every day; they were my consuming addiction. Real humdingers and ring-stingers he'd managed too, red savinas, habaneros and nagas. Half I would eat with my food, half I saved to graze on throughout the day. Eating a pepper was like having molten iron poured into each ear canal while someone else fed your tongue through a mangle. I never grew accustomed to the pain, and that was the whole point. Alive, I felt alive when I ate those insane fruits!

I held up a super-strong naga pepper, ran it under my nose like I'd seen people do with cigars in films.

'The helixir of life!' I declared, flourishing the chilli in the air.

He started again, from under the bed ledge. 'Mo,' he said. 'Mo. Mo. Mo. Mo.'

'What?' I snapped. 'Leave me be! I want to . . . remember.' Did I? I wasn't sure that was true.

'Mo. Mo. Mo. Mo.'

36

'Mo. Mo. Mo. Mo.'

'Mo. Mo. Mo. Mo.'

He could keep that up for hours if necessary, days even.

'Mo. Mo. Mo. Mo.'

'Mo. Mo. Mo. Mo.'

'Mo, listen!'

I broke. 'Don't tell me. You want to play hide-and-seek.'

'No . . . stupid. That's stupid, that is. I heard a rumour. On the cell phone. Last night, when you were asleep, a message from the Bombay Micks.'

I sighed and draped my head with my grungy tracksuit top. I knew what was coming. Same manure every day.

'The war will save us, Mo,' he began, his voice quavering. 'The Establishment will surrender to enemy forces before it's our turn, and we'll be swapped for prisoners of war. It's true, it *has* to be true!'

I didn't object, didn't respond. Nonstop wasn't the only one to cleave to incredible stories, a great many did. They spoke of legal appeals and secret deals and amnesties and reprieves . . . as they daily edged nearer and nearer to death's revolving door, the straws they clutched at became ever more frayed. Identical twins they'd never known they had would volunteer to take their place and be smuggled in, a masked hero would swoop down and pluck them to safety . . . stories, just stories; no death sentence had ever been commuted.

I filtered Nonstop out, popped a pepper into my mouth, listened to the rattling fan pumping in corpse-breath air, eavesdropped on the morning's cell phone calls being relayed from door to door or coming over the pipes. The vibrations meant I could sense them even over Nonstop's prattling.

Donk . . . donk, donk . . . Messages from the left informed me of the day's fresh intake of penitents and news they brought from the outside; the ongoing civil war; and the invasion by white-helmeted Peacemakers, international troops tasked with ending the bloodshed. Good luck with *that*, I thought.

After the news, someone transmitted their move in an inter-pen chess game.

One call came through to us.

Hey, old timers, what's it like?

That made me laugh. Same in pen three as in pen seventy, that's what. As was always the case, the novice screw crew were slow and inefficient users of the cell phone. Evetnaully they'd lrean you culod scarmble the lettres of each word as lnog as the fisrt and the last were crorect. Words were always like life, that's what I believed. The start and the end were fixed points, and everything in between was just a confused, nonsensical jumble.

My own beginnings were lost to me. I was only too conscious of my terminus, the width of two cells away. My confused middle? Months and months ago, before we busted out, I'd been rotting in a juvenile detention centre called the Institute, locked up with an orphan girl called Harete and a boy we called The Moth.

The Moth! His name derived from his Institute habit of moving towards any source of light so he could read. Posh, pious, studious, pompous, ridiculous, skinny Moth! Son of a famous judge, an exiled politician, head always rammed in a book, lover of ancient myths and history. Moth and I had celled

38

together, gelled together.

Then I'd freed the three of us, my first – only – big success. We evaded capture for seven days, followed a line of electricity pylons and trekked to the border, where I delivered him and Harete over the razor wire to the Other country. A fanatical guard called Jelly had hounded us every step of the way, hot on our heels, until he got his fingers burned, and much else besides. Jelly . . . just a nick name, a name from the old nick.

So much for old friends. Thinking about The Moth made my intestines squirm like I'd digested a basket of nagas. I'd never forgotten how, hightailing it from the Institute, we came across an old vase glazed with inscriptions; that cracked crock had impressed him more than all the gruntwork I'd put into freeing him. Pottery, not people, that's what rocked Moth's boat. That vase . . . fit for the prize on a fairground hoopla, no more.

Snapback: at that moment, Nonstop was performing a total inventory of his ailments, almost down to the cellular level.

'Course, my kidneys were wrong from birth. No idea *whose* blood I've got, it never felt right in my veins though. I'm sure I should be an O, I feel like an O, possibly an A, but the doctor wrote "AB" on my file.'

'He probably put "omination" after it,' I interjected.

'Nothing's ever worked properly for me in my whole useless life,' he wailed on, ignoring me completely.

''Cept your gob,' I pointed out, closing my eyes. Since Nonstop never listened, you could insult him as much as you liked. 'And your backside.' *Shush now, ignore him. Must . . . prepare. How? Think of people you'd say goodbye to if you could: Harete and . . . and . . .*

'. . . radiation, dangerous chemicals galore in my line of work, little surprise I'm barely still alive. And as for when I worked at the centre, all those damp tunnels played havoc with my chest . . .'

'Beats me why they bothered to sentence you to death,' I yawned. Sleep was good, sleep was easy. Sleep's projectionist would bring a dream-show Harete to me, Harete as I'd never seen her in real life. 'Should have just stood you in a corner and let you fall apart by yourself.'

Beyond my sealed eyelids the light bulb dimmed and its hum dropped in pitch and rose in volume. It did that occasionally; perhaps the generators were low on fuel and they had to reduce the voltage. Shortages.

'. . . great chunks rubbed off, took weeks to grow back. Probably my ringworm. Or eczema. Or scrofula. Or maybe leprosy. Unless it's from a tropical fly that lays its eggs under your skin, then the eggs hatch . . .'

A cell phone message came thumping through the doors, loud and insistent. I ignored it. How important could it be? F . . . I . . . S . . .

'. . . hatch . . . hatch, Mo! THE HATCH, MO!' shouted Nonstop, pummelling on the bed ledge from underneath.

I blinked awake, annoyed, then stunned. The light was low, the hatch in the pen roof was open, and on the end of a long metal pole a metal gripper had reached down and clamped shut around my left ankle.

The entire Spiral was shouting at the top of its voice.

The screws are fishing!

Chapter 4

In half a heartbeat, I was dangling upside down. The long arm of the law was drawing me up towards the dark opening. *A fishing trip* . . . on some days Dexter Manus just couldn't get enough, he wanted to execute more than whoever he found that morning quailing in pen one.

'Help me, Nonstop!' I yelled in abject panic. 'For scab's sake help!'

I bucked and thrashed, trying to grab the spigot, the only fixed object in the pen. My hand brushed it, but the screws read me and thrust the pole downwards. My grip failed and my head powered into the cement floor, folding my neck. Every nerve arced and sparked; I was overcome with zinging bolts of pain, like I was made of a billion jarred elbows.

Deep in the recess under the sleeping ledge I hazily glimpsed Nonstop, howling and fitting in terror, gnawing on his thumb.

The hoist powered upwards, but I had my anchor. My tingling fingers locked around Nonstop's comfort-thumb. He crushed his other palm over my face, drowning me in sweaty putty as he attempted to push me off him.

'Not bitey-thumb, let go, you'll dislocate it!'

The screws wrenched on the pole again, my feet vanished through the hatch. 'Take him, not me, he's the one you want!' Nonstop clamoured.

From above us came a distressed grunting: me plus hefty Nonstop was too much for the screws. The cuff around my ankle cantilevered open, I plummeted down. The light pinged fully on again, the hatch smacked shut with a sturdy *whump*.

Nonstop slithered back into his cave. I had just enough strength to get on the phone, trying to warn the nearby penitents, but the lines were all busy and I couldn't make myself heard.

'Why did I bother to resist?' I wailed, bushed and bruised, limping back onto the ledge. 'I should have let them pluck me out; what possible difference can it make to anything now?'

'My plan worked, eh, Mo, my plan?' Nonstop began to prattle. 'Pull you back down, only, leave it to the last minute, make them think they were going to succeed? I saved you, Mo, I did! Mo . . . Mo . . . Mo . . . Mo . . . you owe me . . . Mo.'

'I only struggled cos I want to see you killed first, you bloated oaf,' I replied, breaking my own rule: discussing *it*, our executions. 'The thought of living long enough to watch you die is what keeps me going, you mumbling, stumbling, bumbling, fumbling Grumblestiltskin.' But it wasn't true. *Habit*, I decided, that was why I'd struggled, nothing more. Talk of dying set Nonstop off on one, but it was all repeats; I listened only to slide in some insults, and because there was no alternative.

Nonstop claimed often and indignantly to have been sentenced to death on account of some discovery he'd made at his work. You could not ask what that had been – you could not strictly ask Nonstop anything, you had to tune in to radio Nonstop and be lucky enough to catch a moment when the verbal onslaught made some sense – but I half-gathered he had once worked in some whack-a-jack laboratory. Or possibly lavatory; Nonstop had been mumbling. A fizzy cyst, he called himself once, and that seemed about right to me. I assumed this was standard prison-issue flannel, the same effect that led to park flashers and bag snatchers reinventing themselves as master pickpockets and safe crackers. The Spiral was a prison, when all was said and done.

Nonstop was still burbling. 'I'm a classic case, Mo, I am, a classic case of the man who knew too much.'

'Talked too much, you mean.'

'I was good, Mo, I really was, back when I still had my health. Pushed back the frontiers of scientific knowledge, I did.'

'Where to? The dark ages?'

I paid Nonstop no further attention. The two of us had to coexist as parallel columns; meaningful communication was unworkable. A shame, because I knew there was some good in the man, and some wisdom, adrift amidst the oceans of blather. He himself had once used a telling phrase, a technical Colliding stuff together, Mo. That was my life's work. Little particles, the building blocks of the atoms. You start with a bunch of particles, and you accelerate them, whiz them around in circles. Circles within circles actually, each one more energetic than the last. Then you bang them together, or smash them term I'd understood without explanation: *signal to noise ratio*, the amount of useful information compared to the amount of background static. His own ratio was smaller than a snake's inside leg measurement. For all I knew, he could have been saying something really critical to my life – what little remained of it – right at that very moment, but how would I have known? Nonstop had no ability to separate the ore from the spoil; a nine-hour anecdote about ingrowing nipple hair would be delivered with the same wearisome bluster, pancake-flat tone and microscopic level of detail as, say, news of how he'd chanced upon a massively important secret of epochal significance. Not that he ever had. He couldn't find his own toes.

Nonstop didn't mean to be cruel, I had to concede that. He was born to be irritating.

into their opposites, their anti-particles. After each explosion, you analyse the debris, see how the bits scatter and break apart. That's how you arrive at truth, how you get to the heart of the matter, the fundamental *points* of existence. I loved my work. Sheer bad luck I should have bumped into him there, in the centre. Odd little chap. Maybe he was my opposite, maybe my bumping into him was the collision! We were both running in circles, now that I think about it. I was late for a meeting, most uncommon for me – I'm usually scrupulously punctual. Oh, apart from that time at my aunt's funeral, when I was late back from a bowling tournament and I dropped my sandwiches into the grave and they had to stop the service for me to retrieve them and the coffin lid broke open and my foot went . . . Anyway, the centre, yes. I got

There was something timeless about Nonstop, his sort had always been around. The kid you couldn't shake off at school, the one who was always bullied and, by sticking to you like paint to a wall, made you a target too. The kid who was always borrowing your books and never returned them, or only after they'd been used to line the budgie's cage; his kind arrived late for every appointment, they made you late, they spilled your secrets to your enemies, they drove you to an early grave, spelled your name wrong on the headstone and then conspired to keel over and die during your funeral, hogging all the attention. Spend too long with them and you might find yourself becoming one of them. The first sign was a tendency to talk at great length about nothing, with interminable digressions into, wow, never noticed that bruise before, what an amazing the impression the little guy was trying to escape from someone. Guess bashing into me messed it up for him. They put him away somewhere safe after that. Wonder who he was? Someone mega, mega important, that was for sure. Couldn't let me go free, not once they knew I'd seen him, knew he was there. That's how I ended up on the Spiral. Thing is, I'm sure I do know exactly where he is, even now. I knew that place inside out, all the door codes and everything. "Often I have said to you, I ain't any Tennessee tunneller." That's how I remembered the crucial one. Never forget that one. Good, isn't it, Mo? "Often I have said to you, I ain't any Tennessee tunneller." Heh. Clever. Not that I told them I knew that, not during my interrogation. They'd have probably just executed me there and then. As a matter of true fact, I never said a shade of purple and all yellow around the edge . . .

thing when they questioned me. Not a word.'

Catching only the end of the ceaseless bore-a-thon, I almost swallowed my tongue in amazement. 'Not a word? That must have been a first!'

'Don't mock me . . . oh! I think I'm going to have another sneezing attack . . . my allergies . . . spider hairs . . . aaaaaahhhh . . . aaaaaahhhh . . . FTOOOO! Did that land in your hair? So much of it too, my tubes are ruined. Use my tracksuit top to wipe it off, find a dry spot if you can, oh, the misery . . . so *grievous* unfair. I am going to be due so much compensation when they release me . . .'

Whatever Nonstop claimed as the reason for his undoing, I had another theory. I think Nonstop was sentenced to death because someone with the authority *met* him. It's the only excuse they'd have needed.

The temperature in the pen rose inexorably, grinding up from 'oven' to 'blast furnace'. I tried to stay absolutely still; the smallest motion was rewarded with a deluge of sweat.

Rest . . . stay calm . . . do that painting later, self-portrait in gravy. Or a still life. No . . . a still-alive. Five-a-Day could always lick it off the wall tomorrow if he didn't like it.

Nonstop broke from his monologue and tried to engage me in an actual two-way conversation. From below my concrete bed slab his plabby hand popped up, waggling that slice of wannabe-cheese from the day's rations.

'Mo, Mo, my friend. My *best* friend. Swap Nonstop some of your chicken for some of this?' he wheedled. 'For saving you?'

'Scab off! I'd rather eat the soap.'

'Mo, don't be so cruel. Old Nonstop's your soulmate.'

'What? You're not even my cellmate. You're just someone who's here, someone I have to put up with.'

'I was popular once. I had followers.'

'They weren't following you. They just couldn't squeeze past you in the corridor.'

A sly pause, then, 'Justice is like cheese. You ever think of that?' Nonstop tried next.

'What?' I snapped.

'Think. It comes in wheels, it's often full of holes, sometimes it's mouldy, and by the time we get to see any it's been cut very, very thinly. Oh, and the stuff they have abroad is usually better than ours.'

It irked me to confess it, but his joke actually made me think for a minute.

'Not bad,' I laughed back, shaking my head. 'Not good either,' I put in as an afterthought. Didn't want the fat lummock to think he'd amused me.

'Holes, Mo. Cheese can have holes, and prisons have holes too, don't they? Gaps in the security? Escape, Mo, you *must* be thinking about it, must have worked it out by now? You wouldn't leave me behind, not old Nonstop, your pal, your mate, your buddy, the man who saved you just now?'

My guts pulsed painfully. 'No escape. Not possible,' I gabbled, spitting the toxic words out, getting them as far away from me as possible. Didn't he understand, even by pen three?

Keep calm, keep the routine. Thinking about escapes was the worst torment imaginable. You had to pack your skull with an unvarying blank numbness, not think about the non-existent future or the mildewed dreams of the past. Escape from the Spiral *was* impossible; it was a closed system, a sealed cistern. You'd not get a mouse through the air vent, the steel ceiling hatch was bolted from the outside, the crap flap was too small, the walls solid. No windows, no way to open the doors, nowhere to go even if you did, except into another pen. No visitors, no parcels. The screws surveyed the food cartons with metal detectors and did fingertip inspections for forbidden items or notes; no stone – or bean or pea or sprout – was left unturned.

Impossible. Say it, sing it, chant it, chew it, swallow it. The Spiral was a slow-motion helter-skelter; you could travel only in one direction: downwards.

Nonstop's harking on this business was entirely my own fault. During the weeks before my trial I'd been boastful, bragged of my desertion from the Institute. *Escape artist*, I'd styled myself, *top-flight*. I'd been full of puff, not thinking straight, my mind still reeling from the massacre I'd witnessed in the marshes. But the Establishment had proved to be a nut I couldn't crack, and the Spiral represented another dimension of impossibility, a self-contained, self-consistent universe that admitted no violations. Privately, I knew I was a poor apology of an escapologist.

'You broke out before. So *you* say anyway,' Nonstop taunted. 'Or perhaps you're nothing but a bully after all. People have always bullied me, picked on me; jealousy I suppose. And because of my size, but that's hormonal, or glandular. Or genetic.

Or environmental. Or . . .'

I sighed and folded my tracksuit more tightly over my head, trying to block him out. Far, far too hot to fight or argue by then. The words that followed wouldn't have reached him even if he'd listened, they were absorbed in the folds of scratchy fabric.

'I don't want to escape. I'm a mass murderer, I deserve to die.'

An hour later, I lifted the sweat-sopped material from my face. I picked up Nonstop's empty meal carton and scraped half of my food onto it, then shoved it back towards him, same as I did every day. He started to snaffle it down without delay, snorting and snuffling with contentment. I took a bite of his fare in return; it tasted of tyres and smelled like dust on a hot radiator.

A cell phone message came over the pipe, hammered out so loudly that the spigot vibrated with the blows, spraying droplets of water across the pen.

LEWD ONE FORGAVE IN TOE VILLA MEN THIMBLES SHIM

Lew done for. Gave in to evil, lament him, bless him.

So the fishermen had their catch; Lew was hooked, Lew who'd protected me in the Establishment, spared me from violations worse than death. Before the Spiral I'd asked him why he hadn't swum to freedom after sinking his gunboat, but he'd laughed louder than a lighthouse foghorn and told me that every shipwrecked tar knew when it was time to let go and shake fins with the sharks, that you should never hang on at any cost. He mimed a punch to my chin with a capstan-sized fist and made me promise I'd do the same when my time came;

funny moment, I got hot muddled and called him 'Dad'.

I sprang to the front wall and drummed against it with my feet, my fists, my forehead, smashing and smashing it until I was bombed and bloodied. I squatted down and pressed my mouth against the crap flap where the metal was thinnest.

'Scab maggots!' I roared, incoherent with rage. 'D'ya hear me, Manus, screws? I'll annihilate you all. I'll strike like lightning's cross-thread kinsman, the H of the horror and the B of the beast beyond all mercy. I'll trick you to the cusp of triumph and raze you with the opposite of everything you are. I'll entwine you in my coils and crush you; I'll turn you to porcelain and pulverise you with a tap of my toe. This I vow, Manus, you worthless coffin fly!'

The metal plate bounced my insults back at me. I crammed my mouth full of leftover peppers to bring on a chilli fury, then howled through the afternoon until the light died and my gums bled lava.

Another life in the day of the Spiral had passed. Outside on the gantry, Atlas bayed in the throes of giving birth to Africa, sweating out Swaziland, practically dying as he passed angular Angola.

I lay down on the floor, spent. Three spiders with abdomens the size of kiwi fruit pattered out from the corners of the pen and settled on my face, drawn by the sweat. I let them slake their thirst. One was starting to moult, her skin splitting to reveal a spider inside a spider.

When I happened to glance at the front wall, my eyes fringed by hairy arachnid legs, I saw that the spy slot was open. Two ravenous, luminous yellow eyes were studying me through a rubbery hyena mask, jaundiced eyes that flickered and fluttered and lusted.

Chapter 5*

No one thought about it, about death, because you *can't* think about it. No one pondered it in pen seventy, we weren't meditating on it in pen three, we wouldn't be fathoming its abysmal mystery in pen one.

I had no worries about the condition of death, only about the change of state, the transition from living to dead. I hoped it would be quick and not hurt.

Do you fret and vex about where you were or what it was like before you were born? No. So you can't worry about where you'll be after Dexter Manus lays his hand upon you. Everyone who'd gone before us on the Spiral said at one time or another, 'When I get to pen one, I'll think about it.' I bet they didn't. I bet they tried, but come the day all they could think about was the shabbiness of the food and how hot they were and how very much they missed and how hugely they wished.

The Numbers tried to prove it to me once. For them, the silent, tattooed people who lived in the boggy estuaries and watery margins of the Fartherland, everything was mathematics. *We're all marquetry in carbon, or paper dolls gummed by arithmetic onto the pages of a scrapbook, unable to escape the flat world we live in or even view it properly. Only an outside agent, someone external to our reason, can look down, see the full picture and prise us from the page. But we can never know her, never know if she's even there at all, for there's a curt girdle around what can be shown to be true*, they claimed. Incompleteness abounded, confounding all human labours.

The Numbers never took frit about what lay beyond the black bladder of reality, or bent a knee or doffed a cap to it, and they'd come closer than anyone to pressing their faces into the membrane, stretching it until it assumed their shapes, and they its. Where their foreheads had brushed it, it scorched in a triangle, a *delta* sign, the mathematical symbol for *difference*. They patrolled the marshes on glass stilts, fought like thieves and thought like professors, fickle as flick knives, muscular as marlin, fleet as kestrels.

Dead as dinosaurs. When I gave up The Moth and Harete to the Other country, the Numbers took me in and sheltered me. They tried to teach me their history, about their ancient empire. They even endeavoured to school me in their language, a voiceless tongue called Sandscrypt they said was gifted them by someone called Thoth, but learning it drove me sick and pained my think-sponge. No loss though. What use to me of all people was a language in which it was completely, irrefutably impossible to tell a lie?

Soldiers from the Fartherland put them down. On the night the hovercraft arrived, the Numbers hid me in the sett of all setts, buried me under stooks of reeds. Then they broke apart their knives and scythes and sickles and adzes and strutted towards the rays of tracer fire, smiling and laughing.

They *welcomed* their extermination.

I don't know why.

I don't . . . know . . . why . . .

A pioneer squadron dug me out, dragged me back to the Fartherland. I was tried for treason and errorism. Not for escaping from the Institute or helping The Moth, but simply for having lived among the Number.

Why were the troops there? Because of the civil war. What caused the war?

Have you ever damaged something valuable? Swished back a curtain too fast and toppled an heirloom, borrowed a friend's bike and absent-mindedly parked it in front of a road roller, that kind of thing?

I smashed a country.

Oops. Sorry. Didn't mean to.

The Moth had been imprisoned in the Institute to silence his parents, especially his exiled dad. When we liberated Moth – my plan, my idea, my fault – his folks had been free to speak and tell the world what the government of the Fartherland had been secretly up to over the decayed decades.

Bad things. Bad, bad things. Don't ask me, I don't know. Glimpsed the smouldering leftovers once, no more.

When the world learned, you could say it became . . . cheesed off. We'd all expected the old leaders to scram; we thought that Moth's father, the judge, would return and run the country properly.

Wrong. Wrong with a capital R. Rather than park up the ship of state and surrender the wheelhouse keys, the old rulers chose instead to steer her into the whirlpool of civil war.

I was no traitor, but I was a mass murderer. An accidental one, yes, but the first link in the chain that had led to the culling of the Numbers. The ruination of the Fartherland was sticky with my fingerprints.

And to crown it all, Moth was back in the Fartherland.

The intelligence had come to me in pen twelve, sender unknown, a pen-seventy newbie.

MOTHISBACKACHEDDARESAYTORETURN

'Mo, this backache . . .' No, that wasn't right. 'Mo, this back a Cheddar esay tore turn? Hang about, "essay" isn't spelled right, even I know that, and I've never written one,' I wondered out loud, 'and certainly not one about backaches and Cheddar.'

'Cheddar, Mo? Did you say something about Cheddar? Old Nonstop loves a bit of Cheddar. Queen of cheeses is an actual Cheddar, especially if ripened properly. Never store it in the fridge, that's the mistake people always make. The ideal temperature, on the absolute scale, would be . . .'

Try again. Mo, this . . . no . . . oh. No!

Moth is back. Ached, daresay, to return.

WHERE MOTH, I'd responded, tapping so fast my knuckles split.

My reply came at once:

CENTRE OF EVERYTHING CENTRE OF POWER

I could guess what that signified, but I had to know for sure. WHAT MEAN, I pounded back.

The answer came by return of knock, the last I heard from that particular pen pal; he must have been taken by anglers:

HER U LES THE FART HER LAND HI SWILL BED ONE

He rules the Fartherland.

54

His will be done.

I couldn't eat for a week. Harete and I had risked mutilation and death to free that kid from the Institute and sneak him abroad, damn near lost the gamble. For him to come back . . . that wasn't a case of Moth throwing our sacrifices back in our faces, it was more like he'd stapled them to a wrecking ball and was pounding our bodies into raspberry jam with them.

The centre of everything. Like a spider on its web. *Oh, I'll bet he ached to return,* I thought. Like father, like son, Moth was a conniving politician from his skin in, from his heart to his farts. Moth had really been Caterpillar; Harete and I hadn't recognised the larval form. My taking him to the Other country had been a ruse, a safe place for him to pupate, nothing more. The instant his wings had hardened, he'd fluttered back to feed.

The centre of power. Generals, politicians, lawyers, businessmen – Moth's kind. Plotting, scheming, directing and profiting from the war, divvying the spoils.

He rules the Fartherland. Moth was only a teenager, but he'd never been just a teenager. Born middle-aged, elbow patches on his Babygro, a shattered country was a perfect apprentice piece for a trainee tyrant. He'd returned, he was in charge, or working alongside those in charge. And he'd abandoned me.

Escape?

Screw it.

Death at the hands of Dexter Manus terrified me, but I couldn't deny it was deserved. Besides, if life outside was that bent, I no longer wanted to participate.

When people passed into pen one, by tradition the rest of the

Spiral left them alone. Lying to each other, we said it was out of respect. Really though, pen one was irredeemably contaminated with the ruinous, urinous tang of despair.

The men in pen one usually sent a farewell signal at the onset of their final day. By far and away the most common goodbye message tapped out was simply this:

Cheers, lads. See ya.

You'd be the same. You'll be the same. We're all on the Spiral. Some people's Spirals are just a bit tighter than others, that's all.

Chapter 6

The light was already on when I woke up, air was filtering down through the vents, the Spiral was chattering and clucking and hammering to itself as it booted up for another day.

I rolled off the ledge I'd been perched on during the night and plonked my bare feet on the crumbly cement floor, a taste like dirty diesel swirling in my mouth, globules of sweat as big as peanuts dripping from me. Rush hour would not happen for another thirty minutes or so, I had the time to myself.

Swirling the flotsam of my dreams around my mind, I tried to pierce the illogic of that disarranged domain and reconstruct the visions that had seduced me throughout the dead of the night: penumbral, tattooed panthers rough-sawn from brawn and algebra; the slaughtered Numbers.

{Good morning, Mo. A leak has developed. I can speak with you,} trilled an off-key voice in my head, a flute with a split reed, an organ with congested pipes.

A voice in my head?

I punched my face, hard. And again. Two and a bit days to live, and the Spiral had finally succeeded in sending me round the bend. Thumb on my wrist, I timed a minute with my double-pace pulse, but there was no reoccurrence of the interloping voice. A daydream . . . though eerily clear. *Freaky*.

Nonstop was still snoozing under the ledge. Asleep, awake, it made little difference. Most penitents didn't bother to stir until the manciple knocked for the slop bucket and warned them of the coming move. None of us were permitted access to books or radios or any form of entertainment or distraction. We had nothing to get up for, apart from the cell phone or, for those with a passion for pain, fighting. Or chillies. The stiflingly hot pens kept us permanently drowsy; we spent most of the day looking forward to the relative cool and absolute darkness of the night, then most of the night dreaming about the non-events of the day. That was the unintended, twisted brilliance of the Spiral: it was the perfect training ground for empty eternity, an infinite loop of dreaming about dreaming about . . .

Running on empty, my mind dropped a cog, turned inwards, backwards.

I didn't have a lot in common with other seventeen-year-olds, not even my age. I'd lied so frequently about my date of birth and my real name I'd forgotten if there ever had been definitive answers to those questions; the truth was a balloon whose string I had long ago let run free through my greasy digits. Let other people hunt it, I gave not a fig.

Numerically I couldn't have been far wrong, no more than a year or so either side. No point asking my parents. Mum was smoke – perhaps I was breathing in a few molecules of her right there and then, brought over in one of my clouds. Dad was an assembly of dubious memories I couldn't decide if I liked or despised or even believed.

What's more to say? My life in the Fartherland was nothing but years of soggy food and grinding boredom alleviated by running rings around my pa, running away from home and from homes, run-ins with the law. When everyone's legs grew tired of all the running I was crumpled up like an empty crisp bag and flicked into the Institute, and that's how I made the acquaintance of The Moth and Harete.

Harete . . . what name did I have for what I felt for Harete? We'd not seen each other since the day I helped her across the frontier. She had been the ablest of the three of us, wiser, kinder, braver, stronger, cunninger. On the run, we'd made up stories. Pretty much anything's tolerable if you've got a story to read or invent. For us – cold, hunted and so hungry the sight of a leather shoe made us salivate – stories were the vitamin S that had sustained us, kept us alive and sane. The best story had been Harete's.

Just saying 'Harete' caused a gyroscope to spin up in my chest, a device that pointed towards her no matter which way I was oriented, dragging me off-centre. Was that strange force symmetric, would she be thinking about me, wherever she was, safe in the Other country?

With death so close, my infatuation with a girl I'd never see again infuriated me. Thankfully, Nonstop announced his return to consciousness by noisily rearranging some mucus, braking my tobogganing introspection.

'Kyyyyyyyyach. Kyyyyyyyyyach-ach-ach-ach.' The reveille endured for many minutes, each blast a hammer blow on the sugar-glass bubbles of my fatuous musings. After that came a lengthy analysis of the morning's nasal output. Then we had our daily fight; I opened with a roundhouse kick – where better than the Spiral for one of those? – Nonstop brought things to a close with his thumb-biting routine. We always scheduled our fights for first thing in the morning, knowing rush hour would provide an excuse to quit before any real damage was caused.

Rush hour came and went; pack, squeeze through the turnstile, unpack.

Pen II. Another pair of Is facing us, the penultimate pen.

Forty-eight hours left of *being*. However many times I recycled the words, that truth refused to mesh with the gears of my comprehension. Chillies burned my lips, the bright light scoured my eyes like a wire brush, Nonstop bugged me endlessly, but even on oblivion's doorstep, death remained as imponderable as the square root of minus two. There was no sense of difference about the day, no sensation of life leaking away, nothing arcing towards a crescendo.

Another day. How to pass twenty-four hours when you're sealed in an airing cupboard with a man who regards mucus as one of the major food groups?

The meals arrived.

'You're right,' I laughed to Nonstop, examining my pen pal's meagre ration of rice and beans. 'Justice *is* like cheese. You ain't got none of either.'

From under the bed ledge came . . . nothing. No talking, no snoring, no snorting, no whining, no whinging, no bitching, no snitching. Alarmed, I rolled to his side and shook Nonstop where he lay motionless.

'Nonstop! Are you all right?' I asked, tentatively prodding

his flank with my fingers. Could it be a stroke? Heart failure?

Nonstop sighed, visibly sagging like a punctured paddling pool, and slowly rotated his face towards mine. The soggy pastry skin around his eyes glowed an angry orange where he'd been rubbing, but the eyes themselves were wider and darker than I remembered ever seeing them.

'What's the matter, Nonstop?'

His answer came quieter than a gecko's echo. 'The matter? We're going to die, Mo,' was all he said. Then he shut his eyes and turned away from me. The unceasing geyser of meaningless sound had finally run dry; his inert figure became a font of the most profound, churchlike hush.

All at once, I felt terribly, terribly lonely. Many empty minutes scudded by.

'Some hero you turned out to be,' Nonstop mumbled at last, still not facing me.

'Hero?' I gulped.

It took an effort to hear him. 'If you only knew how much I'd bribed the manciples to be put in a pen with you. You were famous, Mo, a legend in the Establishment. For escaping. I thought . . .'

'Sorry. No chance, Nonstop, not from here. Everything was different in the Institute, you see there we –'

'Oh, will you SHUT UP your blethering neck hole for just this once!' thundered Nonstop. I almost fainted, bewildered and acutely hurt.

A parlous silence orbited inside the cell, trailing un-mouthed antagonisms behind it like the dusty flecks of a comet's tail. Nonstop shuffled over onto his broad side and looked at me.

'What will you miss?'

I jolted at his question. 'Miss?'

'Miss. About your life. That . . . girl?' The question was risible, the dead can miss nothing, the time for regrets was then, not later. But I knew what he meant.

'Yes. That is . . . no,' I said, slumping down. 'I never really knew Harete, Nonstop. I just made up . . . fantasies . . . in my mind about how things could have been between us. You know? Stories.'

'Oh, yes. I know that *very* well. Why don't you paint her?'

'Can't,' I replied curtly. I had tried to paint Harete many times before, working on the wall in a moistened teabag, but it had never worked. There was a line I sought, a curve that kinked just so, a path that prescribed the bight of her neck and the ease of her cheek, especially how it had looked whenever her head was half turned away from me. Yet the true line always eluded me. Without exception I'd scrubbed the pictures away, exasperated at my inability to delineate the girl whose memory I'd exalted.

It occurred to me then that I knew virtually nothing about Nonstop. 'What about you? What will you, ah, miss?'

'My sister,' he replied instantly. 'And decent cheese. I like cheese. Like*d*, I mean,' he said, stressing the d.

'You've a sister?'

Nonstop's face creased up and he thumped his thighs. 'I should have looked after her better, Mo,' he said. 'That's an older brother's duty, isn't it?'

Nonstop with a sister? Nonstopella . . . Nonstopina . . . Picturing that took an effort; imagining Nonstop doing anything other than wallowing on the floor of a prison cell like a beached manatee was not easy: Nonstop at home, Nonstop as a child, Nonstop caring for someone else . . . the images struck me as incongruous as a grandfather clock in a sombrero. I'd always taken him for the sort of solitary, deviant sneak whose idea of boyhood fun had involved maiming hedgehogs with an airgun.

I asked him, 'Were you close?' That's how people always phrased it. I remembered Harete asking me, 'Were you close to your father?'

'Only when he walloped me,' I'd always replied.

Nonstop put his two index fingers together, side by side, touching along their length. The fact that he of all people chose to communicate this without speaking leant the gesture an additional weight.

'And you . . . ?'

Keeping the fingers erect, Nonstop flung his arms wide apart, clobbering me square in the face.

'Steady!' I protested, testing for blood. 'Huh. Drifted apart?' I said.

Nonstop snatched me up by my tracksuit with both hands and jerked my head close to his. An infrequent user of the spigot, his face was a shocking mess: tears had excavated pale slug trails through sixty-nine days of dead skin and grime, and his neck and chest were raddled with circular blotches of ringworm.

'*Drifted?*' he steamed, angrier than I'd ever seen him. 'Did that look like a *drift* to you, Mo? Did it? *Torn* apart we were. My parents sent her away. And I did nothing to stop them. I should have spoken out, but I didn't. I bit my lip, held my tongue.'

Nonstop huffed and pushed me away. 'No one ever mentioned her again, Mo. She wasn't spoken about. The silence did for my parents in the end,' he said softly. 'Water boils in a vacuum and they boiled to death in their own silence. Serves them right.'

Sensing the truce between us would not endure, I posed a question that had long bothered me. 'Why do you bite your thumb like that when we fight?'

Nonstop's answer surprised me. 'When we were toddlers, me and my sister used to scrap like rats in a sack. She spoke funny, you see, she was special like that, and she'd get very frustrated. I was the only one who could understand her. I bit her once, got a humongous roasting for it. So after that, I used to bite myself, and sort of . . . project the wound onto her. Guess I never grew out of it.' His words drifted out like the last doleful puffs of smoke from a damped-down grate.

My suspicions were right, the window of clammy intimacy between us could not be held ajar, yet we knew we were just playing well-rehearsed roles; all the spite was spent. Nonstop was like a cell phone message, I decided, there was a different content there that could be extracted if you took the time to delve in deeper and rearrange the boundaries . . . but I had no time.

By mutual, unspoken consent, the rest of the day passed like the rest of the days. I got online, lying on the floor and jamming my hand between the water pipe and the wall, monitoring communications without participating. Arguments about footie, more chess moves, newer news about the war, now so distant and irrelevant it could have been an arm-wrestling competition waged between robotic octopuses for all I cared. According to Flat Pack, people were falling over themselves to join strange, new apocalyptic cults that were smothering the land like knotweed; in other regions, people were concentrating on slaughtering their neighbours with garden implements just because of the shape of the building they prayed in or the way they pronounced 'scone' or 'bath'. That's the thing about civil wars . . . long suppressed hatreds fizz out like the gas from a shaken pop bottle.

'Well off out of it,' I said to myself.

Some personal messages dribbled in from Five-a-Day and others, saying goodbye to me. None came for Nonstop.

The heat stuck to us like a second skin. A numbness descended, a soft blanket of fatalistic acceptance. The day felt like the end of a long, long Sunday afternoon, when no work has been done and all plans have crashed in the heart and you ease up on your futile labours and blissfully relinquish hope.

'We've still got tomorrow,' I sighed.

'And that's all we have,' Nonstop burst out. 'Tomorrow. There'll be nothing left of us soon; no one will miss us, Mo, that's what I find hardest to accept.'

'I know.'

'Feels like we're about to hand in an important homework assignment, or sit an exam. Only we've done no revision. We're going to flunk.'

I had vanishingly small experiences of home or work or exams, but I understood what he meant.

When I passed him his share of my food, our hands bumped. His fingers hooked around mine, hesitantly at first, then, when I did not oppose him, more securely. I found myself wondering how long it had been since that hand had touched someone who had needed him, not despised or pitied him. We pulled apart after a moment and nothing of our momentary skin-ship was mentioned.

Clang . . . clang, clang, clang, clang, clang

Clang, clang, clang, clang . . . clang, clang, clang, clang, clang

Clang, clang . . . clang, clang, clang

The message was coming through loudly. Unusually loudly. Startled, I looked around our cell, trying to locate the source of the sound: not the pipe, not the door either, not the spy slot . . . the ceiling? The vent in the ceiling?

Impossible. The vents did not connect with each other; no one could transmit via the vent, they'd have to be on top of the pen, accessing from the gantry . . .

Outside. That hyena-headed guard, Thera . . . no, Urethra . . . what had Atlas said he was called?

I listened to the signal and decoded the pattern of knocks. UXLUNAQSARARAGNAM

And twice again, the same.

Gibberish. But all the same, through force of habit I hurriedly made up a silly sentence to help me remember the sequence, a trick I had perfected from many hours of piecing together cell phone messages.

Uncle Xerxes loved Una. Quite something, as round and rough as Granny's nutmegs, always magical.

'Not a message. Just the fan making a noise. Bearing's gone,' I concluded after puzzling it over for some minutes.

The excitement over, the bulb blinked out, ticking loudly as it cooled. The black dragon of night roared down, fanning us with his tattered, leathery wings, wafting us towards the last day of our lives.

Chapter 2π

That night, my mind ran around in circles.

I was on the periphery of something, but I couldn't break through to the centre.

Why send that message? That was no wonky, shonky fan bearing, it was an intentional communication. Why climb onto the roof of the pen and hammer out a piece of mumbo jumbo?

{Think it through.}

That off-key voice again! Backchat from a daydream? My imagination had more imagination than I'd imagined, surely the product of a mind under pressure.

{Not a dream. Stop wasting time.}

Huh, bossy little delusion. I humoured it. How did that message run, let's think: *Uncle Xerxes loved Una. Quite something, as round and rough as Granny's nutmegs, always magical.*

UXLUNAQSARARAGNAM

That end piece is well strange: 'aragnam'. Funny, because it's an anagram of 'anagram'. An anagramagram. The r and the n are swapped around, that's all.

{So . . .}

Make the same substitutions elsewhere and experiment with spacing the characters out. Now we could have . . . yes:

UXLURA QS AN ANAGRAM

Qs? That would make sense if it was 'is'. So perhaps Q and I are interchanged as well. What do R and N and Q and I have in common?

I pictured the cell phone grid. An R was position 3-4. An N was 4-3. Letter I was 4-2, whereas Q was 2-4.

The columns and rows are swapped over! All the letter positions are, what is the word?

{Transposed.}

Right! The sender must have not been aware that the penitents send messages column first, then row. He'd muddled it up. So the ones on the diagonal – A, G, M, S, Y – remain the same, the others sort of reflect about that line, and the real message becomes . . .

ETHERA IS AN ANAGRAM

Ethera is an anagram, a puzzle inside a puzzle!

Ethera is a rearrangement of . . . The era . . . At here . . . Reheat . . .

One word was all it took. A keyword, an *ignition* keyword, the sensation of it turning in my mouth was sufficient to twist my life around in a flash, to instantly invert me around my own diagonal and send crashing down the columns that had propped up my despondency.

I'm not usually a screamer, but I screamed. I screamed and I shook Nonstop awake, fumbling for him under my bed.

'Nonstop, wake up! There's someone out there who cares for me. We're going to bust out or die trying, and we've only got one day to prepare!'

But how to escape?

A nucleus of thought started to grow in me, spreading out its fronds like ice crystals growing on a winter window.

Chapter 7 *

The light was already on when I woke up, air was flittering down though the vents, the Spiral was chittering and clacking and hymning to itself as it boosted up for another day.

I tumbled off the edge I'd lain on during the night and smacked my teeth onto the gritty floor. My mouth felt as if it had been stuffed with used bandages, a paste of sweat encased my face like a visor.

Rush hour would not happen for another thirty minutes or so, I had . . .

'Hand it over! Rush hour in two minutes, yuk-yuk!' barked Atlas. He was outside on the gantry, impatiently toeing the crap flap for the slop bucket.

Overslept. Down to my last day of life, and I'd overslept. Not surprising; I'd nodded off only a couple of minutes earlier. All through the night I'd been busy thinking, thinking like I'd never thunk before. I was *exhausted*. I groggily reviewed my plan for the day. What was it, now?

TO DO:
Escape

Save life
Save Nonstop's life

I hurled myself at the door. Everything depended on my speaking to Atlas and gaining his cooperation.

'Atlas, Atlas,' I shouted through the flap, 'it's our final meal today.'

'I know, yuk. Sorry, Mo.'

'We can request something special, right? That's the tradition, isn't it – the condemned men can have what they want for their last repast?'

'Sure, Mo. As long as I've got it, yuk-yuk. We're in a Mother Hubbard situation out here, so don't go requesting monkfish and baked Alaska. Yuk, Alaska, that brings back some memories, too many mountains!'

'Sure, sure. Listen, Atlas. Listen very carefully. This is what I want.'

Atlas heard me out, his lack of yuk-yuks telegraphing his bafflement. 'You're sure that's what you want? For real and actual?'

'Yes, Atlas. Exactly that, or as close as you can improvise.'

I hardly had time to deliver my strange order and pack before the call 'Move through!' was heard and we shuffled over.

Pen I.

Twenty-four hours to live.

Unless I could pull off the most hare-brained, most hopeless and worst prepared-for escape ever devised.

I began to pace the pen, which, on account of its compactness, amounted to no more than standing in the centre and turning

71

around, facing the left door then facing the right door in ever quickening succession. I spun round and round, pounding my head to loosen more ideas, ideas packed into my skull like yellowing earwax.

My overriding thought was, *this is too good to be true*.

More ideas jockeyed for consideration.

A dream. You're not yet awake. No, the smell. My dreams never had smells. The cell honked of raw, rude reality. I could smell Nonstop's breath, see where the sleeves of his tracksuit were brittle and crusty from two months of nose wipings. Those details were never present in dreams.

A trick. What for? *To keep us busy on our final day, to take our minds off our impending executions.* The notion had plausibility. Then why had no one else ever mentioned it before on the cell phone? *Same reason you haven't. In case it's real, and you don't want to alert the screws.*

No, that muddled message was too personalised, it would have signified nothing to anyone else.

You've gone mad. Your brain can't accept the fact that you're going to be horribly killed in a few hours.

Yes. That was credible. Couldn't counter that.

But one thought overruled all others. *What's the worst that could happen?*

'Mo, calm down! Unwind!' Nonstop called out from under the ledge, his first words of the day. He hadn't believed me when I'd roused him during the night. For once, it had been me who'd done all the talking; he'd have needed a chisel and sledgehammer to break into my feverish rambling. He'd dropped off after a few minutes of listening, snored like a rusty chainsaw. He'd doubtless written off the episode as a dream, or a bad case of sleep-talking.

My energy dissipated in the pen's crippling heat. Beneath me was a pale, dusty patch where my feet had worn away a layer of the cement floor.

Hope was a catastrophic gift to bequeath to people in our position. If this was all a cruel joke by Atlas . . . with my dying breath I'd curse him with giving birth to Brazil every night, or Russia sideways on.

My heart was in my mouth, but I think it was only a diversionary tactic to allow the rest of my insides to mount an escape bid from my opposite end. Even Nonstop began to waft a hand in front of his face.

'Hurry up with that blasted food, Atlas!' I fretted, acutely aware how perverse it was to be actively wishing away time on this, the last day of my existence.

Not a moment too soon the day's meals arrived. Atlas posted the food boxes through, and I ripped them from his hands, desperate to learn what he'd managed to obtain from my shopping list.

'See you around, Mo, yuk-yuk,' was all he said. I grunted back some equally anodyne reply, aware that, for all he purported to like me, I was nothing special to Atlas, that he saw people off every day. The meals I held represented the end of our deal and his obligation to find decent food. If anything he'd be glad to be rid of me.

Nonstop lumbered over on all fours, salivating lavishly. 'Our final meal,' he exclaimed. 'Bound to have pushed the boat out, pulled out all the stops, even for mine. I mean, it's a tradition, isn't it?'

'Wait, Nonstop,' I told him. 'Don't touch, and whatever you do, don't eat what's inside. Important, savvy?'

I popped the cartons open, one by one, and together we stared down at the food, each with our own very different expectations.

Nonstop's jaws repeatedly gaped open and hinged shut. On his face, disbelief fused with confusion, bled into disappointment then turned to pucker-lipped peevishness. Nonstop had clearly been setting tremendous store by the prospect of our last supper.

'Bunch of rancid, blister-licking tightwads!' Nonstop seethed through clenched teeth. 'No justice for me, and none for you either today,' he added bitterly. 'You must have finally exhausted your credit. You'd have thought they'd have saved *something* nice . . . this day of all days. Grievous it is, grievous unfair. I mean, how hard would it have been to rustle up a wedge of Brie or a slice of Stilton for old Nonstop?'

The meal was indeed the oddest mishmash of foodstuffs I had ever seen served together.

And it was *exactly* what I'd asked for. Almost – one item was missing; I wasn't surprised at its omission, it had been a substantial ask.

'Nice one, Atlas!' I declared. Silently I admonished myself for my earlier waspish feelings towards the sorry young man and regretted not saying a proper goodbye to him.

The food: a mound of glistening beetroot slices took up the majority of the first carton, all cut into neat circles. The second tub was full of . . . Nonstop dipped his finger into the brown powder and licked it clean.

'Coffee!' he spat, screwing up his face at the taste of the bitter granules.

That wasn't all. There were fistfuls of individually wrapped toffees, perhaps as many as forty sachets of vinegar such as you might find stacked by the tills in a cafeteria, and a fiesta of sparkly boiled sweets in pastel pink and orange and yellow. I tossed one to Nonstop.

'Pear drops,' he informed me, sucking on it. 'I remember these. The taste takes me back. That's *something* nice, I suppose.'

And my chillies. Lots of those, the largest number I'd ever received in one helping, every one of the shrivelled beauties a naga, the most ferociously spicy variety.

I took a pepper from the summit of the pile and bit into it. *Feel this*, I instructed my body, *feel this while you can still feel something*.

Nonstop laughed, began to sing. 'Peter Piper picked a piece of pickled pepper –'

'OW!' I cried, clutching at my cheek. 'Ow! That hurt!'

'Hot?'

I shook my head and spat into my hand. 'No, sharp!'

'Sharp spicy?'

'Sharp *sharp*,' I replied, and I held out my hand for him to see. Cached inside the chewed-up pepper was a thin, pointy-ended plastic stick: a toothpick.

The missing object! Atlas had even managed to secure that, and come up with a terrific hiding place for it.

Nonstop was almost in tears by then. 'I don't understand, Mo. Was it because I defeated them when they came fishing for you? Have we annoyed the screws, did you fall out with

Atlas?' he cried. 'Why, Mo, why this cruddy spread?'

I squatted next to Nonstop.

'It's not a cruddy spread, Nonstop,' I told him. 'It's exactly what I requested. Atlas has just delivered us . . .'

I hesitated. The next three words were almost too big for our tiny pen.

'An escape kit.'

Chapter 8

A lifeline. Just before Dexter Manus sounded out the final syllable of our death sentences, I'd written the pair of us a lifeline. Atlas had delivered the props, now we had to perform.

Nonstop was wittering and twittering. 'Food. It's all just food. No guns, no knives, no screwdrivers or files, no hammers, no saws. What use can food be, other than for eating?'

'Food for thought, eh, Nonstop?' I laughed nervously back. 'We've spent so long obsessing about the *when* and *how* of our deaths, we've totally forgotten the *why*. Why the Spiral? We knew from day one there was no reprieve. So why not kill us on day one? There must be something beyond the Spiral, else it's entirely pointless.'

Nonstop blinked that big blink people reserve for greeting provocative ideas received from people they'd thought dimmer than themselves.

'Something beyond here? Like . . . what? You've heard the rumours on the cell phone, Mo, the worst of all possible deaths. What could Dexter Manus be planning to do with us?'

'Anything. But whatever he does, I can't believe he does it here in these pens. So there has to be a time between us being in pen one and being there, wherever "there" is. Agreed?'

'I . . . yes. Perhaps, maybe.'

'This kit represents our best chance of making use of that opportunity, being escorted to Dexter Manus. A chance in a million, no more, but it's better than zero. Only food, yes, but that's in accordance with the golden . . . no, the plutonium rule of escaping: *use what you've got*.'

'So, how does this rubbish help us? What are we going to do – bribe Dexter Manus with a bag of sweeties and a cup of coffee? Hope he's intending to bite our necks and give him a toffee to loosen his fillings beforehand? Pray that he has an allergy to beetroot?'

I scratched my fluff-smothered chin and thought how I could explain my ideas to Nonstop. I barely grasped them myself. 'All escapes follows a basic formula. What's that chart thing scientists use, the one that lists all the ingredients of the world? You know, the . . . the spasmodic stable of the elephants?'

'The periodic table of the elements, Mo. The ancients thought there were only four: earth, fire, air and water. Actually, there are –'

'Right! Well, the periodic table of escaping contains only five elements,' I said. 'The first element is to break open a lock, for which we have a pick. A toothpick, but that'll double as a lock pick.'

'But what lock? The turnstiles?'

'No, they have no visible locks. At some point tomorrow we're bound to meet with handcuffs or padlocks. If we do, we'll pick them.'

'And the rest?'

'The other elements are to fight past guards, for which we need some weapons; to climb over barriers –'

'We'll need ropes and grappling irons and ladders!'

'Not necessarily. To evade capture, for which we need a disguise.'

'But . . . but . . . but . . .'

'And finally, the most vital element of all. The element of surprise.'

There was no time for further discussion. 'Take off your tracksuit,' I commanded Nonstop. 'Take it off, and shove it in the slop bucket. *Now!*'

Chapter 9

As Nonstop undressed, I shed my own clothes and dumped them in the plastic slop pale, squishing them down to give them a thorough soaking.

Active in body and mind, the bewitching Spiral stupor that had for so long impregnated my every pore began to sweat itself out. *Escaping from prison is much like kissing a girl*, I hypothesised. *Or a boy*, I supposed, *depending*. I'd done each exactly once before – one kiss for Harete, one escape, I mean – so I felt I could speak from experience. The first time you spend forever preparing for it, thinking what to say, how to begin, steaming with worry about what you'll do if it all goes wrong. The second time, you don't care so much, it just comes naturally. You pucker up and go for it.

Not that we were being cavalier about the operation, not by any stretch. But when I thought back to how long Harete and Moth and I had taken in the Institute to get ready for our escape that time, I cringed. What had we been playing at?

There was no point in even thinking about an escape unless we could change the appearance of our clothes. Thankfully, neither of us had been to the lavatory so far in our new pen which meant the slop bucket was full of strong, clean bleach. By drenching our Spiral tracksuits in the bucket, I hoped to remove, or at least subdue, their virulent, fluorescent orange colour, colour that would be a giveaway if we ever did escape from the Spiral. We left the clothes to soak and set to work on the other items.

'Crunch up the toffees,' I instructed Nonstop, 'and grind in the boiled sweets. Work the gunge into a sticky ball, add water if it starts to set too hard. Eat *nothing*.'

I began mashing and tearing the chillies, reducing them to a squishy pulp with my fingers.

We worked for hours without resting. Normally, it amazed me how every diminishing portion of my remaining life zoomed up and expanded to fully occupy my consciousness, each thin sliver a snug refuge against the rising deluge; seventy days ago, seventy days had seemed an age. Now, down to the last day, I sought solace in the thought that I still had the rest of the morning, the whole of the afternoon, all of the night. But that day, trickster time intrigued against me, pedalling faster than ever before, winding up my life's yarn at an ever accelerating rate.

I washed out our soap dispenser and filled it with a mixture of vinegar and the ground up chillies. The vinegar was a strong one, each sachet smelled like the essence of an entire chain of chip shops.

'One blast of that in the face, and you're down, blinded for minutes,' I explained to Nonstop. Forcing home the dispenser piston with my thumb, I sprayed a jet of the fluid across the cell and watched with satisfaction where it splatted against

81

the wall and trickled down. My fingers were still glowing from contact with the fruits despite a protracted wash under the spigot; I had to repeatedly remind myself not to put them anywhere near my eyes. Or elsewhere. Getting even a tiny smear from an oily chilli in certain places was breathtakingly painful even to a hardened naga addict like myself.

By kneading it directly under the air vent, I softened the ball of crunched-up toffees and boiled sweets Nonstop had made. I tipped the mushed-together confection into a plastic bag and sealed it.

'Glue,' I explained. 'Well strong, too. Did you ever know a situation when it wasn't useful to have glue to hand?'

Nonstop scrunched his grimy features into a distinctly unfamiliar configuration – silent deliberation. Thinking, he breathed noisily through his open mouth. Was he beginning to comprehend my plan?

We tipped the bleach from the bucket before it rotted the tracksuits. I poured on fresh water from the spigot, threw in the beetroot and coffee granules.

'The orange colour's almost gone. Now we dye them,' I said. 'They'll look like normal Establishment kit then, mucky brown.'

I bagged up some leftover beetroot slices. Novel, diabolical possibilities raised themselves for almost everything I looked at. I was deep into my escape mindset, every object I viewed presented itself to me like a cell phone message, capable of being twisted and anagrammed and punned into new interpretations.

'We're going to have to see it through, Nonstop,' I told him. 'Come face to face with Dexter Manus. And hope we can know when it's the right moment to act.'

Nonstop nodded enthusiastically. 'We'll know, Mo,' he assured me, 'just like in my experiments. We probe deeper and deeper until we experience the collision. Then we scatter. Told you all this before I did, countless times, but you never listen to me, you're always too busy putting poor old Nonstop down.'

'Too busy picking him up,' I rejoindered, thinking about the morning bucket ritual. I had no idea what he meant, that talk about his experiments.

When our tracksuits had steeped sufficiently in their dun-coloured soup, we hauled them out and let them steam themselves dry in the hot cell. They looked a muddy mess, a reasonable approximation to the overalls worn by the Establishment's surface denizens.

Impatient, I dressed in my still-wet clothes, filled the pockets with the bag of glue, the chilli spray, the toothpick. Could I pick a lock? Why not – I'd heard enough people describe how in the Institute and the Establishment.

We had only to wait. We must have been well into the evening, and we were both starving hungry, having not eaten any of our escape kit meal. I'd saved two cones of dry coffee granules, intending we'd scoff them as soon as the bulb went out; the caffeine buzz would keep us alert for surprises.

We could still hear some cell phone messages, but none came for us. We were shunned, too close to death for others to want to acknowledge, beyond the slop pale. All I could think to send back to the other pen-sioners trapped on the Spiral, our winding staircase to death, was one final cry of defiance:

NEVER GO STRAIGHT

My insides felt they had contracted to the volume of a

pinhead, and my juiceless throat developed that sucking sensation you get before you vomit. Dying was so easy, by far the easiest thing I had ever prepared to do. All it needed was to lie back and wait; I wasn't sure I possessed the courage or the right to resist. Surely this squall of activity was all so much snow in May, too late to take hold, the whole idea too desperate? Was this why the thought of my death had never done more than nibble me lamely with filed-down fangs, because all along I'd secretly believed some fresh hope would gush up? That was madder than trousers for trout.

I struggled to occupy myself in those last minutes of light. My belly was locked solid; my limbs prickled with alternating currents of excitement and doubt, tension and despair. *It can't work. It must work. It can't work. It must work.*

I rested on the bed ledge. A bizarre debate raged in my spinning, sleep-deprived head. One voice was mine, the other was a lilting, looping, musical voice that skipped from key to key and instrument to instrument, bouncing from zither to clarinet, from saxophone to hurdy-gurdy. I identified my interlocutor as the dream voice who'd encouraged me to solve the mystery of the transposed cell phone message. Whatever it was, it seemed to be sticking around.

{This will work.}

How? I still don't know what's beyond the door!

{If it works, you will live. If it doesn't, you will die and know no more. Therefore, it will work, because that is the only option that still leaves a you to be aware.}

That's lunacy. Circular reasoning.

{Perhaps. The Spiral is an equation – a soluble one. All life is mathematics, Mo. Don't you remember what you were taught?}

The Numbers taught me that, yes . . . an equation. Nonstop and me must be the two terms, so that would make it a . . . what did they call them? A quad-erratic equation.

{Have confidence. You've succeeded before.}

Last time I had two trusted friends and I knew what lay beyond the walls of the Institute. Well, one trusted friend and a . . . Now, I've a blundering ox who can hardly walk, I'm deep underground and I've a date with Dexter Manus, our unmaker – remember? I'll meet him very soon. What will he be like? Been wondering that for ages.

{Mo, you always were a poor student. Be very careful when you set your heart on discovering something. Every story has a twist!}

Oh, that. The *twist*. The Institute had taught me all about the *squeeze*, that habit life has of crushing you between two equally hostile forces. The Numbers were too canny to fall victim to squeezes, but they went a bundle on the twist. The twist, they said, was the universe's tendency to deceive you, to dupe you, to lead you up the garden path and dump manure on you. What was that funny football phrase I'd heard on the cell phone, for when a player kicked the ball between an opponent's legs and left him gawping like a dummy?

{I know nothing of these trivialities!}

Who cares, footie was never my game. The point was, the more you desire something, the longer you seek it, the greater will be the twist. Whatever it is you want, you'll find the reverse of it, or a skewed-around version of it. Nothing is ever straight or easy. Better to just give up then, admit defeat.

{Of course it's not! Nonstop understands. Getting to the truth often involves going round in circles until you collide with the opposite of your expectations.}

I don't want to get to the truth, I want to escape!

{Do you? Far more rewarding to go deeper, get to the heart of the matter.}

But I caused the war, the death of the Numbers. I deserve to die.

{No! No cubed! You have the right to live and grow to be a man, not exist as a carcass turning on a spit. Beyond the Spiral, the sour, ambiguous pleasures of adult life await you. You are old enough now to swap honey for hops, to dare, to err, to map the fickle nap of velvet, to love.}

Oh, love, now is it? Get me! Any more demands? A crystal mansion on the moon, a mariachi band to serenade me at the breakfast table, a hand-gilded platypus egg? What do I know about love? Slop buckets and vomit, that's what I know about, ale houses and jail houses; not that I'd ever drunk beer, but Dad used to park me in the corner of rammy pubs when he met his cronies. He didn't drink either, that had been Mum's exclusive pastime, he went to play his arrows. I could even then recall the brown smells of the grown-ups' ciggies and stout, the thunk-thunk-thunk of darts landing in the sisal board. Those darts games used to bug me. I could never understand why it wasn't the centre of the board, the bullseye, that earned the most points. So tempting, right, slap-bang in the middle . . .

{Yes, Mo. A dart straight to the heart!}

And after, the lung-pricking nick of the cold when Dad dragged me outside and we walked home together through concrete canyons to the high-rise hutch we inhabited. Not much more than an above-ground Spiral, that flat.

Dreaming. I jolted awake, livid with myself.

The onslaught of sleep-borne memories was a peerless agony. I wolfed down my pile of dry coffee granules. Still-nattering Nonstop waved his away so I scarfed down his share too, revelling in the burst of zesty bitterness and alertness they brought me.

The light winked out.

Chapter 10

Time to kill.

I wasn't going to risk being caught napping again. The coffee would keep me awake, these might be my final hours alive. I tucked my knees under my chin and propped my back against the wall, settled in.

My ribs were bending against the strain of my pumping innards; I felt my heart might disintegrate under the load and erupt through my chest like an over-spun flywheel. Life, not death, was quickening me, the prospect of a fight and the pin-thin chance of adding new chapters to my own story.

The heat in the pen was phenomenal, the darkness total, the only sounds mine and Nonstop's rough, irregular breathing. Atlas must have not been on duty that night. For a while I thought Nonstop was chanting 'I'll do anything to stay alive, anything to stay alive,' but concluded it was just the rhythm of the clattering fan incorporating into the chuntering of my own phantoms.

The light came on, went off, came on, went off, over and over.

I snapped to attention, not knowing if fat hours or skinny minutes had elapsed. This was it.

Time to die.

I roared, every corpuscle of my body rebelling, and I cried out the only words there ever are to say, the chorus of the cosmos. 'I DON'T WANT TO DIE! SAVE ME, MUM, DAD, NONSTOP, LEW, I ONLY WANT TO LIVE!'

Chapter 11 *

The left-hand door opened by itself. Behind it, another turnstile, only this one had looped bars that glowed with a golden sheen. Beyond them, a glare it was impossible to look into.

Nonstop tumbled out from under the bed ledge. I helped him upright; we stood shoulder to shoulder under our strobing bulb. Nonstop shook the drips from his nose, brushed his hair out of his eyes, straightened his top, slipped on his trainers. He sucked in his chest and bunched up an expanse of loose material at the front of his oversized trousers. 'We should try to look our best, Mo, whatever happens,' he said, his tone serious, grown up. I made a final adjustment to my plan.

'Slip this under your tongue,' I instructed, passing him the toothpick. 'That way, you can spit it into my hands if they cuff them in front of or behind me.'

A hidden loudspeaker exploded into life directly above us, belting out mechanised commands: 'Out! Out!'

The noise was beyond human tolerance. Scrabbling to be first we crashed one at a time through the golden turnstile.

As soon as we passed over, the noises quit, and we were engulfed in a dense freezing fog. Edging forwards, we saw that we had entered a narrow corridor with pure, blank white walls, white floor, white ceiling. The fog dissipated in seconds, and I understood then it had been caused by the sweat-laden air of our foetid pen contacting the icy atmosphere in the passageway.

A figure bore down on us, moving from the direction of the taintless light we could not bear to gaze upon. I tried to perceive him through a palisade of fingers stretched across my eyes. His shadow was long, he walked along it, rolling it up in a few brisk strides. I slipped a hand in my pocket and made ready with my chilli spray.

Death wore a hairnet.

Chapter 12

And yellow rubber gloves. And a quilted top. And around her neck on a lanyard a laminated badge with her photograph on it and words that read: HUMAN RESOURCES.

Screws flanked her, but held back.

Still holding up his trousers, Nonstop blew into his free hand. 'Are you D-D-Dexter Mmmmmmmanus?' he stammered, pressing close to me.

The woman looked Nonstop up and down and pulled a face whittled by revulsion. She was squat and dumpy, with wire-wool hair modelled on a roadkill badger snared under a yellow hairnet.

'All in good time,' she said, frowning. Then, briskly, 'You're lucky, we've vacancies. We usually do, mind, turnover is shocking.'

'Turnover?' I heard someone say. Probably me, I couldn't be sure; I was shivering in the fierce cold, my teeth were vibrating, I felt disconnected from everything, my body included.

'Starfish shoes,' she replied matter-of-factly. 'Why are your uniforms different?' she asked.

'We're category Z,' I said, hoping that made sense to her,

that it implied we were due the least severe form of whatever it was we were destined for.

She nodded incuriously. 'As you say. Second shift despatch are short, but they don't start ops till five. Hmm. We've two slots helping out in the deception hall, I'll assign you there.'

She stabbed at her clipboard with a ballpoint pen, tutting when the pen refused to write. She *hhhhhrrrred* on it twice to warm it up, each time exposing a mouth like a vandalised cemetery, then tried again.

'Ooh!' she said. 'That's odd. Which one of you is known as Mo?'

'H-h-he is,' said Nonstop. Was he dobbing me in? What lay in store, extra torture?

'Only, I've a note about you in this encyclical.'

'A *what*?'

'A circular letter,' said Hairnet, holding up one that was blatantly rectangular. 'There's a preservation order on you. You're to be recirculated, put back on the Spiral. There's luck! What I always said. It's all about who you know.'

Incredulous, Nonstop and I both choked.

'No, thanks,' I told her. 'I'd rather stay with my pen pal. See it through. I can't stomach going round again.'

I meant what I said. I was psyched for it, whatever *it* was, prepared, equipped. And that was a minor consideration; three days earlier I'd wanted to throttle Nonstop. Now, separation from him was unconscionable.

Hairnet did a double double take but said, 'Your choice. I can't make you. Once you pass over, there's no coming back.'

'No. Please, just get –'

'Sentenced to death?' she asked brightly. Ridiculously, Nonstop and I both nodded.

The woman stepped to one side, pushed open a white door set in the white wall. 'Well, here it is then, ducks,' she said, and we walked meekly through.

Chapter 13*

Everything happens at once.

Time ceases to flow, becomes a basalt slab on which all events are immutably etched. Everything there is to see, we see, frozen in the viscid ever-now, and all illuminated by a vile, bile-green light.

People, everywhere in the hall. Children, teenagers, old men and old women; suitcases, baskets, holdalls, handbags, rucksacks, carpet bags, walking frames, crutches, wheelchairs, monsoons of thrown-away documents; a seething, heaving tumult of people and possessions and paperwork swirling around us, basting in heat and terror. I don't know why, but I feel we've arrived seconds after some appalling disclosure has been made.

A hooter blasts, right by my ear. From the shadows appear scores of men in khaki-coloured outfits, some wearing rubber boots, most with towels wrapped around their heads. 'Summoners, to work! Get them up! Get them moving! More care consumers in five minutes, no bonus if we don't clear this lot before then, penalty rations!'

Nonstop pulls me aside, flattens us both tight up against the wall. Up they go, the men and the women and the children;

the summoners – *did I hear that word right?* – grab them by their arms and lock them into handcuffs, a moving conveyor of shackles that runs in a line overhead. 'You two newbies, there by the wall, get cracking! It's us or them! It's them or you!'

We fossilise, not understanding. The sound in the hall is a waterfall, a concussing boom of fury and confusion. The evacuees' arms are manhandled into the conveyor's dangling shackles, their luggage hurled aside. Some lash out, resist, but most are too old, too young, too weak, too stunned by whatever calamitous deceit they have fallen to. I recognise them now; they are the unloved, the unfortunate, the unproductive, the unassuming, the unhealthy, the ill-limbed, burdens to their relatives, to the Fartherland. And I see why the summoners wear towels around their heads, to protect against flying kicks and involuntary showers of liquefied panic as they hook up their victims and send them on their way.

'Latecomer, on express checkout. Summoners attend!' We spin, agog, aghast. At an opening in the wall beside us appears a woman with a puckered pink tunnel of a mouth, well-dressed, snooty-looking, face like a happy cat's backside.

'Here's one for you, needy little bitch,' she screeches, 'greedy cuckoo. Well, I mean, the cost of her medicines! Hard enough to keep one car running with all these shortages, with all this war on, let alone two.' Something small and bony is propelled through the doorway, pivots over Nonstop's shoe and spills onto the ground. Cat-Bum-Face hurls a second object straight at me, a little box. 'Have 'em, no use to me now, can't even flog 'em on the black market,' she says.

Cat-Bum-Face again, catatonic: 'This is the Compensation

Camp, isn't it? Where's my bleeding compo then, my coupons? I'm doing the Fartherland a favour, aren't I, one less useless mouth? Give me my fuel tokens!' Two summoners race up. Who are these creatures? Their clothes resemble Spiral tracksuits, except they're olive coloured.

'Get her up,' they shout at me and Nonstop, 'get your hands dirty, prove you've the will to live.' One of the summoners starts to box my head, but I don't react or defend myself, I stand there dumbskulled.

Nonstop kneels by the bony thing. 'Hey now, 's gonna be all right,' and she shows him her face, it looks bean-green in this sickening light, and she says:

'I'm sick, not thick, they're going to kill us, everybody knows that, only idiots believe they're really going to be cared for.'

Through the doorway, green-lit vampires elbow Cat-Bum-Face aside. I spot fit bodies in fashionable garb, plump bellies, suntans. 'Give us our gas tokens, our tax vouchers, our sugar coupons! We've handed them over like the adverts told us, we want our rewards. Compensation, compensation!' they roar, pounding on the counter.

'Com-pen-sa-tion!'

'Com-pen-sa-tion!'

'Last chance,' bellows the summoner, pointing at the girl. 'Get her shackled on the dead-line!' And Nonstop stands up, straightens up, first time I've ever seen him stand properly unaided; he's still a huge bloke despite his time on the Spiral. His face has rucked into a knotted whorl of fury.

'THE SCAB I WILL!' he yells and he headbutts the summoner square on the nose. The struck nose explodes.

Nonstop's trackie trousers fall down around his ankles. No undershorts.

And *that's* the moment.

That's the precise moment when The Most Irritating Human Being Who Ever Lived becomes my New Best Friend.

'Mo,' he gargles, 'I've swallowed that toothpick. I'm sorry, I'm sorry.' He's choking badly, it's stuck in his throat, his face turns black. Summoners whoop and jump on us from all angles. I'm chewing shoe; my nads are stamped until they're pulsating sacks of agony. I'm up on the dead-line, hands shackled above my head, trainer toes scraping the floor. Nonstop's suspended behind me, the beating's dislodged the pick but our precious tool is lost. Behind Nonstop hangs the girl; there are two others in front of me.

The dead-line moves, the shackles slide along the rail, we're off. I glimpse a summoner riding a mobility scooter; he's going round and round in circles, bawling into a megaphone: 'Give me your tired, your poor, your huddled masses.' Other summoners are scavenging from the abandoned luggage, wolfing any food they find; two of them plunge into a drum of biscuits like it's a high-divers' splash pool.

We accelerate, glide out of the departure hall. I see skips heaped high with wheelchairs, a tepee of toupees. I peer down into mossy-hued side halls where lines of women sit at trestle tables and sort through spoil tips of suitcases, slag heaps of handbags, pyramids of spectacles. A banner headed DELIVERING TREATMENT SOLUTIONS boasts that THE COMPENSATION CAMP HAS A SEVENTY-FIVE PER CENT RECYCLING RATE. We pass a long galley with a floor-to-ceiling window; I spot a familiar dog-head guard in clumpy boots and a rubbery gas mask on the other side of the glass. He fist-pumps as he watches us whoosh by, and I call out to him, to no avail.

I'm a dangling dead-weight, my arms aflame with pain. The girl's wailing.

'What's your name, your name?' Nonstop demands but the girl doesn't reply. 'Where're they taking us, Mo?' he asks, and I tell him:

'We're going to the dead end, the terminus, the last word, the Manus crypt.'

Chapter 14

The dead-line diverges; the people ahead of us fork away to the left, our group of five is switched down the right-hand track. Before us stands a curtain of opaque plastic slats. There's a clock on the wall to one side, nothing else to see. Under the slats howl jets of wickedly frigid blast-chiller air. The hurt in my shoulders, the sickly green light and the teeth-splitting cold are all I can think about.

The dead-line stops; we jerk and jiggle as it judders to a standstill.

'Mind the gap,' an automated voice intones. The dead-line squeaks, the first of our group separates and is dragged by his shackles through the slats. The old, shoeless man does not resist. His socks don't match, I notice, one plain, one diamond patterned.

The sound reminds me of an office stapler, or the lever on a fiddly toaster being pulled down hard. *Thurrr-wock.*

My head droops; I'm writhing desperately to stretch my toes downwards to touch the floor and take the weight off my stricken shoulders, but I can't manage it.

'Mind the gap.' The next member of our group glides

forwards. Her eyes are closed, her head bobs and nods but it's only recoil from the movement. She's wearing nothing but a paper shift done up at the back, turfed out of a hospital bed I suppose. She nudges against the slats, they impede her movement for a fraction of a second before they divide and she vanishes.

The stapler fires again. *Thurr-wock*.

'Mind the gap.' The line starts up. My turn.

'Manus!' I scream. I'm not going to die easy, I'm going to gob into death's eye, kick out his teeth, bite his face. I squirm, try to mess myself, make his task as loathsome as possible, but it's too cold and nothing happens.

'Here I come, Dexter Manus, you glob of discharge! Fight me!' I'm overwhelmed by a tsunami of indiscriminate sensory desires, a violent fervour to taste fried onions, smell paraffin and creosote, feel damp sand, see turquoise.

Music. They're playing music, over the speakers. Chintzy pop tunes, music to murder to. *Shalalalala oooh baybee why durnt ya lurve me yeah . . .*

The dead-line clanks, stops. The slats part with a slapping sound.

Dexter Manus walks out.

Him.

. . . Wanna bee with yooo ma baybeee . . .

We stare at each other, me dangling, him standing. Did he recognise my voice? It takes me a few seconds to mentally shave off the matted deadlocks of his beard, strip away the rubber gloves and padded jerkin, restore shape to the imploded cheeks. His eyes are two burned corks dropped into mushy,

101

week-old kerbside snow.

'Oh, Lew,' I sob. 'My Lieutenant Lew. How can you be Dexter Manus; I don't understand, what are you doing here?'

Lew waggles his left hand at me. It's bound by a plaited wire cord that winds its way back through the slats.

'I'm a left-tenant now, Mo,' he croaks. His right hand grips a metal implement the size of an electric drill, fixed to a flexible hose. He lifts the tool for me to see, points it straight at me.

'Time to meet Dexter Manus,' he says, his voice expressionless, his face deadpan. He moves closer, stands right by me. His breath is icy, colder even than the gale from beyond the curtain.

'I held on too long, Mo,' Lew says dreamily. 'Should have let go right from the start, like you did. Good boy, Mo. I'm proud, very –'

Lew stands to attention and salutes me. With his right hand he touches the tool to the side of his head. His thumb moves to cover a button on the top, flexes; I scrunch my face and look aside, do a half-swallow, half-yawn to swamp my ears with the buzz of my own blood rush.

Thurr-wock. Lew falls, crashes down at my feet, his hand flaps free but the tool stays fixed against his demolished skull, held in place by a metal bolt impaled deep into his cranium. A puddle of liquorice-black blood spreads rapidly out in a halo for my dead friend. Looking straight down into the pool of leaking head oil, I see myself reflected.

. . . *Life's gurnna bee so gurd togeyther, yeah yeah yeah* . . .

Black blood?

Because of the green light, of course.

And if blood appears black, then bright orange tracksuits would look . . . drab olive?

The summoners were us, people from the Spiral. My world turns inside out like a rubber glove, right becomes left, Dexter becomes even more sinister.

The people who ruled the Fartherland understood a thing or two. Tell someone for seventy days that they're going to die, then at the last second offer them the deal of a lifetime: do the worst job imaginable, dispose of those we deem worthless to our society, live until you can bear it no longer, then die by your own hand. *Sentenced to death.* Those were the words of the Praxidike, the judge who'd convicted us. Nothing about being executed, I realise. Those who accept the offer are sentenced to death for the rest of their lives, to organize it, live amongst it, distribute it. The guilt would be theirs, the Establishment could convince itself its hands were clean.

The worst of all possible deaths.

'Mo! This is it,' Nonstop yells, 'the moment of collision. Time to escape, Mo, we've got to get out before they replace him. That's what they meant all along, we die by our own right hand!'

Or those of a friend, someone else from the Spiral. No time to ponder it, or to regret Lew's capitulation. Our arms are cuffed above us, and our lock pick is lost. What I'd give for another pair of hands! I glance at the clock on the wall. It's a proper clock but with a digital display inset, a clock within a clock. The second hand ticks; the clock reads precisely

3:14:15

{It's Pi time we were getting out of here, Mo,} strums that odd, discordant musical voice, emanating from somewhere inside me.

The clock hands!

I rock energetically on my shackles, back and forth, ignoring how the metal rings chomp into my wrists. Lew's body is right below me – did he plan that? I silently thank him and use him to kick against, to raise my legs higher. I aim a foot at the wall, catch the clock just below the six, hoof it free from the wall. The clock drops, lands *smack-crack* on the floor, rolls, *STOP IT!*

The transparent cover pops off and spins away like a wheel trim from a car that's cornered too fast. I pinch the clock between my feet, manoeuvre it on top of Lew, its face covering his. With my left foot, I scrape off my right trainer at the heel. The second hand's too thin, the hour hand's too wide, only the minute hand will do. *Goldiclocks*, I laugh to myself.

My exposed toes are thin and nimble, *Use chopsticks with his feet, that one could*, Dad's voice, *he could change a light bulb with them*. I grip the clock's minute hand between my first two toes and bend upwards. Harder! The hand snaps off at the spindle, almost pings away.

'Mo, what are you playing at?' shouts Nonstop. The freezing breeze pouring from the slats is turning my foot blue; my toes are numb and difficult to control; I have to pretend my foot isn't my foot, it's a machine, a device, the pain isn't mine. I kink my leg, lift up the shaking foot with the clock hand gripped between the trembling toes and offer it to Nonstop's mouth.

He accepts the proffered object between his teeth. *Don't speak now, Nonstop, whatever you do, don't speak, don't swallow.* I shunt myself closer to Nonstop, jolting my handcuffs backwards along the overhead rail to bring the two of us marginally closer together. Nonstop copies me, works himself in my direction. I stretch out my neck, Nonstop cranes his, offers me his mouth.

I clamp the broken-off clock hand between my teeth and take it from his.

I have to use Nonstop again, walk up him like a blubbery ladder so I can bend my arms and pass the clock hand from my mouth to my fingers. It's desperate. One last heave and I do it, I get my face right up as high as my hands, just below the level of the rail. My frozen digits have it!

Next, I explore the surface of the shackles, feeling them, reading them. Standard handcuffs, for all the business of them being attached to the motorised rail. My college was prison; time to apply my ear-learning, the trade tricks I've overheard discussed in workshops and shower blocks, find where the curved bracelet enters the body of the cuff . . . *easy!* Force the minute hand down that gap. Not picking, *shimming*, slipping the bendy plastic strip in between the two interlocked parts of the cuff, sliding them apart. So unbelievably stiff, *push, push, squeeze it down!* Now the tricky part: with the other hand, reach over and actually *tighten* the shimmed cuff, compress it inwards. That drags the shim down into the mechanism where the smooth plastic would act as a wedge, prising open the serrated sections.

One click, two clicks.

That's my kind of music. I flex my wrist and the cuff flies open. One hand free. Nonstop ogles me in amazement – 'Escape artist!' he gasps. Now the other hand, same procedure. I have to twine my legs around Nonstop for support as I work on that one.

I drop the short distance to the floor, land on Lew, earn myself a bath in Lew's brains. Nonstop's actually crying. 'The girl,' he shouts, 'free the girl next.' I'm rubbing my arms, my hands, restoring circulation. I pull on my trainer, race around, the first chance to look at her. She's dressed in a baggy cardigan and trousers, travelling clothes, all part of Cat-Bum-Face's deception. What is she, twelve? Thirteen? Her face is narrow and bloodless, her hair is fair, her eyes shut, but she's not a goner because I see her shiver.

I can't free her, I'm not tall enough. I dash through the slatted curtain. A stool! I drag it, stand on it and shim the nameless girl's cuffs, easier and quicker to do hers than my own but still not instantaneous. 'Leave me,' she protests, 'without my medicine I'm dead anyway, rather it was quick than drawn out and painful.' My trackie top rattles as I work, odd cos the zip's plastic. No, in the pocket is the box Cat-Bum-Face threw, forgotten I'd stowed it.

'These?' I cry, waggling the box, a medicinal maraca.

The girl opens her eyes. 'My pills! Yes, yes, yes!'

Her cuffs spring apart. She drops to a rumpled heap. Two down, one to go.

Clanking, grating, a hundred hamster wheels in need of oil – a new batch of victims suspended from their cuffs trundles into sight, pulls up and stops. A locomotive of the damned.

Pandemonium. The people all see what I'm doing. I turn my back to them and begin work on Nonstop's cuffs, inoculating myself to their pleas. 'What's going on, where are the doctors, they told us we'd be looked after, please find my wife I know she's here somewhere, my wife, have you seen my wife, help us, we've money, don't leave us! We've been tricked, why are they doing this, our own families brought us here, help us, FOR THE LOVE OF –'

The plastic clock hand's almost useless as a shim now, all worn and frayed. Nonstop's cuffs stubbornly refuse to cooperate, they're shiner, newer, stiffer. I've released one cuff and am starting on the second when we hear:

'Mind the gap.'

And Nonstop jolts forwards, first in line. They must have found a new operator; he's come in from the other side of the slats. I'm clinging to Nonstop, my legs wrapped around him, still working the final cuff.

Worse, I turn and see that Hairnet's back, with two summoners this time, pounding along the passageway from the direction of the deception area. The people suspended from the dead-line go berserk, scream and swear and kick at them. They're suffering from no illusions now; a sofa-sized woman with a ripped dress swings from her shackles and with a swipe from her broad hips she smacks the queue brutes down. 'Save yourself, sunshine,' the big woman shouts at me, 'save yourself.'

Below me, the girl sits up, blinks around her, notices what I'd forgotten: the dead-line's moving but the new guy's not retrieved the bolt gun from Lew's crumpled skull. Just as Nonstop and I brush through the flaps, the girl comes to life, races through, holding the device in both hands. *Thurr-wock*.

A scream, the condensation of agony. Nonstop's second cuff gives at last; he falls, taking me with him. In the dark chamber I catch the briefest glimpse of a man in a tracksuit rolling lamely on the floor, a hole where he once had a kneecap.

We run. The roar of dismay behind us tears through my body like a plough, but still we run. Nonstop's unravelled himself from his trousers, has them around his neck. He's pulling the girl along by her scrawny arm. Through the killing zone we lumber, out the other side. The cold is marrow-snapping. I ban my eyes from looking; I don't shut them but I mentally sever the connection to my brain. Surprised people spin around as we race past; we burst through swing doors, dodge forklift trucks hauling piles of bodies with barcodes printed on the soles of their feet.

'Unexpected items in the tagging area,' blares an automated alarm. Summoners and hairnet women converge on us; I pull out the chilli spray and souse them in their faces, one blast apiece. Astonishingly effective, they crash away, blinded by the edible napalm. Nonstop's raving like a trouser-less ogre, battering anyone that comes near us with his gammon joint fists.

We barge through double doors into a narrow gallery, like the one we passed earlier. To the side, a green-tinted pane of glass, stretching from floor to ceiling. At the end, a second door – solid, unbreakable, locked from the other side. Nonstop leans against the door we've just come through, coughing out his kidneys, fit to expire.

Trapped.

On the other side of the glass, a dog head – Hyena-chops, Novice Ethera. Seen in his entirety, not just a masked face at the spy slot, I begin to doubt my earlier unscrambling. Can it really be? Yellow eyes and a hydraulic physique stirring under the fatigues argue against me, but the motions are hangdog, subversive, his body is speaking my language.

I can't run any more, I'm broken with effort and fear. Hyena picks up a fire extinguisher from the corner of the room on his side and whirls around with it, smashes it into the glass. I duck,

108

shield the girl from the ribbons of glass I know are about to rain on us, but the extinguisher just bounces off the window, sends Hyena reeling. He tries again, no difference. A gang of people has gathered on the other side of the door, they start to barge it. Nonstop shoves back, putting his weight to good use.

'I think we can trust him,' I bark at the others, pointing at Hyena, 'he's on our side.' Except he isn't, he's on the far side of that wall of armoured glass.

The girl runs to the window, breathes on it, mists the glass. In the fog she hurriedly scrawls something with her finger; it looks to me like '22AlP 31OH'.

The girl stabs repeatedly towards the bottom corner of the window. Hyena slaps his head, pulls something small out of a pocket. He pushes it against the glass on his side, right in the corner, grinds it into the surface of the window. The girl tells me the window's double glazed, you have to hole it before it will break, the corner is the weakest spot. I jerk her to my side. She weighs nothing, light as a shadow's shadow.

Where Hyena scrunches the object into the window a craze of fine cracks propagates. He picks up the fire extinguisher and slugs the window once more, a mighty strike, breaking through the very instant the summoners barge through. The door slams inwards, shielding us three from the cataract of angular fragments that explodes into the room, a jangling cacophony of pirouetting glass scythes.

And light – true, white light – relief at last from the maddening green!

Carnage; the summoners who crashed through are hosting a jubilee, a gala of burst eyeballs and sliced arteries, but we don't stop to participate, we leap from behind the protective barrier of the door and through the remains of the shattered window. Hyena-head is gesturing for us to follow him; I park all doubts and do so. He's still holding the little tool he used to puncture the window – I catch a suggestion of silver and a splash of red. I delay only to pick up the fire extinguisher he's dropped; its weight and function scream *useful* at me.

We blunder along a steeply downwards-sloping corridor. Summoners appear at the bottom of the incline, eight, nine of them. In the white light, their punch-the-eye bright orange tracksuits confirm my theory: they're all penitents from the Spiral, and the Spiral is the Establishment's second cruellest deception, a loom for weaving murderers. Did I know these men? Had I joked with them on the cell phone? They've a mineral look to them, a famished anger, a crushing want to share their shame. I yearn to tell them, I said it too, I said I'd do anything to stay alive, we all did. Only . . .

The summoners are brandishing what I take to be pickaxe handles. What's their punishment if we escape?

'Ever go bowling, Mo?' shouts Nonstop. Not even time to tell him darts was my game before he's thrown himself onto the floor and is rolling down towards the summoners, gathering speed. His rotund body almost fills the corridor.

Strike!

They're down, *flab*bergasted, crushed and scattered. We vault their prostrate bodies, haul up Nonstop.

Hyena swerves left, through a door, and we follow him. We bolt the door on our side, luck with us at last. Now there's a flight of stairs, leading upwards. And up is always hope.

Chapter 15

Hyena's in the lead, his heavy boots clumping up the stairwell. There must be hundreds of steps; I lean back but see no indication of the top.

Trouser-less Nonstop blunders after him, creaking like a windmill in a whirlwind, hawking out foamy pats of phlegm every few paces, but I think he's stronger than he realises. He's gripping the handrail in one hand and the girl in the other, hoisting her under his arm like a rolled rug. She's weird looking, with starey-boggly onion eyes and is painfully skinny; I don't think she'd make it on her own. I follow behind, meaning I have to look up at Nonstop's filthy, naked backside. I wonder if I should help with the girl, but Nonstop seems to have made her his own. 'Come along, little sis,' he's saying, 'your bro Nonstop's gonna look after you.'

For the first time the girl speaks, her voice *uh-uh-uhing* as she's bounced up the stairs. 'Myristica,' she says, 'that's my name, my-wrist-icka, fifteen,' she adds, so older than I thought, older than she looks.

'Who was that woman, the one who brought you? Was that your mum? Why did she do that? Why would anyone do that?'

Nonstop demands. 'No flagging now,' he says, 'we're almost there, little sis, almost at the top.'

And we are. A bucket, brooms, a mop; the room at the top is a janitor's den. The door's propped open by a chair; Hyena crouches and looks around, scanning the terrain with his yellow eyes. How are they yellow? The fact is inconsistent with my theory. I push forwards and take a peek too.

Outside!

Out-scabbing-side!

I laugh, for I never thought I'd see it again. It's dark, very early in the morning; the sky is a heavy, creased tarpaulin of blackcurrant blue, the humid air reeks of combustion, a pink sweep to the east shows us all there is to see. We're out on the surface, the top of the Spiral, in an overlooked ventricle of the pitch-dark heart of the Establishment.

Hyena can't speak; he slumps, looking dithery and despondent. I see why. Across a wide quadrangle is a wall, a towering blank bank of concrete topped with rotating spikes, the sort you cannot grab because they spin around and throw loose your hand. A tall metal pole stands right by it, resembling a lamp post but crowned with a frizzy nest of barbed wire. A clutch of cameras peeks out from the nest. In other directions the situation looks even more hopeless: searchlights, watchtowers, flood-lit buildings. Harsh triangles of cold yellow light and shadows sharp enough to shave with, paint it all with marker pens and highlighters.

So close. We're so close.

'So you think you're an artist,' I cajole myself. 'Time for your masterpiece. This is what you do, this is what you're about, defeating walls and cracking locks!'

Tiredness ambushes me, eats me, my view of the world shrivels to a distant white disc as I sledge past its tonsils. I strike my head against the door until I regain alertness.

{Think it through, Mo. Use what you've got. Your rule.}

What have I got? A breathless, wobbling Nonstop, lying on his back at the top of the stairwell, melting into his own sweat like a blob of lard in a frying pan; a sickly, silent stick of a girl; Hyena-head; a fire extinguisher; the things in the janitor's cubby hole . . . the chilli spray; the glue.

The glue's the clue.

I scrabble around the cleaner's store until I find what I want, a tube of plastic bin liners. Someone – I forget who, but know it was Moth – once told me about a man called Archie Medes who'd said something like 'give me a long enough lever, and a pivot to rest it on, and I can move the world'. I feel the same about bin bags; a roll of those and I'll escape from *anywhere*.

I explain my plan to the others. They look at me like I've told them we're going to fly out by lassoing penguins with moonbeams. Myristica wilts into snivels, Nonstop cries, but they roll into action regardless. Just as well, for the instant I finish talking the Establishment blooms, and the day knows a second dawn. Sirens wail, hooters honk, the searchlights go mental; it's death-camp disco.

The fire extinguisher's a gas one, carbon dioxide, Nonstop calls it. Hyena squirts blasts of the gas into bin liners, inflating each to capacity in half a second. Myristica ties the tops of the filled bags, seals the necks with a dollop of my toffee-and-pear-drop adhesive. I roll up my sleeves and trackie legs, slather my skin with the home-brew glue. I grab two fistfuls of the bags and pelt out towards the camera pole, launch myself at it, shin up. The metal's smooth and slippery but the glue is superb: I have to tear my forearms and calves off the pole where it gums me to its surface. The pole stands right next to the wall; I climb until I'm higher than the rotating spikes, just beneath the crown of cameras. I take a couple of those circular beetroot slices and slap them over the camera lenses, it's like they were made to measure. Drunken searchlights dazzle me, the space beyond the wall is an invisible void. I know the drop on the far side will be a long one, that's the only reason why this stretch of wall has no walkway, no guards. But how high?

Nothing to lose. What's the worst that could happen?

I bunch the inflated bags in front of my face and leap, counting:

One second, two seco—

Crunch. The ground hammers upwards. My bin bag crash mat puffs out, for a second becomes as unyielding as pig iron, then bursts, job done. I roll for an age, come to rest plastered around a boulder. Teeth are missing, I've bitten through the tip of my tongue, my limbs carol with pain. I make a wild lunge at consciousness as it roars by me like a freight train, just manage to climb on-board.

Nonstop's next. The podgy loon is carrying the scraggy girl on his shoulders. At the top, he knots his trousers around the camera pole, leans outwards. Myristica releases a carpet of stuck-together bin bags; it floats free, Nonstop lets go and they plunge together, Humpty Dumpty plus one. He lands spreadeagled on the bags; *WHUMPF*, she lands on him, a superior cushion. Before they even touch the ground, Hyena has overtaken them; he's tacked two more bags to the soles of his boots as extra shock absorbers. He's on his feet lickety-split, a real urban athlete; perhaps he's just lucky, perhaps I'm witnessing hard-core parkour.

I don't have a watch, but I know it can't be more than ten minutes since we left pen one.

The voice in my head thrums, mocking me:

{Out of the frying pan.}

Part 2:

Breakdown

Chapter 16

Down the mountainside we fell, we Jacks and Jills, all busting our crowns and scattering our pails in the pink and crimson dawn.

We began by clambering down a narrow ravine, a pew-smooth chimney of a cleft in the cliff. No one sane would have taken that route in daylight with ropes, but somehow we did it. The glue helped, sticking us to the rock like we were flies on a wedding cake. After that, we bum-surfed and belly-slid down a succession of scree slopes, riding tides of shale, grabbing at bracken to brake our descent, then pin-balled uncontrollably between tall pines. Every few seconds I checked and rechecked my pocket for that box of Myristica's pills, because an artist is never sloppy, never slipshod.

Kings' horses and kings' men we did not see. It would have been madness to pursue us during our suicide steeplechase and besides, the job had been outsourced, automated; throughout our long fall we were buzzed at a distance by one or more wide-winged, cigar-shaped aircraft too small to hold crew.

Gravity finally finished toying with us and rolled our mangled bodies onto a wooded plateau. There, we flaked out. From exhaustion, yes, but more I think because we needed a span of sobriety to transplant the fact of the Compensation Camp into our minds, and for the graft to take.

How could that abomination exist? Wrong question. Sometimes, the biggest shocks are the easiest to absorb. You might grow up believing legends that say you live on an emerald platter floating in a sea of camel spit, that speccy wizards can redress the most naked of wrongs with runes and hokum and backwards Latin; reality spanks, but it always explains. Of course the Fartherland had that camp. Why else that pervasive, slovenly contempt for liberty and charity that coddled under the meniscus of every facet of life? Why else the miasma that exuded from between the grains in the substandard mortar of every cheerless tower block and frowning town I'd ever visited? The adults had known, or suspected, and the knowing had defiled them.

The camp made total sense. We were inhabitants of Murderworld.

We enfolded the truth.

One of the mini-aeroplanes shot overhead at treetop height, as if hurrying to report our revelations to its masters. Hyena pointed up at the machine and air-wrote with his finger.

'DR ONE'

'Doctor one?' I said, looking up at him from where I lay amongst the pine needles. My words whistled through chipped and missing teeth. Nonstop lay comatose beside me, his arm curved protectively around the mysterious Myristica. Sliding down the scree slopes head first had stretched his baggy trackie top halfway to his knees, a blessing for the world. Incredibly,

Nonstop had not uttered a sound during the entirety of our turbulent descent; the big man's words had become as rare as winter wasps.

Hyena's gas-mask helmet was trashed, the eyepieces smashed. He began to decouple it from where it fixed to his uniform's collar; the process took a while.

Off came his helmet.

Standing between me and the sun he was in silhouette, but it didn't matter. I'd wrestled with drawing that line enough times to recognise it at once, the geometric perfection of the neck's curve and the wonderful discontinuity where it cut to the jut of jaw and the swell of cheek.

The anagram I'd solved in pen two. But I had only half-believed my solution; it had been too abstract and cerebral. Like the existence of the Camp, despite all the clues you diagnose in retrospect, it needed to be experienced in person before the impact was felt.

Ethera = Harete.

Harete.

My Harete.

She'd come for me from the Other country, it really had been her all along, she really had been thinking about me as much as I'd been dreaming about her!

'Drone, you intercontinental mental lentil, they're pilotless drones!' she cried, her flushed face cut and bruised and sparkling with sweat. 'Oh, Mo. You never change, do you? You always did get mixed messages.'

Harete. There could be no keener pivot on which to set the long lever of my sorrow, no finer way to prise my thoughts from the Camp.

I floated upright; I felt on cloud nine hundred and ninety-nine raised to the power nine. I smiled, and another traumatised tooth dripped out. Time to cement the reunion, I reckoned, with my second ever kiss. I homed in, but my foot must have hooked itself under a hooped root, because I ended up stumbling into her, sending us both sprawling.

'Watch out, steady!' she said. 'Can't you walk – is your leg broken?'

A fragrance of vanilla and rosemary wafted to me from her hair. Harete sighed, patted my back. Little, hesitant pats, the ones you give to a muddy dog who's bounded over to greet you after splashing in a scummy pond.

'Ugh, you stink,' she grimaced, shucking me off her. She began to shed the screw's shapeless uniform, revealing combats and camo gear underneath.

We both began to speak at the same time, a hurried, choppy interchange tempered by our pressing need to be elsewhere. Our words overlapped, twisted around each other in corkscrewing threads.

Can't believe it's you, Harete, really you! *And I still can't believe it's you, Mo.* How did you find me? *How did you fail to recognise me?* Why were you pretending to be a screw? *Why were you on the Spiral anyway?* Had you known about that place, that Camp? *So afraid you were going to be executed, or worse, turned into a summoner.* Couldn't you have got us out earlier? *What do you want, a refund? You chose to do it the hard way, Mo. As ever.*

We straightened ourselves out, and this time our garbled

thoughts reformed into overlapping rows; the seeds of one long, angry row, as it transpired.

'Have you heard about that fiend, The Moth? He's scum, back from the Other country.'

'Have you heard about our friend, The Moth? He's come back from the Other country.'

'And causing terrible trouble. The new leaders are brutal, murdering bandits; Moth's arrival here . . . he's a traitor.'

'And of course, in terrible trouble. The new leaders are brutal murderers and it's Moth, a rival here, who's in danger.'

'There was always something tragic about Moth. He's an ogre, as wanted as a pressure sore.'

'There was always something magic about Moth. He's an augur, hunted like a precious ore.'

'That's what I feel. He came back to help himself, it's evident. He's up to his neck in this. Someone should find him and capture him. Not us, naturally.'

'That's what I fear. He came back to help, self-evident. He's risked his neck for this. We've got to find him and rescue him. Us, naturally.'

Our lines decoupled.

Harete gawped at me. 'Have you lost your marbles?' she said. 'You're calling The Moth scum? Mo, I know you've been through a terrible ordeal, but what is all this?'

Gabbling like a spooked goose, I tried to relate the news I'd received ('He's at the centre of everything, the centre of power,') but she stalled me with a blocking palm.

'Well, what does that mean? That could mean anything!' Harete blustered. 'We don't have time for this; save it for the later time of never. You're wrong, Mo, wrong.' She produced a tube like a marker pen, and began patterning her cheeks with wavy green lines.

'Rescue Moth?' I mouthed to myself again, drooping down onto needle-strewn soil as dry and powdery as crumbled crackers. 'Rescue Moth?'

Harete's mere presence by my side surpassed in enchantment my entire storehouse of fantasies, but I could not accept it as a shilling for a press-ganged mug. My creditors were harrying me for payment; all my deferred shock and tiredness and hunger welled up and subsumed me, abetted by memories of our previous escapade; the looming trees looked reminiscent of encircling soldiers, and of those interminable pylons. Not again, I thought, I simply couldn't face going on another dangerous journey. Escaping was my forte, and punning with matter, finding different meanings for the objects around me; rescuing someone sounded much too much like hard work, and Moth was a double-crossing back-stabber, he didn't want or deserve rescuing. We should have been running as far and as fast as we could away from our former friend.

'Don't worry, Mo,' Harete reassured me, her hands on her hips, looking magnificent, martial, managerial. She scanned the sky for the spying drone, peered quizzically at Nonstop and Myristica as if she had only just then noticed them for the first time, and stepped into the forest. 'We're the hunters now, not the hunted. It won't be like last time, I promise you that,' she said.

As it turned out, she was right.

It was much, much worse.

Chapter 17*

We didn't get out of the woods unscathed, there were casualties. How could there not have been? The weakest always pay the highest price. I should have known it would happen; the Numbers had tried to teach me, they'd lived simple lives out in the marshes, but they'd always kept a proof over their heads: the *twist*. You never find what you want, you always end up being blindsided by events.

Midday, in the forested foothills of the Establishment's mountain lair, the high pines buffered us from the dazzling white tablecloth of the sky, the sun was a fiery plum, a spiteful, rotten fruit that oozed burning juice onto us each time we crossed into a clearing.

Harete dished out her orders, and who were we to disagree? Get down off the hillside, make our way to the Facility –

'The Facility?'

'A refugee site. Doctors, beds, food.'

– she knew lay not far away, rest and recuperate there. 'Try not to be seen by those drones,' she warned. 'They're not armed, but if they spot us, their operators will start to shell the area.'

I've had better days, I really have.

Pop, pop, pop!

'Run!'

Bombs exploded close by, or maybe they were shells; don't ask me, I'm not an expert. Not the sort of cheese-puff explosions you see in movies, all drawn out drum rolls of thunder, gorgeous chrysanthemum fireballs and your heroes tumbling end over end in slow-motion somersaults. Real explosions are Bang!, simple as that, no fuss, no colours, lasting no longer than a balloon kissed by a lit splint. Louder, though, a loud that hooks your lungs up your neck, a loud that feels like a ball-peen hammer to both sides of your skull. All that, and a shower of stony muck.

'Wait!'

Harete had wagons of stamina, but Nonstop and I hadn't eaten or slept for nigh on two days, and who knew what Myristica had been through. We recovered under a limestone ledge, listening for whistles.

Nonstop had taken to carrying the slight Myristica on his shoulders, and was cooing a stream of reassuring nonsenses to her. It creeped me cold. So did the clinging Myristica. Her receding hairline and straggly, thinning locks were a disconcerting mirror of Nonstop's, her taut, tracing-paper skin more blue than white. Alone, each of my companions was a disturbing sight, but it was nothing in comparison to the Nonstop–Myristica amalgam, a two-headed, four-armed biped with naked, jiggling buttocks, overhanging belly and thighs like two basins of papier mâché.

Pop, pop, POP!

The tree nearest our den started to do that haunted-house

126

creaky door thing; we couldn't see which direction it was going to fall in, so –

'Leg it!'

The thermostat of my emotions was shot. Fleeing, I sampled elation, the most refined extract of happiness I'd ever tasted. I no longer minded that Nonstop, a man I had daily supported over the slop bucket, a man who claimed to be suffering from brittle bones, a curved spine, arthritis and piles, now seemed capable of jogging with a teenager on his shoulders in the course of an artillery barrage.

I didn't care. I'd earned not only my freedom but my wings; I was a true escapologist, a twice-lucky skedaddle rabbit; I was outside in the sun and fresh air and feeling and alive!

Breaking out, that's what I'm good at! Better than the first Saturday after the last day at your last school, better than jacking-in a jerky job at some nerd-infested berk circus and beginning a six day lie-in. Better than . . .

'You've never actually been to school, or had a job,' Harete corrected me from her side of the dusty hollow we'd slithered into. 'Until now.'

Had I been speaking out loud? Harete! There, with me! So much for the Numbers' philosophy, that mystical, mathematical flatulence about how you can never find what you set your heart on; I'd found exactly what I wanted.

Only . . . only . . .

Only, she'd grown. Taller, and much more besides. Since the last time we had seen each other, Harete had metamorphosed. What was she now, seventeen, eighteen? I'd grown, but she'd grown up. Whereas I was only an unchanged extension of my earlier self, the same but fractionally bigger, Harete seemed to have become someone new, a fact transmitted by her every movement and gesture and look. No wonder I was a master of escapes, I realised, I was weightless and stateless, able to melt through matter without interaction. Harete had ingested some magic particle, something that bestowed poise and maturity and mass upon its absorber. Not podge, but gravitas, for she was as flexuous and elegant as she'd ever been, with copper-coloured eyes and long, brown hair, tied back in a swishing ponytail. Graceful. Mesmerising.

She mattered, in a way I never could. Looking at her, I felt small and grubby and undeveloped.

'Job? What job?' There was no need for that sort of language.

'Finding The Moth, of course! RUN!'

POP!

The loudest yet. The blast bounced between the trees, fleecing one of its bark. We all fell down. White-hot steel peelings zinged past; one nicked my hip before slicing deep into a trunk. The forest floor smouldered where the metal rinds took root.

We waited, but no more shells fell.

Shortages?

The trees became denser, the cover better. I couldn't keep my eyes off the darting Harete, which was problematic because she was so well camouflaged I frequently found I was ogling a shrub by mistake. The rare sights of her I caught were as troublesome as they were delightful. Nothing in my grey life had prepared me for the disruptive effect induced by her bounding contour. Were the changes all hers? I wondered if I was suffering from a sickness, some hangover from my time with the Numbers and their obsessions with form and connectedness, topology . . . bottomology . . .

I tried to maintain pace with her, haranguing her with questions as she led the way, slinkier than the meander of a salamander. How? Where? What? No answers! I caulked the silence with a condensed version of my own story, telling her everything that had happened to me since we'd said goodbye at the border with the Other country: my time with the Numbers, their destruction, my capture, life on the Spiral.

No responses. Why was she being so elusive?

Harete located a stream, a smart trick to find your way downhill – if it had had any water in it.

'Uh! My sucky luck!' she cursed, the first glint of the old Harete, my Harete, fallible, human Harete.

I earned my keep, pointing out that the way twigs and stones had piled up against ridges and roots showed the direction water had once taken. My remuneration was terse answers, grudgingly shouted out as we followed the dried scar of the watercourse.

She'd done well for herself in the Other country, had been fostered by a family, gone to college. 'Stuck up? Not a collage, Mo, a college.' No, not with Moth, he'd lived somewhere different with his judge father and professor mother. He'd not been in touch with her for, oh, donkey's yonks. She'd watched the news, seen our secretive nation contract a mortal dose of civil war, implode, explode, disgorge millions of refugees. Next came word from the judge: The Moth had vanished, he'd somehow persuaded a team of Peacemakers to fly him back to his homeland, reason unknown. And not a word from or about him since.

'Typical. Who else would have friends with helicopters?' I snorted. 'He always did move in elevated circles.'

How had she found me? Her story had a familiar ring to it. The ring, the one Moth had gifted me, the one I'd paid Atlas with, the one whose hard jewels Harete had used to perforate the double-glazed window. Harete had learned of it being sold at auction in the Other country, brought over by a refugee. She'd quit college, sold everything, borrowed and begged and –

'Stolen?'

Beneath her camo-stripes, her cheeks flushed as red as the ring's rubies. No – red diamonds, apparently, the real deal. Tracking the ring from buyer to seller through refugee sites, she'd traced it back to the Spiral and Atlas and me.

Bloody amazing! What a champion!

'All on your own? What about the people you lived with, your new family?'

'Yes, on my own. I didn't need their permission, I'm not a child, I'm a woman. I don't need you or anyone else to hold my hand.'

'How did you get yourself into the country? It can't be easy, not during a war.'

'It's not like it was, Mo, no barbed wire or border guards now. The barriers have all been torn down.'

'How did you get a job as a screw?'

'They weren't fussy.'

I understood. Shortages. The Establishment would surely have pounced on any able-bodied person who'd requested to serve, especially for a job on the Spiral.

I was so unbelievably tired by then, it felt like a dog had crawled under my skin and was chewing my bones from the inside. And burning them, operating a charcoal clamp. The afternoon heat was blistering and the only moisture I'd seen for hours was the permanent drip on the tip of Nonstop's nose.

The stream bed forked.

'Wait here,' Harete instructed me, 'I need to see which way is best. Don't move until I fetch you. Can you manage that without messing up?'

She slipped away; the Nonstop–Myristica blancmange blundered up to me, swaying, more than my equal in exhaustion.

The lower head clucked, 'Mo, Mo, who is that angry soldier girl? Why was she pretending to be a screw? Why is she so mad angry bonkers cross? She scares the goolies off me.' The perspiring, tottering creature stooped to separate into its constituent parts.

'That's Harete. She's –'

'Harete?'

'Yes, you see –'

'Your girlfriend, Harete?'

Girlfriend? I took the word for a test drive. I liked it. 'Yes? Yes. Yes!'

'The one you spoke about all the time,' continued Nonstop, 'and tried to draw and moaned about in your sleep? Kept me awake that did some nights, never liked to say, not being one to complain as you know, on and on and on you'd go about her. Very selfish of you actually now that I think about it, but hey ho, my shoulders are broad.'

'Uh . . . right. She's angry with me, Nonstop. Apparently I wrecked everything.'

'Everything? What, Mo, what did you do wrong?'

Everything.

She'd spelled it out as we'd crept along. From her growly, sedimentary tone I felt I should have made notes.

What I got wrong (again)
By Mo, aged 17+/- a bit

For starters, when on the Spiral I hadn't deciphered the Hyena-headed screw's jumbled name until it was almost too late. Could she have made it any more obvious? Perhaps she should have printed up some business cards, or hired cheerleaders with pom-poms, _Mo_. Nor had I recognised her fevered blinks as being cell phone signals, left eye for rows, right eye for columns; Harete had even worn luminous yellow contact lenses to make her eyes more noticeable in the brightly lit pens, but did I twig? Did I nipples. What had I thought she was doing, a sponsored tic? A shame, because if I had paid proper attention, I'd have been able to cooperate with my own salvation and let her pluck me out through the hatch, but I didn't so I wasn't so she couldn't. Together, we could have raised out Nonstop (dubious, I thought), and might even have rescued the occupants of a few other pens, gathered together enough people to overpower the screws and then free everyone. But oh no, we had to do it my way. The wasteful way.

There was more, but that was the gist.

'So it was _you_ who tried to catch me that time, during the fishing trip!' I shouted, loitering behind my own reprimand.

'Yes. But I wasted so much time fighting against you, other screws came along. I almost got rumbled that time – we were meant to operate in pairs.'

'And you went on to catch Lew.'

'That wasn't me in person. I'd wanted to spare you the horrors of the Compensation Camp.'

'Instead, you hastened Lew to it.'

'It wasn't easy for me! Three days I had, that was all, with the likelihood of having to watch you die, unable to get word to you; I . . . I tried, Mo. He'd have ended up there anyway, you know that.'

'Guess.'

Harete had been incensed. 'It's you all over, Mo. Always thinking about yourself and your mad schemes, never thinking there might be other people to help, or other people trying to help you, never *listening*, getting all your words muddled and bent.'

What could I say?

Un Burr Leave A Bull.

I had dreamed that the Spiral was a quad-erratic equation. That meant there were two solutions, two routes. I'd worked out the trivial one. Typical of Harete to have performed the more detailed calculation, to have come for me and then expanded her plans to save other people as well.

Escape artist? Nah, I was nothing more than a scarper craftsman, second class.

What mattered now was that I was together again with Harete, my Harete, that indefatigable combination of velocity and felicity. Her churlishness was just a temporary blip; she'd traversed a country to find me, now we could start again where we'd left off.

She'd come for me. Therefore she loved me, just like I loved her.

What? The word whacked my bush and boozled my bam; I hadn't expected the bloody L word. It struck me at that point I had never used the term before, never annotated my feelings for Harete in that way. But it was the right word, just as 'girlfriend' had been. Love was a mirror, that was right, wasn't it? You saw yourself in it, the angle of coincidence equalling the angle of introspection.

I felt dizzy around three different axes.

Harete returned, beckoned silently for us to follow, and we trooped off. The drones were back in force, and I became grateful that we had dyed our tracksuits; the original orange would have made us stick out like stilt walkers at a dwarf's funeral.

Put-put-put-put!

A different type of drone ambled overhead, a unit with stubby wings and a smoky motor that spluttered like a tubercular moped. The machine circled us twice before throbbing away.

The wood changed in character, the pines fraternising with slow oaks and beeches and hazels. I picked up a long stick; you can't take a walk in the woods without a stick.

'Look,' cried Nonstop. 'Nuns! Nuns, in a tree!'

He was bang right.

The lofty tree was dripping with nuns like two-tone pine

cones, three skewered neatly in a line along a branch. They were a very long way above us in the canopy; I could not see if their habits were shrouding white bones or melting meat. We walked on, curious but not frightened, possessing the dazed insouciance of day trippers who have accidentally wandered into a city's iffier districts. Soon we encountered trees drizzled with gaping clamshells of burst-open suitcases and metal seats. Underfoot crunched a carpet of grated aeroplane: everything from socks to circuit boards, plus larger pieces such as shanks of hydraulic machinery and sections of curved fuselage. In wonderment we skirted a tract of uprooted trees at one edge of which sulked a jet engine, concertinaed like a beer can, a thing big enough to host a hoedown. But no more bodies.

'Mo. Mo. Mo. Mo.'

'Yeah?'

'Rats, Mo. This plane must have been carrying three, four hundred people. Look at all the luggage. Look at all the seats. Where are the corpses? Think how big the rats must be around here.'

I stopped. 'Surely . . . someone must have collected the bodies?'

'Who? And why'd they leave the nuns?'

'Where are the clothes and bones then?'

'Rats don't take off the wrappers and they're not bothered about hard centres. Eat anything, they will. Relentless, destroying mouths.'

'Relatives of yours?' I asked, but we all started to trot much faster. The air was still, no hint of a breeze, yet something was definitely rustling in the undergrowth.

Harete un-melded herself from the background. 'Whoa, wait up, look here, everyone!' she hailed us, pointing at an oblong resting in the fork of a low tree branch – a slim metal trolley on caster wheels, upright, intact and resplendently defiant of both the devastation around it and the obligations of gravity.

I had no idea what it was, never having travelled by air other than when being launched across a room with a size eleven shoe up my jacksie, but Harete obviously did. From her perch on Nonstop's shoulders, Myristica was able to waggle the bough; eventually the big box rocked and dropped with a very loud and whimsical tinkling sound, combine-harvester-meets-crystal-chandelier satisfying.

'Sheesh, look at the scratches on it. Rats, Mo.'

'Aw, get bent!' I protested. 'It fell out of the sky and landed in a tree, it's bound to have a few dings and dents. What is it, anyway?'

Harete set about attacking the trolley, and with some assistance from Nonstop she wrenched open a door in its side.

Biscuits!

Chocolate!

Drinks! Drinks! Drinks!

'Wahay!' we all cheered together.

Harete gutted the box, pulling out armfuls of bottles and packets, and we shifted into the shade of a tree to consume them. She told me the box was a sort of snack cart designed to be wheeled up and down the aisle of the aeroplane. My first chocolate bar for a year! I sucked the water out of a plastic bottle so hard it started to crumple up.

'After save lotion,' I said between gulps, and I cracked open

136

a second bottle. Harete's eyes crossed over and she made a growling noise like a peeved cat. When Nonstop had an attack of belches and hiccups, she looked like she was going to weep. All I could do was suck in the sight of her, and flash her my top-drawer smile, gussied-up with a cheeky wink; *you and me, Harete. You and me.*

Nonstop brushed a column of red ants off a tree stump and plonked his bare backside down, Myristica dismounted. He continued with his tedious thesis. 'These peanuts and chocs are all still in date,' he said. 'This airliner can't have been shot down very long ago, that's what I think. So the bodies can't have rotted, they can't have. Far too much luggage for just those few dead nuns. How much luggage can a dead nun lug?'

'What's that? A tongue-twister?' *That smell. Hmm!*

The miniature bottles of booze inside the trolley had all smashed; the air was saturated with the chromatic aromas of hard liquor. Droplets of oily orange fluid were stuck to the outside of my water bottle. I licked them off. Yuk. Licked a few more to confirm the nastiness, and the ones from my choc wrapper.

When Myristica finished her drink, Nonstop fed her squares of chocolate, posting them into her mouth one at a time. She ate them all, saying nothing, staring at me with her forget-me-not blue eyes. The vision was disquieting. Her head was too big, I decided, and too bulbous and too veiny. Her silence and passivity irritated me, which I knew was unfair. Why did I dislike her so? Everything about the scene irked me.

'Hey, any of those little crackers with cheese slices in there?' Nonstop asked. 'They sometimes have those on-board planes. I love cheese. Oh, if they had some cheese it would be simply perfect. Have a shufty for me, someone, see if there's any cheese. Any sort would be grand – I like Cheddar, Stilton, Brie, Halloumi, Camembert, Port Salut, Marscapone . . .'

Harete's patience with her motley team expired. 'For pity's sake, belt up. And *do* close your legs when you're sitting down!' she rebuked him, shielding her own eyes. She looked in the trolley anyway, but there was no cheese. She did find a torn skirt though, spread over a bush, and threatened Nonstop with impromptu field surgery unless he put it on.

'I've no dignity!' he wailed, speaking through a hailstorm of nut dust. 'This is grievous not fair.'

'You cannot go about like that any more. Not when there's a young girl around. Or me, for that matter. I can't see any trousers, just put that on for now.'

He did, and we all had a snigger at his expense. Old Mother Nonstop. The skirt was a baggy, brown drape that reached to his ankles. He twirled around in it a few times before declaring it satisfactory.

'Actually, not too bad,' he grumbled. 'Quite cool. Thermally, I mean, if not in a fashion sense. Yes, old Nonstop can manage with this.'

Other finds: a small rucksack that Harete loaded with supplies from the raided trolley, and in a side pouch, a pocket knife.

'Bagsy that,' I said. The knife was nothing deluxe, just two folding blades – a straight one and a rinky-dink little saw – but it felt well-made and very at home in my palm and in my pocket.

Put-put-put-put! Bwarrp! Put-put-put!

The sky moped, back by unpopular demand. Harete donned

the rucksack. 'I don't like the look of that thing,' she announced. 'That's not a spotter, that's some sort of . . . missile?'

Nonstop squatted down on his haunches; Myristica used the tree stump to climb onto his shoulders.

Maybe the heat had stewed my brain in its own juices. Maybe the chocolate was too rich and had upset my sugar balance, maybe it was lack of sleep or those few licks of liquor, I don't know. My mood skewed a one-eighty.

'Aw, give the guy a break,' I yelled at the skinny girl. 'You don't need to be carried. It's boiling hot out here – you're half-killing him. Walk by yourself, you lazy tyke!'

Nonstop rounded on me. 'Out of order, Mo, well out of order. She's ill. The medicines, remember, and what her mum said?'

I shouted back, 'For all we know, she suffers from nothing worse than split ends. She's taking you for a ride! I mean . . . you know what I mean.'

'That's Nonstop's business,' said Harete. 'Don't be a tool, Mo, she's plainly not right. I mean, not well.'

'A tool? Tools are useful, in case you'd forgotten.'

We almost missed Myristica's contribution. 'Not my mum,' she said. 'Dead Dad's wife number three. Dad was killed by tank fire, months ago.'

'Uh, whatever,' I carried on. 'Stop mothering her, Nonstop, you hen-pecked pile of puff pastry. She can talk, she can walk. We'll move faster if she does it by herself. You're gonna pass out if you carry her any longer in this heat.'

Bwarrp, bwarrp, put-put-put-put! Put-put-put-put!

'Don't listen to him, sis, Nonstop'll take care of you, Nonstop won't ever let you down.'

'She's not your damn sister!'

'I ran away with my brother and his girlfriend, but I got lost and had to make my way home. She always resented me, my stepmum did, I knew she'd evacuate me, take me to the Compo Camp. Everyone knows what really goes on there.'

Harete was having a conniption. 'Clever up, clod knockers! We could be attacked any second. Mo, get off his back.'

'Yeah, Mo, yeah, get off my back, Mo. Do what your girlfriend says.'

What was she getting at me for? 'It's her you should be saying that to!' I snapped.

Harete gasped indignantly. 'I'm not his *girlfriend*! Did he tell you I was?'

'Yes. Been bragging about you for simply ages. That's my girlfriend, we're in love, mwah mwah, kissy kissy, I'm going to marry her. He never shuts up about you. On the Spiral when he thought I was sleeping he used to say your name and put his hand down the front of his –'

'Mo, how dare you!'

'But . . .'

'I am ill, though. My brother said I'm dying of arithmetic. There's a lump growing in me, another life inside mine. Its cells are just dividing and multiplying, doing maths. The size of a nut, for now.'

'Dying?' I switched my head from speaker to speaker. 'You're not . . . I thought . . .'

'Mo! No, surely – oh, Mo, *Mo*.' Harete's copper eyes widened and her hands cupped a dome over her mouth.

'You know your problem?' demanded Nonstop, his pink,

recessed eyes flaring like rubbed match heads, jabbing me on the breastbone with a chubby finger as plump as a peeled eel. 'I said, d'ya know your problem? No? Nonstop'll tell you then, since you're obviously blind to your own faults.'

Bwarrp, bwarrp.

'That flying thing's coming back, Mister Nonstop, Miss Harete.'

My chest felt like I'd swallowed a bell. A big, bronze bell with a whetted rim that hollowed me out as I swallowed it. A bell that clanged and rang out and said, 'Look at this squalid little imbecile, everyone! He actually thought she was his girlfriend, ha-ha-ha-ha-haaaa!' as it sank through me.

A dumb-bell.

'I knew that,' I choked. 'I just meant, I meant, you're my friend, and a girl and . . . well, you've sure come a long way to boss me around, you car-boot commando!'

'*What?* What do you mean by that?'

'You're jealous, because of Myristica. Yeah, that's what you are. Jealous,' Nonstop huffed. 'Cos I'm not taking care of you any more, not protecting you like I did on the Spiral. Well, tough tonsils. She needs me more than you do, she's young and sick.'

We held a ten-second truce. Multiple strands of confusion crocheted themselves into a carpet of misery.

Not my girlfriend. *Not.*

Dying.

Jealous.

'SCAB OFF, the lot of you!' I screamed, and I swished my stick through the air, scattering my companions. 'Fat knackers to you, you bladder of blubber, you and your shrivelled shoulder mole. And to you, Harete. One green marker pen and a bargain-bin camo-shirt and you think you're a super-secret agent. You're not even good enough to be a thickening agent!'

Sand on the ground, my rage had traction. I blasted on. 'Bog off! I don't need any of you!'

Jealous? Protected by Nonstop? How deluded could that oaf loaf be?

Not my girlfriend.

'Please can I have my pills back?' asked Myristica. 'It's mainly the pain they help with, but I do need them ever so much. They didn't drop out, did they, tumbling down that cliff?'

'Whaddya take me for?' I fumed. 'An amateur? Some brand of low-grade pill-losing loser?' The box holding the foil sheets of blister-packed tablets had remained safe in my trackie pocket, checking for it had become a reflex action. Before ferreting it out, and to emphasise my anger, I high-kicked a wedge-shaped flap of shiny alloy that was embedded in the ground, some flake of the aircraft's epidermis.

Bwarrp –

The metal sail folded over, caught the sun, reflected it.

– *bwarrp. Put-put-put-put!* –

Flash!

So, so bright. I cringed at the crinkled image of the metal-reflected sun.

Flash!

– *Put-put-put-put!*

The puttering drone must have spied the sun flashes; the machine reacted as it was programmed to do, no doubt exactly as it had done when the airliner had drifted into its patrol zone.

Blue. That's all I saw, a vertical lake of pure, beautiful, restful blue. The blue held, then turned black.

And that's the last thing I saw.

Chapter 18

A puzzle.

Someone had sneaked up without my noticing and stubbed cigarettes out all over my face. Most unnecessary.

And it was night-time. One second ago it had been afternoon, now it was indisputably night, a night as unutterably dark as any on the Spiral. An eclipse? Good, yes, but that wouldn't explain the burned face.

I was definitely still outside; I could smell the woods and the smashed whisky miniatures and sense a puffy, irregular wind against my raw, sore, tender face.

And I was standing on top of a pillar. I knew I was on a pillar because when I prodded around me with my stick, I felt nothing; the end of the stick waggled in free space. Unless . . . unless someone had dug a trench around me, and I was standing on a little island in the middle.

'Mo. Mo. Mo. Mo. Speak, Mo!' Nonstop, of course. Very close to me, the puffy wind was his breath.

Harete's voice next. She sounded in a terrible palaver, like something awful had happened, the stroppy, mardy moo. 'Mo, are you all right? Can you talk?'

'Yes, I'm fine,' I replied shakily. 'Never weller. Although I am now completely blind. And the end of my stick's broken off. Can someone find me a new one, please?'

Chapter 19*

'A laser. That drone fired a laser at you, when it detected the flash off the metal you whacked. We saw it, a cone of bright blue light,' said Nonstop. 'An anti-aircraft weapon, to dazzle the pilots.'

'Right.'

'Blinded, Mo. You've been blinded by science.'

'Right, yes. Thanks.'

'Your skin's all burned as well. Very brown it is.'

'It was brown before, Nonstop.'

'Yeah, but it's now a sort of cooked brown, all crusty with black bits. Do you feel something on the bridge of your nose?'

'Yes?'

'Reckon that's one of your eyelids. Wonder what sort of laser it was? Optics was never my field, you know that, particles was my field. Not too hot on optics and lasers and masers. Wavelength must have been about –'

'Nonstop?'

'Yes, Mo?'

'Will I be blind forever? Or will it pass?'

'Forever, Mo. Old Nonstop was wondering that as soon as

he saw the blue light. *Will the damage be permanent, or lead to only temporary scotomata?* I asked myself, and as soon as I saw your face, I thought, *no, that's definitely irreversible.* Burned to a cinder, I should think, your retinas. Crisped up like deep-fried noodles.'

'Right. Thanks.'

'Wah!' Nonstop yelped, and I sensed Harete had shunted him forcefully aside.

'Mo, does it hurt? What are we going to do? What do you need?' She sounded spooked; I could imagine her wringing her hands, biting her lip.

Good. Serves her right. I got a mean little tingle from that idea, a warm, wet squeeze in my vitals.

I thought hard. Those initial moments were a crucial crumple-zone of planning time before shock gained hold, like that bubble of sober clarity you experience when you cut yourself badly and you can view the gushing blood with cool, stop-motion objectivity.

'Um. I'd like a new stick, I really would. And . . . a rope. Find a rope, so someone can lead me, because we're not completely off the mountain yet, and I don't want to fall down a cliff.'

A good stick was found within seconds and passed to me. Almost a small branch from the length and weight of it; it had a pleasingly sinuous structure, like two snakes entwined around each other. I clasped the stick with both hands in front of me and felt immediately better.

'That any good?'

'Terrific. Out of sight,' I joked nervously. I'd show them. I'd show *her*. Mo's blind, but he's not down and not out. 'Seems

147

like you *can* get the staff these days.'

'Nonstop, Mysterica . . . Merist . . . both of you, come with me,' I heard Harete say, her brief panic over and her authority restored. 'There's more wreckage in the trees over there – help me look for a length of cord or a piece of cloth we can cut up and make a rope from.'

'And, Mo –'

'I know, I know. Stay where I am, don't move. What sort of an idiot do you think I am?'

'Guess you'd know the answer to that better than me,' she replied coldly.

I heard them crash away through bushes. Tapping around with my new stick I located the tree stump and gingerly manoeuvred myself onto it. I was sure I was going to lose control any second, blub, fly completely to pieces. Yet, sweating, sitting peacefully in the scorching sunlight, nothing happened. I remained totally tranquil. Daunted, yes, anxious, naturally, and fearful. But calm. Blindness was a practical matter, a massive inconvenience for sure, but . . . well, I'd known a blinder in the Institute, and he'd done all right for himself. It had been quick and painless and the blackness was almost comforting . . . I started to worry that I wasn't more worried. What on earth was wrong with me? Why was the only pain I felt the one in my chest? Didn't I comprehend how serious this all was? *I was blind!*

Harete; the heart of the matter, and the matter of the heart. Funny how they called it heartache, heartbreak; the pain seemed more digestive, or respiratory. Well, she'd have to look after me now, wouldn't she? So maybe my condition was a disguised blessing . . . a twist with a happy ending, yes! This could bring us together. She'd see how bravely and selflessly I coped ('it doesn't bother him at all, he still loves his awful jokes') and . . . what a goon I'd been; *of course* she wasn't my girlfriend, how could she be? We'd been apart for well over a year, hadn't known each other particularly well even before then, but that didn't mean she didn't love me. I'd freaked her out with a bad choice of word, that was all! Girlfriends you took to the flicks or cafes or showed off to your mates, or, did, well, other stuff with. I'd hardly been in a position to do any of that, being on the Spiral. She wasn't my girlfriend, but she obviously felt the same powerful attraction for me that I experienced for her; the irrefutable evidence of that was her presence.

Round and round my notions and emotions whizzed. A new paradigm for myself congealed; I was an adult now, numerically and in all other regards. That was why my blindness did not overly perturb me; with time and patience it was conquerable, as were all matters of matter.

Sorted. Tidy. Crisp.

TO DO:
Wait for others to come back
Get to that Facility place
Return with Harete to the Other country
Live together – a couple!

See? No need to get in a tizzy. A new, scary, sightless world awaited me, but Harete and I would conquer it together. With her, I could cope with anything the world could fire at me, I could master the art of darkness.

Noises. One of the three had returned and was pacing around me, shuffling through the rubbish underfoot.

'Whoozat?'

No reply, therefore Myristica. Time to man up and apologise.

'Hey, Myristica. Myr? Maz? Look, uh, I'm really sorry about, you know, all those things I said before. And I'm really sorry about your illness. I was out of order, like Nonstop said. Overwrought, and . . . well, you know.'

She continued to shuffle around me and did not dignify my ramblings with a reply. Couldn't blame her.

My embarrassed, drumming fingers located a forgotten chocolate bar on the stump. I propped my staff between my legs and unwrapped the confectionary. Without invitation, Myristica sat down on my lap. Light, she was, half what you'd expect from a kid her age, and fidgety, but it was a congenial if slightly awkward display of forgiveness. I leaned back, not wishing to be overfamiliar. Also, she smelled rank.

The girl started roughly tearing chunks off the bar. *Bit rude*, I thought, *but hey*. Her hand was wet and warm. I shifted my weight; Myristica squeaked in protest.

I stood up, ejector-seat fast.

The massive rat clung onto me, dug in its claws. It must have been the size of a lamb.

I flinched my entire body, trying to fling the vile thing off; I grabbed my staff and began to beat my own legs, *thwack*, *whack*. The rat clawed its way up the front of my tracksuit. The beast was so heavy it almost pulled me over, its face reached mine, its whiskers brushed against my chin. The rat's back claws were still hooked into my thighs, that was how long it was. The chocolate! I hurled the bar away, and the rat detached itself and leapt away in pursuit.

Stay calm, very important not to panic. My heart was firing like a nail gun. Damn my blind eyes, damn them. I was so helpless, so vulnerable.

'HARETE!' I called. 'NONSTOP!'

Nothing. I called them again, five, six, times, top-of-my-voice, jaw-busting shouts, shouts that left me drained and headachy.

No reply. And they'd been gone an awfully long time, it occurred to me.

Many more rats. I felt them brush past my legs, heard them scratching and bruxing. Tens of them, dozens, a gross of rats scurried over my foot. All were scampering off to my right. What was there? The trolley we'd opened, still loaded with snacks and gin.

Rats; rats that had gorged on four hundred dead passengers and crew, left not a trace of them behind, and grown to monstrous sizes in the process.

Thoughts: *get away else you will be ripped apart and eaten by those rodents. The others have gone, killed or captured, dead, or good as.*

I was blind – blind and marooned in a sea of man-fattened rats.

My second death sentence of the day.

Chapter 20

Cool, Mo, keep cool.

I probed forwards with my stave, aiming for the groove of the stream bed. That would be my way out of the woods. The sun's rays were useful now, no mistaking which quadrant of my face they were toasting. I used my face as compass and sundial: afternoon, heading south-west.

The rats had been used to eating dead people, not live ones, so maybe I wouldn't remind them too much of past meals as long as I –

Over I went, *crunch*, head met metal.

I got up. *Tap-tap*, step-step, *tap-tap*, step-step. Over, up.

'Where's that scabbing stream?' I roared. I remembered a game we played in the Institute, out in the big yard. Grab a kid and blindfold him, get him to walk in a straight line. Same result every time – he'd end up blundering in an ever-tightening spiral. We're all on the Spiral, hadn't I always said that? But I could not afford to travel in circles, I *had* to reach that stream.

Over. Up. Every time I fell, I discovered new objects to scratch me and graze me and bash my bones against. Wet stuff, jagged stuff, stuff that dipped away like a see-saw when

I stepped on it and catapulted me into more pointy stuff.

Over. Up. For how many hours I progressed like that I cannot say.

I bounced down a steep slope. The dry stream? Rats poured over me; I was lying in a rodent road, a rat run, their hairs and claws and the powerful stink of their sticky urine was everywhere on me. I ripped around me with my blade and stave, lashing and slashing. A humungous specimen pinned my knife arm to the ground. I rolled towards it, planning to throttle the creature; by luck my free hand found its neck, too wide for my fingers to encircle.

'Die, queen rat!' I yelled, and squeezed hard. The rat must have been the queen, it had smooth skin, and when I twisted myself on top of it and took a face full of its long, silky fur, I found it did not stink of excrement and earth but of:

Vanilla.

Rosemary.

A bulb of dark clarity detonated inside my head.

'Mo, you no-nads crapsack, one of these days I swear, I'll do for you.' Harete. Hot, cross Harete. Very cross. Crosser than a game of noughts and crosses played at a crossroads in a crosswind.

I wept, 'You're not dead? Harete, all of you, you're alive?'

Several dirty hands clamped over my mouth, heaved me up, dragged me from the stream bed and into the undergrowth. Someone wrested my stick from me and began to beat away the rodents.

'Shut up!' multiple voices stung me. 'Shhhh! Soldiers, in the wood. That's why we couldn't answer your shouts. They're still around, somewhere. Be *quiet*!'

I cried, openly blubbing out my heart and viciously cursing my blindness. My body twanged like a schoolboy's ruler as repressed shudders of revulsion and sickness rippled through it. I started to explain what had happened, but Harete slapped me around the face. *Slapped* me.

'Yes, yes. Never mind that, Mysti . . . Myeri . . . the girl, she needs her pills,' she told me. 'Get separated, run away, scab off for all I care, but at least return her medicines.'

Smarting inside and out, I located my pocket, patted it for the cardboard box. The box was there. Phew. Imagine if I'd dropped it amongst all the plane wreckage, all those rats!

The pocket was open. Because I'd opened it earlier, of course, when Myristica had asked me for her tablets.

The box was open.

The box was empty.

Total loser.

Chapter 21

We searched, of course we did. Nonstop and Harete backtracked along the stream bed, scoured the woods. I waited, an invariant darkness before me and in me. *Scab. Scab. Scab. Slabs of knacker scabs.*

What chance of finding three small, silvery sheets afloat in a wood bescumbered with diced passenger jet? The rats had probably eaten them anyway.

Harete returned, took control. 'The Facility, the refugee camp. They'll have medicines, or they can take her to a hospital that does. We just need to walk there faster than I'd planned. Can you manage?' The query was directed at Myristica.

'Probably. Three provisos,' replied Myristica, sounding wobbly. 'I will need carrying because my legs always fail first. Don't be hard on Mo. And never call me brave.'

A wretched journey ensued, the slow-roast torture of desperately needing to be somewhere fast but being completely unable to hurry.

Harete navigated up front. All the road signs had been looted for scrap so she steered by studying the angles of satellite dishes and the layout of churches. Clever clogs.

Nonstop followed behind, dragging me like a dog on a lead using a rope he'd found. He was supposed to employ those never-resting jabber jaws of his as a substitute for my eyes, provide me with a continuous commentary on my surroundings. He was worse than worse than useless. Not even that good.

Deliberately, of course. He couldn't forgive me for losing the tablets.

'You shouldn't have played with those rats, Mo, that was a grievous brainless thing to do. You should have listened to old Nonstop.'

'I've a choice?' I cried.

'Weil's disease, Mo. You've probably contracted that from the rats. Or bubonic plague. Or typhus. Or hantavirus. Ooh, that's a seriously bad one to get, incurable too. The signs are chills –'

'Check.'

'Aches, fever –'

'Got those, check.'

'Shortness of breath.'

'Check.'

Terrific. Blind *and* riddled with diseases.

{Ignore him.}

Oh, and mad, forgot about that one. Voices in the head.

'Hope you've got *all* those diseases, Mo, and some ones unknown to science, really nasty ones that give you knob rot and nad rash. You deserve them, blind or not.'

'Thanks, mate. What about lockjaw, Nonstop? Any chance of that?'

'Hmmm, not sure if rats carry tetanus.'

'I meant for you, Nonstop. For you.'

He whip-snapped the rope, I crashed. Knees like burger patties I had by then, knees like pizzas with glass-and-gravel toppings.

Myristica took over the job of guide; she had the best view from up on Nonstop's shoulders. She did the job admirably, despite Nonstop's tireless and tiresome fussing over her. Of the three of them, only she bore me no resentment.

'Mo, grassy bank, uphill, twenty degrees. Paved road, kink left, that's it, well done. Careful, fallen masonry, dodge left. Half a Labrador, you're past it, just a little on your shoe. That must have been a supermarket over there, but it's all . . . melted . . . you're doing grand.'

I'd been handed a rag to use as a blindfold; it seemed important for me to advertise my condition, and the pressure of the material on my face felt soothing. Harete would have been happy for me to wear a dunce's cap, had we found a traffic cone from which to make one. My panicky behaviour in the woods hadn't impressed her, my losing of the pills far less.

Pallets o' scabs.

Whenever I spoke with Harete I kept picturing a pair of magnets, like the ones I used to amuse myself with as a kid if I got hold of a smashed-up loudspeaker or a motor from a toy. I'd tease one magnet by prodding at a pole with the like pole of the other, north versus north or south versus south, loving how it twitched and skated away over the chipped Formica of the kitchen table, repulsed by an invisible flux that was as strong as it was impalpable.

Several times I tried to make a breakthrough, speak without

157

repelling her. No joy.

'Wha'? What's occurring?' I remember spluttering, bobbing up from a meagre doze, six winks at most. I felt beyond terrible. Days and nights were virtually indistinguishable to me, two subtle gradations of darkness and heat. I had lost track of time, of reality, couldn't always tell if I was walking, sleepwalking or dreaming of walking.

'I'm bloody sick of bloody peanuts. I'm giving all mine to the birds,' Harete said. I heard her rip open packet after packet from our supplies and tip the nuts out. 'Bloody starlings keep fighting over them. Eat, damn you! There's plenty for everyone so stop fighting and eat!'

'The world in a peanut shell, Harete. The drought must be hard on them too.'

'The weather's all wrong, Mo. Worst heatwave in living memory,' she said next. There was a stiffness to her voice, a rigidity I suspected arose from small talk bowing under the pressure of bigger feelings.

'Um.' What did she want me to say?

How I wished I could see her. All those weeks on the Spiral spent cobbling together phantasms, and there she was, her flesh made flesh, yet still removed from me. Doubly, trebly removed, inaccessible by sight and by degrees of inapproachability I was only then starting to comprehend.

'Perhaps we caused that too,' I sighed. 'The civil war and the uncivil weather. Could the fighting have bust the weather?'

'We *did* start the war, didn't we, Mo? That idea's been terrorising me for a long time.'

'I dunno, Harete. It's possible it had already begun before

we smuggled Moth over the border; we wouldn't have known in the Institute.'

'I don't believe that. Moth's father was a very important man. Once his son was free and he spilled the beans, that's when it all began.'

'Guess. P'raps.'

The weather? Politics? She was stalling. I knew fine well why: the persistent ripple caused by my clumsy use of the word 'girlfriend' the day before, and its ramifications. Every time we spoke we skipped over it like a ruck in a rug, neither of us wanting to lift up the corner and straighten out the matter for fear of what else we might discover concealed beneath it, squished into the underlay.

'What were the delta gypsies like, Mo?' she asked. I brightened, happy to share.

'The Numbers, you mean. They weren't gypsies, they never called themselves that. No shame in being a gypsy, just not who they were.'

'But what were they like to live with?'

'Rough as sandpaper bog roll. Swearing, spitting, boozing, fighting – naked, bare-knuckle boxing, that is – smoking, all that kind of thing,' I informed her. 'They'd thieve the bogies from your nose. And yet they'd take the last crust from their children's mouths rather than see you go hungry, they'd die before they betrayed you, and they never, ever lied. I adored them.'

'Naked boxing? Spitting? What about the women?' Harete quizzed me.

'That *was* the women, Harete. The men were like living

statues, they did nothing but stand around and think all day. Proving theorems and, well, contemplating maths stuff.'

'Lazy beggars!'

'No. Only their real parts were inactive. Their imaginations were whirring away. They were complex people, Harete.'

'They don't sound entirely rational, if you ask me. You didn't make any, you know, special friends, then?'

'No. Just as well, considering what happened to them all.'

So that was her angle: special friends? The phrase disinterred a possibility I'd dared not consider before then. If the pure Harete I'd known before had changed, perhaps it was because she'd become alloyed with some other substance. Another boy.

A man.

'What about you, Harete?' I asked, dreading the answer but owned by an impulse to know. 'In the Other country, did you, was there, is there . . . a boy, or . . .'

'Let's move on, Mo.'

She woke the others. Preparing to depart our shelter I had an idea. 'Harete,' I asked, 'will we tell stories as we walk, like we did the last time?'

'Oh, those awful stories,' tutted Harete. 'Don't remind me. We've no time for stories, Mo. We've got to be completely serious now. We must get My-wrist-icka to the Facility.' She was getting the hang of the name, at last.

'No stories? A little story never hurt anyone,' I grumbled. 'I mean. What's the worst that could happen?'

Harete had changed, but in this regard it was a sure turn for the worse. Running and hiding soon became banal, even given the added piquancy of blindness and Myristica's predicament.

160

Without stories, we'd have nothing to relieve the tedium but boredom, nothing to vary the boredom but monotony. I cast my mind back to the stories the Numbers had taught me. There was the one about petals and seeds, pine cones and snail shells:

One, one, two, three, five, eight . . .

No, it didn't satisfy me. Nor Nonstop. 'Fibbing Archie's series,' he called it.

Dead, dead, everywhere we walked through was dead. People think war is noisy, but that's not so, at least not for ninety-nine per cent of the time. Think of the really rough districts in a city, the sort of neighbourhoods where householders take their doorstep in at night and even the traffic bollards go around in pairs. Those places are always eerily quiet, even in the middle of the day, no pedestrians, no cars, the shops all shuttered. It's the safe places that hustle and bustle. War's the same; sure, every once in a while a dart-shaped aeroplane flashes overhead, cracking open the sky; occasionally a sparrow hops on a landmine, a shell crumps listlessly into a play park. But in the main, it's disquietingly quiet.

And scary. Rocks-in-your-guts scary, lumpy-gravy-in-your-keks scary. Just because the others never saw anyone didn't mean there wasn't anyone to see. Day and night we kept eyes and ears and noses pinned wide for dog packs, rat packs, killers, guerrillas, escaped gorillas, partisans, artisans, malicious militias, conscripts, convicts, desperados, deserters; any threat or foe our hyper-heightened sense of fear suggested might be eyeing us up with a view to beating us, eating us or cheating us.

Waste of time. The trouble with trouble is, you spend so much time checking over your shoulder for the threats you

161

anticipate, you don't spot the uncovered manhole leading down to the sewer.

We'd been crossing a car park when vehicles around us began bursting open like roasting chestnuts. So I'm told. What did I know? I was nothing but a sack of spuds, tugged left, jerked right, then bashed against rustiness, my nose tickled by the smells of brake fluid and sun-softened tarmac.

Snipers. We'd ambled into their crossfire. They were using rockets. And every time Harete tried to lead us deadbeats clear – *whizz bang*, an explosion close enough to rip open my tracksuit top like an overfamiliar gym teacher. A cell without walls, new one on me, invisible bars of fear and indecision. Which way to run, which way?

So we stayed put, quaking behind a sideways-on minibus. Whose snipers were they? There was no way of knowing. We were in a civil war. It did not have two sides like a sheet of paper, it had twenty or more, like one of those honky-tonk dice Moth used when playing his favourite board game back in the Institute. Heavy on the dragons, as I recalled, and kingdoms with names with too many Zs in them. Roll a six to invade, a double twenty to, I dunno, rescue the enchanted prince and win the damsel's hand. What had he called the shape of his die, an eye-cosh—

{Icosahedron, Mo.}

Right, thanks. I worried at a splinter, an extract of hatchback in my neck. *Sorry, voice, been meaning to ask, what exactly are –*

'Pssst, Mo,' throated Myristica, pinching me on the elbow.
'Yeah?'

'What's the worst that could happen, Mo?'

162

'Say what?'

'What you said earlier. I made up a story for you; I heard you tell Harete you liked stories. You want to hear it? I am sooooo bored.'

I was bored too. War is boring. It's boring like you cannot conceive, boring like a rainy Tuesday afternoon spent in a launderette with nothing but old washing powder boxes to read. That you might be dismembered at any instant does nothing to make it more entertaining. There is no excitement in war, only grinding boredom, and then someone close to you dies.

'Are you up to it? I mean . . .'

'Kiss my sweaty cleft. Would I have offered if I wasn't able? Do you know how incredibly dull dying is, how lonely?'

I've spruced it up a little, removed all the 'umms' and 'erms'. And to be sure, there's some of me in there; the teller and the listener always stick to the story like bubblegum to a spaniel. But this is her story, and scab anchors to anyone who says otherwise.

'What's the Worst that Could Happen?'
As told by Myristica
(As remembered by Mo)

Ed Long was an impetuous youth who never paid attention to warnings or advice. He ran with scissors and knives, skated on frozen ponds, never ate fruit.

When challenged about his dangerous ways he'd always reply, 'What's the worst that could happen? A cut, a soaking? Constipation?'

One day, Ed was repairing an electric toaster. Too lazy to find a replacement fuse, he was jamming a nail into the plug when his far-sighted friend Claire Voyant found him. Claire lectured him on the perils of his reckless action.

'You have a devil-may-care attitude,' she told him.

'Let the devil care! What's the worst that could happen? A shock?' snorted Ed.

'The toaster could catch fire,' Claire replied. 'The house could burn down.'

'We're insured. Anyway, the carpet's torn, the neighbours are awful, we've damp in the basement and squirrels in the attic. We'd not miss it.'

'The fire could spread to other houses in the street,' Claire pointed out.

'This neighbourhood's a slum! If that's the worst that could happen, I'd be doing the town a favour.'

'That's not the worst. It could all take place during a firefighters' strike. The fire could burn for days. The entire town would become a raging flame pit.'

The new reasoning gave Ed cause to pause. 'Seems . . . farfetched,' he gulped. 'But that is definitely a worst-case scenario.'

'Far from it,' continued Claire. 'What if the heat from the burning city caused a disturbance in the rocks beneath it? Maybe the town sits on a fragile cap above an underground magma chamber. A great plume of lava could spew out, reducing the country to a desert of pumice.'

'Now you've definitely strayed beyond what is possible!'

'Scarcely the beginning! Don't you know that once things start to go wrong, they inevitably continue to do so? Are you such a dunderhead that you do not know of the *chain reaction*?'

'You mean, worse could yet happen?'

'The eruption could cause sympathetic vibrations, igniting volcanoes across the globe, leading to the destruction of all human civilisation in a suffocating rain of molten rocks and sulphur.'

'All humanity eradicated? A dramatic finale!'

'An overture! Just as air from a puncture causes a balloon to career around the room, the Earth could be thrown from its orbit in reaction to the rocketing lava.'

'Don't tell me. It would crash into the moon?'

'At first. Next, the planetary detritus would be sent tumbling into the sun. Unknown stellar processes could mean that, upon impact, the sun itself is put out.'

'Put out?'

'Poisoned. First it would explode into a supernova, then collapse into a black hole.' Warming to her theme, Claire grabbed her friend by the lapels and shook him violently. 'A black hole, I tell you! And one that grows in power as it gobbles up planet after planet, the nearby stars, the Milky Way and beyond.

All the galaxies, countless billions of them, would be sucked into the maws of the never-sated vortex. The entire universe, dragged into the crusher, squished into the volume of a full stop!'

'I give in! Let me go!' screamed Ed.

'No! Not only the fabric of reality, but the stitches too. Time begins to run backwards. And who knows what might happen then? I put it to you –' here, Claire emphasised her words by bashing Ed's head on the ground as she spoke each one, '– that what happens is this: tipping into the black hole, the soul of every animal, alien, human that lives or has ever lived or will ever live becomes preserved in an instant of time particular to that creature; every soul is forced to re-experience its greatest moment of terror and shame and loneliness and humiliation and pain, magnified infinitely – forever!'

Claire ceased cracking Ed's head on the linoleum, and Ed quit struggling. Both rested for a while, musing on the horrific idea.

'Every creature on every world in the universe . . . that lives or has ever lived . . .' murmured Ed.

'Forced to endure time frozen at the precise moment of that being's greatest despair,' said Claire.

'Forever.'

'And ever!'

'But that would truly be a living . . .'

'Don't say it, bad luck would follow. But that, I think you will agree, definitely *is* The Worst That

Could Happen. Of course, I am playing devil's advocate here.'

'Since you put it like that,' said Ed at long last, 'perhaps I could fetch a thirteen-amp fuse from the shed.'

'We've run out,' sniffed Claire, rummaging in the bread bin. 'Stick that nail in the plug; I'd murder for a toasted teacake.'

'A chain reaction. I love that, sis,' Nonstop said. 'A chain reaction ad absurdum. Or do I mean ad infinitum? Or is it ad nauseum?'

'Whatever you wish, Doctor Science. Personally, I always react very badly to chains,' whispered our storyteller, done in by her recital. 'That's why I'm so grateful to you for releasing me from the ones in the Camp. The story was my present to you all.'

'Even me?' I asked. 'Busting story, by the way.' That was an understatement of my esteem. For the duration of its telling I had been the equal of my peers, blindness had been no impediment.

'Especially even you, dum-dum. Quit beating yourself up, won't ya? Those pills would always have run out sometime. Besides, they weren't anti-rocket tablets.'

The story stayed with me, particularly the way everything had . . . spiralled . . . out of control. I asked Myristica for another, but she said no, we weren't in a multi-story car park, and we all had to laugh.

Not for long though, because Myristica began to die. Minute

167

by minute, we discerned her slight footprint on the beach of life being washed away, her voice ebbing, the insurmountable pain screwing her down. She'd said the story was a present; she must have meant a going-away gift.

The snipers changed tactic, blasting cars at random and leaving long, purposeful, nerve-knapping lulls between each shot. Nonstop was doing everyone's crust in with his gasbagging pleas for Harete to *do* something. That's what I remember most, not the rockets, but that filthy, air-bending heat, and Nonstop's endless whinging, on and scabbing on and scabbing on.

'All reds gone. Then yellow,' whimpered Myristica. 'Green one . . . brown . . . blue, yes, and pink. Next will come . . . will come . . .' Her mind was coasting around a deranged rainbow visible only to her, a prismatic death rattle.

'Sis, sis, I'm here for you, hush now,' nagged Nurse Nonstop, the distended duffball. What a toss wad. Yeah, my new best friend, but still a toss wad. I hated him, hated Harete, hated the snipers, hated my shut-in, shut-off world, the flies crawling in my ears, my smashed teeth, waiting to be shot at, waiting for Myristica to die, waiting, waiting.

My nut was baked, my lemon was twisted, my melon was bent. I cracked.

'This is all Moth's fault!' I screamed, clawing at the asphalt. '*He's at the centre of everything*, remember? *The centre of power*. This country is rotten to the core, and the core is where he's at. I hate that gutter maggot!'

'Lies!' spat Harete. I heard the helplessness in her voice. 'Prison whispers! Moth was the cleverest and . . . fairest . . . and . . . he's our friend! I'm positive he came back to mend things, but met with misfortune. *We* caused all this, when we helped him away from the Institute. Only right I try to repair the damage. If I can get us out of here.'

'You're made of ten scoops of mad!' I groaned. 'With a layer of whipped lunacy on top and idiot-sprinkles and a pillock-flake. Us, trace one boy in a warzone?'

'Not us. Me. Not now you're –'

'Blind. You can say it. I'm blind.' Even I wasn't used to saying it, much less to being it. 'He was never our friend. He dropped you soon enough, over in the Other country, you said so yourself.'

'He was . . . busy.'

'Get real! Moth's true friends are people in places so high you'd need to wear an oxygen mask just to shake hands with them. He's back, nobbing his hob and browning his nose and wagging his chin with the people in charge.'

'You revolt me, Mo; you're eaten up with envy because Moth's smart and principled and you're . . . you're tower-block trash, high-rise riff-raff.'

Blood bags burst in my skull. No laser or shell could have floored me more effectively, if I hadn't already been lying down. 'You're living in a fairy tale,' I laughed at her. 'Ooh, ooh, watch me save the world and rescue my likkle chummy fwom the baddies and then we'll all have cakes and lemonade. Face facts, girl, woman, whatever you call yourself. Moth's gone wrong, and you'll never find him, and even if you did he'd throw you on the Spiral, and who cares anyway, because you can't even get us out of a car park and we're all going to die, we're all going to die!'

I was tanked on anger. I had to get away from that death-trap car park and from Harete. I made a wild break for it. One step, two steps, I fell – or was felled – and received an instant makeover: lip gloss, eyeliner and foundation, all in shades of pavement. Another tooth flew the coop. Blind luck is a myth.

SCAAAAAAAAAAAAAAAAAAAAAAAAAAAAAAAAA AAAAAAAAAAAB.

There's always someone worse off than yourself. Myristica spoke in a voice as thin as cat lips, poppycock posted by her delirium. 'Snooker. You know snooker, Mo?'

'Sure, sure,' I comforted her from a puddle of blood and gravel. A white lie; darts was the only game I followed. 'You play anything you want. Pool, poker, snakes and ladders, we'll have a turn on them all.' Poor, sad, dying bulb-headed runt. I began to giggle uncontrollably, like I'd smoked a bale of laughing cress.

'No, Mo. Bazooka snooker. They're shooting cars in the order you pot balls. Pink SUV was last . . . one every minute . . . next due about . . . about . . .'

Harete heard her, gasped. 'What ball comes after pink? Think!'

Nonstop said, 'Black, seven points for the black.'

'What colour's this bus? I can't see; someone tell me, tell me what colour!'

'Black-ish! Well, more of a dark slate, actually. Reminds me of a pair of brogues –'

'. . . about *now*.'

Someone hoicked me clear of the minibus barely a second before a sniper spotted it and potted it, igniting the fuel tank.

The vehicle blew with a stupidly immense, chest-compressing force. Harete executed our escape route – white car to gold to grey to striped to silver, all non-scoring colours. In two minutes flat we'd cleared the car park and were safe, screaming out our brains, fugitives once again from the casual cruelty of men and their games.

Danger drained, I came to my senses. First I came to my sense of touch, scratching at ringworm on my elbow and fingering one of the three foils of pills I thought lost. It had slipped through a hole in my pocket, migrated along the lining and was hibernating in the sleeve. That made me at once the most loved and most hated member of our quartet. Didn't give a scabby badger's nadgers. The other sense I came to was when I recalled the fireball made by our mutilated minibus as it was hit by the rocket.

I'd *seen* the fireball. Through my blindfold, through my eyelids, I'd seen it.

Chapter 22

Cautiously, I tested out my eyes, not letting on what I was up to.

The fireball had been no hallucination, but I did not know if my eyes were sensitive to anything of lesser brightness. I eased my blindfold upwards and dared to open my right eye. Unsealing my eyelid was an effort in itself; the sorry fold had become fused to my cheek with gunge.

When I tore it open, I found the central part of my vision occluded by a smudgy black disc that obscured everything apart from a thin ring of clear sight around its edge. Below the lower rim of the inky moon I could make out the darting stubs of my trainers. Sight through my left eye was interrupted by a gambolling host of smaller blobs of unstable, unnameable colours. Looking through either eye for more than a bare second gave rise to a sensation akin to an ice-cream headache magnified to planetary proportions, the pain being in direct proportion to the brightness of the ambient light. Nevertheless, my blindness was not complete. My bones turned to butter and I tottered like a bandy-legged wino. I had not been sentenced to a life of darkness, but to one of nebulous muzziness.

Any initial urge to share my news with the others (and

nah-nah to Nonstop about his inaccurate diagnosis) soon subsided, censored by my innate sneakiness. Without any clear idea of how, it struck me that there must be advantages in being thought to be blind when one wasn't.

I persisted with my experiments.

Angling my head about me and looking through the blindfold, using it as a crude sunscreen, I obtained fragmentary snapshots of our surroundings. Around us lay lifeless suburban precincts, tornadoes of bluebottles buzzing over the residues of former inhabitants. Two graceful, swan-necked warplanes jousted high overhead, each probably costing as much as a cure for cancer. In front of me, impatient to depart, stood Harete.

Harete – her face, her cheek, her neck, that delectable line that twined around my chest and connected her with perfection. I had to shut my eyes again, almost wishing they had been destroyed totally rather than function only well enough to tease me with glimpses of the unobtainable.

I took stock.

TO DO:
Get Myristica to safety
Stop Harete killing herself on lethal errand
Make her love me again
Rest eyes, hope they improve

Slog on.

Nonstop was pushing Myristica in a wheelbarrow he'd found; I was traipsing alongside, one hand on the barrow. We were on a wide carriageway, and no longer alone: hundreds of evacuees had spilled out and joined us from a side road. Everyone was on foot, heading for the Facility. Lamentations of helicopters belonging to the Peacemakers drubbed above, dicing the leaden air with their twin rotors, each underslung with a swaying cargo net bulging with supplies.

No one spoke to anyone else; we all knew we were in competition for limited resources.

Us or them.

Only the babies and toddlers cried. And cried. And cried.

'Daddy, will dolly be all right?' A child's voice.

'Throw that piece of trash away!' a man growled back. 'We carry only what we can eat. Here!'

I heard something being smacked out of a small hand and smashing onto the ground. The child broke into a terrible scream. 'Not dolly with one arm, I want dolly with one arm, I love my dolly with one arm, no, Daddy, no!'

The child's grief clawed into me like a cat on curtains. My toe scuffed against something. I let go of the barrow, squatted down and patted around for the object. I plucked it up. A plastic doll with frizzy hair and one arm missing. I held it horizontally; the doll's bristly eyelashes tickled my palm as the eyes rolled shut.

'I've got your doll! Hey, girly, I've got your dolly with one arm!' I yelled, standing up and turning around. Where were they? Useless, they'd gone. 'I'll look after it, I promise I will!'

'Mo! What's that crappy thing you're holding there?' Harete asked.

'Just some girl's doll.'

'You lose vital medicines, you pick up junk, what's with you?

Throw it away, for pity's sake,' she admonished me.

'The scab I will!' I shouted at her. 'It was loved once, so it has to be loved forever. That's the rule.'

'What rule?'

'One I've just made up.'

For me, the found doll and its lost owner encapsulated the banjaxed, Moth-eaten world. I refused to stomach the doll's loss. It had no life, but it had once been enlivened by affection and had enhanced a life; it deserved to be spared. At that moment, I empathised more with the one-armed toy than with any living person; it seemed to me to be the last, true innocent entity on Earth.

'Uh, as you wish,' grumbled Harete, reconnecting my hand with the barrow. I tucked the doll safely into the waistband of my trackie trousers.

We plodded for hours in the roasting heat. The humidity skyrocketed, the air became metallic. At Nonstop's request I removed my top and arrayed it over Myristica to prevent her from becoming burned. My darker complexion was scant protection, the skin on my neck and chest fell away in sheets the size of pantiles, leaving the newly exposed layers to be violently irritated by the lacquer of grit and sweat that glazed me.

We rested up. Harete scouted ahead, Myristica and I chatted. The pills from my sleeve had tamed her pain, bought her another day or two. Rented, rather.

'She your first?' asked Myristica from the barrow. 'Harete?'

'Come again?'

'Your first crush,' she giggled. 'Your first lurrrve!'

'Me? No. Nooo,' I told her. 'Latest in a line as long as . . .'

I tried to think of something long. A bus queue; a German sausage; a politician's speech.

'Thought she was. Always the hardest, your first. She is lovely, mind. Gutsy and good looking. Bitch! She's worth falling for, Mo.' She spoke kindly, her insult I knew to be a joke.

'Um. You're right. Never known any girls before. They've always been on the other side of the wire.' I scratched my forehead. Under my blindfold a whopper patch of itchy ringworm had sprung up, slap bang between my eyes.

'Don't take it too hard, Mo. She thinks a lot of you, I can tell.'

'She hates me.'

'Yes. But it's the right flavour of hate.'

I felt the need to unburden. 'I'm bonkers for her, Myristica,' I blurted. 'Every thought I have is about her. It hurts, a real, physical pain, growing bigger inside me.'

'Tell me about it. Which means, don't. I'm way ahead of you on the things-growing-inside-you-and-hurting front. Waaaay ahead.'

Her illness. 'Oh . . . I didn't mean . . .'

'Forget it. I've a good sense of tumour.'

'What can I do, Myristica? Is there an answer?'

'Yes. I have it, but you don't want it. It never ends, Mo. Dad told me that. He was a sucker for falling in love. You remind me a lot of Dad and wife number two,' she sighed. 'That was my mum. They were potty about each other. Never stopped them arguing though.'

'What happened to wife number two, Myristica?'

'Not sure. I think wife number three killed her. Before she was number three. Try to find some distractions or a hobby.

176

Maybe get yourself a girlfriend to take your mind off being in love.'

'Very witty. It's not just the . . . you know . . . thingy side of things I'm thinking about.'

'You mean, sex?'

'Shhh! Don't say that word!' I said guiltily, worried Nonstop had overheard us. The topic was not one I wanted to discuss with any girl, certainly not Myristica, and particularly not within earshot of her self-appointed guardian. 'Um. Yes. I mean, no. A bit, but . . . when I think about Harete, it's not like that. Well, not only that. More about . . . eh . . . well, there's another side to it. But she doesn't feel like that about me, I know it.'

'The blind leading the blind. Oh, Mo, I might be only fifteen, but I've had to pack a lot in, there being a shortage of time for me. You haven't, er . . . written any poetry, have you?'

'Poetry?'

'You know:

Harete, Harete, I loves ya like spaghetti.
I'm totally crazy, like sauce Bolognese.
My linguine is teeny, my vermicelli smelly,
Lookin' at your ravioli is killin' me slowly.

Or are you pasta that stage?'

'Huh. I've that to look forward to?'

'Maybe.'

'Grim.' I wished for guidance through the turbulence. 'Should I tell her, Myristica? How I feel?'

'Sure,' she advised me. 'And why not give her a big bag of cement to carry while you're about it? The poor girl's only leading three cripples through a war, it's not like she's got much on her mind or anything.'

Harete padded over. 'The Facility is up ahead. We'll be safe there. That's where we'll split up and go our separate ways.' Her tone was brusque, businesslike.

'We've made it,' whooped Nonstop. 'By the skin of our teeth, sis, we've made it!' He hugged her and me; I was forgiven and readmitted to the ample, sweaty folds of his friendship.

So that's that, I thought.

The End.

Myristica would receive the medicines she needed. Harete would leave and look for The Moth, and fail and probably die. I would be shipped off to some . . . home . . . for the blind where I'd learn to make wicker furniture and read bumpy books. Nonstop would become a scientist abroad. Moth would eat baked-bean canapés and run the country from an amethyst palace in the stratosphere.

My theory of The Bad Moth had been largely developed off the cuff, but the more I thought about it, the more it felt right, like my pocket knife. I pictured him riding in a 'copter, wearing those trousers that levitated so far above the tops of his shoes you could have parked a bus in the gap. He'd have that board game on his lap, and the dice: throw a nine, a treaty I'll sign; a two and an eight, become head of state.

My disappointment at Harete's imminent departure slid down my throat as easily as a spoonful of quicklime, but I couldn't deny the allure of a stay in the Facility. Beds, decent fodder; it must have been over four months since I'd changed my underwear, it occurred to me. And, best of all, safety at last for Myristica.

The ringworm on my forehead was itching like mad.

{The twist! You've not got to grips with the twist.}

Him again! *Who are you, head voice?* I asked. Was it mad to converse with figments of your own insanity? Might not talking fertilise the monster?

{Call me . . . call me the Kernel.}

You can't spell, Colonel.

{I can spell, Mo. Danger, up ahead. Terrible danger.}

Chapter 23*

The refugee site was locked shut.

A town-strong crowd of agitated people had compacted up against the perimeter; I heard them shaking the fences and clamouring.

'Let us in!' they demanded. 'Let us in! We want food, we want water, we want doctors!' Others raged about their rights being infringed, how they were going to file for damages. 'We want lawyers!' they shouted. 'We want compensation!'

We pierced our way through the throng to the front. There was a noticeboard affixed to the gates. Harete read the words aloud for my benefit, shouting to be heard over the crowd, but I couldn't make head nor tail of the language. It sounded superficially like the one we all spoke, only somehow much less so. 'DPCRM Facility. Dear Service User, welcome to the South-West-Central Region Displaced-Person Care, Resettlement and Management Facility (North-East sector). We look forward to being of assistance in meeting your emergency accommodation and revictualisation expectations.'

'What does that all mean?' I howled.

Harete translated. 'Hello,' she said. 'That's all. Welcome.'

She read out the remainder of the note.

'Service users are advised that, due to staff shortages and the intensifying regional security landscape, internal operation of the Facility has been tendered out to qualified local care enablers (QLCEs).'

Harete sounded mystified. 'Absolutely no idea what that's about. Anyone?' she asked.

'It says "tender",' Myristica said, 'that might mean something to do with being soft. That sounds promising; I could do with a lengthy session of being softed up.'

It hardly mattered; a siren blew, the gates grated open. The crowd hollered their approval and heaved forwards, washing us through with them. Even had we changed our minds, we had no choice but to enter. We next had to queue for many long, thirsty hours as the crowd was funnelled through the main gates and then compelled to diverge into numerous separate aisles for de-lousing, inspection and a sworn declaration by each of us that we agreed to something called the 'Terms and Conditions' of entry.

The wheelbarrow was confiscated by a Peacemaker soldier; Nonstop and I had to carry Myristica between us.

'Health and safety,' explained the white-helmeted confiscator, although whose he did not specify. Suspecting we might be searched for weapons, I slipped my pocket knife inside Dolly-with-one-arm, dropping the folded-up blade into the hole where the missing limb should have connected.

'Window number seven, please,' chimed a sing-song recorded voice. Our group schlepped wearily forwards to a glazed booth occupied by yet another man wearing a white helmet and a blue uniform underneath a reflective safety tabard. Without interest he speedily registered our names (only Myristica's was real) and occupations (we said 'school student' for Myristica, 'scientist' for Nonstop, 'hunter' for Harete, I chose 'retired escape artist'). The last selection was for something he called 'personal belief and value system'.

'You've a choice of three. Neo-Patriot, Ultra-Disillusioned or Mothodist,' drawled the man, reading from a list.

I couldn't contain myself. 'Mothodist, Harete, he said *Moth*-o-dist!'

'Probably his foreign accent,' Nonstop suggested. 'CAN YOU TALK MORE CLEARLY?' he boomed, rapping the glass with his knuckles. 'DOOO YOOO SPEEEK OUR LANGUIDGE?'

'I'll put you down for Mothodism. That's the most popular in here,' the man informed us.

'But what is Mothodism?' choked Harete. 'I've never heard of it, or those other ones.'

The Peacemaker sighed heavily and said, 'Oh, you know, one of those new crazes. It's sweeping the nation.'

'I don't want to sweep the nation. Sounds like hard work,' grumbled Nonstop. Nevertheless, the others consented to the recommendation. But not me; unwilling to be associated with anything that sounded Moth-related, I insisted he write down 'Nun of the above'.

'Proceed to hanger five. Health and safety,' concluded our be-boothed bureaucrat, a phrase I then understood to be a salutation. A buzzer buzzed, a barrier swung upwards, we stepped into the Facility. It was early evening and my eyes were able to function briefly in the subdued, dusty light; we were

182

standing on the edge of a wide concrete apron studded with rows of green barns – the hangers, I guessed – that stretched into the distance until hidden by a quivering heat haze that lifted in waves from the sun-kicked concrete.

'Right, everyone,' said Harete, 'immediate priority, a doctor for Myristica. I'll stay the night, I'm bushed. I'll push off tomorrow after breakfast.'

The word 'breakfast' set Nonstop's chops wobbling. 'Wonder if they do cheese for breakfast?' he jabber-gabbled, 'Whaddya think, Mo? Could it be possible? Real cheese?'

'Dunno, Nonstop. Perhaps,' I murmured.

'Can you see a sign to the gift shop? Will there be a swimming pool?'

The wire fences were off-putting, the hangers looked daunting and soulless. Still . . .

Food!

Beds!

Medicines and doctors!

Health *and* safety!

None of the above. The exact opposite, in fact.

Chapter 24

In accordance with the screeds of all nightmares, our residency in the Facility started with a good thing, a deceptive, invigorating cardamom pod of happiness to bite into, before transposing itself into an undertaking that surpassed in horror everything we'd known to date.

Even the good thing began with a disfigurement. We'd hardly crossed into the Facility when we were set upon by a leopard and a she-wolf. That's what it looked like to me, seen through my two nuked eyes and the fuzzy gauze of my blindfold.

'That's my sister you've abducted!' snarled the leopard, and he pounced. I ducked; he hacked off a wedge of my ear with a billhook. The she-wolf laughed. 'Sick him!' it screeched.

The loss of my ear meat happened too fast for hurt to register. I went for my own knife, but I'd forgotten I'd hidden it, and I pulled out Dolly-with-one-arm in error. I ended up lying on my back and jabbing the broken toy at the cleaver-wielding leopard. Nonstop coiled up into a ball and bit his thumb. Bad thinking.

Or maybe inspired. The leopard was destabilised, it roared, 'Whaaaat, what are you?' and was so put out that its second swing with the blade arced through the empty air between us.

Harete sprang forwards onto her hands and mule-kicked backwards, catching the leopard under his chin. The cleaver spun loose, but the leopard rolled adroitly and unsheathed two daggers. I guess leopards are like disposable shavers, the best models always boast three blades. Before you could say, well, 'knife', he was behind Harete and had a dagger driving towards her jugular.

Myristica rescued us. 'Lonza, no, they saved me!' she cried, and she threw herself at him. In her condition, it took a lot to do that. The leopard released Harete, grasped Myristica, and the pair of them cried like professional onion peelers as we looked on, bemused and confused and bleeding.

'Every day for months I've waited by the gates,' roared the leopard, beside himself with happiness, 'just in case you'd survived, wound up here. I can't believe it, you're alive, it's my wonderful little sister and she's alive!'

'Lonza, my big, strong Lonza!' Myristica replied. 'Too good, it's too good to see you, my heart's going to pop!'

'We're all together again. That's marvellous, only, I wish it wasn't here. Anywhere but here.'

'We're together, surely that's what matters, almost a family again!'

'You don't know what it's like. This place, it's . . . it's the worst place in the world. The worst possible things that can happen all happen inside. I wish you weren't here, Meg. I really do.'

What a fool, I thought, trying to staunch the flow of blood by making my blindfold double as a bandage. The worst place in the world? There was a five-hour queue outside the gates!

'Eww!' said the she-wolf, disgusted by the display of affection. 'Hello? We've gotta get back to the hanger. We've gotta make the cut, Lonza. The cut.'

The cut? Was she talking about my ear?

We understood nothing, but we learned fast.

Part 3:

Break Time

Chapter 25

Lonza, the leopard was called. Eighteen years old, he claimed; in form he was tall and gracile, with charcoal-coloured skin and refrigerator showroom teeth and frosty, violet eyes. Strong too: his arms and shoulders rotated up knots of muscle whenever they stirred, making you think he'd taken to concealing tennis balls inside his sweat-stained shirt. His svelte body was sintered from sinew and obsidian.

Lonza was Myristica's older half-brother, the one she'd run away from dead Dad's wife number three with, before becoming separated, returning home and being dumped into the Compensation Camp. He always referred to his sister as 'Meg', never 'Myristica'.

She was called Lupa, she was Lonza's girlfriend, and she was pregnant. Within two seconds of meeting her I could tell Lupa was going to be an acquired taste – like toenail clippings, or having your gall bladder removed through a tear duct.

'Hello? Did your mam never learn you it's rude to stare?' said Lupa, and with a raised middle finger she tugged down the skin underneath her left eye and leered at me: a doubleheader insult, the evil eye and the bird. Her bump was a compact semi-sphere blooming from her abdomen; when trotting along she rested her hands on it like it was a parcel shelf. 'Lonza, why does the blind one keep staring at me? Can you, like, slit him up or something? And I don't like this lardy fatso in the skirt. He looks like a perv, Lonza. I can always smell pervs, an' he's one.'

We hastened to hanger five, directed by Lonza. 'We need to get a bustle on,' he said, 'talk as we walk. You first, Meg.'

Myristica explained about us, what little she knew, and the Compensation Camp. Lupa received the news with a dismissive snort. 'Pah! *That* place,' she spat. 'Where they do for the gadgies and spazzies and dib-dobs an' that. We used to watch them being collected and chuck stones at the buses as they drove by. Best place for her if you ask me. She's, like, practically dead anyway. Why do we have to take her in, Lonza? It's me you should be caring for, you dumb rinser.'

'Shut up, Lupa,' growled Lonza. A mismatched couple, I thought, as dangerous as an unbalanced wheel. More: I recognised fellow super-survivors when I met them, knew from myself how villainous and felonious they could be, especially if cornered.

An echoic voice barked out from loudspeakers. 'Performance Review in five minutes!' it crackled. 'Proceed to your home hanger for Performance Review.'

'What's the hurry?' puffed Nonstop, struggling to keep up. All around us, other people were being chivvied and chased into the cavernous hangers. 'Is it dinner time? Is that why people are hurrying? What happens if we're late, do we miss pudding?' he fussed.

Lonza didn't exactly put us in the picture, he clobbered us over the head with it, left us with strips of canvas and broken frame dangling around our necks.

'Don't take this the wrong way,' he began. 'But I've got to tell you. Tough girl, you'll be all right. Fat man, you're probably not going to last long. That skirt won't do you any favours, it'll count against you at the Performance Review. The management won't like it – they're upset by anything suss. Meg, don't worry. Whatever happens, I'll help you make the cut. Lupa's sorted; the Peacemakers give her masses of extra rations because she's pregnant. And she can get your drugs. She doesn't have to lift a finger.'

Except to insult me, I thought.

'Blind boy, I'm sorry . . . you ain't got a chance.'

Harete jumped to my defence. 'What's that supposed to mean?'

I could hear the shrug in Lonza's voice. 'He'll not pass the Performance Review, he won't make the cut. He can't possibly work, can he? There's no way we'll be able to scrape together enough to keep him. That's how it is here. You work, or you . . . leave.'

Harete tightened her grip on my hand. 'Then we'll go, right now,' she snapped. 'It's all of us, or none!'

'Pah! You know, like, scab nothing,' sneered Lupa. 'Anyway, you're too late.'

We all stopped walking. I could tell from the dip in temperature we were in the shadow of one of the giant hangers. Hundreds of other people were already there; I heard them shuffling and coughing and spitting, hurriedly arranging themselves to stand in line, murmuring and muttering, stammering and stuttering.

Lupa growled at us from the side of her mouth. 'Shut up now, colon-kissers. It's Performance Review time, here come the management. Not nice knowing you, blind-eyes. You're out for sure. You too, chubber-chops.'

My heart plunged to the bottom of an abyss. Three days it had taken us to toil our way to the Facility, and now I was about to be evicted?

The line fell totally silent. We were being inspected; there was a group of people I couldn't see moving slowly along the line ('The management,' whispered Lonza). Occasionally they stopped and spoke to certain people ('Other team leaders, like me.'), sometimes arguing with them, slapping and punching them. From time to time selected individuals were pulled forcibly out of the line and corralled into a bunch ('Didn't make the cut.').

The hanger's managers were approaching; I could hear them whistling and tongue-clicking, using their own private language to talk amongst themselves.

I seized up, tar in my arteries. My heart began to burrow deeper and deeper, setting course for the Earth's core.

That Whistle-Click language could only mean one thing: we'd successfully delivered ourselves body and soul into the hands of most violent criminal tribe in all of the Fartherland.

Fractions.

Chapter 26

Our turn. The management team began to sniff out Lonza, Lupa and their new associates.

There were nine of them, men and women. My eyes sizzled like frying eggs in the evening sunlight, but I forced myself to study them, taking snapshot after snapshot through my blindfold.

Their favoured dress style was feathered turbans and head cloths, crossed-over belts of large-calibre bullets, sandals, and a snazzy automatic weapon slung on a strap or tossed about nonchalantly in the arms, as if it were an everyday thing like an umbrella. Popular accessories included grenade launchers balanced on the crown of the head, plastic sunglasses and tatty T-shirts bearing abstruse foreign slogans: 'Fuzz Pod GO Boy', 'Say !Hi! Juicy', 'Slummin' It Low End: Godda Prob?'.

Some of the Fractions were pale skinned and wearing black face paint, others were dark skinned but made up to look paler, a few piebald members seemed to be both. 'Morris men with machine guns,' was Nonstop's description, lost on me.

'Mo,' hissed Harete, 'can you speak their language?'

'No,' I mumbled. Her guess was fair, just wrong. Fractions

193

were said to be the distant relatives of the dead Numbers, but they didn't know Sandscrypt, didn't carry the triangular delta mark on their foreheads. What they mainly shared with their deceased relations was a similar delight in violence. Similar, but enhanced to the nth degree, and never employed for noble ends.

Most of us in the Fartherland had encountered improper Fractions at one time or another in the towns and cities; they worked in ways that let them put their inherent faculty for mathematics to bad use, grafting as loan wolves, cardvarks or crooked bookies, tickling society's flaccid underbelly with a dirty fingernail and making it purr as they picked its pocket. But these were something different, a denomination wholly unknown to me.

Barbarians; prehistoric forest lodgers whose peaty reek and token clothing screamed: *We shun the town and all works of mind and kindness; we are we, and you are not. We are what came first, and what will be left.*

'Ey. Oo is? Oo is, Yonza?' spoke the lead Fraction, gesturing at us, the newcomers. Lonza explained: new intake, fresh blood, his team.

'Let them prove themselves, One-for-Sorrow,' beseeched Lonza on our behalf. 'You can't make a man fail the cut on his first night.'

'Ey, Yonza! Two, tree 'undred come 'ere a day, split many 'angers! We can chuz oo we lak!' was the gruff response. 'Oo not tell us, we man'gement!'

One-for-Sorrow was patently the leader of the tribe. He had a haughty bearing to him and a high, domed skull like a freshly risen loaf; his face and bare arms were painted in black and white checks.

'W'cha darn 'ere? Oo wanna wuk for us?' began a different, much shorter man, very aggressively. He skipped about, jabbing his gun butt in our faces, enjoying watching us flinch. 'Need figh'ers, not scardey chicka-chicks! Need 'ave sum'ing inside oo!'

Lonza tried again. I felt grateful for the lad's efforts. 'Please, Two-for-Joy, they want to join. I'll support my sick sister, work harder, and you know Lupa brings in a heap of freebies just for being pregnant. This new girl's tough anyway, a canny scrapper!'

He pointed at Harete as he spoke.

Two-for-Joy slobbered with approval. 'Vey smarty shape girly. Maxo maxo do'ble!' he said, and he stepped nearer and began to caress Harete's cheek with a finger bunged up with gold rings as big as horse brasses. My heart walloped, faltered. He mimed squeezing her breasts, pressed his gnarled hands onto her front. There was a brackish taste on my tongue; Harete must have been itching to punch him out, but I had to prevent that at all costs. They'd never forgive an insult like that.

I coughed and scuffed my shoe on the ground, hoping to distract him, draw him to me. No need, the Fractions had already locked onto a much more gainful target: Nonstop. He was chewing his sucky-thumb and turning slowly around on the spot, flapping at his assailants with his free hand.

'Mo. Mo. Make them stop, Mo!' he pleaded, but there was nothing I could do. I blink-watched uselessly, dying inside, a flavour of slow self-evaporation I knew so, so well.

'Yey! Fatta man, is oo womb-man, is oo wep-man, yey? Fatta man, oo be ma wif?' they teased him. Some of them used their guns to hook up his skirt at the rear and mimed crude,

195

crotch-thrusting motions at him. Nonstop limply batted them away, chewed his thumb, spun around faster. More Fractions joined in. I got terrible shakes; it was a scene I'd witnessed countless times in playgrounds and exercise yards, only this time with cheap Chinese rifles thrown into the mix. One of the taunters was getting excited, scenting fun and blood.

'Ans' me fatta man! Oo prop man? Yey? Yey?' he screamed into Nonstop's tearful face. 'Ans' me o' a KILL oo! A KILL OO NOW!'

What could I do?

The synthetic rage fizzled, they tired of Nonstop, let him be. He was a lodestone for bullies, but too obvious a patsy to provide good sport. The group switched its interest to me, the next in line. Rough hands patted over me, stroked and nipped my burned face. A woman pinched my nose and punched me hard in the groin. I cried out and realised it was a trick to force me to open my mouth so she could inspect my teeth; she was either assessing my health or prospecting for gold. Then the woman rolled up my blindfold, stared straight into my eyes. She wasn't a fool, she could see the damage.

'Not bad, but 'im bland, wat oos 'im?' sniffed the woman. 'Dead in ice.'

One-for-Sorrow nodded, cocked a buttock and passed judgement and wind simultaneously.

'Fit girl stez. Sick girl stez, but oo wuk extra for 'er, Yonza. Fatta man, bland boy go,' he pronounced. That was that.

'Wait!' yelled Harete. She dug into her pockets, produced the ring – Moth's ring, my ring, Atlas's ring – and proffered it in a shaking hand to the lead Fraction. But the once-fantastical

196

bangle wasn't in tip-top condition any more; when Harete had used it to break the window back in the Compensation Camp the soft platinum had bent under the pressure and most of the diamonds had fallen out. All that was left was a buckled band and two lonely jewels. Junk. One-for-Sorrow looked offended, swatted the object away.

'Oo lot, back in 'anger for slippy slip,' he barked. The management team threw open the hanger doors, people started to file in. Not me, not Nonstop, we'd failed the cut; we were pulled out of the queue and pushed into the reject's group.

What faced us, I wondered, quaking where I stood. A night sleeping rough with no evening meal? A beating? Expulsion from the Facility?

One-for-Sorrow turned to us and smiled.

'Tam to put out a rabbish!' he said cheerfully.

'Mo . . . I've got a grievous bad feeling,' fretted Nonstop. So did I.

One-for-Sorrow slipped his gun from its strap, a machine pistol with a rotary magazine. I knew the type – they were named 'burp guns' after the noise they made.

He slid back the gun's bolt, cocking the gun, priming it. *Kerrrrrlink* creaked the spring. I could smell the oily contraption, hear his rings tinker against the steel barrel.

Lupa shouted out her fond farewells. 'Tough twinkies, losers!' she jeered. 'Ya gonna be killed to death. Pah!'

Up came the gun.

The Kernel's voice ripped through me. {MO! Tell them a story, you fool!}

197

Chapter 27

I think the Kernel must have put himself in the driving seat, because I don't remember much after that.

I do recall One-for-Sorrow's bemused expression when I stutteringly asked him if he'd like to hear a story. And how Seven-Wives spontaneously offered to eviscerate me with a bayonet as punishment for my effrontery, that bit has stayed with me too (as well as the rest of my bits). But not quite how or why One-for-Sorrow came to agree to my suggestion, whether he hungered for novelty or just valued a moment to relight his pipe before executing us.

Nevertheless, agree he did, and this is more or less what I told them, although why and how I never did understand. They all listened, all the tribe of Fractions and Lonza and Harete and many others.

'The Sons of Two Squires'
As told by the Kernel
(With assistance from Mo's mouth)

Once, there were two sons of two squires who lived on adjacent sides of a triangular meadow. One son was a lover of words, the other was a son of numbers. Regularly, they would meet up and contest the merits of their hobbies, crossing the sward to cross swords.

'Words are more interesting than numbers, because with words I can write stories,' announced Lex, a smidgen too pompously for that time of the afternoon.

'You mean *lies*,' replied Logan grumpily.

'A crass assumption. Stories are only superficially fictional. They always hold truths – truths about the writer, the reader, the worlds they both inhabit.'

Logan had heard it all before. He banged down his glass on the log table. 'Very derivative. You might as well say that a cake contains truths about the baker and the eater,' he scoffed.

Lex thought for a moment. 'Perhaps it does,' he said. 'Like a story, a cake may have many layers. And hidden surprises inside, like a fifteen-forint piece.'

'And they may both have too much filling,' sighed Logan. 'Or be all sponge and no fruit. And have irritating, sugary characters balanced on the top. Besides, it is wolves that have lairs, not cakes.'

'Well, I do d'éclair you could be right!' laughed Lex. 'Then tell me about numbers. I know they have plenty of practical uses. But do they tell us anything about human lives?'

'They are the bread under the jam of reality,'

proclaimed Logan. 'The paper under the ink. They have much to tell us about everything.'

'But they are so *linear*. Zero, one, two . . . and onwards to infinity. From dawn to yawn, a tedious line of digits. Zzzzzzz.'

'Don't be so negative. You have forgotten that for every number there is its twin, its minus, lurking on the opposite side of zero. Four and minus four . . . two and minus two . . . the anti-numbers, the mirror numbers. Put a number together with its minus version and . . . poof! They vanish. You are left with nothing.'

'So?'

'For one thing, it tells us that symmetry is boring.'

Lex shook his head. 'I disagree,' he said. 'There are some fascinating gravestones in our local ones.'

'Symmetry, not cemetery!' groaned Logan. 'When two sides balance exactly, the net result is nothing. Everything interesting comes from the leftovers. The universe is made from such scrag-ends, minute residuals that the Big Bang forgot to lick its pencil and strike out.'

'You are unbalanced.'

'Proudly! It's still more complex than that. There is another entire set of numbers. I shall not explain the details – those skilled in my art call them *imaginary*. They live on their own line at right angles to the *real* numbers, crossing at zero, the origin.'

'My brain is becoming very warm,' goaded Lex.

'Must be because my eyes have double-glazed over.'

'Listen. This means that numbers don't reside on a boring line, they live on a field defined by these two axes.'

'Now we are crossing axes, not swords!'

'One day, I shall show you a painting I made, a portrait of the entire universe and all who live in it.'

'A painting by Numbers?'

'Yes! It's very beautiful. Forms like chameleon tails and spirals abound . . . and the magical thing about the picture is this: study the inciest, winciest feature with a microscope set to look down the eyepiece of another microscope, or fly to Pluto and use a telescope to assume the grandest field of vision; in either case, you would see the same, rich level of detail.'

'Hmm. I have heard it said that the "devil is in the detail". If the whole is as detailed as any part, does that mean that the devil is everywhere?'

'I would have thought life demon-straights that to us daily. The devil is in every twist and turn of life's journey.'

'Meaning?'

'All quests are futile. No journey can ever be a matter of trotting along a straight line, keeping on the right side of zero and avoiding those pesky negatives. No, life is a confusing, zigzagging expedition. Maybe you'll get shot off to infinity, or trapped in a never-ending circle. You might set off with the finest intentions and your best spotted handkerchief on the end of a curtain pole slung over your shoulder, you might have made the most detailed preparations. But it's guaranteed you'll fail. You'll meet the opposite of what you sought, or a sort of twisted-round, right-angled version of it. Or nothing at all. The harder you seek something, the greater the twists will be.'

Lex was a little shaken by this promulgation. 'All quests are futile? If I go looking for a dragon, I could meet . . .'

'An anti-dragon.'

'What would that be like?' Lex asked.

'A kitten?' suggested Logan. 'Or a reptile that sucks in fire and liberates maidens?'

'A nogard. And how would a twisted-round, right-angled dragon look?'

Logan thought. 'Not sure. A savage, fire-breathing kitten? A scaly, winged animal that does nothing more irritating than stuff avocados into the shoes of Norwegian sailors? Something you never quite expected.'

'All quests are futile . . . you have proof of this? You number-scrunchers live to prove your theorems. Without a proof, what you have is not a fact, it's not even a hypothesis, it's . . .'

'Conjecture?'

'A story.'

Log$_n$ looked depressed. 'I have spent my life seeking confirmation of my idea,' he explained. 'Hence, I have failed. This is itself a clue that my idea is correct, but not definite proof.'

Lex thought long and hard, then short and soft. 'Perhaps the proof is in the pudding. Or cake. We must journey through this maze, seek the unexpected, and when equal and opposing forces have cancelled each other out, forge what life we can from the remainders.'

'Well said, word-burglar. A noble philosophy.'

But Lex had not finished. 'Hear me out. You failed to prove your theory with the scalpel-like precision of numbers. Your chosen tool was too fine for the job, it was like trying to pick up anvils with tweezers. Let us step back and take a broader view, search for the proof you seek through the wide-angle lens of stories.'

'A why-dangle lens?'

'The knotty, loopy yarn of a hangman. Better – of a hanged man. Once upon a time,' Lex began. 'Once upon a time . . .'

A robust, industrial-grade silence wafted down upon us, a silence permeated only by splintery blasts of gunfire coming from outside neighbouring hangers.

'A sort a lak,' declared One-for-Sorrow after due consideration, sucking in the evening air and nodding.

Seven-Wives added his two pennyworth. 'Story wa gar gut. Vair confoos in parts, but a lak, cos wa abart nummers and laf. An menshun deffil-man, 'im gut to haf in story. A lak deffil-man.'

One-for-Sorrow clapped his hands, ending all discussion.

'Fatta man, bland boy, slip in 'anger for night,' he ordered. 'But oo wuk, or bang bang morrow!'

I don't remember me and Nonstop stumbling back to Harete, going inside the hanger, finding a space on the floor, sleeping, but we must have done all that. Don't remember hearing the burp guns firing as the Fractions set about killing the other people who'd failed the cut, but after a few days you got so used to that sound it ceased to register, like a neighbour's dog that barks in the evenings, or the hum of a fridge.

Chapter 28

A new life began for us in hanger five, a life as intimate with death as the bee is with the comb, as the worm is with the earth.

Hanger five was a family business. The Facility's other hangers were controlled by different groups; every hanger was set in opposition to every other. Within each hanger, people were grouped into teams, each team working in competition with every other team. Every individual inside a team was out for him or herself. Rivalries within rivalries within rivalries . . .

The food arrived daily on those big white helicopters, cargos of international aid donated by other countries and intended for the millions of people starving in the Fartherland's civil war. Not only food: medicines, blankets, tents, clothes; everything you'd need to stay alive if you biked back from the swimming pool with your mates one afternoon and found someone had installed a spiffy new crater where your street used to be – the dog was on fire, Dad was wearing his lungs for a waistcoat and the man who used to serve at the sweetshop was exhorting your sister to strap a bomb to her chest and run towards a tank. That kind of thing: civil war stuff. Turn on your telly, open a newspaper or switch on one of those smarty-pants portable phones or tutti-frutti computers they have in rich places, you'll find a war like ours going on somewhere. Betcha.

The Facility was a distribution centre, a place where the food aid was meant to be collected before being stacked onto trucks and driven out across the country to be given away to the needy.

But that's not how it actually worked.

Instead, each hanger was operated by a different group of gangsters. Every day, the teams under their control went out and fought each other to bring back as much of the supplies as they could. This was hoarded in the hangers, then periodically taken away and sold at vast profit, all the money going to the criminals. If you didn't scavenge enough food to hand over to your hanger's management, you'd fail the nightly cut.

Blam, blam.

As far as I could tell, only our hanger was run by Fractions. Other hangers were managed by clans, gangs, mobs, foreign corporations, soldiers, all sorts.

That first morning, Harete and Nonstop and I tried to leave. Myristica wasn't in a fit state to be moved; the exertions of the past days had taken their toll and she was skirting the hems of consciousness. Besides, she was with Lonza and mumbled that she wanted to stay, nothing Harete said would change her mind. No one could work that day because there was too much smoke for helicopters to fly, so no one stopped us leaving the hanger when the doors were opened. We ran as fast as we could all the way to the main gate. When we got there, Harete did the talking.

'Let us out, please,' she panted to the Peacemaker on duty. He was sitting behind thick glass in an air-conditioned kiosk; the controls to open the gate were right by his elbow. 'And we have to report some murders. A lot of them. Get your supervisor!'

The guard did not look up. 'We regret, egress from the DPCRM Facility is not permissible during this presently instantiated chronological juncture,' he said, addressing his own nipples.

'Sorry? What?'

'You can't leave,' explained the Peacemaker, his voice muffled by the kiosk's window. 'This is a designated quarantine area. The Facility is rife with cholera, dysentery, typhus. Once you're in, you're in. Oh, and don't rush the fences, they're electrified. For hygiene.'

'But! But!' we protested as one.

'You agreed to the Terms and Conditions of entry!' the guard reminded us.

Taking no chances himself, he picked up a spray bottle of disinfectant and squirted the section of the window nearest Harete. Then he yanked down a blind over the kiosk window, saying, 'Your statutory rights are not affected. Health and safety!'

So that was that. As we were soon to learn, the small team of foreign Peacemakers on the site were entirely redundant, as much use as a bunch of parking wardens. They owned the buildings and guarded the gate and flew the helicopters, but they had no control over what went on inside or around the hangers. Their only positive contribution to affairs was to make sure no firearms were deployed during the daily free-for-all battles for a share of the deliveries, to keep that part of the horror gun-free.

More or less gun-free, that is; give or take; by and large.

We trudged back to our hanger, dismayed, terrified, confused. Groups from the other sheds glowered at us mistrustfully. We'd asked Lonza if we could run away to a different hanger, but he'd told us the others were no better.

'What are we going to do?' cried a tearful Harete. She sounded very, very afraid. Her despondency troubled me more than my own. I'd grown used to being scared for my life, the novelty had long dwindled. Observing its effects on Harete was deeply unsettling, reinforcing my feelings of abject uselessness. Her condition degraded me, further exposed my riotous obsession with her as folly. *If I cannot help the girl I claim to love, what use am I to anyone?*

'Just like my story,' I said bitterly. 'We sought sanctuary, so found its opposite. Or a skewed-around version of it.'

'How you made up that story on the spur of the moment, I'll never know,' Harete said, pulling herself together. 'I thought you'd really lost the plot, hardly understood a word of it.'

I blew up. 'You don't understand? Why should you? What gives you the right to think that the world or your life can be understood, or that understanding comes easily? Perhaps you'll understand in ten years' time, or a hundred, or on your deathbed, or never. That's how things are.' The vehemence of the outburst shocked me, but I applied its reasoning to itself and refused to question it.

'Was it something you learned from the delta gyp— from the Numbers?'

'Not sure. I'm in two minds about that,' I said, thinking about the Kernel's input. He'd saved my life, but I hadn't enjoyed being turned into a ventriloquist's dummy. He? *He* was *me*, surely . . . yet he knew things I didn't. Was I fated to be forever in two minds?

'I understood some of it, Mo. *Fractals*,' Nonstop said, a word I didn't know and didn't appreciate, it sounding very too much like 'Fractions'. 'Think of cow parsley and coastlines, the way any small part looks exactly the same as the whole.'

'Give it a rest, man!' That was Harete.

'What about the next working day? How will we make the cut, Mo, how?'

How?

We slouched back into the teeming sweatbox of hanger five. No bodies, I noticed; someone had at least carted off the corpses of the people the Fractions had murdered the night before.

The giant metal shed was nine-tenths filled with crates of food, but none of it was for us. Workers were all kept permanently starving, apart from elite scavengers like Lonza. We'd been warned: to so much as let your eyes linger on that stolen freight for too long was to risk being slaughtered. When not working, the hanger's hundreds of workers were forced to rest and sleep on the bare floor of a cordoned-off region at one end of the shed.

'I never did like open-plan offices,' grumbled Nonstop. 'At least on the Spiral we had our own cubicle.'

Our bosses, the thirty or so fractious Fractions, reclined leisurely in hammocks slung above us. When they wanted to relieve themselves, they did so over the hammocks' sides. The stench and the heat and the flies in the hanger were beyond the reaches of imagination, not that they seemed the least bothered by those things.

'Well, well, look's who's returned back,' Lupa greeted us. 'The slapper, the blind bard of the hanger and the sidekick's sidekick. Decided to stay, did ya, rinsers?'

'We liked the company,' I said. Lupa alone looked and sounded well-fed. Exactly as Lonza had described, by some quirk of the Peacemaker's rules, Lupa's pregnancy ensured she was supplied directly by them with ample food, more than enough to sustain her and to pay her dues to the Fractions. She was also permitted access to doctors and the dispensary.

I rested, listening in to short-range and long-range hubbub. I reckoned my sight would improve, but slowly. In the meantime, it was critical to restrict use of my frazzled eyes, a considerable challenge when faced with so many new dangers. My snapshot method of looking was better than nothing, but I paid for every minute of sight with an hour of skull-crunching headaches.

Lonza was talking with Harete, explaining to her what would happen when the weather cleared, the helicopters arrived and they had to go to work. Their conversation was rapid, professional, shop talk for natural fighters. The two of them had a good rapport, I sensed that at once.

Other voices reached me through the dark. Unfortunately.

'Hey, blind eyes,' screeched Lupa. 'Is that slag Harete your girlfriend?'

'No,' I told her. 'She's not.'

'No way she's your girlfriend. You're a skank. She is out of your dimension.'

'I said she isn't.'

'Nah-huh. No way is she.'

'That's what I just said! Don't you listen?' I exploded.

'Right. So tell your slut girlfriend to stop smooching with my boyfriend. Know what I mean?'

'Shut up, Lupa,' growled Lonza. That's about all Lonza ever said to the teenage mother of his unborn child. It demonstrated good judgement. There was certainly no point arguing with hard-faced, tight-eyed, foul-mouthed Lupa. To do so was to swim permanently upstream inside a sewer pipe.

'You. Mo-ron or whaddever you're called. Blind Ally.'

'Yeah?'

'That story you told was a pile. I didn't get none of it, and I've, like, got sustificates and that. Also, I hate it when stories try to teach me stuff. If I ever wanted to know stuff, I'd get Lonza to stab the crack out of someone who knew whatever it was I wanted to know until they told him. So don't ever try and teach me with a story, cos I'm already smart, the milk of the crop. Not like you scum, you're all as thick as thieves. Know what I mean?'

'Right, Lupa. So what kind of stories do you like?'

Lupa thought for a long time before replying. 'I'd like a story about a owl what swears a lot and then it, like, rips a person's face off, right in the actual face. That would be awe-perspiring.'

'I'll . . . I'll see what I can think up,' I said, regretting that the drone had not deafened me also.

With no warning, Lupa grabbed my ankles and pulled off both my trainers. 'Your shoes are gooder than mine. We're, like, swapping,' she said.

211

'The scab we are!' My fist soared and drew back. I homed in on her voice, itching to bust her waxy face like punching a spoon through the seal on a jar of coffee.

'Oi, sphincter-licker. Pregnant! You even touch me, and it's like you're actually murdering a baby infant. Besides, who else is gonna get sick-insect's druggy-wuggies?'

That was the clincher. Without those medicines, Myristica had little life to speak of. My fist was barking at me to let fly, but I spent my punch on my own thigh.

Lupa hooted and said, 'You are so gonna learn who's boss – you are totally gonna learn to cow town before me.'

I learned, we all learned. Lupa was untouchable in every sense. Not only by us and the other workers; the Fractions too had an inviolable respect for her condition, as if it were something miraculous, a mode of reproduction wholly unknown to them.

Her crumbling trainers were two sizes too small for me. And both were lefts.

That first full day in the Facility wore on. No helicopters meant no work, which also meant no night-time cut to survive; but it also meant no food, and nothing to do. Arguments were breaking out everywhere, the nerves of the Fractions and the workers alike were elongated far beyond their normal breaking points.

Nonstop entered a decline as profound as Myristica's, but whereas hers was medical, his was emotional. Lonza jealously shielded his half-sister from everyone's attentions but his own. One use of the word 'sis' by Nonstop had been sufficient for Lonza to smash his face, causing that titchy nose to flatten

212

out and fountain blood. Nonstop was banned from speaking to her on pain of, well, pain.

He took his demotion badly. 'Useless half-brother he is anyway,' he pointed out to me. 'He's the one that lost her in the first place; it's me that rescued her, like I rescued you. Grievous unfair.'

'Here,' I said, and I pulled Dolly-with-one-arm out of my trackie waistband. 'She's yours. But you've got to promise me you'll guard her. What's been loved once must be loved forever, remember?'

I'd only meant it as a silly joke, but Nonstop willingly accepted the toy. 'Thanks, Mo. I will. I really, really will,' he said. Dolly soon had a friend of her own: when Lonza had his back to us, Myristica nudged Nonstop and with a wan smile palmed to him a tiny toy bear. I think it had once been a decoration from a key ring.

'For my secret brother,' she whispered.

Nonstop put the bear inside Dolly, along with my knife.

'Your sister, Nonstop, I mean your real one, do you think –'

'Yes, Mo. That Compensation Camp place. That's where my parents would have taken her. I'd always suspected something of the sort.'

I swallowed hard.

'I envy her, now,' Nonstop added. 'I do, I envy her.'

The Fractions found it no easier than the rest of us to cope with the dragging boredom. They relieved their executive stress by promenading casually around the hanger, seeking people to pick on. The air in the claustrophobic hall became as opaque as wallpaper paste, a filthy fug of sweat and terror.

All working eyes fixed on the swaggering Fractions. Everyone in our team shrank down, stared at the floor, trying to make ourselves invisible, inaudible, unremarkable. It was absolutely critical not to stand out from the crowd in any way.

'Oi, Pick-Up-Sticks! Come over here and play, I'm bored off me head!' bawled Lupa.

'Cram your crevice!' hissed Lonza. 'You might be protected, but we sure ain't.'

'Pah! Up-shut yourself and drink sick. They won't waste an ace worker like you, just these other slit-rinsers.'

I was desperate to know what was occurring. 'Where are they? Can you see them?'

'Supriss, surpiss!' a guttural voice licked at my ear. 'Ay is rat be'ind 'oo! Lez speel!'

Pick-Up-Sticks sprang up like a heavily armed jack-in-the-box. The Fraction had a blue-painted face and, immune to the heat, appeared to be wearing all the clothes he'd ever owned at once, T-shirts layered over T-shirts, wigs piled on top of wigs, sunglasses balanced on glasses. The jackdaw jackanapes sniffed us over like a miser buying pet-shop offal.

He spotted broken Dolly clasped in Nonstop's trembling hand. I winced. Nonstop's card was already marked from the previous night; this was surely a provocation too far.

'Waz is? Fatta man lak play dolla? Oo not prop man!' screamed Pick-Up-Sticks, spitting with black-eyed fury. He stabbed his gun barrel hard up against Nonstop's temple. 'Fatta man go boom boom splat!'

Nonstop squirmed and emitted a pitiful 'nnnn nnnn nnn nnnn' noise and farted cataclysmically. It smelled terrible. I felt ashamed on his behalf, then ashamed of my ignoble shame.

Pick-Up-Sticks's finger hooked around the revolver's trigger. I blink-watched the crescent trigger curl, the hammer yawn back.

The trigger finger tightened.

Relaxed.

Tightened – really tight. I'm certain I could see the hammer fluttering at the extent of its travel, ready to snap back. The temperature in the hanger felt like a thousand million degrees. Nonstop shook so hard the tiny key ring teddy bear popped out of Dolly's arm hole and landed at his feet.

The Fraction's pellet eye rotated downwards to the dropped toy. His face lit up like a coach lantern.

'Eyyyyyy, a lak!' he cried. 'Dolla in dolla, es gar gut!' He immediately holstered his gun, replaced the toy bear inside Dolly and fussed around Nonstop, pressing Dolly against his chest, his head, his arms, as if striving to arrive at some more satisfying configuration. He finally settled on putting the doll down the front of Nonstop's trackie top, then stood back to admire his creation, jigging and hopping with unrestrained delight.

'Bear dolla insid baba dolla insid fatta man, ey!' he bubbled, his pidgin talk barely comprehendible. From behind my blindfold I blink-looked the happy savage over, trying to get some handle on him and his kind. What warped, misbegotten urge underpinned this excitation? His brown teeth were decorated, I noticed; he'd had digits painted on them: 2 7 1 8 2 8 1 8.

The voice in my head delighted at the dental scrimshaw, buzzing like a comb and tissue-paper harmonica. The Kernel was hugely aroused by these extraordinary people; I'd been hearing him chunter and witter to himself all day, his thoughts bleeding into mine, making my forehead itch.

{Look at his t-*e*-*e*-th!}

Pick-Up-Sticks sauntered off in search of other people to play with. Nonstop and I breathed out together, liquefying in our relief.

We'd survived another brush with our pantomime hosts. But we were both familiar with the mechanics of luck, understood how it sticks and stacks. Every escape was merely a delay, nothing more.

Chapter 29 *

The weather was too bad for flying for the next three days as well.

Because we weren't working, we weren't eating. Lupa reluctantly doled out some of her stocks of baby food, although only after Lonza twisted her arms. We bolted the vegetable-flavoured putty and supplemented it with the remains of my glue, set as brittle as glass in its plastic bag, but still edible. It was nowhere near enough.

Late on day two the crowded hanger became suffused with a delicious aroma of cooking. From the management's private area behind a barrier of piled-up food-aid boxes wafted the sumptuous scents of frying meat and boiling vegetables.

'Don't eat the stew,' Lonza warned us. 'No matter how hungry you are, don't eat it.'

'Why shouldn't we? I'm so grievous hungry,' whined Nonstop. 'Surely if they're offering us food we should accept it?'

'Don't eat the stew,' repeated Lonza. A quick flourish of his largest blade drove home the point. I knew the young man well enough by then to appreciate he was not taken to wasting words; lean Lonza was impervious to sentiment, hard as boiled boots. Nevertheless, he was looking after all of us, I could not deny that.

He supplied no explanation. The hanger buzzed with the same advice from old hands in every corner: *Don't eat the stew.*

Once prepared, the food was taken on a tour of the workers' part of the hanger in stockpots propelled on a trolley by One-for-Sorrow, dressed for the part in a chef's tall hat.

'What's in it?' asked Harete, sniffing deeply. 'It smells fabulous!'

'Ghoul hash, some call it,' Lonza told her. 'Be strong, Harete.'

The hanger charged up with anticipation as four hundred hungry people sampled the diffusing aromas and weighed up their cravings against the advice. The smell of the food was making us all salivate and writhe.

One-for-Sorrow trundled close by with the trolley. He lowered one of the big metal pans onto the floor and removed the lid.

'Com get! Es gut fo' empty tums,' he cackled. 'Ol pram cuts. A bite make free!' The other Fractions took that as their cue and started to sing in unison, 'A bite make free! A bite make free!'

We looked at the pot. Everyone around us looked at the pot.

'I smell cheese sauce,' Nonstop pined.

'I smell onions and carrots and garlic,' mewed Myristica.

'I smell gravy!' growled Lonza. 'Real gravy!'

But it was Harete who cracked first. I was so hungry and tired that the sudden inrush of rich, foody smells gave rise to a sort of savoury overload; yellow nausea washed over me, all of a sudden I couldn't have swallowed so much as a teaspoon of water, my own spittle became repulsive in my mouth. Myristica was too ill to take the food, Lonza and Lupa too experienced, Nonstop too slow.

Harete's appetite was still coupled to physical strength. She crawled on hands and knees closer to the pan.

'Just want to look,' she said. 'No harm in that.'

I had to switch to strobo-vision, angling my neck to see around my eyes' black discs and taking snapshots. I saw Lonza haul Harete back by her ankles, drag her across the floor like a sailor pulling up an anchor; but she kicked free and joined with a band of people drooling around the rim of the pot. Two-for-Joy stepped over and started to ladle the steaming, sticky mess over their heads. Instead of running away, scalded and screaming, the recipients of the gravy benediction cried out with pleasure.

'Meat!' moaned Harete covetously. 'Oh, such wonderful meat! I want it, I must, must have it!'

Scandalised by Harete's abandonment, I inhaled more deeply; this time I detected a structure to the smell, a bass note odour that had bypassed me until then. Myristica had it in her nostrils too.

'Like catnip!' she said. 'Drives some cats wild, others ignore it! Must be some sort of . . . psycho salsa?'

I took another snapshot. Harete's hair had become liberated from its ponytail and was hanging down in greasy cords, matted with juice. She was threshing, jiving, revelling in the sensation of the lumpy sauce cascading over her, tumbling from her chin. Her mouth opened, she raked the backs of her hands slowly down her cheeks, almost – but not quite – channelling rivulets of the cloudy sauce in over the threshold of her lips.

Some people had yielded fully and were already scooping handfuls into their mouths, crying and grunting with uninhibited ravishment. The crazed scene was repeated everywhere the pans had been placed. The hanger was in complete uproar; everyone was stamping and shouting, 'Don't eat the stew! Don't eat the stew!'

Harete made her choice. She dipped into the pot, brought her cupped hand to the brink of her gaping mouth. I had to long-blink my stinging eyes; someone moved between us and for a vital moment I missed what was happening. The next I knew, Harete's face was ricked in a silent scream and she was frantically flicking the gruel from her fingers. I watched as she passed out and sank under a tidal surge of newcomers determined to join in the rapture. At the last instant before she disappeared from sight, Lonza tunnelled through the crush of diners and hooked his arms around her.

When he'd dragged Harete back to us, he lay her down and prised open her jaws. I thought he was about to administer artificial respiration; instead he inserted his nose into her mouth and breathed in. He was sampling, I understood then, learning if she'd eaten, if she was contaminated beyond redemption. She hadn't, she wasn't. Harete rolled away from him, retching, wretched.

Hours later, small rings of empty space opened up around the men and women who'd supped the stew. No one approached or spoke to them. The damned hugged their knees and rocked backwards and forwards, humming blissfully to themselves. Over the course of the day their skin turned the colour of pewter and garlands of white, weeping lesions erupted around their mouths, neither affliction detracting from the euphoric daze in which each seemed permanently sealed.

'They'll not make the next cut,' Lonza told us. He was busy trimming off Harete's adulterated tresses with a knife, cropping her hair until it was not much more than a crew cut. Lonza worked with great care and dexterity, gliding the blade around her ears, coaxing Harete back to life and humour as the two of them talked. I shuffled around, not able to tolerate the thought of his hands trespassing on the hallowed curves of her neck.

Once, I heard them both laugh; not the knowing, rusty caw used to greet and appease calamity, but genuine laughter, as unexpected as a plump blackbird in December. How those two had found anything to laugh about in hanger five was beyond me. Not only me:

'What a dumb slut. Your girlfriend is either mental or both,' Lupa grumped, speaking from where she lay on the floor beside me.

'How many times? She's not my girlfriend!'

'And she never will be, skank. Pah!'

Don't ask me what Harete found in the goulash. I was too far away, my eyes too damaged. But I guess everything blends eventually, if you've a big enough mixer with a tough enough blade.

No bodies, I remembered. You never saw what they did with the bodies.

The night after the goulash, a pernicious cough did the rounds. Once a person caught the cough, pretty soon everyone around them started quacking and hacking along too, their staccato coughs reverberating like timpani rolls in the tin-topped hanger. The cough trailed a rumour behind it: it was the overture to *barn dance*.

221

'Starts with coughing,' explained Lonza. 'You get all jumpy, can't sit still, have to leap madly about, but you're dizzy and lose balance. Two days of that, then you lie down.'

'Then what?'

'Then nothing.'

'Best bit is when they snuff it in the night,' sniggered Lupa. 'And their mates shake them to see if they're awake. The disease, like, liquefies the brain into . . . liquid. You can hear it go *slosh-slosh* in their skulls. That's so totally awesome cool.'

'You're making this up!'

Lonza grimly corroborated her account, saying, 'It's true enough. Their insides turn to emulsion. The sickness comes from the goulash-noshers I reckon.'

'Hope you and fatso and slag-face get it,' Lupa said. 'Oh, that would be bang lush. I'll empty your heads out through your lug holes. I won't get it – I'm like immune.'

'No brain,' explained Lonza.

After that, we were all permanently alert for the first tickle in our throats.

Sleep was nigh impossible because of the overcrowding, the noise and the stinking heat, but we all managed some in fits and starts and stops. Not being able to get to sleep was bad enough, worse was waking up and listening to the hushed conversations of others who couldn't sleep, or didn't want to.

'Is Lonza your surname?'

'No, Harete, it's my given name. '

'Hope you kept the receipt!'

'Ha! Back at you with that.'

'Lupa's . . . different.'

'What do you think of her? Honestly?'

'She's, um, the salt of the earth.'

'She's that. But who wants salty earth?'

'Lonza! You must love her really. She's pregnant with your baby after all. Yours and hers, I mean.'

'She's a survivor, I'll grant her that. You want that in a mother. I'll forgive her anything if she keeps herself and our baby alive. She wasn't always as nasty she is now, she changed. Can you blame her, being pregnant and living here?'

'But what will happen when she gives birth?' asked Harete. 'There aren't any other preg . . .'

Wet a spoon-back with dew, float it one light year above a first birthday candle and wait for the drops to boil.

That's how long the silence lasted.

Listen.

That's the sound life makes when wolf truth devours it.

They carried on talking.

'You really care for Myristica though, don't you?'

'They've not minted or mined the word to say how much.'

'Is there any way to get out of here? Could we wait for the trucks that collect the food and smuggle ourselves out in them?'

'Been tried, never works. You do know, don't you, that if one person tries to escape, the Fractions will plug the whole team? You have to believe it, Harete, life here is like life anywhere else. We stay, we endure, we look after each other. There's no way out alive.'

'That's so bleak an outlook. I don't think I can go on if

that's true.'

'You'll find your way. Harete? Will you let me hold you in the night?'

Dynamo heart, turbine heart, reactor heart. Say no. Say no. Say no, say no, say –

'What about Lupa?'

'She won't care, I promise you that. Please?'

'Yes, Lonza. I'd like that very, very much. I'm so hungry to be held.'

I thieved a look.

By the light of an overhead tube, I half-watched Harete's face glow and break and admit to another self, submit to another person. *That look!* My insides shrivelled like a crisp packet on a bonfire. Foul Lupa had been right: Harete would never love me, my feelings towards her were misspent currency. It wasn't a simple matter of mixed messages or petty squabbles. Lonza was a fighter, a protector, a lover, a father, almost. I was a cowardly, immature, teenage jailbird, citizen of the Institute and child of the Spiral. I'd never looked after anyone, was incapable of caring for anyone but myself. All I'd done in my low-rent, bottom-shelf, cut-price life was run away from my problems, invariably ending up facing more than I'd started with.

Reality had been laying siege to me for several days. I had denied it access, although I had known it intimately. Now, flooding over the ramparts, the understanding macerated me. That Harete did not love me was a given; during our travels and travails I had become secretly addicted to the doctrine. The deeper I thought about it, the more absurd the notion appeared; indeed, for her to have expressed affection or respect for me would have severed that bond she had with perfection and lessened her in my defective sight. But never had I thought she would take communion with another person, and so readily, so quickly, and under such appalling circumstances.

My connective tissues melted, I began to decompose.

'Mo. Mo. Mo. I can't sleep, Mo.' On that occasion, I was grateful for Nonstop's interruption.

'Try rocking yourself to sleep.'

'Haven't got a rock.'

'Try counting sheep.'

'We are the sheep. I . . . I miss the Spiral, Mo. We didn't appreciate what we had.'

'We had nothing!'

'I know. And we didn't appreciate it.'

I nodded. Nonstop was right. I missed the Spiral, too. I missed the food, I missed Atlas, I very much missed having only Dexter Manus to worry about. Above all else, I missed the old Harete, my Harete, the one who'd been a heady pressing of memory and infatuation and possibility. Not this one, this . . . solid, confusing, relentlessly independent one, this one who'd given up her cushy life in the Other country to rescue me, yet who did not love me.

'Help me, Kernel!' I begged. 'I don't know how to live any more, nothing makes sense to me. The wicked are loved and the lovable act wickedly. I've lost my way!'

No answer; my madness must have been burrowing away inside his thoughts; no – inside *my* thoughts.

On the fourth day the helicopters returned.

Chapter 30

The hanger was peaceful that fourth morning, the workers' living area was empty.

After spending so long cooped up with the Fractions, angels bearing angel cakes would not have been greeted with more jubilation than the overdue helicopters. All the workers had gone to market, the Facility's term for the scrum-cum-bloodbath that ensued when those aerial caravans descended with their pendulous cargo nets filled with food, and close to two thousand people swarmed in and fought for a share.

Nonstop, Harete and Lonza from our team had left with the others. Before they'd departed, I'd hugged Harete and back-slapped Nonstop; they'd been too battened-down with apprehension to say much. Lonza had been coaching Harete for the previous four days. He'd even devised a role for Nonstop: guarding the team's secret weapon, an old wheelie bin. The bin was normally kept chained up outside the hanger; at market time it enabled Lonza to transport much more booty than was possible using folded cloths or arms alone as most other teams had to.

I'd volunteered. I'd even charily admitted to the true state of my vision, explained how by twisting my head around in low light I could see around the blank spots in my eyes, for brief periods at least.

For once, Lupa had voiced the truth.

'Oh, lend me your brain, I'm trying to build a moron!' she'd groaned. 'You wouldn't last two minutes out there.'

With the workers gone, Lupa toddled off to the Peacemakers to be issued with her free rations. No sooner had she departed than I felt a stringy arm hook around my neck and I was dragged to one side by a Fraction, He-Played-Three, in appearance a hybrid of hobo, clown and gunslinger. He was young, maybe only thirteen, but no less callous or rapacious than his elders.

He-Played-Three made an unexpected demand of me:

'Pruv oo is bland,' he said. 'Pruv me, you no-see-can-able.'

'How? ' I replied.

I sensed He-Played-Three flap his arms and wiggle his fingers around in front of my eyes – I felt the displaced air play on my lips and face-fuzz. As it happened, at that precise time I was effectively blind; tiredness and overuse meant I was having a bad-eyes day, and the brash morning light was far too strong for me to see anything.

'How man fings I 'old up?' He-Played-Three said.

'I don't know. I can't see,' I said, quite honestly. The super-thick Fraction grunted, but even he knew the assessment lacked clinical rigour.

'Oo got ice,' he reasoned aloud. 'Oo not need. A stub cigar out in oor ice, then oo deffo bland.' I heard him strike a match and smelled the dungy flatus of a large cigar being lit and puffed on, stoked to full heat.

Emergency; I had to act or have my recovering eyes burned out forever. With no regard to the consequences, I lifted my blindfold, worked out whereabouts in the sky the sun hung and aimed my face straight at it, eyes wide open, holding the pose for fully half a minute.

The pain in my eyes was excruciating. I can't think having the burning end of that fat cigar ground into them would have hurt much less. It needed immense discipline – and fear – to force myself to stand still, hoping my clenching and unclenching fists would not give me away.

I broke off, aware of the damage I'd done. My eyes were both as dead as poached eggs; it was too much to hope they'd recover a second time.

'Yey, gut. Fan, oo bland. Jop for oo,' said He-Played-Three, satisfied by the demonstration. A stinking pall of cigar smoke hung around my head. I spluttered, and trusted that would explain why my eyes were watering so much, if he thought to ask.

He didn't. He marched me into the Fractions' own quarters at the far end of the hanger and I was set immediately to work. Another malformed junior called Went-to-Mow issued me with a jute sack and a bag of bait soaked in rat poison. My duty was to re-bait all the rodent traps and deposit dead vermin in the sack.

The Fractions must have thought me a laggardly worker. But movement was difficult. A sulphuric toxin had percolated throughout my body, wasting my muscles and swelling my joints: hatred; matchless, blind hatred.

They'd needed a sightless person to preserve their privacy.

But I could still listen. A minute blue spark sprang forth in my mind – a pilot light. *Learn as much as possible about the Fractions, learn how to hurt the little scabbers.*

I applied myself studiously to this task. My blindness assisted, I was free from all distractions. The brother Fractions were stocktaking, repeatedly counting and re-counting the stolen foodstuffs. For them, to be was to count; theirs was the counter culture.

Some spoken snippets I overheard were decidedly curious.

'Ey. Wat in tin? Bif? Wat is bif?'

'Bif is type eaty mit. Is cow metal. Lak pok is pig plastic.'

'But wat bif made from, ey?'

'From . . . an'mal stuffs, innit?'

'But wat is? A muz know!'

'Dunno. Ey, look! Mit in tins. Tins in box. Box in crate. Crate in pallet. Pallet in truck. Truck in hanger. Hanger in land. Land in . . . in . . . big land.'

'Ey, a luffin' they divven levels!'

Or:

'Oo've nine tins. Is three-bi-three. Only. A got seventeen.'

'Pram! Pram! No way, only seventeen-bi-one!'

'Pure.'

'Bless they prams. Pram nums is like . . . nummer mit.'

The rest of their communications were conducted in Whistle-Click. It was obvious to me that if I was to learn anything to keep me from becoming an ingredient in the zombie pot luck, it was that strange language I needed to master. And that was surely hopeless. Bilious depression sloshed in the dirty dishwater of my back-brain, diluting my earlier fury.

I learned but one secret. Padding through the private volume I realised something was shadowing me. The clomping footsteps were more reminiscent of hooves than feet, and the musty, musky odour was definitely agricultural. The snorts of pungent breath issued from too high up for it to be a goat; I decided the Fractions had tethered a llama there, except that hardly seemed a fact worth hiding from prying eyes.

Job completed, He-Played-Three dumped me back into the workers' space; I was given a broom and the job of sweeping out the area. I knew that in a few hours the workers would return. Then there'd be a Performance Review – our team would have to demonstrate it had salvaged enough food to justify its size, else someone would fail the cut. My life lay in my friends' hands. And in their wheelie bin.

Myristica came over to assist, steering me as I swept. She'd rallied that morning, benefiting from her new supplies of tablets.

'How's it going, Mo? Not been able to talk much to ya lately,' she said as we patrolled the hanger, up and down, left and right, driving the broom together.

I related to her the setback to my vision. 'How are you in yourself, Myristica? Are you still in pain?'

'Only always, Mo,' she replied. 'The "theatre of war", that's the expression generals use, isn't it? I've the best seat in the house for this production. I'm the theatre.'

She didn't mean the Fartherland's civil war, but the one going off in her body. Under the care she'd received while her father was alive the tumour's advance had stabilised, then reversed. Without treatment, the arithmetically minded lump's cells had resumed dividing and multiplying, accelerating to make

230

up for lost time.

'The pills, they stop you dying?'

Myristica half-gulped, half-laughed. 'Show me the drug that can do that! They do lessen the pain though. When Lupa can be bothered to collect them, that is.'

Urgh: sucking up to Lupa and keeping her sweet. Even amidst the slaughter of hanger life, that necessity still grated.

'Your bro and Harete are clicking well,' I said. The statement brought no catharsis; it felt more like trying to cure a mouth full of boils by chewing on salted razor blades.

'Yup. That . . . bother you?'

'Nah,' I lied. The lie sounded lonely, so I found it a companion. 'Happy for her. If . . . I really love her, I should be glad she's in with someone who can look after her. I can't even look *at* her, I'm no scabbing use.'

'Mo, my brother won't leave Lupa. He knows it, she knows it. He only wants to be Harete's friend. Good luck to them – there's little enough friendship in this place.'

'Friendship? But that's cheating!' I gasped, mortified. 'That's not real love! Real love is feeling like you're being asphyxiated every time you think of a person, it's a . . . a vulture feeding from your ribcage, it's pain deep in the marrow, it's missing someone like you'd miss your own arm if it were severed!'

Myristica shrieked with laughter, a peel so loud that the Fractions by the door ceased whistle-clicking for a minute, stepped inside to investigate. We worked the large broom side-by-side in silence until we heard them depart and resume cleaning their guns and smoking their hookah.

'You're so jealous!' Myristica teased me.

231

The broom collided with something immovable: a body, one of the several people who'd expired during the night. I hurled the broom aside and sat down, unable to reign in my rampaging misery any longer. I felt sick to my pits.

Did I envy Lonza? I turned the conceit over for examination like a foreign coin slipped into my change. He was so patently superior to me, envying him for his mutual affinity with Harete seemed witless.

Not since pen two had I felt so lost. Love belonged with explosions and fights, I thought, another outpouring of misdirected violence that in no regard matched its depiction in fiction. Perhaps for the good-looking it did, maybe it was positively rigid with possibilities and excitement for them. For the left-behinds and losers and everyone else, it was just another of life's incontestably nasty discouragements, no more nourishing than a gassy belch that tasted of last week's egg sandwiches.

I must have looked singularly pitiable – Myristica perched herself beside me.

'Not sure you really know Harete at all,' she said. 'I don't either, but I'll bet she doesn't want to be a limestone effigy, being slowly eroded by your drool as you marvel at her beauty. I think you fell for a mirage, like one of those heat hazes that forms above a road on a hot day. You know, where the air goes wobbly and you think you're seeing water, but it's actually a distorted image of the sky. An optical illusion.'

'You're right,' I sighed. 'That's exactly what happened. I built a Harete in my head from a collection of scrapbook cuttings and set her to wander around my dreams. But it wasn't the real her.'

'Strikes me, you didn't learn the lesson of your own story. What was it you said: all quests are futile? You made Harete the object of an expedition, like she was an old cathedral or a new continent.'

I nodded. 'Of course. And so I didn't find her. Instead, another version, not the opposite, just . . . different. And the worst of it is, even though I know that, it still hurts and I still love her.'

Myristica persisted with her line of thought. 'Who knows, though. Maybe you'll bump into an equally unexpected but enticing thing. Perhaps you've already met it. Do you think?'

'No, I don't think so, Myristica. On this journey I've met with nothing but hatred, violence and death.'

'Oh,' said Myristica, for some reason sounding timorous, a touch disappointed even. 'Well. There's none so blind . . . take heart, Mo. I know I shall,' she added after a long hiatus.

The conversation had reached a pinnacle of ridiculousness. 'Who cares anyway?' I sulked. 'We might as well debate the rising price of peacock beaks in Venezuela. Today, tomorrow, those Fractions are going to shoot me. Then Nonstop. Then you. And if Harete or Lonza break a leg and can't work, all of us.'

Myristica refused to give up. 'So let's do something about it. The others are going to be busy from now on. It's up to you and me to work out how to survive this place. Or even . . . escape.'

'Don't start on about escapes,' I rebuffed her. 'I'm blind, you're ill, Lupa's up the duff, we're hemmed in by electric fences, watched by trigger-happy trolls. Anyway, every time I escape I end up somewhere worse. I'm done with escapes. Through, finished, over.'

'Survival, then. Will you settle for that?'

'Prolonging the agony. Postponing the inevitable.'

Myristica sounded angry. 'Just like the others!' she fumed. 'You don't think I can do it. I'm not just a dying little girl, a pity pet, a worry-sponge for Lonza and Nonstop. Boo-hoo, I've got bitch-bastard cancer, pat me on the head and feel sorry for me. This is *my* chance to fight. I want to show I can take risks to help people I care for, instead of being the one who's always carried. Lame ducks can fight too, you get me?'

But I didn't, not until Myristica led me by the hand.

'Being in lurrrve, Mo, remember? The part that isn't lust, the missing element? It's when you grow up and, for the first time in your life, you don't want to be looked after. You're ready to step through the looking glass and be the one who does the defending. Even if the other person doesn't appreciate you're doing it for them, even if you suffer in the process.'

Myristica's appeal moved me. The way I read it, she wanted to prove herself to Lonza, the brother she loved so deeply, show him she was no longer the child he took her for.

'Oh, whatever,' I relented. 'Get your thinking cap on then.'

'Barn storming! Let's think of more stories, Mo. That crazy tale you told the Fractions worked, and it's a head-trip Harete that's made you more melancholic than . . . than . . .'

'A melon with colic?' I suggested.

'Absolutely. And a complete drip to boot. No offence.'

'None taken.'

'Your story had a hitch at the end,' she said, sounding thoughtful.

'A hitch at the end?' I gasped. 'It was full of mistakes all

234

the way through – I didn't know what I was saying for most of the time!'

'No, not an error, like a trailer hitch. A place for us to hook up another episode. So let's tie up the Fractions with a long story, buy us some time. For seed corn we'll use your own experiences on the Spiral. We'll show them . . . show them the pun is mightier than the gun!'

'The pun is mightier than the horde!' I laughed. 'Myristica . . . Meg . . . uh, it's . . . I've . . .'

'Enjoyed talking to me?'

'Yeah. Been good,' I sniffled. Right then, Myristica's voice was the one welcome entrant in my sightless universe.

'Almost as good as talking to Harete, huh? Wait for the burnout, Mo. These crushes always crash and burn. After the burnout, ya can get to know and love the real girl.'

But our plan came unstuck at once. The Fractions began shooting into the air to signal the return of the work details, hours earlier than expected. We had no time to prepare any stories. Whatever our friends had recovered would be weighted and counted; once more my life hung in the balance.

Chapter 31 *

Things had not gone well.

Or rather, they had gone well, and then Nonstop had messed up. A grim-spirited Harete filled us in: the fighting had been a carnival of barbarity, hundreds of people at a time rushing forwards, crawling over the dropped cargo nets, snatching up whatever they could, fighting with staves and blades and slingshots to ward off competitors. The Peacemakers had monitored the melee from afar, meticulously noting down every breach of regulations on their digital clipboards. Lonza had ably done his part, dashing to and fro. Harete had played second stop, relaying whatever Lonza brought back to Nonstop. He'd guarded the wheelie bin by sitting on it, biting his thumb. Only during the race back to the hanger had Nonstop tripped up, his foot catching in the hem of his skirt. The bin had emptied out, half of everything they had scavenged had been sent rolling over the concrete, swept up by the swift.

We queued outside the hanger. The Fractions were already progressing along the line, inspecting the productivity of each team. Harete defended Nonstop the best she could. 'He did well, Lonza, up until then. He'll improve. Were you perfect on your first day?' she argued. She sounded shaken and frail, I think more from what she'd witnessed than from accumulated injuries. Still, she was a whale for sympathy.

Lonza was a sprat. 'He's a scabbing danger to us all!' he growled. 'And now we'll fail the cut. That's the way it is, Harete. One of those two is going to have to go. Not my rules, theirs!'

Nonstop himself was gibbering like his mind was trying to dig its way out through his teeth.

'You've never seen anything like it, Mo. Not my fault. Grievous bad it was. The ground was uneven, there was blood and food and ick and sick and muck and yuck everywhere underfoot. Poor old Nonstop wasn't made for this.'

Lupa was bouncing with glee. 'Oh, but this is the best. THE best!' she squealed. 'Pervy-skirt or fertiliser-face. I just gotta see who gets it. I'm gonna ask One-for-Sorrow if I can, like, have something off your skellington as a souvenir. Know what I mean?'

The lead Fractions approached: haughty One-for-Sorrow and shorty, paunchy Two-for-Joy. I heard them sift through the bin, assaying the material for quantity and quality.

'Oo short, Yonza. Way short,' said One-for-Sorrow, scratching his domed igloo of a head. 'A ready took baba fud from pregga girl in'o account. Oo got to give up one for shootin'. Mebbe bland boy, mebbe fatta man.'

Harete broke down and Lupa cried out, 'Yessss! Result! Back of the neck!'

Lonza stood behind me. I sensed his paw hover over my shoulder, float to Nonstop, move back. I didn't resent him, I pitied him. Eighteen years old and being forced to choose

237

someone to be put to death.

Me or Nonstop . . . me or Nonstop.

I sweated in my lightless silo, expecting to be pushed out of line any second. The babble of the people in the queue dropped away faster than the ground seen from a soaring hot air balloon. The nerves in my fingers and toes lit up; I felt I was streaming needles of blue plasma from my extremities. Without seeing it, I knew Lonza's deciding hand was still fluttering between me and Nonstop – I swear I could feel a heat radiating from it like it was a flatiron.

'Excuse me,' Myristica interrupted. 'We've a new story we'd like to tell you. A story like a life, a story for a life.'

I inhaled so forcefully I sucked up a passing mosquito – how had she managed to invent a story so quickly?

From the Fractions came no answer. Not a whistle, not a click. I focused my ears on a single sound: the chirp of a reversing alarm on a Peacemaker's tank.

'This vehicle is reversing . . . this vehicle is reversing . . .'

'Na,' said One-for-Sorrow. There was to be no quarter from the Fractions.

'Oo tell story, sicky girly. We not lak story, *oo* die. Un'stood? Not bland boy, not fatta man, oo!'

'Deal!' Myristica answered without hesitation.

Lonza exploded. 'No, Meg! You're safe, don't gamble your life for these deadbeats!' he exhorted her, but Myristica ignored him. I understood the rule: the jeopardy had to be held by the storyteller, else people might deliberately tell lousy stories to dispose of other team members.

'Are ya toting your guns comfortably?' started Myristica,

speaking quietly but confidently, unfazed by the wager she was taking on. 'Then we'll begin. You'll remember from the end of Mo's story that Lex and Logan, the son of words and the son of Numbers, had determined to prove life's inherent screwiness using stories. This is Lex's story, these are his words.'

And I honestly think they are. They're not mine, not Myristica's. Maybe I spiced it with a pun or two, but when I replay that story, the voice I hear doesn't belong to anyone I know or knew. Can a story speak for itself, does it live like a person?

'A Stay of Execution'
As told by Lex
As retold by Myristica
As remembered by Mo

All fights deserved

Once upon a time, there lived a man called Nestor. Nestor resided in a country of very fair and reasonable people. He himself wasn't very fair or reasonable however, despite having a cushy job in a toy factory that made Russian dolls. He was a restless, angry, violent person, never satisfied with his lot, always wanting something different to what he had, always seeking but never knowing what he was looking for.

As if these faults were not serious enough, he was also a very jealous man. He treasured his wife dearly, but could not bear the thought of her ever leaving him, which she often threatened to do on account of his terrible behaviour.

He came to believe (quite wrongly) that his wife was in love with a neighbour. Seeing the two of them chatting happily together one day he leapt over the fence and began an argument. Soon, he and the neighbour were having a right old ding-dong. It ended when Nestor picked up a garden spade and whacked the other man over the head with it, killing him instantly, eventually.

Nestor was arrested, tried, and sentenced to death. He was taken to prison and locked in a cell on the infamous death throw, which is like death row, but everyone is a lot more agitated and keeps waving their arms around and hurling their food all over the place.

The prisoners all had a date set for their executions, and over the course of many months they were led out one by one and taken to their deaths. Oddly though, none of them knew how the executions were performed. A common belief was that the condemned were dropped into a water tank housing a many-tentacled sea creature that would shoot poisonous darts into their heads. According to the gossip, this sea beast was called the Firing Squid. But this was only rumour.

Eventually, the day came for Nestor's execution. What annoyed him most was the way in which the day arrived with no sense of occasion, just a day like any other. Even the weather refused to cooperate – he'd wanted tornadoes and thunder and lightning, but all he got was light drizzle with a sixty-five per cent chance of heavier showers moving in from the south by the afternoon.

The guards came to escort Nestor to his place of legal execution. He waved goodbye to his fellow prisoners and meekly allowed himself to be led through an iron door and down a long corridor. In front of the last door on the left stood the prison governor.

Nestor looked over the governor's shoulder. A sign on the door said: HANGING ROOM.

'So that's how it's done,' said Nestor, relieved that he'd found out at last, but annoyed that it was only at this very late moment.

The governor looked up from his papers and noticed what Nestor was reading.

'Sorry!' he said, and he moved a step to the side. As he did so, Nestor saw with a jolt that the sign actually read: CHANGING ROOM.

'Get him inside and get him changed!' commanded the governor. The guards pushed Nestor into the room and made him take off his prison uniform and put on a new suit, new shoes, a waterproof coat and, most puzzlingly of all, a life jacket. Nestor was now very confused. Was he to do battle with the Firing Squid after all? His fear was terrible.

The governor took Nestor by the hand and led him out through a second door. 'Don't worry!' he said, which struck Nestor as the silliest advice ever given.

'The thing is,' continued the governor, 'we don't actually have the death penalty at all. It's the most secret secret there is in our country – only a handful of people know the truth. The general population thinks that we do, but none of us in the prison service could bring ourselves to enforce it.

'Instead, you are to be deported to the Island of Disgrace where all condemned prisoners are sent. You will live out your life in that society as a free man. You may never return, nor send home any form of communication. Nor will anyone visit you – the island is held in total isolation. As far as everyone here is concerned you are dead, and nothing more will ever be heard of or from you.'

Nestor almost fainted with relief. A reprieve! A second chance for life! He wept with joy and willingly allowed himself to be strapped into an automated boat that set off at high speed across the long sea for many hours before depositing him on the shores of an island far from his homeland. The boat caught fire and sank as soon as he stepped from it, as it was programmed to do.

My journey is at an end, thought Nestor, *here I shall live out my days in tranquillity*.

But Nestor was wrong. He couldn't have been more wrong if he'd added two to three and come up with the answer 'discount carpet warehouse'. His terrible journey had barely begun.

To be continued . . .

I listened to One-for-Sorrow's jaw click as he mulled the story over. 'In'restin',' he announced. 'Wan ear-hear mo'. Garn!'

'No,' said Myristica. 'Not today. Another time.' And from that position she would not budge, not even when Nonstop and I were unstintingly dusted with punches and kicks.

'Ol rat, sobeet,' the Fractions grudgingly agreed once they understood Myristica could not be swayed. We were going to ration their stories just as they rationed our food. 'Slong as story not end: "Wen we wok up, found were all dreamy-dream." You end lak that, we shoot all oos. That *terrible* endin'.'

They moved on, the spectators dispersed. We'd made it through another day.

'Meg,' I croaked. 'You are as beautiful as fruit. Love how you recycled my own story.'

'Lame ducks rule, mate. You'd do the same for me.'

'You bet.'

The cost of our achievement was Lonza's support for me.

'You're a liability,' the panther purred in my ear, away from his sister. 'You leave my Meg out of this from now on, got that? Else I'll cut you.'

I understood. As always, Lonza wasn't being cruel, just realistic. From then on, at every failed Performance Review, I knew he would always select me for destruction.

The next time, it would be my turn to placate our fickle masters with a story; it was my skill at continuing the fiction that was worrying me, my lie-ability.

Chapter 32

How did we cope?

Lonza had said it best: life in the Facility was like life anywhere else. We lived by routine, that indispensable handhold on sanity. Anyone can endure any kind of existence. All that's required is that he or she can point to a timetable and say, 'This is when we rise, when we eat, this is the slot for wickedness, this is when we sleep.'

For us, every day began when we awoke from the florid aberrations of our nightmares, and immediately felt homesick for them.

To market, to market, for the three able-bodied people. Me, I'd attend to the rat traps in the morning, sweep the hanger in the afternoon.

Home again, home again. Performance Review, the cut.

Every day, the Fractions butchered people nominated by their fellow team members as being the least productive. Adults yielded their elderly parents; lovers fell over themselves to make the first sacrifice, or debated if that was not in fact the easier option; parents daily faced the hardest dilemmas: themselves, or a child, usually a child who would not in any case survive without them, or a judgement between children. All choices were made mechanically, dead-faced, there was less anguish expressed than you might imagine. Besides, after a few days in the Facility, people no longer suffered from emotions. They – we – became bone robots.

More refugees arrived daily to fill the vacancies, unaware of what awaited them. The Peacemakers looked away and taped foam rubber over the rims of their helmets, lest anyone nick a finger.

We got used to it. You do, you do. The drip-fed put-downs, the bricks through the window, the screams in the night, the men in the spinney: whatever it is, whatever ails you and nails you. You get used to it.

Or you go to the wall, fall at the fence, and then you're not around to say, 'How did we live? We got used to it.' Only others are, the ones who did.

Every day, snide Lupa grew a notch larger, Nonstop a touch slimmer, Harete a shade more withdrawn, Myristica a tad weaker.

Every night, Lonza and Harete slept a little closer to each other, Lupa a little further away. How did I know? Myristica told me, but only because I pestered her to report. The gossip served as a replacement for my chillies, a slug of pain taken willingly to rouse me.

Lupa did not object to the change in arrangements. She demanded isolation, could not bear to have anyone touch her. 'Not even the Peacemaker doctors; I don't let them examine me or nothing, rinsing bunch of foreign pre-verts,' as she put it herself. We didn't think it strange; in the crowded hanger, seclusion seemed an understandable indulgence to hanker after.

A quaint by-product of the kinematics of our nocturnal fidgeting was that Myristica's head somehow always ended up on my shoulder, no matter where she and I began the night. I welcomed it. To us hanger-rabble, kindness and companionship were like gold leaf: each minuscule speck that fell our way had to be hammered flatter than a plumber's whistling to spread it as wide as possible. A cheesy joke from Nonstop might make me smile for the rest of the day, a squeeze of my hand from Harete could last me a week.

Before we slept, the evening meal, our only one of the day.

We didn't eat the food the workers brought home, that was all handed to the Fractions to go into their warehouse. We ate much poorer fare distributed according to a team's performance: damaged tins, rusty tins, tins whose best-before dates would be of interest to archaeologists.

Lupa played Mother.

'Eeny, meeny, miny, mo,' she went. Eeny was Lonza, meeny was herself, miny was Myristica, mo was – this was Lupa talking, remember – Nonstop. She'd chuck Harete her tins without saying a word; I took whatever remained.

'Hope it's cheese,' Nonstop always said when he took his can, but it never was. 'Even macaroni cheese. I could murder some cheese.'

'Pah! I could murder a fatso in a skirt,' Lupa would reply.

Knowing I couldn't read the labels, and that I had little to contribute to our collective welfare, snickering Lupa always arranged for me to receive the worst tin in the pile; whereas the others usually landed corned beef or beans, peaches or

246

pilchards, I had to contend with dog meat, fermented fish fins, obscure foreign fruit that tasted like congealed sneezes.

I didn't complain. Yes, Lupa. No, Lupa.

One meal I remember well. I fingered the contents of my open can, risked a look. My eyes were recovering again, but the second bout of damage had been significant: the dead spots were still there, and bigger, and what wasn't black was milky and fuzzy, as if I were looking through frosted glass. All I could tell was that the things in the tin were thumb-sized, with shiny, graphite grey carapaces. Fishing bait? They looked like they were going to be crunchy, obscenely bitter and indescribably nasty.

I put one of dead wrigglers in my mouth.

It was crunchy, obscenely bitter and indescribably nasty. I had to hold my breath and chew it very quickly, willing back the rising chimney of puke that surged up. My chilli spray was long gone by then; a shame, it might have made the meal palatable. Patting through my pockets for the bottle, wondering if I could scratch out a little dried-up residue, I located my rodent poison. The bag held a number of cubes made up from dried meal and a toxic additive. Nonstop had examined the cubes and named the bum ingredient Arse Nick.

So easy to crumble one of the cubes into my tin, I thought, chewing on another leathery bug. I touched a cube to my tongue, savoured the saltiness. What an abso-scab-bloody-bing-lutely atrocious choice, a dinner of rubbery pupae or rodent poison; but then again, not so raw a choice as which child to surrender to the raucous rattle of the burp gun.

Why was my life like this, a journey through a series of nested shells, each more violent and deadly than the last? War, Spiral,

247

Camp, Facility . . . the Fartherland had too great a quotient of woe, more than could have arisen just by accident. Surely someone was responsible for all the suffering?

The centre of everything. The centre of power. It had to be him. The bait cube melted appetisingly in my mouth. *I could swallow it,* I thought, *end all the misery and mystery.*

{No! SPIT!}

My hand was bashed away from my mouth, my lump of poison went flying.

'Who's that?' I yelled. Not anyone from my team; I could hear them scarfing noisily from their own tins, oblivious to me. Someone clapped their hand on my shoulder; I shook it away, deploring the uninvited intimacy.

'Pilgrim!' hissed a boy. 'Do you follow the pylons?'

'What the scab are you on about?' I shouted. 'Who are you?'

Squinting, I saw three kids barely in their teens smiling at me. Smiling? What did they know? They looked gaunt, green: three limp sticks of asparagus.

'My name is Moth,' replied the nearest blur. 'My friends are Mo and Harete, and we are here to save you, pilgrim. Do you know the story of The Moth?'

With those words, the tinned grubs became only the second worst taste in my mouth. The Spiral had been overrun with spiders and ringworm, the Facility had its own creeping infestation: Mothodists.

Chapter 33

Hanger five was a hive of feverish, frenetic disputation. So was the entire Facility, but nowhere more so than hanger five. 'The seminary of the slaughterhouse', some workers called it.

Lonza knew, but his permanently pragmatic bent and lowering mien meant he'd paid it no heed, and stupid Lupa was too duff dense to take an interest in such abstract matters. Still, it was inevitable we would encounter them, for the Mothodists were everywhere, and wherever they were, they argued. Or preached. Or tried to rope you in on debates about what *they* called politics or theology and what I called 'what I did last autumn'.

Day and night you'd hear believers shout out, 'The Moth is returned!' Queue for an hour to drink at the hosepipe, one of the buffoons would be bound to buttonhole you. 'Pilgrim, follow the pylons! Freedom is within thy grasp!' they'd cry, and if you weren't careful you'd be biffed from your place and have to start queuing all over again. Try for half a minute's privacy in which to relieve yourself in the drain, you'd have barely lowered your trousers halfway to your ankles before some bearded creep strolled up behind you, slapped you heartily and roared, 'Glory, Pilgrim! Hast thou heard the news? The son of the judge lives, he who scaled the scaly serpent of the Final Fence, he for whom justice is just ice, to be dispensed with a cool hand to all who desire it!'

When the hanger filled up with the fagged-out survivors of that day's market, we'd overhear them feuding, voices and hackles raised. Often they sounded on the verge of fisticuffs, as if their dodgy dogma was more important than their physical survival. They argued about whether the characters in the story of Moth's escape from the Fartherland really had been chased by a giant pig, if the hedges and pylons and the great fence of razor wire were solid or symbolic, if the tractor that ran over Harete had been a physical, diesel-slurping puller of ploughs or was a parable for . . . but there were as many interpretations as there were ways to make a baby cry. Take your pick, and hit one of them with it.

Some held the story to be true in every word and detail, others maintained that it was only a series of instructive metaphors. (Nonstop explained to me what a metaphor was; I'd never met a metaphor before. Thanks to the Mothodists, I was one. It didn't feel right, and thinking about it gave me terrible trots; Harete had said I must be suffering from an allegory.)

Unadulterated bladder-splash, every word of it. Yes, there had been a super-sized sow, and a fence of razors waiting for us at the border. A bloody big tractor with bloody big wheels did drive over the top of Harete. Moth and I had thought that she'd died, an honest mistake . . . but there had been no magic, no miracles. None of it had meant anything.

Somehow, the tale of our escape from the Institute had evolved legs, broken free and transformed into a rollicking, frolicking monster.

Harete found it all as unsettling as I did. Our names raised no suspicions. Lob a rusty tin of tuna in any direction, chances are it would bounce off the bonce of someone who shared our now commonplace tags. There were multiple Mos, hordes of Haretes, myriads of Moths; a significant portion of the cultists had restyled themselves after their heroes. Lonza had assumed we were followers of fashion, rather than the genuine articles.

Harete and I shrunk from contact with the Mothodists. We knew the events of the story they were talking about. We'd walked them, lived through them, experienced them in the ice-pinched, helicopter-hounded flesh; only too vividly did we remember our seven days of dog and bog and hedge and sludge.

'How, Harete? How did this all start?' I asked her one night, as we overheard sundry Mothodists bicker over how many angles danced within a pylon, whether The Moth ever carried money, how many substances and natures he possessed.

'Beats me,' she replied. 'The only people I told in detail about our escape were the police in the Other country. I didn't even get my photo in the papers. No one there made a fuss, Moth and I weren't celebrities. They were more het up about giving us tetanus jabs and placing us in schools. They say The Moth is good, Mo. Let's be content with that, our friend is well spoken of.'

Her answer did not placate me. 'No one could know so much about those incidents on our journey, except for him, me and you,' I reminded her. 'He must be the one who's wagging the tale, with himself in the starring role. Of course he's putting it about that he's good. Did you ever hear of a despot who had it circulated that he was a slime-clad maniac? He's using these people, Harete.'

'Or they're using him,' she said. 'Or someone else is using them *and* him.'

'Pshaw! Think: kids who spend their weekends playing five-a-side want to become soccer stars. Those that tinker with motorbikes dream of speedway. Moth loved reading about legends and myths, gods and conquerors. Stands to reason he'd want to become one.'

'So what did you used to dream about?' Harete's question annoyed me, it was irrelevant.

'Escaping,' I answered, thinking about me and Dad and the dingy high-rise tower block we'd once called home.

'That figures,' she sighed. I could almost hear her eyes roll.

What followed was too hurtful to relate, one of those dreadful treadmill arguments, exertion without progress, where you begin by defending views you don't even hold and end up running around in circles.

My memory prefers to squeeze the words together like garbage in a trash compactor.

What's your beef? *You know. Your One Big Idea, escaping. It's just another word for running away.* You calling me chicken? *No. I want to stop the evil forever, close this death depot down, end it for everyone.* No chance! Another of your impossible dreams, like your game of Hunt The Moth. *Better to spend your life running towards someone than to be always running away from something.* Gee, guess you can hang up your running shoes

252

now you've found your someone. *Do what?* He's a ham if you ask me, that Lonza. *What's he got to do with . . . what are you saying?* Does it need saying? And right in front of his pregnant girlfriend too. I never had you pegged as the trashy type. *How dare you say that!* Oh, be honest with yourself, Harete. You think we don't know? *Mind your own business! Anyway. Maybe I do feel for Lonza. I don't have to justify myself. You know why I like him?* Ooh, I dunno, Harete. Would it be those indigo eyes, that deep voice, the way he brings home the bacon? *No, because he cares! The way he cares for Myristica, the baby, even Lupa. When we go to market, he throws food to weaker teams, helps them survive the cut. He doesn't know I see, but I do.* Well, I've felt his hand above my shoulder, lost half an ear to him. You'll forgive me if I don't swoon. *But he has no choice. How many other teams support a blind person? He cares for you more than you'll ever know.* Yeah, yeah. Probably only says that to suck up to you. *In a funny way, Mo, he reminds me a lot of you. Not so self-centred, of course, but then who is?* Self-centred? *You heard me. Self. Centred.*

My rhythm disrupted, the treadmill slowed. The spiteful slanging didn't bother me; wounding words were like ulcers in the mouth, they felt vast to the touch at the time, but, examined later, I knew they'd be exposed as inconsequential pimples. *He reminds me of you.* Harete was in love with someone who reminded her of me. But not in love with me. By the scabs on the scabs on Satan's rump, how did that work?

I had to ask. 'Why did you bother to rescue me, Harete? Why did you give up that wonderful, ordinary life in the Other country, that life of homework and toast and telly and beautiful, beautiful boredom, and fight your way to the Spiral to free me, self-centred, cowardly me?'

Harete gulped as she dismounted the wheel. 'I traced the ring.'

'I know.'

'Moth's ring.'

'I know. The one he gave to me on our final day together, at the border with the Other Country. "You keep it," he said, "it's tainted for me." Remember?'

'But I don't remember. Not that part,' she mumbled, the words slinking out of her mouth like bishops from a brothel.

'*Oh.*'

Oh.

Harete had not known the ring had been in my possession. *All along, it was The Moth she had been tracking down, it was for him she'd renounced her hard-won life of liberty.* She had sought The Moth and found me. That was well bent; twisted.

When, about six thousand years later, I got around to breathing again, my loss was partnered by lucidity. Much of what had passed between us since our first encounter made some sense now.

'Sorry, Mo. For everything,' she said. 'All we can do is make the best we can of every day. Seek any happiness.'

The soft-soap platitude grated, I was sure those were Lonza's words she was flannelling me with.

Harete had more sympathy with the believers than I could muster. 'Can't you understand the appeal of Moth's story?' she asked me, minutes later. 'People have lost everything: their homes, their families, their country. The old Fartherland was nothing but a circle of lies and fear, a voodoo loop. Once Moth crossed that border –'

'Yeah, yeah, and his father, the judge, blah, blah, scabbing blah.'

'No,' Harete said, braking me mid-flow. 'I've changed my mind. I think, when people learned that three crummy kids in rags had outsmarted the Marshalls and the border guards and escaped, they realised the country was no more substantial than a meringue case. The Fartherland dematerialised as instantly as belief in the tooth fairy, taking all its myths with it. A new story was sucked into the vacuum: our story, Moth's story.'

'But there isn't one story any more. There are hundreds of variations.'

'So there should be. A good story is like a life: it grows and feeds from others, it spawns. The story of Moth's escape and return is all anyone owns any more. Cities burn, people burn, books burn. Stories don't burn, they endure. Don't begrudge these poor people the only thing they own, the only thing that ties them to each other. A story of freedom and hope.'

I couldn't argue with that. Really – I didn't understand it.

'You've done all right out of the damn thing anyway,' I grumbled. 'Second billing. I'm a . . . a footnote. A footsore footnote in the fable of my own life. There's hardly a mention of me at all.'

That was true. No version of the piecemeal story we heard contained more than sparse references to myself. 'And Mo came along too,' ran the ending of a typical recital. Or, 'Mo fell asleep under a pylon.'

All that was from the previous few days. Chewing my way

through my tin of bugs-in-brine, I was faced with the latest trio of devotees angling to reel in a new recruit, a mock Moth, a fake Harete and, most contemptible of all, a phony Mo. To judge from their phlegmy coughs and the way they jiggered about as they spoke, they were already seriously sickened with barn dance. I stretched my trackie top over my nose to guard me from their germs.

Sham Harete tried first to inspire me. 'Isn't The Moth simply wonderful?' the dippy girl gushed in my aching face. 'I know he will save us all, he will surmount all obstacles set before him, just as he overcame the hedges during his long journey to freedom!'

I was tempted to tell her about The Moth I knew – the shy, owlish dunker of digestive biscuits into condensed milk, the soppy, jug-eared tucker of shirt into pants, the sports-abhorring knowledge-box I'd roomed with – but I thought better of it. The more I was forced to re-remember The Moth, the less he resembled not only the Mothodists' alleged super-being but my own reassessment of him as the adolescent autocrat skulking at the centre of the vortex. Neither model sang true.

'If he's so whoop-de-doop powerful, why are we all stuck in the Facility then, working until we're booted outside to be shot?' I challenged her. 'Why are entire families being murdered, every day?'

She could only simper at me. Hearing the young idiots talk like that broke me up badly. I felt sorry for the doomed kids and at the same time incredibly angry with them.

'Listen to the real Mo, you cranks. Learn from him: escape, flee while you've still the strength!' I implored them. 'Grab a gun, bribe a Peacemaker, short out the electric fence, dig a tunnel, do whatever you can, and do it *soon*!' I cried, flashing tears, but they laughed at me and said story Mo was the joker, the jester, the patsy, the fall guy, the quipster, the quitter, the left-behind, his character had nothing to teach anyone.

They broke away, still tittering.

'Scabbing lunatics! Save yourselves!' I shouted, but they were gone.

What really rankled me, what really got on my goat and up my nose and twanged my wick like a washtub bass was this: when we'd fled across country that winter, it was me who devised the way to cross the hedges, not Moth; *me*.

Chapter 34

The Mothodists had their story, we had ours. The evening after my visit from the three missionaries our team failed another Performance Review. One of us was going to be for the chop. Guess who?

Not Nonstop's fault – fresher teams from the other hangers had proved irresistible. They'd taken the pick of the helicopters' loads and left everyone else battling for the dregs: split bags of flour and beans, bales of manky blankets. Lonza had been rolled, battered with a blackjack (a sock full of batteries), had lost all his precious knives – one stuck in an assailant's thigh, one dropped and one bartered, traded to prevent Harete from being . . . but they were vague on the details: the knife had been accepted, she was unharmed. Lonza was gashed and bloodied, no longer stalking like an onyx lynx but limping like a ragged alley cat barely escaped from a detour into the dogs' home.

The Fractions in charge of our hanger were sore-headed too.

'Too many pips in 'anger is 'avin it sicky wi' barn dance,' muttered stout Two-for-Joy. He sliced through the twine around a cube of blankets in our team's pile. They were for children; perhaps they'd even been donated by children. Swivelling my head to peer through a clear spot, I discerned multicoloured dinosaurs and chubby-faced steam engines smiling back at the irritable Fraction. The silly, happy things pained me greatly, their uncorrupted gaiety as jarring as party balloons at a funeral. The contrast between the blankets' old and new homes was mortifyingly stark; not far from where we stood right then, a child young enough to enjoy those blankets was being given over by his family. Their team bedded near ours – the boy was deathly sick, limbs like cocktail sticks, his cough had been driving me bonkers for the last three nights.

His mother was saying her goodbyes; I heard the Fraction attending their team impatiently slapping the floor with a sandal as she did so. *'Settle now, you'll be seeing Daddy soon, Mummy will join you when she's ready, yes, yes, you go on ahead, I have to stay behind and look after your brothers, you're so terribly weak with that cough now . . . think of The Moth, the boy in that story you like, he'll be there to guide you . . . you're going over the fence to a better life.'*

Radio voices. That was my trick, to pretend it was all just the soundtrack of a radio play blaring from a receiver. Tune it out, turn it down, switch it over, exercise that secret muscle inside you that you tighten up when you turn away from the bad stuff.

Lupa sighed. 'Boring!' she said. Harete keened uncontrollably; sullen Lonza pulled Myristica towards him and crossed his arms over her. Sadness redlines at quite a low level, I'd discovered. If you're X sad when your budgie dies, you're only 1.6X sad when your granddad dies, and when they line your entire family up and shoot them one by one, it's hard to manage more than

2X sad. Strange. Also, I might be wrong, but I don't think any of us entertained fantasies of revenge; we weren't tensed and clenched and needing to be restrained, we saw and heard the same and similar every day. You really can get used to anything, anything at all, your mind and body will not permit you to be constantly revolted or scared. Ask the sewer-man, the mortician, the bomb disposal expert.

Besides, we had ourselves and each other to worry about. That's how it worked.

That's how they always make it work.

Them, not us.

You, not me.

Tomorrow, not today.

You'll see. You'll learn. Whoever you are, wherever you are, whenever you are, I tell thee: *you're so scabbing near someone who's lived through something like this, seen it all first hand.* A short plane ride, a bus journey.

Believe me.

Two-for-Joy finished picking through the blankets and the rest of our team's contribution. He was a dwarfish, portly man, criss-crossed with ammunition and tinsel, halfway between a harlequin and a Christmas tree: primeval, prime evil.

'Is oll shizzy rabbish!' he screamed, and he tore up the blankets in a fit of temper, reducing them to felt strips. Two-for-Joy turned on me.

'Oo! Mus mek gar, gar fan story. A well, well unhapp now. Story no gut, def gonna slot oo. Unerstan'?'

I understood. I was still dizzy from the shock of the blankets, they had perturbed me more than the condemned child.

Too easy, with the Fractions, too easy to write them off as paramilitary ragamuffins, too easy to misdirect the malice we felt for our suffering onto the other teams, or each other. That was their trap. The Fractions meant business.

I carried on with our story, hitching another wagon to the train, adding another day to my life. Never spared another thought to the little kid.

'A Stay of Execution, Part II'
As told by Lex
As retold by Mo

All wrongs re-served

On the Island of Disgrace, Nestor carried on with his life much as he had lived it back home, working in a factory that made collapsible tube telescopes. The island was somewhat smaller and a little bit more backward than the land he had come from, but not enough to make life disagreeable.

You might think that it would be a horrible place to live, since the entire population was made up of convicted killers. The fact was, in most cases, years spent on death throw followed by the shock of the last-minute reprieve had transformed the inhabitants into placid people who valued life.

In most cases. But not in Nestor's. After some years on the island, he got into a fight over an unpaid bill and pushed a man off a cliff. Nestor found himself in court, then prison, then in a cell on double death throw. You cannot imagine the magnitude of Nestor's bleakness and despair, for this was a man who had killed twice and who had thrown away the most precious thing there is, a second chance at life.

Once more, Nestor had to await his day of execution. Once more, he had to endure speculation as to the method that would be used to end his life.

His last day came. Another walk along a corridor, another governor standing in front of another door, thumbing through his paperwork. Nestor was most despondent to see that the sign on the door read ELECTRIC CHAIR and that this time the governor was not partially obscuring it.

'Tsk! Silly mistake!' said the governor, following the direction of Nestor's gaze. Bending down, he picked something up from the floor and applied it to the sign, sliding the letters along to make room for the one that had dropped off. The sign then ran: ELECT RICK, CHAIR.

'That's Rick Shaw – he's standing for election as chairman of the prison transport committee,' the governor explained. 'Can't say I approve of the location of his campaign posters though!'

Nestor's mind was turning somersaults. It was numb with terror and illuminated only by a minuscule glint of hope whose existence he dared not admit to.

He need not have worried. The governor handed

him a life jacket and led him to a jetty where one of the robot boats was moored. 'We couldn't implement the death sentence. As a nation formed of people who had escaped the hangman once, who were we to employ executioners? It's a one-way trip to the Island of Double Disgrace for you, my lad!'

Well, you can imagine how things worked out after that. A new life on a new (and slightly smaller, slightly more primitive) island, a few happy years to settle in, a job peeling onions, a regrettable incident with a pushy beggar and a chainsaw, and Nestor was in a cell on triple death throw. By now, he was fairly relaxed about things. When at last he was led to the governor, it was with no dismay or horror at all that he greeted a sign on the door saying BEHEADING CHAMBER.

Nestor didn't even wait for the governor to correct the mistake. He leaned forwards, blew away the dust that concealed the rest of the words and adjusted the spacing himself. MAYBE HEADING TO LUNCH, AMBER.

'A note from my wife,' mumbled the governor, patently embarrassed by such flagrant abuse of an official noticeboard.

Nestor grabbed the life jacket from where it lay on the floor, crashed through the doors and hurled himself into the automatic boat that would carry him to the Island of Triple Disgrace. Only by now, he really had had enough. He tore apart the boat's control console and set about disabling the machinery that lay hidden beneath it. More by luck than judgement he managed to gain some sort of control over the craft. 'Let's see where this farce ends. Let's find what lies at the middle of this fakery!' he said, and he sent the boat surging ahead.

For more than a week he haphazardly roamed the seas, passing by the islands of Triple and Quadruple and even Pentuple Disgrace, the latter no more than a sea stack, a tall column of rock jutting up above the ocean on top of which sat one man clothed in a loincloth. 'I'm innocent!' the man cried, as Nestor's boat roared by. 'I'm innocent, finally!'

Intrigued, Nestor turned back.

'Hey, you!' said Nestor. 'Give me your name!'

The old man looked deeply offended. 'Give you my name?' he said. 'Then you would be called Simeon, and what should I be called?'

Nestor moored the boat at the base of the sea stack and engaged Simeon in conversation, bellowing over the noise of the wheeling seabirds.

'Can you tell me where we are?' Nestor shouted.

'We are directly above the centre of the Earth,' came the reply.

'That's information's useless!' protested Nestor.

'Not a bit of it. It is never wrong. There is little that has that to commend it.'

'It looks very narrow up there,' commented Nestor next, marvelling at the needle-like rock pillar. 'Make sure you don't overbalance.'

'Overbalance? You think my life is in danger

if I have too much balance?' Simeon called down, standing on tiptoes on the very edge of the sheer drop. 'I should think you would want to warn me not to underbalance.'

Nestor had no desire to split hairs on that topic. He shouted up from the boat, 'Are you the end? Is this as far as it goes?'

'No!' replied Simeon. 'And if you want my advice, you'll never go looking for such a place. Climb up and I will tell you why.'

Nestor made the hazardous climb to the summit of the rocky pillar and squeezed into the driftwood shack that was Simeon's home.

'It's vital you listen to my story,' Simeon warned him, 'literally a matter of life and death. And when I say "literally", I mean literally literally, not just common or garden figuratively literally. Do not allow your wits to be diverted. It is so easy in this life to be led by the nose, made to ride white elephants and fish for red herrings, go for walks with shaggy dogs, become sidetracked, waylaid.'

Nestor knew the message must be one of great importance. I'd better pay very close attention, he thought. But then his eye was caught by something stirring under a blanket on the tiny bed in the corner of the room . . .

To be continued . . .

I waited. The uncertainty was murderous. I felt as if every part of my body and its surroundings had been sprinkled with explosive dust, that a detaching eyelash could detonate the world.

Two-for-Joy and his thuggish subordinates whistled and clicked, perhaps comparing notes.

'Sgoodnuff, fo' now,' he reported. 'S'pose.'

I breathed again, my heart restarted, my strangled tripe unknotted. Survival tasted of ammonia and pencil shavings.

'Oo live. But warn oo, pay-shuns thin. Not lak string-along. Next tam, wan' better. Wan more. This team too big an'way, too many slackies.' Two-for-Joy loaned me a punch that almost snapped my breastbone, then his deputies gathered up the day's substandard takings and moved on to the next team.

Lonza came over to me. Was it time for a gold star, a pat on the back?

'We're up crap creek now,' he said, 'and you've paddled us there.'

'Eh?'

'If the stories are no good, he'll kill you. If they are good, he'll want more and more. We'd easy brought back enough today, those blankets were fine, he deliberately made us fail so he could listen to more story.'

I hadn't thought of that. Like feeding chocolate drops to a dog, it was something that was likely to prove hard to stop now that we'd started. What we'd intended to be only occasional stopgaps to help us avoid the cut on thin days now looked to be demanded of us every day.

The Kernel had gone quiet on me. I felt withered and wearied; my capacity for invention was nil, my mind as hollow as my stomach. Staying alive was all down to me, and I wasn't sure how much longer I could keep going.

Chapter 35

I cracked it. Five days, that's how long I needed to decipher Whistle-Click. Not bad, though I say so myself.

All I'd really needed to do was *listen*, properly listen, during my morning duties, baiting and resetting the rodent traps in the Fractions' private zone. Funny how widespread is the belief that we hear with our eyes, because I'd noticed with other people too, not just Fractions, that once they accept you're blind, they assume you're deaf as well. More: if, in their opinion, you're only a disposable machine made of meat, somewhere between an electric whisk and a pit pony in terms of labour-saving usefulness, they have scabsolutely no cares for what they say or do in front of you. No one blushes if they finger their backside and sniff their armpits in front of a lathe or if the lawnmower spies them undressing.

Already blind, I had become invisible.

Listen. The whistling part of Whistle-Click . . . three tones, either rising or falling, but the highest tone only ever rising. That made five altogether.

The clicking part . . . either a single or rapid double-click. One kind was made with the tongue against the roof of the mouth and the mouth closed, another by flicking the tongue towards the teeth, mouth open. (Those were the sounds that showered you with baccy-sodden spittle if you were standing too close.) The last, rarer kind was a wet pop made entirely with the lips. That made another five, except that clicks and double-clicks came paired – any click or a pop followed by any other click (but never a pop). So really, there were twenty combinations.

Guess. Whistle-Click wasn't a language, it was a simple spelling code, hardly different from the cell phone! Whistles for vowels and the click patterns as coordinates on a grid of consonants.

Test. Make one of the Fractions whistle-click something, trick them into using a particular word.

Myristica helped. Every few minutes she'd shout out a word from a list I'd suggested. 'Cat!' she shouted the first time, her voice plainly audible over the high wall of boxes. I strained my ears, trying to commit the surprised Fraction's reaction to memory. My theory was, if a stranger ran up to you in a park and shouted 'Penguin!' that seven times out of ten the first thing you'd say back would be 'Penguin?' I had to discount the idea you'd say 'Where?' or 'Three, ta,' or 'Up ya notch!'

Interesting . . . clicks but no whistles.

'Coat!' was her second word. Ten minutes later, 'Cut!' No whistles, no change at all to the pattern of clicks.

Refine. The clicks were consonants, but the whistles weren't vowels. When they spoke in code, thy spk lk ths, mnt thy cld tlk mch fstr. Myristica wondered if they used facial tics or hand gestures to express a vowel if the meaning wasn't clear without it.

So the whistles were . . .

'Cat! Cat!'

A whistle, clicks. Of course! *The whistles were numbers.*

The puzzle unravelled over successive mornings. Myristica said she felt like a crazy-cake, shouting out 'Zebra!' and 'Bat!' and 'Mink!' and so on, but I needed to chart the grid of consonants; they were cleverer than we'd been on the Spiral, they'd devised a time-saving measure we'd never thought of, putting common letters in lower grid positions. One click-one click mapped not to B (no vowels, remember) but T. Letters like N and R and S enjoyed a similar status. I never sussed the number system completely, but near enough.

They say learning another language broadens your mind, but then again, so does sleeping with your head under a steam hammer. My sneak peek into the private thoughts of the Fractions proved not as advantageous as I'd hoped for: less a case of throwing open a window into another culture, more one of uncovering the keyhole into a lavatory.

With one exception. The Fractions were seriously narked about the latest outbreak of barn dance, and the effect it was having on productivity. Not to worry – a solution lay close to hand. If things did not improve within a few days, I learned, they planned to steal one of the Peacemakers' tanks, park it outside, run a hosepipe from the exhausts under the barn door and rev the engine.

Push in choke, advised Three-Bags-Full, *make smoke thicker*.

Fumigate the entire barn.

With everyone in it.

Gas us all, and start afresh with a new crop of disease-free refugees.

I needed to warn the others, the people in my team, everyone in the hanger. There was no reason not to stage a massed attack on the Fractions – riot, rebel, rush the gates, however substantial the losses. The idea was terrifying. Exhilarating.

Wincing and cringing I scoured the crowd of workers returning from market, hoping to spot my mates. We'd all been rubbing along a lot better of late; Lupa had reigned in her attacks on Nonstop, while Lonza had mellowed towards me, acclaimed my partial mastery of Whistle-Click.

I found Nonstop with the bin, but he didn't know what had become of Harete and Lonza. I waited a while longer. And longer.

And longer.

They never turned up. I groped my way out the back of the hanger. Not there. Performance Review was ten minutes away, where could they be? Had they rubbed a Fraction up the wrong way and been shot? It happened; most days I learned of good scavengers being topped on the spot by testy or bored Fractions, discarded like toothpicks.

At my side stood a roped-off quad stacked with quaggy trash sacks waiting to be burned; sometimes people farmed them for cockroaches to eat. Seriously worried, I waded to an open space I knew lay in the middle of it, following liquid sounds. I thought to anticipate all possible outcomes, lick the twist. Who might be there?

Harete.

Or Lonza.

Or neither.

Or both.

No other option remained.

Wrong. False. Untrue. The twist twisted me.

Harete and Lonza, yes, but two into one. Kissing, and not with the sort of childish lip-biff I'd once printed upon Harete. They were squeezed together so tightly you couldn't have shimmed them apart with a crowbar.

I spied, hidden behind lumpy, sun-roasted bin bags, a symphony of stinks. My friends undocked after five minutes. The confirmation busted me up sick, gouged potholes in my soul. *Make the best of every day . . . seek any happiness . . .* Harete's bromides tasted no better reheated. I slunk away, vibrating with hatred for myself and the world.

Of the plan to fumigate the hanger I said nothing to anyone, fearing more than ever how far people who had nothing left to lose might go.

Chapter 36

Lonza had guessed right.

Two-for-Joy, that short-arse, bug-ugly, half-formed toad, was a storyholic.

The following Performance Review, Two-for-Joy and his henchies swanked directly to where our team waited outside the hanger, bullet belts clinking, sandals slip-slapping. The wheelie bin had been brought back crammed full with rock-hard bags of rice, water sterilising kits, packets of dried soups.

'No way can he fail us, Mo,' whispered Nonstop. 'Market was mayhem, but we did well, even I did well. Didn't I, Harete? Nonstop did well today, no mistakes, no slip-ups. Good boy Nonstop, oh yes.'

Two-for-Joy made no pretence about his demands. If the day's haul was insufficient, he didn't actually say. He gobbed out a wad of chewed leaves, gripped me by my throat and pulled me into a headlock.

'Story,' he said. 'Noo rools. No gut, we slot oo an' we slot sicky girl 'swell. Two fo' one. Slot one, slot one free. Bargain. Oo lak noo rools?'

'Yes,' I creaked. His thumbs were as strong as spanners and

pressed so deeply into my windpipe it was hard to talk. 'Very fair,' I added, fearing I would black out before I'd begun to deliver my story. I'd been rehearsing all that day; I knew exactly what I was going to say. I took a deep breath.

'Nestor walked over to the cot in the –'

'Ay, no' oo!' interrupted Two-for-Joy, ramping up the pressure on my throat. 'We 'ear nuff fro' oo. We wan' fatta man tell necks part story.'

'Ay. Fatta man! Fatta man!' shouted Ten-Green-Bottles and Fish-Alive. 'Skirty fella mus be cannable tell gar gut story, 'im maxo maxo fun-sized.'

'Me?' spluttered Nonstop. 'But . . . but . . . I'm no good at public speaking, I'm the shy, silent type. Tell him, Mo, I hardly talk at all, do I? I'm practically mute, I can't tell stories, oh, please, please don't make me do this.'

Still restraining me in the headlock, Two-for-Joy drew out a bayonet. 'Story fro' fatta man. Or we see wot bland boy ackshlly made of.' The bayonet was stabbed into my navel; he was preparing to screw it downwards and dig out my bowels. 'We ol lak findin' out wot fings made fro'. Big in'erest.'

I flapped a hand at Nonstop, wanting him at any cost to persuade Two-for-Joy to let me tell the story, but only squeaks and gurgles could escape my throttled neck.

'What things are made of?' wittered Nonstop, spinning around in a thumb-biting tizzy. He repeated the phrase several more times, playing for time. I despaired; Nonstop was a blabbermouth and a bore, not a storyteller.

'Story mus' be bes' evah. Las' one war dullsy. Bes evah o' we insidy-outsidy bland boy.'

The bayonet dug in deeper. I ceased breathing. Temperature, time, emotion – everything stopped for me. This was to be my end, and the last sounds I'd hear would be Nonstop's infernal squeals.

'What things are made of . . . yes . . . all right . . . let me see now. Yes, yes, I think I have it. I do, I do, I have it!'

And to all our amazements, he did. Big time.

'A Stay of Execution, Part III'
As told by Lex
As retold by Nonstop
As remembered by Mo

All right(whale)s preserved

'Wait a minute,' Nestor said to Simeon. 'We're not alone.'

Stepping over to the cot in the corner of the tiny shack, Nestor tore back the blanket. There was indeed someone there: an old man with a ketchup-red face and a beard that looked and smelled as if he had knitted it from hairs pulled out of the plug holes in public washrooms.

'Who is this?' roared Nestor. 'A spy?'

'Don't listen to him!' said Simeon. 'It is me you need to pay heed to. My curse it is that I must share this island pillar with him. He is a trickster, a time waster – his lies are as obvious as a mandrill's violet rump.'

The frightened old man in the bed cowered away from Nestor. 'Do not hurt me, young man! I'll tell you anything you desire.'

'Who are you, and what could you know that might interest me, old man?' demanded Nestor.

The bearded man beckoned for Nestor to stoop closer. 'Have you ever wondered what things are made of? Really made of? What is the nittiest grit that makes up all the bigger nitty-gritty?'

Nestor frowned. 'No, I cannot say I've ever had reason to worry about that. But now that you mention it, I suppose it is an interesting question.'

'Aha! Then pull up a stool. Mine is a story that may intrigue,' said the old man. 'My name is Higgs, and before my exile to this devil-forsaken needle, I was a sailor, a bosun. It was my luck to learn a secret from the final words of a shipwrecked scientist I rescued. The scientist had been sailing in his dinghy, Jonah. One stormy night, the Jonah crashed into the prows of a sinking ship, and the scientist was thrown overboard and swallowed alive by a whale.'

'What sort of a whale?'

'A right whale. There are very few left.'

'Go on.'

'The whale was in turn swallowed into the hull of a whaling vessel named *Sistership*.'

'Boo!' interjected Simeon, who, despite himself, was listening avidly to Bosun Higgs's story.

'Fortunately, that ship was swallowed by an anti-whaling-ship ship, *TSINATS*, which stood for "This Ship Is Named After This Ship".'

'Hurrah!' cried Nestor and Simeon.

'Which was dragged into the maws of an even greater freighter, the anti-anti-whaling-ship-ship ship, *Brotherhood*. Now, *Brotherhood* was the sister ship of *Sistership*, and of other ships called *Sister's Hip*, and *Hip Sisters*, but since they don't appear in this story, we won't mention them.'

'Double boo! And good.'

'*Brotherhood* was gobbled bodily into the capacious hold of another craft belonging to the whale-savers, *TADSFI*, that name meaning "This Acronym Doesn't Stand for Itself".'

'Problematic,' agreed Simeon and Nestor.

'And still more: the whale-haters largest boat, *This Ship Contains All Other Ships That Contain a Ship*, ate up that ship. Regrettably, the captain of this final ship hated the name of his vessel to be inaccurate, and, having now eaten all other ship-eating ships, he determined to force that leviathan of an ark to engulf itself. This enterprise ended badly: the ship sank. It was on the remains of that hulk that little Jonah first came a cropper.'

Nestor raised a finger to pause the story. 'Something is amiss. The first vessel, the row boat, crashed on the wreckage of the last ship. But the last ship did not founder until after it had ingested all the smaller ones. Isn't this something of a . . . what's the word I seek? A paradox?'

Higgs dismissed Nestor. 'There was not even one dog present, let alone a pair of them.'

'A coincidence, then?'

'If it is a coincidence, it's only a coincidence that it's a coincidence,' replied the Bosun. 'Now, listen!'

'The scientist had but a few minutes of life remaining to him when I dragged him from the whale's guts; his lungs were awash with salt water and his mouth was filled with bladderwrack. There was far too short a time to teach me all the hyper-complicated mathematics needed to comprehend his field of study. In desperation, he expressed all his life's findings as a story. This is his story.'

Two-for-Joy didn't ease up on the bayonet, he ground it inwards even harder. My belly button popped out like a toadstool and a lacework of blood leaked down my flank. If either of us had coughed, I'd have been disembowelled.

'Dipper! Oo mus' go dipper an' farer in story, mus' go ol' way to cen're!'

Ten-Green-Bottles menaced Myristica with a machete. 'Ay, wat inside? Wat heart taste lak?' she bayed, showering us with strands of mucus and saliva.

Nonstop swilled in air and dabbed his streaming brow. He sounded completely worn out. Did he have it in him to continue with his concoction?

He straightened out his skirt and carried on.

'What Am I Made of?'

As told by Bosun Higgs (who learned it from a scientist) to Nestor

As retold by Lex

As re-retold by Nonstop

As remembered by Mo

A goatherd from Gothenburg (with a mother from Gotland and a father from Scotland) was busy making cheese in his dairy when a thought sprinted athwart his mind's eye with the speed of fox fleeing across a motorway. Swerving at first to avoid the thought, the goatherd found himself drawn towards it, running over it, absorbing it.

'What am I made of?' he asked himself. The question struck him as the most important ever asked.

He repeated the question to his best friend, Primrose Twinkle-Pansy, who lived in the little white cottage down the lane with the thatched roof and the roses round the door. Primrose pondered long and hard. Finally, he yawned and scratched his stubbly chin. He'd not long come off night shift at the steel mill, and was dog-tired.

'Since you eat nothing but cheese, and drink nothing but milk, and since cheese is made from milk, you are made of milk,' he gruffly ventured. 'Now bog off.'

'Wait,' insisted the goatherd. 'What is milk made from?'

Primrose groaned. 'Think it through. Milk comes from goats, your goats eat only grass, so milk is made of grass. And water.' Then he slammed the shutters and retired to bed.

The goatherd did think it through, but the answers in no way satisfied the cavernous want that had opened in his being. 'I must go deeper and deeper, get to the heart of this matter,' he said to himself, 'I must gorge until my obsession is satisfied, until I know for certain what I am made of.' Walking along the lane he bumped into a Kurd whom he knew to be expensively schooled in many subjects.

'Halloo, you!' he hailed him.

'Halloo, me,' replied the Kurd. 'Does something whey upon your mind?'

'Please. What is grass made of?'

The Kurd smiled. 'Chemicals,' he replied. 'With long, horrible names, like carbon dye-oxhide, sulphur so-good, sulphur what-the-hecksaflouride, methane, youthane, polly-put-the-kettle-on-3,4-knock-at-the-door, things of that ilk.'

'And these chemicals? From what are they composed?'

'Elements, from the periodic table of the elements.'

'Can you name some?'

'Can I? Certainly. The full table runs as follows: hydrogen, helium, shelium, moron, alluvium, geranium, irony, gymnasium, hafnium, haf-notium, nasturtium, odium, opprobrium, sanatorium, and pandemonium.'

279

'Why do so many have names that end in "ium"?'

'I . . . um . . . don't know. Go away – my patience is exhausted. If you wish to know more, you must ask the sage, Derby. He is one of the Big Cheeses around here.'

The goatherd felt dissatisfied. He waved goodbye to the Kurd, but it was a pretty poor salute. He journeyed farther afield, seeking the recommended soothsayer. They met at a village feta, where the wise man was playing the traditional games of Pin the Tail on the Donkey and Mask a Pony.

'Eh? What's that you ask? What are the elements made of?' grunted the sage. 'They are made of atoms, every man-jack of 'em.'

The goatherd had the feeling he was being continually fobbed off. 'And the atoms? Is this the end? The name implies so – a-tom means un-bloomin'-splittable, like auto-tomic means self-splitting, as of a salamander that severs its own tail if nabbed by it.'

'Alas, the a-toms were named in haste. They are themselves made of smaller particles, building blocks as it were.'

'Such as?'

'Oh, let me think now. Protons. Croutons. Elections. Stiltons, I think.'

The goatherd sighed long and low and let a cool Bries play over his hot head. 'Take that proton you mentioned, for example. Have you finally got to the point?'

'Nope. Some of these subatomic fleas have smaller fleas upon their backs. Smash apart a proton – another proton will do the job just peachy – and you'll find a soup of things called glutens, if memory serves me right. And quarks.'

The goatherd almost had a thrombosis. 'Quark!' he roared. 'That is a German cheese. Are you really a sage, or some Käse Kaiser? I should royally thrash you!'

'Stop! Do not hit me, young man. You are on a fool's errand. You should never have given up your employment in the dairy to become this itinerant seeker after ultimate composition. Did you not know, the devil makes work for idle hands? If you want to proceed, take your enquiries to the only one who can assist you – the gorgon, Zola. And tread Caerphilly.'

An arduous adventure ensued, involving prodigious amounts of seeking and searching. The trail led to a wild and windy country, and to remote hills therein.

The goatherd was set upon by bears, but every one of them was only a common bear, very runny.

Finally, in a deep cave, the goatherd located the gorgon, Zola.

The gorgon looked the goatherd up and down. 'Well?' he asked.

'Long have I been seeking an answer,' replied the weary goatherd. 'Long have I drilled ever deeper for the innermost truth that lurks inside the garb and garbage of outer truths, hoping to penetrate at last to the stuff that underpins all other stuffs.'

'Then be prepared for a hammering anti-climax,' said Zola portentously. 'Fromage to age people have sought to patch the void in their souls with quests for grails and girls and leavers and lovers. They have become pilgrims for sanctuary and science, for enlightenment and entitlement, for art and for heart. They have stalked fact and decried it as imposter legend, they have laboured long to photograph chimeras with cameras, have stared so hard down telescopes that they have seen nothing but the backs of their own necks. They have never learned that the whole of the whole is in each part of each part, that everything is made of everything else.'

'Sorry,' said the goatherd, 'I wasn't actually listening there, had to shake a stone out of my shoe. Anyway, what I wanted to know was, these point particle thingies that make up the bigger particles that make the atoms of the elements that make the molecules of chemicals that make the milk that makes the cheese that makes me. What are they made of?'

'Strings, possibly. Little, wobbly, vibrating loops. It's always circles, isn't it? Nature seems to love the blessed things. That's the latest idea, but there have been others and doubtless will be more yet.'

The goatherd was frantic. 'Loops within loops! But loops of what?'

The gorgon sighed. 'Time? Energy? Art? String cheese? Maybe they're not made of anything. Are you going to be long? Only, I have to feed my hair and telephone my good friend Jack Hughes on Devil's Island.'

The goatherd broke down, feeling at last the oppressive awfulness of many wasted years spent travelling and, especially dreadful to remember, queuing. The gorgon took pity on him.

'Perhaps you have asked the wrong question,' he suggested. 'Perhaps you should be interested not in what cheese is made from, but what can be made from cheese. I've a recipe for a souffle here – perhaps it might interest you? First, take an egg –'

'An egg!' cried the goatherd. 'An egg. I wonder what that's made from? Inside the shell is the membrane, then inside that is the albumen, then comes the yolk . . .'

Fortunately, a plait of the gorgon's hair (which was made of snakes) reached over and strangled the goatherd to death before he could waste any more of his or anyone else's time.

His body was cremated and, in a manner he was no longer around to fully appreciate, returned mainly to water and carbon dioxide. These substances were spread around the planet and taken up by plants, some of which were nibbled by yaks.

One day, a yak herder from Yalta (whose father was from Yekaterinburg and whose mother was from Malta) was . . . but we have already been here, before and later.

Nestor snapped from his reverie. 'That diversion was just a load of nonsense,' he cried. 'You have wasted my time!' He was about to do injury to Bosun Higgs when the pillar of rock on which they all stood lurched horribly, threatening to collapse.

'Don't say I didn't warn you about him,' said Nestor. 'You have received a lesson in how easy it is to be deflected from your mission. Now our time is truly short, and you have yet to hear my own advice, words that may very well save your life!'

To be continued . . .

If a snooping rat had twitched an ear it would have sounded as loud as a Lambeg drum at that moment in the queue outside hanger five. What did you do in the war, Daddy? I listened to an obese man tell a funny story about cheese, then waited to discover if I was going to have my entrails slashed out.

Two-for-Joy withdrew his bayonet point from my belly, released me. A lone Fraction began to clap slowly. *Very* slowly. I crawled back to my teammates, pulled open my left eye and cocked my head to half-see the events that unfolded.

A second Fraction began to clap, slightly faster. Another Fraction copied him. The clapping snowballed, and soon every one of them was clapping and cheering and crying and braying at the tops of their lungs. More than one raised their burp gun aloft and blasted entire magazines of bullets skywards. They skipped, bared their chests and breasts and fell at Nonstop's feet and kissed them. No people have ever greeted any speech with more uninhibited, rapturous and impassioned jubilance.

'What's going on?' cried Harete. 'Why did they like that insane story so much?'

I shouted back, 'I don't know. I doubt they understood a word; I think it's his courage they're applauding.'

One-for-Sorrow appeared. He stood adjacent to Nonstop and made his own Whistle-Click speech, too fast for me to translate. Then he turned to Nonstop.

'Oo lak chiz, fatta man?' he said. 'Oo rilly lak chiz?'

'Chess? Jazz?' puzzled Nonstop, his brow lines deep furrows of confusion.

'Cheese!' I yelled. 'He's asking if you like cheese, you Cheddar-head!'

'Oh, yes! ' Nonstop enthused, licking his lips. 'I LOVE CHEESE!'

One-for-Sorrow clicked his fingers and a minute later a lackey Fraction appeared bearing a plastic lunch box with a press-seal lid. One-for-Sorrow prised up the lid and proudly conducted Nonstop on a tour of the delicacies inside.

'Iz naz, tha 'un. Tha spesh naz aswell. Tha 'un med wi' urbs. Oo lak, all oors!' So saying, he gifted the entire selection box over to Nonstop.

Then the Fractions departed, talking and whistling amongst themselves.

All of us fell to the ground in disbelief and relief. We hugged and backslapped Nonstop; Myristica and Harete kissed him. Nonstop wasted no time before tucking into his gift. Before we'd finished laughing and cheering he had hamster cheeks and something yellow that ponged of gangrenous feet dribbling all over his chin. 'Have some!' he cried, waving a wedge under my nose, but I demurred.

'You earned it, Nonstop, you eat it. Your story really hit the spot with them,' Lonza congratulated him, the first occasion Lonza had said something positive about Nonstop. 'Besides, that looks like those yellow cubes they put in urinals.'

'Do I look like I eat gone-off stuff?' Lupa dismissed him. 'Be usual, why can't ya?'

'Your loss, this is top-rank cheese,' Nonstop sniffed, popping a squidgy lump into his own mouth.

'Rank being the operative word,' I said. At that instant, I felt something approximating hope. If Nonstop was able to tell good stories too, that would lift the pressure on me and Myristica (Lonza had forbidden her to tell them to the Fractions, but she could still work with me to invent them). Could we amuse the Fractions enough for them to spare us if they decided to fumigate the hanger? I dared to think we had a chance of a chance.

TO DO:
Tell more stories with help of others
Stay on right side of Lonza
Try not to think about Harete
Survive

'Nonstop, you're full of surprises,' I told him when we squeezed back into our space on the bustling hanger floor. 'Every time I think you're going to let us down, you pull something special out from under your skirt.'

'Thanks, Mo. Talking doesn't come naturally to me as you know, puts a grievous mental strain on me, actually. But I thought from what we've learned about them they'd appreciate a story inside a story.'

I had to think. 'A story in a story in a story. The goatherd's story within Nestor's story within Lex's story. Surely?'

Nonstop used his podgy fingers to check my reasoning. 'Oh . . . yes. Will it be enough, do you think, Mo? Can we sing for our supper indefinitely?'

'I don't see how, Nonstop,' I had to confess. 'But the stories are gaining us breathing space.'

'Funny,' said Nonstop. 'I find myself daydreaming about Lex and Nestor and the other characters. Did you know Lonza and Harete have been thinking up stories during lulls at market?'

'No?' I boggled. That must have been Harete's doing; all along she'd been prepping material to save me if I dried up!

'Only rudimentary ideas, of course. They need old Nonstop to tutor them, but then I've a natural flare for storytelling, always said so.'

'You're a real mate, you know that?' I laughed. 'Helping Harete and Lonza at market, and the way you put up with this place, hardly ever complaining nowadays. I scarcely recognise you from the Spiral. You're a changed man.'

I never imagined Nonstop to be blessed with even minimal powers of self-analysis, but what he said next made me reconsider. 'I suppose I was a bit of a bother on the Spiral. The good old Spiral, the good old days, best days of my life . . .' he yawned. 'All I wanted was to be friends with you, but you never wanted to know, you were so bound up in your own misery, moping about the past and Harete. You couldn't see past my size or clumsiness. I think I irritated you deliberately just so we could fight, because at least we talked when we fought. Silly, I know, but a noisy war can be more bearable than a lonely peace.'

That brought me up sharp; I wasn't sure what to say in return. 'Sorry I let you down,' I mumbled.

The evening ended with an unsatisfying, truncated coda. The Mothodist girl I'd met a few days before limped over to us. She was alone; I didn't ask about her friends, I assumed they'd died. She was hawking leaflets, hand-copied tracts I'd seen Mothodists pushing on converts.

'P-p-pilgrim, c-c-can you spare food for my l-l-leaflet?' she begged. 'The c-c-cover shows The M-M-Moth's a-p-p-proved likeness.'

She was crawling on her elbows and knees, her last legs. One of her limbs convulsed outwards, reminiscent of a lizard resting on hot desert sands. Dead before daybreak, I knew. And fiercely infectious.

I couldn't even see the damn leaflet, and I waved her away, but Nonstop gifted her a generous triangle of cheese and received a flyer in return.

'Huh. Well, well, well,' he said after examining the sketchy pages. 'Well, well, well. That answers *that* question. Fancy finding that out here. Here, of all places, Mo. Mo.'

'What?' I asked irritably. 'What does it answer?'

'Not bad. Not bad at all, just as I remember him, they've even got his trousers right – way too short they were. He must have liked draughty ankles,' Nonstop rambled on. He sounded drowsy; he was slurring his words as he spoke.

I sat up and attempted to inspect the crumpled paper, but the Fractions had dimmed the hanger lights; I could see nothing.

'Nonstop, what do you mean? She said that was a picture of The Moth. But how do you know it's a good likeness? When have you seen The Moth?' To my recollection, I'd never seen a photograph of the boy.

Nonstop yawned again, breathing out a gruesome cocktail of cheese fumes. 'That time I bumped into him at my work. Told you all this on the Spiral – typical, you never listen to old Nonstop. Never listen, never . . .' His voice crumbled to a rumble, then revived. 'Didn't know his name then. Just a wee skinny lad he was. "Help me," he said, "tell my friends . . ." something or other.'

'At your work? Where?' I pestered, shaking him, pinching his earlobe to stop him from nodding off.

'You know all this, Mo. Moth's at the centre of everything. You said that yourself. He is too, I know he is. That's where I met him. Ooh, lovely cheese that was. Luvverly . . .' He removed Dolly-with-one-arm from his waistband, and held the toy to his mouth. I wondered if he was about to kiss it goodnight; instead he whispered to it. 'Often I have said to you, I ain't any Tennessee tunneller. That's right, isn't it, Dolly? Our little secret.'

Nonstop smacked his lips in memory of his cheese, rolled over and started to snore. I badgered him with more questions, but he was gone from me. Once Nonstop was asleep, nothing short of a bonfire lit on his crotch would rouse him.

I resolved to ask again in the morning. I'd long decided to

289

sever any connection with my treacherous ex-cellmate, yet Nonstop's information played heavily upon me. *The centre of everything* . . . That was a figure of speech, a turn of phrase, how could Nonstop have met Moth there?

'Sweet cheese dreams, Nonstop. I'll never let you down, not after all we've been through, never,' I told him, hoping he could still hear me through the armour of his sleeping, and I meant it.

Words.

I hate words.

And they hate me.

Chapter 37 *

There's no way we could have prevented it. We'd lived on borrowed time for weeks; we knew the debt would be called in, repayment demanded with interest and penalties.

It wasn't my fault.

Most things turn out to be, but not this time.

Performance Review, the day after Nonstop's story. Another early evening queuing up outside on the scorched concrete under that heartless late summer sun.

I had the next chunk of story committed to memory, but I knew I wouldn't need it. The haul was huge, more than could be fitted into the bin; almost forty 'copters had arrived that day alone, and fully a third of the hangers were completely out of action, ravaged by barn dance. The latest strain of the disease was very fast-acting; thousands had been stricken overnight. Terrible . . . but that's how things were, and we had to look at it that way: their suffering strengthened our survival.

'Never seen anything like it, we had to leave stuff behind,' Lonza told us. 'We could have filled the bin three times over.'

Harete was pleased too. 'We didn't have to fight; I even saw teams helping other teams,' she said. 'Why can't they always share stuff equally? It could be like that every day.'

Her saying that made me happier still. Harete would never be perverted by the Facility. She could never comprehend the idiosyncrasies of evil, the ways it has of making dirt simple things inordinately intricate. The rival criminal organisations that ran the different hangers could never cooperate, even though it would have meant more wealth for them all. Peanuts and starlings.

Two-for-Joy couldn't fail us that evening; the stuff we had was manifestly more than adequate. To fail us and demand a story would have looked suspicious to his own team. I was anxious for him to hurry up and give us the nod; I'd not had a chance to speak to Nonstop all day and I wanted to pick up our conversation from the night before, about his claim to have met The Moth. It was right there on my list, underlined:

TO DO:
<u>What did Nonstop mean?</u>

Two-for-Joy duly turned up. Sure enough, he had no desire to fail us; every surviving team had come up trumps, and he was a happy little Fraction. He inspected our contribution, clicked his approval, signalled for it to be collected and stowed. Turning to leave, he hesitated, touched a stubby finger to his stubbly chin.

'Sham no story to-nighty, bland boy,' the stocky ogre said. The sentiment sounded a touch sheepish, a public confession to a guilty thrill. 'War lookin' fo'ward. Mebbe oo let Two-fo' tell story lumpling soon? A is avin' plen'y 'ead doodles. F'rinstance,

Nestor-man need do babymaker dance wiv a curly girl, ay? Ey gar gut story need that.'

'Uh, sure. If you say so,' was all I could think to reply. Was the man suggesting what I thought he was?

'Ay. Yonza team all gut fellers. Spesh fatta man. Oo and us, we like *that*, cos of story,' he said. At the word 'that' he interleaved the stumpy, ring-notched fingers of his two hands. The meaning was clear: solidarity.

The revelation astounded me; I blenched. I needed to think how to exploit the news. Could our diversionary saga be a path to cosying up to the Fractions, becoming hugger-mugger with the bloody buggers? And then what?

Freedom?

Two-for-Joy shambled away, his weaponry clunking.

'Oh . . .' cried Lupa. She clutched her stomach, grimaced, leaned forwards. 'Oh, no, not now. Get back in, you little turd, not now!'

Lonza rushed to her side. 'Get away from me!' she screamed. 'Don't touch me!'

She began to waddle back inside the hanger as quickly as she could, bent double.

'The baby's not due for another month!' Myristica whispered. 'This is really, really bad. Whatever happens now, don't let the Fractions see. We'll have to deliver it in secret and hide it.'

I gulped and nodded, dreading the impossible-sounding idea.

But it was too late. It's always too late.

Two-for-Joy spun around, alerted by the commotion. Whimpering Lupa had duck-scuttled halfway back to the hanger. We encircled her, tried to shield her. Two-for-Joy thrust his way through us.

'Ey, preggo girly, oo no go 'anger, oo come wi' me, pissmocker docker, 'ee see babba come out tidy good!' he babbled. 'Wan watch, wan see summin' inside get come outside, is lak magik, we ol wan see insidy outside babba person.' The pocket monster was panting exuberantly; this must have been a moment he'd been looking forward to for a long time.

'Leave me alone!' bawled Lupa, batting him away. She grabbed at her thigh. She was wearing leggings, crusty and holed, unchanged and unwashed like all our clothes. 'Not now, get back in!' she cried again.

Dimly, I could see a small bulge sliding slowly down Lupa's leg, trapped inside her tights.

'I can't look!' wept Myristica, and she buried her head in my chest.

Two-for-Joy knelt in front of Lupa and began pawing at her, groping her. Harete and Lonza tried tugging at him, but the muscular little Fraction was too powerful for them. I heard the slick *shhhhhhhh* sound of his bayonet gliding from its greased scabbard.

'What's he doing with that? Someone help us!' I called out. Not a baby; he couldn't kill a newborn baby, not even him.

Peacemakers! Two of the smiling troops happened to stroll around the corner at that very moment, smart in their starchy blue uniforms, spotless white helmets, reflective hi-vis tabards.

'Help us, help her, in the name of everything you claim to believe in, help!' I pleaded, running to them and prostrating myself at their safety boots. They came, they saw, they –

Conferred.

'Interfering would constitute a protocol violation,' said the first soldier. Her words said that, her yo-yo tone told me she too was appalled at what she was witnessing. She hefted her automatic rifle nervously, stepped forwards for a closer look. 'Mind, it does appear to be a prima facie case of common assault. Perhaps I could escalate this to a different solutions pathway.'

Her colleague barred her progress with his arm. 'Don't be so hasty,' he gruffed. 'This could be a valid form of ethno-cultural expression. Like a traditional dance. We must respect diversity.'

'Of course,' sniffed the female soldier. 'Try to embrace inclusivity, young man. You and your little chums should workshop your racist tendencies. Health and safety.'

They one-eightied and blowed out. By then, Two-for-Joy had pushed screaming Lupa to the ground, and his deputies had raced back and smashed Harete and Lonza away. I heard slashing and grunting; Two-for-Joy was snuffling and snarling and slavering, a starving dog at its bowl, a snouty dog in the manger.

Two-for-Joy stood.

'Congra'layshuns!' he smirked. He held something small and bloody in his hands, wrapped up in Lupa's torn leggings where he'd cut them from her with his bayonet.

'Congra'layshuns!' he said again. 'Is an 'am.'

Chapter 38

It was a ham.

A big, triangular tin of ham. Lupa had stolen it, stuffed it into the top of her leggings, but it had come lose and ridden down. She must have pilfered it from the bin, withheld it from what had to be surrendered to the Fractions.

That was a calamitous error.

'We had loads today, they wouldn't miss it. I wanted something different – it's to help my baby grow proper,' she begged. 'Fed up with baby food. That's all those Peacemaker spew-chewers give me, and I haven't got a baby yet!'

No dice.

The Fractions were boiling mad. One-for-Sorrow was summoned. We were frog-marched into the hanger, herded into a corner. I could feel the rage emanating from them. The fact that all the food was stolen by the Fractions in the first place in no part lessened their mountainous swell of injustice.

'Ees death! Slot 'er!' demanded Two-for-Joy, supported by Hickory-Dickory and many others. Some members of the tribe saw things differently; I caught snatches of their Whistle-Click. 'Bad team, kill all, stop rot,' they suggested. Lupa's condition could no longer protect her. Or could it? There was a touch of hesitancy about the Fractions.

Harete pleaded, her complaints were dismissed. The nearest she received to an explanation came from Went-to-Mow. 'We oll 'avin' boss fellers too, bosses o'er us. We don' make ur quota, we get slumbered, bang bang! Get out news we softy chaps, allow nickin', we double dead fellows.'

'But –'

'No! Someone die. No stoop story save, not fo' this.'

I was clustered with the others, rigid with alarm. Lonza was grating his teeth in powerless rage. Vile though Lupa was, I couldn't countenance the thought of a pregnant girl being chopped in half by blazing burp guns. That was too much; we all have a limit, that was beyond mine. The Numbers, I'd seen that very thing happen when soldiers had killed the Numbers in the marshes. Never again. Never. Never.

And then there was the consideration of Myristica's medicines, for Lupa remained the only one of us who could acquire them. If she died, Meg would die.

Not for the first time, Harete's words repeated on me. 'Self-centred.' The phrase sat on my heart where she'd pinned it, oxidising.

So I did something I'd never done before. It felt easy and good. I sensed it was expected of me too, and if it wasn't, it should have been. None of the others spoke up, not so that I heard anyway, not even the Kernel. When your free-ranging insanity knows something is right, you know it's really right.

'I stole the ham,' I announced, putting up my hand. 'I stole it from the bin and passed it to Lupa. She didn't know it was

297

swiped – I told her One-for-Sorrow had awarded our team a bonus.'

A flurry of hissing and commotion. One-for-Sorrow barked for silence, spoke directly to me. 'Oo, bland boy?' he asked. He was wearing a bowler hat, headgear reserved for official duties.

'Me. Don't need eyes, I can still feel things.'

'Oo tek respons'billy?'

'I do.'

'Oke. Punshment is oors.' He didn't believe me, I knew, and he didn't need to. The Fractions could save face, Lupa's baby could live, this was the best fit to everyone's difficulty.

Almost everyone's.

'Na! Bland boy lie, he no sticky nicker. Pregga girly is pincher peep, she die,' Two-for-Joy insisted, apparently taking the theft as a deeply personal insult. Other Fractions murmured agreement, but they were the minority and the decision was not overturned.

The Fractions began to usher the other teams in from outside; they needed to make an example of a thief. The workers were herded in, moulded around us. There was no willingness among them – they came under protest.

Finally – my turn for peace, so often postponed. No tears, no fuss, this was how it had to be. I felt happy.

And I couldn't remember the last time I'd said that.

Seventeen and a hero; a good time and a fair way to die.

One-for-Sorrow separated me from the others. 'This oor punshment. Oo chuz oo die.'

'What? You don't understand! I die! I stole the ham!' I shouted.

'A un'stan' perfec. *This* pun'shment. Oo chuz oo die. Not oo. Not chuz self. Ten secs, else kill oll team.'

'No!'

'Nine.'

'No! No!'

'Eight.'

'PLEASE!'

'Seven.'

He meant it.

'Six.'

Burp guns were cocked, the audience pulled back, stampeding to get far away. Fractions marshalled them forwards at gunpoint. Attendance was mandatory.

{Choose!}

'I CAN'T! I CAN'T!'

'Five.'

Not Lonza. Without him, the team would all fail the cut. Not Harete because she could take over if Lonza was injured and because I SCABBING LOVED HER no matter how true all that Myristica had said was. Not Lupa; it was to save her unborn baby I was doing this.

Nonstop or Myristica.

'Four.'

Myristica could tell stories.

Nonstop could tell stories. Nonstop helped with market.

'Three.'

If I chose Myristica, Lonza would kill me.

'Two.'

Myristica would probably die soon anyway.

'One.'

When they fumigated, everyone would die anyway.

Nonstop called out, 'Me, Mo, choose me. What was loved once must always be loved. Myristica's still loved, I'm not. Not since real sis died.'

A young man screamed out, his voice so loud it took sole possession of the hanger, roaring louder than the crowd, louder than helicopters, louder than burb guns.

'I love you, Nonstop!' the man said. The voice was familiar. Mine. Echoes reinforced it. Someone else screamed the same words too – Myristica.

One-for-Sorrow, his face right in my face, lifting my head up by the hair like it was a trophy he'd already lopped off. 'Oo to chuz? Oo?'

'Nonstop,' I said. Only the shapes made by my lips betrayed him, no sound issued from them, no will stood behind them. Shapes. Geometry. Topology. Blame them, not me.

Two betrayals had occurred, one public, one private. 'You knew, didn't you, Kernel?' I whispered. 'You knew they'd twist my volunteering. That's why you didn't stop me. To save yourself.'

{Guilty.}

Chapter 39

That wasn't the end of it.

That was the start of it.

They made *us* kill Nonstop.

They made us kill Nonstop, and they forced everyone else to watch us do it. In that dusty, dirty corner of the crowded hanger, as the punch-drunk summer afternoon fused into steamy, mosquito-blown evening, they made us murder our friend.

Lonza had no knives. We couldn't borrow a gun from a Fraction, no one from another team was allowed to lend us anything. My poison was too slow, my pocket knife was inside Dolly-with-one-arm in Nonstop's waistband, and we weren't allowed to remove it. Fractions' rules.

Lonza took over. His motivation was not desire or wickedness, only efficiency.

But this was an obscene mismatch, a declawed moggy set to dispatch a hippo.

Nonstop knelt down, made suggestions. Couldn't have been more helpful, more cooperative. He assumed the role of demure supplicant to Lonza's unwilling executioner.

In the end, Lonza decided to strangle Nonstop with a rope made by twisting up Nonstop's skirt.

It took forever. Nonstop proved almost indestructible.

I owed Nonstop my obedient observance. I watched, as best I could, peeking through my blindfold and the dead spots in my eyes; I watched through voluptuous waves of crippling brain pain. All I could think was, *it should have been me, I'd have died easy*.

What do you want me to say? Do you want me to wax on about Nonstop's puffed-out, vermillion face? The way his tongue rolled into a tube and stiffened and probed out of his mouth like a great, red, cracked cylinder of luncheon meat? How that titchy, itchy nose transformed into a magical, bottomless ewer for blood?

Scab the scab off, you scabbing scabbers.

Still Nonstop wouldn't die.

Lonza took to clubbing him with the triangular tin of ham, hefting it in both hands, crunching it down into the top of his skull. The young man was soon exhausted, wobbling so much he could hardly stand up.

Our drafted-in show-goers remained respectfully silent, collectively wincing and sobbing with every blow, their juddering sawtooth in-breaths synchronising with the rhythm of Lonza's strikes. Coarsened and dehumanised prisoners they may have been, but they were not criminals, they were refugees, ordinary people, this was no spectator sport for them. The Fractions meanwhile were engaged in a blizzard of trade, exchanging bracelets and rings as they placed wagers on the timing of Nonstop's death, I'll-Sing-You-Twelve-Ho playing tic-tac man.

Whack. Whack. The sound was soft and puffy, like an under-inflated football being kicked against the gable end of a house. Ruefully I thought back to the summoners' killing tool, that head hole punch in the Compensation Camp and the swift end it dispensed. *We should have stayed*, I wept, *we should have stayed*.

Near the end, Lonza burned me a look, Lew's look, the face of a man drowning in air, the face of a man for whom existence itself has become insufferable. He owed me Meg though, that understanding passed unsaid between us, he owed me Meg and his baby and Lupa.

''Nuff,' declared One-for-Sorrow, calling time. Kneeling Nonstop was not dead, but not alive. In transit. His skull was open at the back, a soft boiled egg after the spoon has been applied. Flies, I remember the fat, fuzzy flies and how they hovered around the bloody crater like wildebeest at a watering hole.

Cheers and boos and whistles and clicks came from the Fractions, and there was a final furore as debtors paid creditors, then the crowd of workers was permitted to disperse. They were fizzing with thunderous, electric hate for the Fractions, and I was grateful to them for that.

Harete went to Lonza. He pushed her away.

Myristica and I went to Nonstop. We cradled him, we two held him all the way as he spiralled into irredeemable catastrophe.

There's another thing that isn't like it is in films and fiction. Dying.

Nonstop clung on, took a long time to fully depart. 'It hurts so grievous bad, make it stop, please make it stop,' he kept whining, on and on and on and on. Nothing we said reached him; he was dying on autopilot, confined in his final minutes to a solitary cell without a spy slot.

Listening to my friend's dissolving life was the purest torture I'd ever known.

'Make the hurting stop. Help . . . me . . .'

Shut up, please, shut up. Stop being part of the universe. Why can't you just die?

'Pain . . . help, won't someone . . . sis!'

Shut up! I hate you, I hate you!

'SIS!'

I love you, I love you, my brother, I love you.

At long, long last, the dying died. With nine gasps, Nonstop gave out his being.

Nonstop had stopped.

I picked up Dolly-with-one-arm from where it had fallen. I felt very thirsty. More than anything else, I felt thirsty.

Two-for-Joy wandered over.

'A lak fatta man. Roller poller pal tolt gar fan story 'bout stuff-in-stuff, wa mekkin' a mind smile,' he said. 'Pregga girly shud bin dedded, no fatta man. Wa ma tip-top friend.'

I nodded. I doubt the most sensitive scientific instrument on Earth could have measured the minuscule angle through which my head dipped, but I nodded.

'Oo can kip can,' Two-for-Joy said. He slid the dented, bloodstained tin of ham towards me with the toe of his sandal, then plodded away.

Chapter 40

Who slept that night? No one from our team. Myristica wound up tight by me, cold despite the boiling heat. Harete and Lonza lay side by side, closer than the two ones of eleven, but not contacting.

Lonza had said only these words before we'd all lain down: 'No one can touch me.'

Lupa had her own space; she was as shunned as a goulash-nosher. None of us wished for so much as a trailing thread from a frayed cuff to connect with her.

Morning brought a sun like an open oven door, a hole in the clouds through which heat vomited out. And with the sun, a hanger moon; the Fractions had strung Nonstop's body from the rafters, a warning to others.

Lupa yawned, stretched awake, saw the hanging body. 'Pah!' she laughed. 'That is, like, so humongoose. A new day without that fat fudgeball!'

And that was me.

A snap decision.

Because you don't have to get used to it. And those that do become habituated; maybe they shouldn't, maybe they're

305

destined to become the new tormenters, the throwers of bricks, the men in the spinney, maybe they should have quit sooner too.

It had to be like that. I knew the Kernel thumbed through my thoughts, knew he'd try to foil me if I'd planned for it. Only spontaneous decisions could defeat him, only unthinking fibre and bone could neutralise the parasite.

The hanger doors had been cranked open. I hopped-skipped-jumped over the stirring workers and hared outside. No one stopped me; it wasn't against the rules, there was nowhere to go.

And nowhere was where I was headed: the electrified fence.

I could not live another hour. And I hadn't forgiven the Kernel. My to-do list was short and sweet.

TO DO:
Kill self, kill Kernel

I ran, I didn't need to see, all I had to do was maintain a straight course and I'd run smack bang into the fence, the inner layer of three concentric rings of fizzling, crackling high-voltage fortifications.

Smack *BANG!*

The fences groomed the sticky air with a sparky, static electric emanation, part feeling, part odour, a fairground pheromone. Many other degraded slaves chose the same ending every day, a ride on the last waltzer. They had their reasons, I had mine:

Symmetry. That mad guard, Jelly, had died trying to catch me after I'd helped Harete into the Other country. He'd been electrocuted after brushing against the live power cables carried by a pylon.

306

Logic. Without Nonstop, the team would be less effective at market, the loss exceeding the reduction in the number of hungry mouths.

Justice. I had volunteered to die. The cuckoo Kernel had deceived me. Attacking the Fractions was not possible, they'd have exacted revenge on the entire team.

Run! My fleet feet pounded over the cracked concrete towards the crackle and hum.

{Stop, Mo! This is not suicide, it's genocide!}

'No, Kernel, it's pesticide.'

The Kernel applied the brakes, dug his heels in. No – my heels.

I'd suspected he could control my body; for days, I'd wordlessly theorised that many of the problems with my vision and the after-pains were down to him, that he'd been censoring some sights, sanctioning others, that I was as much his prisoner as I was the Fractions'.

{You. Must. Stop.}

'No! Every prisoner has the right to die.'

{I am not a prisoner!}

'You're a dream or an illness or a story gone wrong, I don't know what you are, you brain-invader. You've been keeping me blind.'

{That was essential! So many dangers here, I couldn't risk you trying to escape. I was keeping you safe.}

'You murdered Nonstop.'

{I can explain!}

'Don't explain, die!'

I tried to shuffle forwards. I was almost within touching

307

distance of the fence; if I hadn't bitten my fingernails I could have made contact, that's how close I was. When I stretched out my hand, I could feel whiskery, vanguard sparks excite my fingertips.

My legs refused to budge, the Kernel was staging a coup. I fought against him. He tried to discourage me, bombing me with mallet-blows of pain; he contracted my muscles and curved my spine backwards, bending me further away from the fence.

He tried to bribe me, his voice dripping syrup. Or sauce.

{I will give you Harete. I will show you how to win her.}

'She is not yours to award, skull-squatter! And she's all shook up and took up with Lonza the leopard.'

{Then I can make her lionise you. You can be with her, but for that to happen you must live, *I must live*.}

A new trick: the Kernel inflamed the ringworm patch on my forehead. The spot burned with what was incontestably the most maddeningly irritating itch I'd ever felt. I had to withdraw my outstretched arms, so near to touching the fence, to rub at it. I pulled off and threw away my blindfold, the better to scratch directly at the throbbing, ridged skin underneath.

The Kernel was not all powerful. Controlling my legs put him at the limit of his powers, and he had to cease regulating my vision. I saw clearer than I had for weeks, the dead spots notwithstanding. I saw clearly the first fence, a wall of wire hexagons. It stood within spitting distance.

Spitting distance. Arms too short, legs paralysed by the Kernel, but there remained one way to touch the fence. I dropped my trackie trousers. I would pee on it; when my yellow salty current joined with the electric one, it would be as effective as touching it directly. My bladder was not under the Kernel's control, although I felt him struggling for it, numbing my groin, trying to deaden my nerves as we wrestled for control.

{Put it away. I have other plans for you, for that!}

I aimed myself at the fence, tried to release. I had to close my eyes, concentrate on relaxing, tune out the Kernel's deafening death throes. He was screaming my head off from the inside, trying to deter me.

{ONE AND ONE IS TWO AND ONE IS THREE AND ONE IS FOUR . . .}

I let go.

Bliss.

Shhhhhhhhhhh.

No pain, no fizzing, and the noise sounded wrong, too soft. I opened my eyes to check my aim and range. I was peeing on a Fraction; he had unwisely placed himself between me and the fence. The man was Seven-Potato-More, the tribe's cook, cropping barbecued carrion from the day's other suicides.

So much the better; an enraged Fraction would kill me as effectively as an electrified fence. I carried on peeing, aiming high up the big man's barrel chest, splattering him liberally, catching the lower fringes of his straggly ginger beard.

Seven-Potato-More stepped forwards. The gobsmacked Fraction stared straight into my eyes, entranced, fascinated to the exclusion of everything else around him. He did not look insulted, did not register my peeing on him.

'One-fo'-Sorrow,' he bawled, 'is 'im, is 'im!'

He slung me over his shoulder like a side of beef and pelted back to the hanger at full tilt.

The Kernel was livid. He swamped my mind with a chlorine hurricane of acrimony and thrummed out his threats.

{You young idiot, my story should never be shared with these maverick imps! We are not ready, you and the girl are not ready. You forced my hand. When opportunity arises I will force yours. I am your enemy, Mo, your enemy within!}

Chapter 41 *

That marked the point when everything became seriously weird.

Seven-Potato-More crashed through the throngs of workers preparing to set off for market, trampling them underfoot in his haste. All the time he ran, he shouted out for One-for-Sorrow. We charged into the Fractions' own darkened area beyond the cordon of boxes. There, the excited cook demonstrated to all the Fractions the feature he had identified in my eyes.

One-for-Sorrow saw it straight away. His chessboard face paint denied me the chance to confirm it, but I'm pretty sure he paled. His tugged nervously on his bullet-case earrings, fiddled with his bowler hat.

'Put blan'fol' back on, mus' nev' show anyone else,' he instructed, all his usual haughtiness dried up. Without delay the blindfold was retied around my head. I was pleased to note that even with the grimy fabric band reapplied I was able to see passably well through the thin gauze; perhaps as much as half my field of vision was functioning. The damage from the sun and the drone had not been imaginary, but now I knew the Kernel had exacerbated the smudginess and the suffering

I had felt when using my eyes – except when it had suited him. No longer; his ploy to clip my wings had ended. All my senses felt heightened. Was that the Kernel's doing too? Had I inadvertently compelled him to boost my strength? His survival required mine, that much we both knew.

One-for-Sorrow spoke again. 'Get bland boy's team, get Yonza, get oll,' he ordered, once in words, once in clicks, both forms causing minions to zip into activity.

Seconds later, Lonza, Harete, Myristica and Lupa were manhandled into the room. Seeing me they all began to shout out questions, but One-for-Sorrow shut them all up with the most extraordinary words I'd heard a Fraction utter.

'Chez. Give oll chez,' he barked. 'Mek comfo'ble.'

Battered seats were unstacked and passed to us. The surprises did not end there. No sooner had we parked our backsides on the cracked plastic chairs than we became aware of clomping sounds, and a musty odour that made my eyes sting. Before I could rise or cry out, a creature like no other I had known was towering above me.

Chapter 42

Earlier, I had wondered from the stink and the clattering of hooves if the Fractions had stabled a barnyard animal in their quarters. Not so – my shadowy companion had been human after all; no giant goat or llama, but she was perhaps a lama of sorts.

The woman – there was no doubt on this point, she was naked from the waist up – stood far taller than any of the Fractions. Her creased peach stone of a head balanced atop a tower of chunky gold necklaces that had stretched her tapering, vase-like neck to the length of a forearm. If the rule was to add one ring every year she must have been . . .

'Eighty-five,' I heard Myristica whisper to Harete.

Stretch-neck's hair was as white and as long as a wedding train; it flowed freely from her head and down her back. Regions within the carpet of hair moved independently, giving the suggestion of dogs or small children scampering underneath it. Her skirt was made of strips of torn newspapers, on her feet: roller skates. Silver, sparkly roller skates decorated with stars and streamers. She walked, not rolled, towards me, the skates making the clip-clop sounds I had misheard as hooves.

Nothing about the woman made sense. Was the creature magpie, magus, magistrate, minstrel, magician?

'I am Origin,' announced stretch-neck. If that was a name or a title she did not make clear. Her voice was crisp, clear, beautifully enunciated. 'I am the mother, grandmother and great-grandmother of all the set of Integers you have seen.'

'Integers!' I gasped. 'We thought you were all Fractions.'

The strange old woman fixed me with a glare that could have passed through a mountain and juiced a grapefruit on the other side.

{The eyes, Mo! (0,0)}

'Fractions?' she spat, elaborately exercising every consonant. '*Fffffrrrractionssss?* Do I look as if I spend my days mugging and drugging and conning marks with games of Find the Lady in beer halls and bus stations?'

I had no idea what a half-naked octogenarian on roller skates looked like she spent her days doing, but I had no desire to offend her.

'N-no, s-sorry,' I replied. Find the Lady? I knew that game. You *never* found the lady.

The old woman clonked closer, lifted my blindfold, repeated the examination her underlings had performed. She nodded, as apparently satisfied as they had been disturbed.

'Do you understand what is meant by the word "origin"?' she asked me.

'Of course,' I said. 'The beginning of everything, where the real and imaginary cross over.'

Why did I say that?

Was that me? The Kernel?

314

I wanted to correct myself, but more questions were fired at me. Origin's olivine eyes cut into me as she rattled them off.

'What are the elements?' she screeched.

'Hydrogen ... helium,' I began hesitantly, dimly remembering what Nonstop had taught me.

'What are the elements?' The same question. Had my answer failed to satisfy?

'Earth, fire, water, air,' ran my second attempt. That must have been some of Moth's learning scuffing off on me like shoe polish on a shiny floor.

'What are the elements?' The same question *again*?

'Two, three, five, seven, eleven,' I began, speaking as fast my lips would permit me.

'Excellent!' cried Origin. 'The primes. All natural numbers can be assembled from the primes.' Another question followed. 'Where do parallel lines meet?'

'At infinity,' I declared, again speaking as if I knew what I was talking about. How could parallel lines ever meet? They were obliged to continue side by side in perpetuity, never crossing, like the two rails of a railway track. I conceived a point, a circle into which many straight lines plunged, converging, dying. Or being born, if you spun time backwards, if the end became the beginning. A tempest of ululating confusion took hold of me, a storm of words and symbols whirling around in my head, fusing, breaking up; circles rolled within circles, words sounded within words, stories played out within stories, the outermost consuming the innermost, everything becoming its opposite. I stood up, reeled around the room, bouncing off the walls, off Fractions {Integers!}. Origin's voice alone reached me, snaking to me through the mania, an umbilical cord, a noose.

'Where is the final number?' she demanded. Her voice was not steel, it was uranium, heavy and deadly. Words shot from her mouth like black sparks, her jawbone creaked like the runners of a cot or the lid of a coffin, her breath reeked of gripe water and formaldehyde.

'Where is the final number?' she insisted. 'Tell me!'

'I don't know!' I cried. 'There is no final number! The numbers go on forever – Moth told me that, Nonstop told me that – they never end!'

Stop.

I was sitting on my chair in the dark recesses of the hanger; I had never moved from my chair. My head cleared, but my stomach took a little while to catch up, returning from riding a rollercoaster on Mars. Whoever I had been, I was back to the me I knew, the Mo I lived in.

'He's the one,' Origin declared, turning from me. 'Not a scintilla of doubt. Three of you must take him out to the Domain without delay, keep him there. At all costs, guard him from the cousins. These other workers are of no interest.'

I was to leave? Why? What was going on?

Alone?

I wasn't going to stand for that, even if I was sitting down. My hands dived into my bag of rat bait and I pulled out a fistful of the salty brown cubes.

'Origin!' I shouted. 'My friends come too, all of them. Give me your word, or I'll eat the poison!'

Fractions lunged at me; I packed three cubes into my mouth. I was so hungry it took an effort not to swallow them.

316

'Leave him!' Origin squawked, flapping her hands at her offspring. 'He's too valuable.'

She addressed me again. 'Very well – your friends will accompany you.'

I spat the lumps back into my palm but kept my hand where it was, ready to re-eat them. 'You give me your word?'

'Better, I give you my number.'

'Which is?'

'Absolute zero!'

'One more thing, long-throat witch,' I said, emboldened by her description of me: *too valuable*. 'Can you raise the dead?'

'No.'

'Thought not, roller-toes. But you can lower them. I want my friend brought down from the rafters. I want his body burned on a pyre, maximum respect, maxo maxo dignity. For this journey, I want food and drink for everyone, not the normal muck in cans and not that cannibal depravity either. And I want a really big supply of the drugs Myristica needs.'

Origin nodded. She had no choice but to agree to my terms, and I had her number.

The Fractions brought everything I'd asked for, including four cardboard crates full of tablets in blister packs; must have been the dispensary's entire stock.

'A lifetime's supply,' murmured Myristica.

'Really, Meg?' gasped Lonza. 'That many?'

'However many I have, it's a lifetime's supply. When they run out, so do I.'

We put them in our wheelie bin along with the food, drinks and the Fractions' own travelling supplies. Then we set off.

317

Part 4:

Break-up

Chapter 43*

The truck wasn't troubled at the main gates. The Peacemakers weren't supposed to let anyone out on account of the quarantine, but they were outgunned by the Fractions – Integers, whatever – and besides, as the Peacemakers explained, they needed a special chitty signing before they were allowed to fire their rifles in case the noise disturbed pelicans during their nesting season. 'But the Major's away on maternity leave. We'll just let you through,' the gatehouse sergeant wisely concluded. 'Health and safety.'

The truck revved up and powered out past sentry boxes and wire fences.

Out.

OUT!

Not free though. We were tied to the truck. And Origin's word was worth her number, nothing, because my bag of poison, my one hold over our captors, had been ripped from my wrists. But the Facility was behind us, diminishing in size by the second. Long queues of refugees had to dive headlong into ditches as the lorry blasted along the road, swerving from side to side. We shouted at the people, but the truck was too loud and too fast for our warnings to be understood.

Lupa was furious with the day's turn of events. The jolting, bouncing vehicle was making her even more irritable than usual.

'You've really blown it now, bran-flake face,' she huffed. 'I'm pregnant with a baby child, remember? Where am I, like, going to de-pregnate? I was safe where we was. Where's my food gonna come from now?'

I shrugged. Origin had mentioned the Domain, and I took that to be the name of their homelands, but she had not elaborated. We knew only that we would be driven into the mountains, then have to walk for some days.

'Shut up, Lupa. We'll manage,' Lonza told her. 'This is the best thing that's happened to us for ages. Wherever we're going to, it can't be worse than where we've been. We're with Mo, and he's special.'

Lupa curled her lip so far she could have used it as a parasol. 'Uh. You guys are so, like, dunce,' she snorted. 'Think about it, you ignoranuses. The Fractions are totally juiced up about things inside other things, and we all know what they like to eat. He's not special. He's *the* special. Know what I mean? And that's just for starters. Or rather, you lot are . . . whores' duvets. Pah! Hope they choke on you.'

I couldn't dismiss Lupa's idea. Yet even that prognosis could not crush my exultation at our release from the Facility. I gloried in the changes to my situation, for I was half-free, half-sighted, and rotated from the bottom of the pile to the top of the heap. Harete and Lonza tried to discern what the Fractions had seen in my eyes, but drew a blank.

'Must be like reading tea leaves in the bottom of a cup,'

said Harete. 'What were all those questions about, Mo? And who are they, if not really Fractions, and how many of these mad castes are there?'

No one could answer her, least of all me. The truck sped up; we shut our eyes and mouths against the stinging dust.

'Crocodiles,' said Lupa, out of the blue, yelling over the din of the rattling, tappety engine. She had on a cockled, constipated look. She was thinking.

'What?' we all groaned together.

'It's sorta like . . . there's crocodiles, right?'

'Yeah?'

'But there's also, um, alligators. Basically the same as crocs, but not crocs.'

'So?'

Lupa sighed. 'Just saying, right? Whenever you think you've got something sorted, like these mingers being Fractions, there's always something else that comes along, just a bit different. Forget it. I'm an interffectual, totally wasted on you spackers.'

'Caimans,' mumbled Harete. 'That's another animal like crocodiles.'

'Said, forget it, *slag*.'

Funnily enough, I knew what Lupa was groping towards. Another manifestation of the twist, perhaps, the way completeness eludes you. Crocodiles, alligators, caimans; Numbers, Fractions, Integers . . .

'Who cares what they call themselves? They're a superstitious bunch of subhuman barbarians,' choked Lonza. The death of Nonstop had ruined him. Overnight, his taciturn broodiness had been supplanted by a chitinous vulnerability. I understood

323

why: to do the deed, Lonza had needed to siphon from his navel a djinn. The spirit lay draped around the young man's shoulders like a grinning fox fur stole. I imagined I could hear it sniping in his ear: 'The fighter has become a killer, yip, yip!' The spirit could never be returned, any more than toothpaste could be squeezed back into the tube or I could banish my own Kernel. Lonza dispatched me a wavering smile and I returned it, warming at last to the too-cool youth. Harete shuffled closer to Lonza, but he slid away, placing himself equidistant along the truck's bench between her and Lupa.

No danger of Lonza's insult being overheard, for the Fractions accompanying us were all riotously larking about in the cab, taking potshots and waving their private parts through the windows at astonished refugees, the driver steering with his bare feet on the wheel. The Kernel was sulking, but he'd cranked all the controls up to maximum before retiring. My splotchy vision glowed with an unearthly acuity, and my ears could distinguish the creaks and squeaks of individual springs in the rickety truck's suspension.

The wind wasn't real, only an artefact of our motion, but it was welcome for all that. I slit open a plastic bag containing a sample of Nonstop's ashes and let them blow away in the draught. His body had been burned on a pyre of tyres outside hanger five not three hours before, they were warm to the touch.

'Goodbye, my brother!' I shouted after them.

'We were really fondue!' said Myristica, then she rolled a soppy prayer:

'*Once you were a scientist, with diplomas and degreeses,*
Obsessed with smashing atoms, talking nonsense, eating cheeses.
Then a captive on the Spiral, then a brother, helper, friend,

324

Never stoic, thrice heroic, please, please help us 'til the end.'

Harete threw overboard a posy of weeds she'd found growing near a leak in the hanger's toilet gutter, with stems like umbrella spokes ending in little white flowers.

'Cow parsley,' she said, 'some call it mother-die. It seemed . . . he had a mothering nature. He cared.'

'Amen,' said Lonza.

'A menace, you mean,' grumbled Lupa. 'Fat prat – I won't miss him. He took up too much room on the floor and he was always treading on my fingers. Clumsy oaf. He was ham-fisted. Geddit? Hey, Lonza, did ya hear me? *Ham-fisted,* I said.'

You could have grated a cobblestone on the face Lonza presented to his girlfriend. He said nothing – the hardest, darkest, weightiest nothing I never heard.

The countryside we weaved through was a desiccated, garbage-bedraggled wasteland; no rain had fallen since early spring, nothing was growing. All the houses were soot-streaked roofless husks, smashed by bombs, sacked by looters. Saddest of all for me was a scene of felled electricity pylons, crumpled tangles of steel looking like sets of jackstraws abandoned by child giants called in for their tea.

Above us congregated a seething brood of beer brown clouds sculpted in the shape of ox hearts. The afternoon ripened and turned dark and clammy, the initial thrill of being outside decayed. Worry settled in, moved out, evicted by boredom.

We drowsed. I dreamed of Nonstop's funeral pyre, woke up with a flame-inspired idea, a choice pastry from the half-bakery of my overheated cranium. The plan foundered at once. Rummaging groggily through the wheelie bin, the only tin

325

of powdered milk I found was almost empty. Myristica was awake; I remember slur-mumbling my scheme to her, drifting off again. When I woke for the second time, hours later, I immediately found a second tin, brim full, right at the top of the bin. Useless scabbing eyes.

The truck jounced its way downwards through the gears and climbed into the hills. The hills became mountains, the road thinned to a lane, a rutted track, nothing. We'd run out of gears. We dismounted, the Fractions divided; the juniors returned with the lorry, three seniors stayed with us: squat Two-for-Joy, his brother Three-Blind-Mice and Four-and-Twenty Blackbirds. Our guards were plainly on edge; all earlier jollity had vanished. Perhaps the hills housed parties of bandits. Hadn't Origin mentioned rival cousins?

Our hands were bound and we were tied to one another with a nylon rope. Before the lid was lashed down, I dropped Dolly-with-one-arm inside the wheelie bin. She was my sole memento of Nonstop; I didn't want her to drop from my waistband. At gunpoint the Fractions directed us to walk, and under no circumstances to speak.

Lonza and I had to lug the wheelie bin, him at the front, me at the back. We tried trundling the thing, but the ground was too rough and both the plastic wheels broke off. Harete had it no easier: she had to alternate between carrying Myristica piggy-back and assisting lumbering Lupa. The path decayed to a sheep track that carved a line across vertiginous granite slopes studded with quartz-speckled boulders.

All afternoon we climbed, higher and higher, with nothing to drink or eat. My eyes packed up again, deluged with sweat.

I converted my blindfold into a bandana to soak away the moisture. The clouds coalesced into a solid flank the colour of bruised muscle; occasionally we heard coughs of thunder, an outbreak of atmospheric barn dance.

Late in the day, a long-forgotten feeling assailed us: being cool. A sublimely invigorating current of air spooled down the mountainside and washed over us, air deflected from higher peaks and refrigerated by altitude.

And my language tuition paid off. I overheard Two-for-Joy whistle-clicking. Many clicks, one terminating whistle.

NXT RST GT RD NWNTD 4

Next rest, get rid of unwanted four.

The final whistle indeed. That would be the lingering aftertaste of the tinned meat; my guess was Two-for-Joy had never forgiven Lupa for the insult of the theft, and he resented Lonza for killing Nonstop. Two-for-Joy had presumably only waited until then to save his men the bother of carrying the heavy bin up the steep paths.

We were scratching our way along a track with a sheer drop to our right and a high cliff to our left, one Fraction ahead of us and two behind. No way out. The fading light was almost too dim to walk safely in by then; our next rest could not have been more than a few minutes away.

I drummed my intelligence out on the wheelie bin using the cell phone code. Harete understood immediately. None of the others knew the code; Harete and I became tightly coupled by the rope and shared awareness.

The glacial breeze bore with it imprints of me and her and Moth on our pylon-guided winter sprint. It whistled uninterrupted through my greasy head, scouring away an accumulation of delusions. Right then, side-lit by orange sunlight ricocheting from valley walls, I realised I was seeing Harete properly at long last, or even for the first time ever. Not one thing about her differed from how it had been the preceding moment, but the effect she produced within me had changed completely. The fever inside me had died.

This must be the burnout, as promised by Myristica!

Who was Harete? An ordinary teenage girl, seventeen, eighteen, I didn't know. Nothing special to look at really, no enthralling curves or bewitching smiles, just an unremarkable girl who couldn't help caring, a girl who deserved blue shoes and job interviews, a choice of hair scrunchies and flowers in bunches. And Lonza, the target of her own wistful sight, reflected in her lustrous copper eyes. She deserved him, if he was whom she desired, but she was too honourable to request him. Lonza in his turn had his gaze pegged to struggling Myristica. Of the two, he looked the sicker, sunken and disordered. Myristica had focused her soft eyes on me. I took the look, turned, closed the pentangle, studied Lupa. Only she was found unwanting, examining and patting and smoothing her bump, centred. She noticed me looking at her and mouthed, 'Cough off, minger.'

Escape, then. Three berserkers with guns versus five half-starved teenagers, one pregnant, one dying and loving life, one strong but sick of existence, one engrossed by a tantalising spectre of the unrealisable, one newly liberated. In other words: five normal kids.

We had nothing, and that's all we needed. I updated my

schedule.

TO DO:
Buy time
Cut ropes
Overpower Fractions
Escape

Item one: time. We had one trick to play, the same we'd been playing for weeks. I drummed an idea to Harete, found her prepared and willing.

'Two-for!' I called, earning a dirty stare and a fist with more rings than a telephone exchange under my nose, but no strike; privilege indeed. 'You want to hear more story when we eat tonight? The final chapter?'

Two-for-Joy readily agreed. 'Ay! For defs story, oo tell, oo fin'sh Nestor story!'

'No,' said Harete on cue, speaking firmly but politely, school mistress to naughty child. 'It's a group story. We each only know a small part, so we have to take turns to tell it. Like a round-bottomed cup filled with wine, the story has to be passed from one of us to the other without ever being put down. We *all* tell the story. Understand?'

Two-for-Joy's face ruckled; perhaps he was struggling to envisage Harete's goblet, or maybe he was annoyed at the disruption to his planned killings. He scratched his groin ostentatiously, agreed, clicked out some new instructions. The details eluded me, the gist was: delay killing until story complete.

Harete's intervention had been perfect.

'Fud in ten mins, e'body,' Two-for-Joy announced.

'What are we going to do?' Harete whispered to me from the corner of her mouth.

'Sup with the devil,' I told her.

'We need a long spoon for that. Got one?'

'No. Only a short knife,' I said, thinking of the next difficulty.

Item two: the ropes. My knife was inside the doll inside the bin. Maxo maxo screw-up. One small plus point, we all had our hands tied in front of our bodies; the Fractions had recognised it would have been impossible for us to scramble over rocks if they'd tied them behind our backs.

As we walked on, I looked out for small, sharp stones, but saw none, only large chunks too big to conceal.

But I only needed to be lucky once.

Walking up front, Three-Blind-Mice spat out a cigarette he'd barely started, needing to whistle-click to his chief behind us. I waited until I drew level with the discarded fag, pretended to stumble, dropped my end of the bin, fell flat.

My face was over the cigarette. I picked it up with my lips, took it into my mouth. For seventeen years people had told me I was too lippy, was heading for a fat lip, was gobby. My mouth was going to save us all, and not a word would be spoken.

My twisty tongue turned the ciggie around, placed the burning tip *inside* my mouth. I sucked the whole thing in, so that the unlit end was flush with my teeth, then I plugged that into the gap where I'd lost a tooth.

I didn't want to smoke the ciggie. Don't smoke, never have, never will. Horrible habit.

I *reverse* smoked it. But only because I had to. Some folks

330

really do that, smoke with the lit end inside their mouth. That pub where Dad played darts, one of his pals did that; some people just can't wait for cancer to catch them, they have to chase after it like it's the last bus home. All I needed was to keep that glowing end alight for a few more minutes. My mouth was on fire. But I held fast. Perhaps the chillies had trained me, a different kind of heat, but pain is pain. I kept my lips shut, starving the foul thing of air, only occasionally parting them a tad to admit oxygen, let the smoke out. We all had fogging breath, so it didn't show.

When Two-for-Joy relented and passed around a water bottle, I could only pretend to drink. *Stay alive*, I beamed to the tiny flame, *your life is ours!*

The path broadened out into a circular patch of flat ground. The order was given, we made camp. Lonza and I dropped the wheelie bin on its side and all five of us collapsed around it, tired beyond any meaning of the word. Myristica's condition looked very delicate: she was hyperventilating, pale, her eyes unfocused.

I spat the cigarette from my blistered mouth into my cupped hands, tied together at the wrists. It was still alight – we had a fighting chance. The Fractions meanwhile built a camp fire. They'd brought along a sack of charcoal in the bin and supplemented it with branches broken from stunted trees we'd passed on the way. No mugs – they kept the small fire a good distance from us, beyond the range of the leash we were all secured to. We weren't going to benefit from any embers that popped out of the fire.

Thanks to my mouth-pouched tumour-tube, we didn't need

them.

Slowly, as unobtrusively as possible, I puffed air onto the cigarette stub. After each blow, I bent my fingers down and dabbed the glowing tip against the nylon rope, melting through it one strand at a time.

When Four-and-Twenty asked what we wanted taking from the wheelie bin to eat, I raised a few eyebrows by requesting the tin of Lupa's formula baby milk.

Lupa had no objections. 'Go ahead. Knock yourself out. I'm sick of the stuff,' she said.

'Prefer a nice tinned ham, would you?' chided Lonza.

Everyone else chose biscuits, a goody we'd never been allowed in the hanger, and easy to open and eat with tied hands. Once the food was removed, the bin was lashed shut again.

I didn't touch my dried milk.

For themselves, the Fractions erected a tripod of metal bars and hung from it a tureen of cannibal casserole to heat over their fire. As it steamed and stewed, they gleefully declaimed their love of what they called in Whistle-Click the 'Brthfgd': the Broth of God.

The ulcer sun threw in the towel and withdrew behind the bulk of abutting ranges; the evening grew dark; the Fractions' fire burned brightly. The three cutthroats squatted close around it, keeping their eyes and guns (two burp guns, one revolver) trained on us, stirring and supping all the while from their broth. They wouldn't shoot me; for once in my life I was valuable to someone. That was irrelevant. After Nonstop's death, I was determined that no more friends would die.

I continued to work on melting my rope, strand by strand.

Harete inaugurated the proceedings. I was in safe hands. Harete could be entrusted to lure the Fractions to the rayless heart of the labyrinth and abandon them there; she'd play the polestar, I'd wield the poleaxe.

Death by story.

'Gentledemons,' Harete said, relishing the moment as much as me. 'I believe we've an unfinished tale to conclude.'

Chapter 44

'A Stay of Execution, Part IV'
As told by Lex
As retold by Harete
As remembered by Mo

Simeon and Nestor conversed as they perched atop the rocky tower, now listing and swaying sickeningly.

'Listen,' Simeon spoke, 'until a few weeks ago I shared this pinprick needle of an island with two other men. One you have already met, the diverting Bosun Higgs. The other was a good friend of mine, a man whose crime was to author puns of such awfulness that people who heard them groaned themselves to death.

'He too was a killer?'

'Yes, although his conviction was not for murder, only for man's laughter. Anyway, one day a third person arrived. I was instantly suspicious.'

'I would have thought you would have welcomed new company,' said Nestor.

Simeon shook his head. 'My watchword has always been: better the devil you know.'

'Better! The devil, you know,' repeated Nestor uncertainly, the phrase being novel to him.

'No! Better the devil you know.'

'Better the devil. You know?'

'Hopeless! It matters not. The newcomer turned up in a deplorable, half-crazed condition. Within thirty minutes of his arrival he had beaten my pun-loving friend to death with a puffin, and after a few weeks on pentuple death row I was forced to exile him to the Island of Hextuple Disgrace.'

'Hextuple, did you say? Not "sextuple"?'

'We call it that to save on the sniggering. Now, before he was exiled, that murderer confessed to me his story. I shall now tell you it, in an effort to dissuade you from a fruitless search for the end, the place of ultimate exile or ultimate freedom. This then, is the story of that man, Yan Tan.'

With a curlicue of smoke, the final braid of the cord around my wrists gave way. My hands snapped free. I breathed one more gasp of life into the butt and applied the smouldering end to the rope stretched taut around the wheelie bin. The Fractions had noticed nothing, they were too absorbed in the story, rocking gently. Harete passed the round-bottomed cup to her left.

Myristica received it willingly. Her body was weak, but her

instincts were brighter than the thorny sparks that spritzed from the campfire. The night was full up, the scenery flats of the world were set close by: us, them, the fire. Nothing else existed. The sky was too cloud-bound for the marionette moon to show her face. Suited me, I wanted no witnesses. I was well up for it. I had a raging hate on, a hate storm that could melt rocks and boil seas.

Myristica spoke and we all plunged in, hostage and kidnapper united by twisty fantasy.

'The Story of Yan Tan'
As told by Simeon to Nestor
As retold by Lex
As re-retold by Myristica

Yan Tan was a peaceable and studious man, a craftsman who made diminutive furniture for the dolls' houses inside dolls' houses.

He was working alone one night – it was Holloween, the celebration of all things concave and empty – in the basement of his basement when a man came bursting in through the door. The man was clearly deranged, with foaming eyes, a swivelling mouth, torn clothes and, most noticeably, his right hand missing. He begged Yan Tan for water and food, and although he was very scared of his crazed visitor, Yan Tan gave him both. The meal was a robust repast consisting of soup-flavoured soup, toad-in-the-hole-in-the-toad-in-the-hole, and roast chicken flavour flavour flavour chicken wings.

At that point, Nestor was forced to break in. 'Whoa. What?'

'It's perfectly straightforward,' replied Simeon. 'You must have noticed how potato crisps never taste of the foods they claim to mimic. Roast chicken flavour crisps taste nothing like roasted chickens. Yet the flavour is a thing in itself, roast chicken flavour flavour. The meat was moistened with a sauce that attempted to emulate that peculiar taste. The jar therefore labelled it roast chicken flavour flavour flavour. You see?'

'I see,' said Nestor.

To drink, Yan Tan gave his guest a mug of Scotch, which as everyone knows is the juice extracted from Scotch eggs, Scotch pancakes and Scotch bonnet chillies. The drink it was that finally loosened the man's tongue.

'My name is Tethera Methera,' said the man whose name was Tethera Methera, 'and I have a shocking story to tell you.'

The rope around the bin burned through. I had to tear my own attention away from the fire and the story, pinch myself to concentrate. The bin lay on its side, the lid nearest to me, none of that by accident. I slipped my hand into the bin, groped around for Dolly, wormed out my knife. The blade was dangerously shiny. I smeared it over with the chocolate cream filling from a dropped biscuit, leaving only the edge of the blade clean.

Lonza took the story cup from his sister. He was restored to alertness, his hunter's eyes dilated. Cleverly, he leaned in towards the fire, simultaneously drawing the Fractions' focus away from me, and at the same time tensioning the rope that connected us, making it easier to cut. Everyone on the team knew what I was about now.

> 'The Story of Tethera Methera'
> As told by him to Yan Tan
> As retold by Simeon to Nestor
> As re-retold by Lex to Logan
> As re-re-retold by Lonza

I was an artist, specialising in painting pictures of people painting pictures of people painting pictures. The work required fastidious attention to detail because my pieces habitually sold for less money than those of a famous forger who had lately begun to fake my work, forcing me to paint in the style of someone copying myself.

This came second nature to me. At nights I played in a pop band called Internal Reflections, formed in tribute to some of the region's top tribute bands. I played lead guitar or double bass. On alternate evenings I dressed up as myself, put on a wig identical to my own hair, and rehearsed with an Internal

Reflections tribute band called Infernal Deflections. There, I played bismuth guitar or double turbot.

One particular night – it was the festival of Shalloween, the celebration of all things cursory and lacking in depth – I was working in my attic's attic's attic when I was roused by a knocking at the door (actually, on the cat flap set into the door built into the gate). Opening my window (to be precise, a pane within a skylight), I looked down and saw a lunatic, who told me his name was Pip Sethera. I cursed, then cursed again – re-cursed, in fact.

'Is that the conman Pip Sethera, the retired door-to-door door salesman?' I yelled. 'Not to mention purveyor of high-visibility camouflage clothing, motorised exercise bicycles and sieves for separating fact from fiction?'

But he said not, that I must have been thinking of his brother's brother's brother (who was a full-time part-time unemployed careers advisor when not working the day shift as a night watchman). Anyway, he had urgent news to impart to me from a visitor he had received.

The knife made short work of the rope connecting me to Lonza. I leaned backwards, pretending to stretch my legs, and rapidly nicked apart the sections of rope strung between the others.

The story cup returned to Harete. I was mightily impressed with Lonza's contribution. Had he composed and memorised that in the Facility, or had it been made up on the fly?

The Fractions were spellbound, their guns no longer pointing at us but aimed any which way. Two-for-Joy was counting on his fingers to keep track of the tiers of the story. His brow was incised with deep folds.

The plan was working. He was lost in the labyrinth.

'E's gar, gar complica'ed!' he muttered. 'Ay is losin' ma mind!'

Harete continued.

Well, this went on for some long time, as you can imagine. But eventually Tethera Methera explained to Yan Tan what he had learned from Pip Sethera (who had been told it by Lethera Hovera (who had received the news from Dovera Dick (who had been educated by Yan-a-Dick Tan-a-Dick))), all about the great execution fraud, how his country pretended to have capital punishment but did not. He went on to describe how each of the islands of exile continued the hoax, banishing prisoners to ever smaller and more remote locations.

'Once I knew this, my life could not continue as it had,' said Tethera Methera. 'I became seized by the idea of revealing how far this continued, and where the mercy ran out. I murdered Pip Sethera (the killer of Lethera Hovera (the slayer of Dovera Dick (who had so cruelly dispatched Yan-a-Dick Tan-a-Dick))), confessed, was sentenced to death and, when the day of my execution came, I was exiled to the Island of Disgrace. Immediately upon disembarking from the boat, I murdered the man who came to greet me, confessed and was sentenced to death. And so it continued!'

'How far did you get? ' asked Yan Tan.

Tethera Methera rubbed his bleary eyes. 'The Island of Novemtrigenuple Disgrace,' he said. 'That's thirty-nine, in case you're wondering.'

'Just out of interest, what was that like?'

'A cavern set in a cliff of guano on an island made of solid acid floating within the caldera of an active volcano. In the cave, it was knee-deep in boiling pig dung.'

'Knee deep? Could have been worse, I suppose,' said Yan Tan.

'It was. The custom among the inhabitants was to stand on their heads.'

'Oo stop, stop plis!' blurted Two-for-Joy, looking fit to rupture his overtaxed bean of a brain. 'Girly, a lost, total lost! Is oos story? Oo spik now?'

Harete explained. 'I am relating to you Yan Tan's account of what he was told by Tethera Methera, as conveyed by Simeon to Nestor, within the story Lex is telling Logan. Do please keep up!'

Slim-witted Three-Blind-Mice was struggling also. 'Is ol var twizzy turny,' he grumbled.

Back to Lonza. As each speaker finished his or her turn, they relaxed back into the swirling shadows and allowed me to bump fists with them, ideal cover for a hasty slashing of the loops tying their own hands.

341

Yan Tan grimaced. 'Yeuch. And, again, just to humour me, what was the fake sign on the door of the execution room that you passed through on your way there?'

'The sign had read "Lethal Injection Cell". Needless to say, when the governor saw that I was looking at it fearfully, he slid the letters along and rearranged it –'

'Let me guess,' interrupted Yan Tan. 'I should say it became "Let Hal Inject I once, ll", an advertisement for the tenth sequel to a popular film about a mad doctor called Harry with a penchant for performing controversial inoculations?'

'Something along those lines,' admitted Tethera Methera.

Tethera Methera was not yet finished. He detailed how Pip Sethera had told him a secret before he had been killed – that the island you were sentenced to depended on which hand you had used to commit your crime.

'Remember those pretend death cells I told you about? Well each has two doors that lead from it. If you enacted your murder with your right hand, you are made to go through the right-hand door and off to one island. If it was the left you used, you are taken through the other door and the boat takes you to a different island.

'Pip had a theory that as long as you always murdered with the same hand – it did not matter which, provided you never swapped midway – you would eventually reach the end, whatever that might be. From then on, I always carried the gun, knife or rock in my right hand when killing my prey, beginning with Pip himself.

Harete flashed me a look, half glare, half despair. *How much longer?*

Myristica, her second go. Her voice was the quietest; the Fractions had to lean forwards to isolate her words from the retorts of splitting wood. Distracted, they didn't see me extricate Lupa's wrists. That was it, all ropes cut. Still my signal event was pending. I was good and tight now, keyed up.

'But Pip was wrong. During that thirty-ninth exile, I raided the governor's office and found a book that logged all the islands. I spent weeks studying that volume, tracing right-hand-only routes and left-hand-only routes between the islands, but never could I work out how to reach the end.'

Yan Tan was fascinated. 'But was there really an end? Or was that too an illusion?' he asked breathlessly.

'It was real! The ultimate island was called the Nub, or the Redoubt of Doubt. The book described it as a place of all-consuming fire, the hearth of matter.'

Tethera Methera went on to say how the discovery had thrown him into a rage. 'I was boiling mad. I had wasted my life taking all these wrong turns, and I was still no nearer to reaching the Nub, except perhaps for the possibility of encountering it by accident. And what use is that?

'In my wanton fury, I cut off my own right hand so that I could never use it again, and determined to retrace my steps, from now on only killing my poor victims with my left hand. But it has been a failure! From the islands I have been deported to since that point, I appear to have been going round in circles. I am lost, lost!'

Three-Blind-Mice removed the cooking pot and kicked away the iron tripod.

That's what I'd been waiting for.

The action was necessary – but not sufficient.

Smart Harete winked at me; I knew she had gleaned the finessing touch I still awaited. Her third and final turn. She dropped her voice, spoke quieter even than Myristica had. The Fractions craned forwards.

Yan Tan was enraptured by the idea of the Nub and the maze of islands that led to it. When he heard that Tethera Methera had not thought to bring the map book with him, he was giddy with anger. He murdered Tethera Methera (with his right hand), and decided that he would make it to the Island of Novemtrigenuple Disgrace, steal the book and solve the mystery for himself.

'And so that's what Yan Tan was doing when he came to this island. Barely an eighth of the way even to find the book, and no knowing how far he was from his destination,' said Simeon. 'Imagine the slaughter!'

Nestor was saddened and depressed by Simeon's saga. 'So there really is no easy way to the Nub. No plan, or system, not even bloody ruthlessness will get you there. Only chance.'

Nestor said goodbye to Simeon, took from him stores of puffin-muffins to sustain him on his now-pointless journey and shinned back down the sea stack to his waiting boat. He revved up the engine and set off, but without direction or purpose. Hardly had he set sail when the sea stack toppled and fell into the ocean behind him, undoubtedly killing Simeon and Bosun Higgs.

The days at sea passed by in a daze, at sea. His supplies exhausted, Nestor fell unconscious, but the boat carried on regardless, driving itself ever onwards across the ocean.

Onwards it sped, increasing in speed, assisted by submarine currents and waves and wind.

Onwards it sped, skating over the surface of the sea, banking left then right.

Until finally, with a smashing, crunching sound –

Harete stopped speaking mid-sentence and turned to me. Her timing was faultless.

The Fractions had their heads pressed close together, and so near the fire it was a wonder their eyebrows weren't smouldering.

'Garn!' shouted Two-for-Joy, pounding his palm with his

fist. 'End! Bland boy end story, mus' know end!'

Still pretending my hands were tied at the wrists, I picked up the open tin of dried milk.

'The story cup passes to me!' I said.

The Fraction's three ugly pumpkin faces were lit as much from within by eagerness as by the fire from outside. They wanted their final helping of the story, they wanted it so very much: the pay-off, the release, the exit from the labyrinth!

Stories as drugs – anaesthetics, narcotics – a lesson from my first escape.

Food as weapons, a lesson from the Spiral.

I hurled the entire contents of the tin straight onto the glowing bed of the fire.

The great cloud of super-fine milk powder detonated instantly. It could have been petrol, so powerful was the fireball; the force took even me by surprise. With their faces so close to the glowing charcoal, and unshielded now that the tureen was gone, all three Fractions received the full treatment, a socking great uppercut of billowing, white-hot flame.

Two-for-Joy was blown upwards, backwards. Three-Blind-Mice and Four-and-Twenty Blackbirds hurled themselves aside, both transformed into flaring torches; their gaudy, hotchpotch clothes had never been selected for reasons of health or safety.

Lonza flowed through the air like a jet of steam from a ruptured boiler. The wheelie bin was under his arms and his violet eyes were blazing so brightly they seemed to light a cone in front of him. He rammed one of the burning Fractions in the chest with the bin, sent him rolling down the slope; how steep or deep it was we could not tell. A second Fraction hared off down the path, back the way we'd come, trailing sparks and trollish oaths, his ringlets and ribbons and feathers all well alight.

Two-for-Joy never stood again; the back of his neck must have struck a stone. His legs kicked, his arms thrashed, he could not right himself. Lonza was drunk on djinn, his tonic. On its return stroke, the battering ram became a piledriver. Lonza brought the bin down vertically onto Two-for-Joy's head like he was mashing a scorpion with a length of two-by-four. The heavy handgun flew loose, skittering into the dark beyond the range of the firelight.

Down came the bin. With each strike, Two-for-Joy and Lonza each cried one word.

'Muss!'	....	'Batter!'
'Know!'	....	'The!'
''ow!'	....	'Devil!'
'Story!'	....	'You!'
'End!'	....	'Know!'

And that was that. A bolt of cold air gusted onto the fire, and in the boosted shine we saw Lonza nodding with the satisfaction of a job well done. For one second I felt a puff of pity for Two-for-Joy and revulsion at his violent downfall. But only for that long.

Lonza wasn't done. He picked up a dropped burp gun and sprayed the killing machine down the slope where the first Fraction had rolled, then along the path after his retreating compadre, sweeping it from side to side until the magazine was spent.

Lupa shouted, 'Are they dead? Did you stiff 'em?'

'Don't know! Too dark to see,' Lonza replied. He was our skipper now, pumped and authoritative. 'Grab the bin,' he said, 'we've got to get far, far away from here.'

We didn't argue. Harete piled stones over the campfire and we raced into the night. It felt like a beginning, but I'd forgotten the Fartherland was twinned with Twist City, that as with a coiled rope, the end and the beginning can lie side by side, confusable.

This was an end.

Chapter 45

Lonza led; his big-cat night vision was superb.

'The Fractions' hideout is only a day's walk away, they must have scouts and patrols,' he warned us. 'We need to cross these hills. We'll be safe over the other side.'

Hills? That was an understatement. And the logistics were horrendous. Once we left the campsite and the path we were properly in the mountains; what faced us was more rock climbing than fell walking. One thing was plain from the off: the ordeal would be well beyond what Lupa and Myristica could manage. Lonza had to choose whom he carried. He vacillated, torn.

'Ya got to look after the baby, bro,' Myristica told him. 'It's the contents that matter, not the packaging.'

'I'll carry you, Meg,' I said. But Lonza had other ideas.

'No,' he flatly insisted. 'You and Harete have to carry that bin. All the food and water and blankets are in it, and Meg's pills. We need all that stuff; could be days before we reach safety, there's nothing to eat or drink out here.'

'I'll make a bag out of my trackie top,' I suggested.

'You'll never be able to carry enough, and you'll freeze once we start to climb. We take the bin. Sorry, Meg.'

That must have been a tough call for Lonza to make. For a girl in her deteriorating condition, a two-day hike in the mountains held no promise but suffering.

Myristica understood. 'Wish Nonstop was still here,' was all she said. Whenever the ground flattened out, Harete and I let Myristica lie on top of the wheelie bin as we carried it between us, ferrying her like it was a stretcher.

I don't know where we went, what direction, anything. There was a bunch of up, a deal of down, scabs of scarpering over escarpments, circling cirques, feeling our way around cwms and cols and corries and quarries.

Splotchy eyes, see? Or rather, I didn't, not well. And the star-starved night was dark, black as barge hulls, black as hearses, black as bin bags.

Lupa clung like a monkey to Lonza's back. His strength was inexhaustible. Unnervingly so: the battery was back in the lad all right, but the wrong type, the voltage too high, the juice too rich.

'I know these mountains,' he fizzed hours later as we fed and watered ourselves, as much to lighten the load as to slake our thirst. 'Meg's too young to remember, but we used to visit here on holidays years ago, back when we were a family. There's all sorts around these parts, secret military bases, the works. Doesn't surprise me the Fractions are holed up in some narrow canyon, these hills could hide anything. There's a valley for us too, our own dale. I know it.'

'What's come over him?' I whispered to Harete. Lonza's charismatic transformation was eerie. Nothing seemed capable of discouraging him, not from walking or talking; the djinn must have carried Nonstop's ghost on the pillion.

'Us! You and me, Lupa, and our baby, a new life! And you, Meg – the clean mountain air will cure you in no time. Live with us, Harete, Mo. Can you make a bow and arrows or a canoe? I'll teach you. We'll hunt for rabbits, fish for salmon, plant crops. We'll find an enclave, a land within a land. We'll *found* it. On love!'

We packed up and scrambled after him, neither disagreeing nor believing.

Daybreak. The underbellies of the clouds changed from molasses to malt extract to pale barley stroked with green. Then the barley thinned and parted, vouchsafing to us a view of the pure blue beyond. The blue fuelled Lonza to still greater extremes, re-tensioned the mainspring of his joy.

'Look at that magnificent sky, Mo!' he commanded, hands on hips, standing on a boulder with his chest thrown out. He'd been posing there for ten minutes already, waiting for the rest of us wheezing sloggers to catch up. I did look. It truly was magnificent: the barren mountains and the wide sky were staggeringly beautiful. I was pulling the wide-mouthed, slot-eyed face of a long distance runner crossing the tape. I tried to reply, but only bloodstained spit made it through the portcullis of saliva strands.

'There's no narrator to define us and confine us, no Lex or Logan. We've reached the top level at last, and from now on only we tell our stories!' he boomed. Once a panther, by then Lonza had transfigured into a windmill, an imposing black tower with madly waving arms, milling golden, wheaten words between his teeth.

He jumped down, slung Lupa over his shoulder and strode off with long, confident strides and long, confident cries. 'My child will know nothing but happiness and freedom!'

Lonza was beginning to frighten me.

Harete was supporting the rear end of the wheelie bin. 'He's amazing!' she laughed. 'We're finally seeing the leopard unfettered, the real Lonza. I always sensed he was in there, Mo, like a sculptor can see the finished statue in the raw marble. And he'll take care of us all. What a father he'll make. We'll farm and fight, not run away! I only wish . . . oh, I wish . . .'

She censored her mouth, laundered her words, but her muscles broke the embargo. Almost imperceptibly she yawed towards him; her mouth pouted out a puff of air, a shallow projection onto the real axis of a far more absorbing event occurring in her imagination.

'Too high,' I said under what was left of my breath, not certain who I was thinking of. 'Heading for a fall.'

Harete hadn't had her burn out, like I'd had mine the day before. For her, Lonza was still hidden behind a screen of her own constructions; he was an illustrious illusion rich in sweet mystique. I spat on my ripped hands, hefted my end of the bin and shunted her to get walking.

We started to ascend another mountain, a whopper. As we went uphill, Myristica's condition went downhill. I don't know how high we were by then, if the air had grown too thin for her heart and lungs, but she weakened by the minute. When the slope grew too steep she had to dismount from our wheelie bin and toil with us on foot, suffering terribly. The angle and the loose, dry stones underfoot made for hard going: trudge two steps up, slide one down. Three hours of that we had, roasted by the sun, chilled by the wind, tanned by both.

Harete took to dragging the bin solo and I carried Myristica, fireman style.

'Had. My. Burn. Out,' I confided, rationing my words, one per step.

'How d'ya feel?'

'Empty. *Good* empty. Clean. Free. Weight. Off. My. Back.'

I stopped and we fell together, flannelling our faces with stones. 'After the forest fire, when the deadwood's all burned away, the soil's fertile. There's room for new growth, carpets of bluebells,' said Meg. She wiped the hair from my face and smiled. I smiled back, thinking: *kind of pretty, I guess*.

'Don't want growth. Enjoying the emptiness,' I told her. 'Never want to feel that way about anyone again.'

'Never?'

'Never, Meg. Rather die.'

Myristica began to laugh. 'Oh, Mo. It's impossible though, isn't it?'

'We'll manage. You're not so heavy –'

'Not *this*. Life. We're all stuck in the cells of our selves, doing solitary, banging on the walls, whistling and clicking like mad. But no one in the other cells understands us. We can't explain the code we're using because we can only speak in that code. Life is impossible, Mo. No one can know another.'

When I tried to answer her, she put a finger over my lips and smiled at me again. I lifted her and we slogged on. During our next rest I asked her to clarify, but she felt limp and

353

unresponsive and sicked up down my back.

The five of us bunched together. To the right of us yawned a practically vertical drop that terminated in a circular tarn. The water in the tarn was prison denim blue and so clear I could see all the way to the bottom, deep beneath its surface. And to the left, beyond the sheer drop on that side, a rolling expanse of arid mountains. Everything was rounded off by spreads-straight-from-the-fridge yellow sunshine and a sky so adorably bright and blue it made you want to renounce the memory of all other colours and go and live with it in a blue bungalow and farm blue chickens.

A bouquet of exquisite happiness swirled over my palate, a flavour I had all but forgotten.

For the final push onto the razor-back ridge along the top we had to pass the bin vertically between us; at times we were almost standing on each other's heads. When I happened to look upwards, I found I was staring straight up Lupa's baggy top where it had come untucked from her leggings and was flapping free.

Lonza looked too.

Lonza saw too.

I saw him see.

Ensconced safely in the attic of my head, lying in a hammock knitted from my nerves, the Kernel hooted with laughter.

{The twist! Oh, what a twist!}

We all made it onto the windy ridge. *Summited*, as mountaineers would say. Except this was a false peak, a swindle. The Fractions had never induced in me such foreboding as I felt just then. What had I always believed?

Natural survivors spell trouble.

My sore feet began to drag of their own accord.

Scab, scab, scab.

We'd have to wait, I knew that; so big a hope lofted so high and so fast might take several minutes to return to Earth. There'd be no soft landing.

Dawdling, I focused on a trio of gate-crashing anomalies that had wandered in underneath catastrophe's mantle. Those people, for instance, those women, marching in single file up that side ridge, coming our way. Who were they? They were wearing flappy red robes and carrying banners painted with pictures of . . . wheels? Lusty singing reached me:

'*Daughter of the fecund prairie,*
Virgin, as was Holy Mary.
Crushed by Satan's rubber heel,
Risen 'neath strong limbs of steel.'

An imperious voice interrupted the singing. 'Sing up, Sister Massey. Watch your step, Sister Ferguson. The pilgrimage of the pylons will be ruined if you fall and break a leg!'

And the rock wall over yonder, hewn into titanic faces. That was worth a peep, surely? Three of the faces were of stern, po-faced men, the sculpted granite probably no less inflexible than their living features had been. The fourth face was that of a woman, and looked gentler than the others. *I've just put the kettle on*, rather than *I've just carpet-bombed a major industrial province.*

Check: *has it begun? No. Not yet.*

And what was that, far away to the left and below me, on a hill-fringed plateau set within a succulent swale, the only

355

green visible anywhere in the vista? It had been hidden in mist a minute earlier, but the veil had lifted. A shimmering sapphire, a jewel the size of a circus big top. How divine!

Yet? No.

The sapphire was remarkable, as was the procession of pylons that queued obediently before it. Six sets of electricity cables ran along the distant valley before converging on that giant gemstone, parallel lines brought together to deliver the power; or perhaps that was where the lines began, they were not converging but radiating outwards? Either way: paradise, that's what I was glimpsing; a giant jewel set in a verdant vale.

I stopped, because ten paces ahead of me it had started, it was happening. Re-entry. Explosive fragmentation. Fallout.

Lonza beheld Lupa and said, 'Why, Lupa? Why did you do it?' Then he punched her, threw a big, black paw at her temple. Smash. Lupa fell down, Lonza booted her in the belly. Her top tore, and the under layers came loose, and all the padding that she'd used to fake her pregnancy tumbled out.

The rangy wolf bayed and leapt up, her hands full of stones. 'Ya dumb rinser, whydya think? To survive! For the food the Peacemakers gave me, and all for no work. My food kept your veg of a sister alive too, so don't come high and mighty with me!

'Oh, I really was pregnant at the start,' she continued, her thin face warping with anger. 'But I lost it, two days after you blundered us into the Facility. It was a bloody mess. A BLOODY MESS, there in the drain. And you never even noticed. I hated you then, I hated you so much. You didn't never love me; you loved it, my bump.'

Lonza staggered around, clutching his head, a man poisoned

and choking at the same time.

'You venal bitch!' he screamed. 'My child, our child! Our new lives, everything . . . all gone. I had to kill Nonstop because of you!'

'Good! I'm glad! You'd rather it had been me, wouldn't you? So you could shack up with *her*. Hard cheese, as that fatso would have said. Pah!'

Lonza lunged at Lupa, gripped her head in his hands, twisted it around, peeled back her eyelids with his thumbs and forced her to look over at us. 'I'm the one that's mis-carried. I could have been carrying Meg up here, instead of you. Look at her!' he yelled. 'Look how ill she is now; that's your fault, you sewer-slag!'

Myristica had shrivelled to a hunched-up ball. Harete wrapped herself around her, covering her ears, shrouding her from the wind and the cold and the fight. The singing women in red robes had crossed onto the main ridge by then, holding their banners aloft.

'*For Icarus she felt great loss,*
Yet slew the three-dog Kerberos
On wings she rose o'er fence of razor
Moth's companion, praise her, praise her!'

The pageant's incantations distracted Lonza. The wolf fought free; she and the leopard tore into each other. They slashed about with fist and tooth and nail and heel, lurching critically close to the precipices on either side.

Lupa sprang back; she snatched open the bin lid and delved inside. Lonza reared up, armed with a rock, poised to pulp her skull.

One bang, quieter than you'd have thought from a revolver as heavy as Two-for-Joy's. Lupa must have retrieved the gun and stowed it in the bin when we'd not been paying attention.

They both stood back, equally stunned.

'I'm sorry, Lonza, I really am. I l-love you, ever s-so much. I do,' stuttered Lupa, tears racing down her shredded cheeks. 'Only, I'm never clever or brave or pretty, not like her. Don't we get a share of love as well, the common and the ugly? I wanted that baby so much. And I wanted you. My bump was the only hold I ever had over you; I never wanted to admit it was gone. That was all.'

Lonza was standing quietly with both hands pressed tightly around the soggy gash in his abdomen. The shot had quartered him; it was an unsurvivable injury. He trembled all over, his teeth chattered, blood was pouring down his leg and soaking into the meagre mountain soil. The cold wind picked at him, he winced with each cuff.

'I know, Lulu,' he said shakily, but without rancour. 'I understand. Come here, Meg. Come to your Lonny. Hug me.'

Myristica did as bidden, emerging from underneath Harete and stepping to be by her brother's side. She put her arms around him. I looked on, unable to marry the passion play to the surroundings, the bright sun, the blue sky, the chanting women. A hideous inertia overcame me, total muscular paralysis. I had to crack long stays of incredulity just to blink.

'I'm going now,' said Lonza. 'Feel awful warm. You'll stick by me, won't you, Meg?'

'Yes, Lonza, I want to,' said Myristica. 'You've always been the best possible brother. I know you'll always look after me.'

Harete always could read faster than me. 'Don't do it!' she implored them. 'We'll look after Meg, we'll get her treatment, we'll nurse her, we'll –'

Lonza lumbered to the left edge of the ridge, supported by his sister. 'Only from duty, Harete. Not from love. It's not enough. Without love, it's . . . nothing,' he said.

They staggered on together; they were one fidget from the lip of the cliff.

'But I love you, Lonza!' screamed Harete. 'I'm in love with you. Stop! STOP!'

'No, Harete!' said Lonza, hard to hear over the cracking of his clothes in the wind. 'You have no idea what love is. An inside flossy feeling, a permanent birthday morning tingle? Love isn't that, it's changing someone's soiled underwear for the ninth time in a day, wiping the sick from their chin, and being prepared to do it forever. You don't know the first thing about love.'

Myristica spoke. 'But I do, and I love you, Mo, have done since you rescued me the first time. You're a cracking lad. Sorry you didn't wise to it, sorry you couldn't respond. Doesn't matter anyway. You'll understand, soon.'

When they stepped in tandem off the cliff, they hovered for a tenth of a second, like two people standing in an invisible lift.

Then they dropped.

Silence. *Scrunch, bump*. A long wait. *Plash*, almost like a sneeze. Atishoo, atishoo, we all fall down.

Gone.

Me too; I annulled the union of mind and body, adopted a new viewpoint.

359

The three meat statues on the ridge remained where they were, swaying. The wind blew strong and cold, but they showed no inclination for stirring, for speaking, for emoting.

The medium-sized one with a burned face and a headband decided to take his leave of the other two. Without urgency he reorganised the contents of a wheelie bin that stood incongruously by him. He emptied out three big cardboard boxes, and puzzled for a while at what he found inside: hundreds of empty tablet wrappers, but no tablets, only powdery, milk-white traces of crushed-up pills.

His next act was to diligently remove and drain a number of plastic water bottles and stow the empties back inside the bin. This completed, he lay the contraption flat and climbed into it, feet first.

The other statues made no move or sound in reaction to the activity, they were both fixated on a spot to the left.

'Go to those marching women,' the medium-sized one called out from inside his smelly rubbish bin. 'They'll look after you.'

With his arms, the skinny boy propelled the bin to the precipice overlooking the tarn. He pushed off. As the bin started to slide along, he pulled shut the lid with a length of rope. In imitation of his friends a minute beforehand who had departed over the opposite side, the bin cannoned over the edge of the cliff. A passing gull heard a boy scream out his brains inside the bin; said she wasn't certain, but she thought it sounded like a war cry.

'Death to love!'

Chapter 46

A bomb made from milk powder, a lock pick from a clock hand, why not an escape capsule from a wheelie bin?

I don't do self-murder. The electric fence, well, that had been an exception. Extenuating circumstances, m'lud. Faced with the same, doubled, I was proud to report that I had no thoughts to repeat the failed experiment, however it must have looked to those I left behind. Remind me again who they were? Just some people I once hung with.

Re-entry was a thrill and a half. The slope had looked smooth as glass from the top, but sliding over it in the bin I realised it was exceedingly rough. Once, terrifyingly, the bin swivelled around, leaving me in danger of falling out through the opening, but it righted just before it skipped off an outcrop and launched itself through the air.

Free fall.

One one thousand, two one thousand – I flashed back to jumps I'd made during other escapes, leaps from walls around the Institute and the Establishment. This put all those to shame.

Six one thousand –

Splashdown!

With a boom like a cupped hand clapping a plump buttock, the escape capsule smacked onto the surface of the blue tarn. The bin's blunt end did not make for smooth entry into the water, braking was severe. The deceleration packed me to the foot of the bin but, as planned, the empty bottles crumpled and soaked up the damage. The bin must have punched under to great depth; the sides bulged inwards as the water pressure squeezed them. Buoyant with trapped air, the bin rocketed upwards. I thumped open the lid and swam out. I swim like a concert piano, but the edge was no more than twelve strokes away; the tarn wasn't really much more than a deep rock pool. I climbed onto a slippery shelf, fainted.

Don't worry about Dolly-with-one-arm. I'd poked her down the sleeve of my tracksuit; she was looking after my knife again.

The sun dried me out. I wandered off. Like Nestor, I had no idea where I was going, didn't care. Didn't look back up the cliff, didn't see any stick figures waving at me, didn't hear a shout reverberating from the cliffs, 'Mo-mo-mo-mo-mo-mo-mo-mo-mo-mo-mo-mo . . .'

I plunged into some pine woods, blundered around, freer and happier than I'd been for . . . than I'd ever been.

TO DO:
Nothing!

'Death to love!' I shouted. That was my battle cry, my slogan, my catchphrase, my jingle. Wasn't it a do-dah though? That thing, where you say the same thing twice. A Tortoise-ology. Because love was death. So 'death to love' was like saying 'nine equals nine'. Love *was* death. And enslavement. What had it ever done for me? Love was a maddening tune you couldn't exorcise from your head; love was the sharp, familiar tang of cack under your fingernails, resistant to soap and scrubbing.

Of all the escapes I'd ever completed, this was my finest and most necessary to date, I concluded.

Coasting in neutral, I ambled downhill along a dried stream bed that wound its way through the sunny forest. From a high tree, a tonal irregularity caught my eye. Annoying, because I was no longer in a mood for anything of mine to be trapped. I looked up.

Nuns.

Nuns in a tree.

Chapter 47*

Full circle.

That figures, I decided after minutes of static contemplation. Hadn't someone told me recently that the valleys hid every kind of perversity? The creased mountain landscape evidently harboured more secret societies than there were nits in my tousled hair, all close by and unaware of each other: the Fractions' Domain, the Establishment, others? I really wasn't surprised at all; spirals and loops and other figures of hate were looming large in my life. Nonstop had lectured of particles being whizzed around in circles, becoming more and more energised with each revolution, before crashing together. Perhaps I was such a particle.

Shock over, I calmed down and walked on, threading my way through the crash debris. I looked out for the airliner's food trolley, but did not see it. Perhaps the rats had eaten it whole. The hot, dry forest was still and deathly silent. Guardedly I scanned the sky for drones, shielding my face with my hand.

An hour later, I bumbled onto a road at the edge of the woods. Not wishing to travel on a highway in broad daylight, I sought out a hollow tree and curled up inside.

I slept longer than intended; it was late evening when I awoke. Bad, because only during the day could I see where the defunct spots in my vision were, and adjust for them by moving my head. At night, I wasn't able to see what I wasn't able see. I rolled out of my woody bunk and set off along the road. Last time, I remembered we had headed right, and that had led eventually to the Facility. I swivelled left.

Rumble, rumble. The sound came from behind me. I spun around, stared, saw nothing, walked on. Nothing could not hurt me.

{A double negative!}

Therefore . . . therefore something could hurt me?

RUMBLE, RUMBLE.

Impact: the nothing, now a something, batted me square in the back, very hard, very heavy, very metal.

I did a roly-poly barrel roll that took me a hundred paces along the road, didn't have time to swear. *Road kill*, I flash-thought, centrifuging wildly. I was down on the pavement; the something was over the top of me. A hiss: air-brakes, a door opening, stampeding feet, exploratory dowels of white torchlight.

Shouty people took hold of me, dragged me out from under the . . . some kind of vehicle; it must have been coasting stealthily downhill with no lights and the engine turned off.

Torch beams rubbed me over, hardy hands patted me down, testing my hurt, miraculously finding only grazes and bruises. I submitted, and tipped back my head to study the front of the vehicle. It was as big as a bus. It *was* a bus. Across the front of the bus were unfamiliar words in an unfamiliar script:

WOBITE TIBbVbX.

No, upside down. And reversed, to be read in a rear-view mirror. Two flips were needed to make sense of it: MOBILE LIBRARY.

I'd been flattened by a library! A scabbing bookstore on wheels!

'Are you librarians?' I groggily asked. None of the shouty people ringing me looked much like book lenders. Bookmakers, perhaps, or their debt collectors. Solid youths in bat-black paramilitary gear. Illuminated by the cab's interior light shining out through the windscreen I spied the kids' close-cropped heads, bulled belts, ball-buster boots. The spit and polish and doormat haircuts said 'hard nuts'.

'The oodyasay?' laughed Youth One, the coconut-headed teenager nearest to me. 'We're not from no Libraria, pal, we're not poxing foreigners. We're the Mothodists.'

My grog dispersed. One word had acted as finings. He'd said '*the* Mothodists', not just 'Mothodists'. These people weren't followers of my ex-friend's cult, they were the organisers! Could that mean – could Moth himself be here?

'MOTH!' I shouted, unable to contain myself. 'MOTH, MOTH!'

'Right! Wanna join?' perked up Youth Two, impressed by my enthusiasm. 'You get a bostin' uniform. Bonza togs. And we've stacks of grub; we get it all for free from a place near here. We need fit youngsters, see, we're the mission militant and martial. Come and join us!'

'I . . .'

'Here comes the gaffer. Talk it over.'

I sat upright, rigid as a nail, my many pains deferred for later enjoyment. Wobbling alongside the bus came four more chunky teens. They were transporting a cobbled-together sedan chair. The long handles were scaffolding poles and the passenger compartment an old coin-operated photo booth. The porters reverentially lowered the litter made of litter to the road, facing the curtained-off entrance towards me.

One shaved Sherpa pulled a coin from his – whoops, *her* – pocket, dropped it in the slot, yanked a handle. The photo booth's timer began to whirr and tick, counting down.

'His eminent munificence and munificent eminence, the Alderman Paracelsus Al-Hakim Hyssop,' proclaimed the burly girl, stamping to attention. 'Acclaimed Archimandrite, Confirmed Bachelor of Herbal Sciences, Universal Man, Blessed Guide and Guru of Mothodists and Mothlims, the Purging Surgeon, Customary Excisor of Apostasy.'

Alderman Hyssop?

{The man collects names like a hedgehog picks up fleas. 'Alderman' and 'Al-Hakim' both mean elder or wise man . . . hyssop, a purgative herb. The oil can cause seizures. The rest is piffle.}

Not Moth, then. Or could it be? In times of war, names were plastic, titles elastic, identities spastic.

A boyish gloved hand tweaked aside the fabric of the booth's curtain, sufficient for the passenger to see me, not enough for me to see him. The legs and shoes beneath the curtain gave nothing away. Except the trouser hems were concertinaed onto the tops of the shoes, no geeky, sock-filled cut-off. Ridiculous, yet I knew: not Moth.

'Yes. Oh, but *yes*!' gloated a thin voice. Dry and papery, the voice would have made excellent kindling, or bedding for a hamster. The voice rustled on. 'Such abundant fortune! Such sweet, rarefied kismet! In this night we give our thanks to most auspicious providence,' it said. The words clashed with the voice, too fruity, too studied.

'Does he join us, Alderman Hyssop?' asked Youth Three. 'Is he Mothodist material?' Neither of them deigned to consult me. I couldn't run – I had the bus to my back, the booth to my front and Mothodists all around me. I wanted to, though. The day had meant to be the first day in a commitment-free, desire-free life. For seventeen years I'd been as popular as lumps in trumps. Suddenly, roller-skating witches and boxed hermits couldn't get enough of me, but not for my sake, for theirs. Harete hadn't wanted me, Myristica had; no, *don't know those people, don't know those names, push them back down, bottle them up, salt them, pickle them, forget, forget.*

'He joins!' rasped the Alderman from inside his litter. 'He must.'

'Shall I prepare his uniform, his membership number?'

The booth's clockwork timer was still tick-tick-ticking; I could hear the coin rattling in the mechanism.

'I know his number already. I have known it for a long time.'

'Your eminence?'

'This boy's number is eight hundred and sixty-five.'

The penny dropped, a bell rang. From behind the curtain pulsed the camera flash.

Eight six five. My inmate number from the Institute.

Funny, how of all the kids and teachers you ever live with

through school, in later years you only ever seem to bump into the ones you really despised. I'm translating experiences, being something of an education-evader myself, but I'm sure you know how it goes: never the goofy kid with braces who happily let you copy his work in return for a packet of nudey playing cards, never the gruff-but-kindly caretaker who let you watch his portable TV in the boiler room. The ones you collide with are the deputy headmaster with the murky past and the abiding loathing of 'your sort', or the in-bred, too-tall twins who extorted lunch money, armed with a metal ruler.

I deliberately deliberated on such matters as Youths One to Four jury-rigged a branding iron, pulled down my trackie trousers and seared my buttocks with my old Institute number: eight six five.

The pain was pronounced and prolonged, so was the bacon sizzle and smell of charring flesh. At the time, I thought it the most unspeakable agony I'd ever endured in my seventeen dog years; I screamed so hard I almost ruptured myself.

Compared to the horror that was to befall me a few hours later, it was nothing, nothing at all; just another everyday pain in the backside.

Chapter 48

Entombed in the matrix of night, the Kernel spoke to me in a dream. *No! Mustn't pander to him. He doesn't exist.* I mean, I dreamed the Kernel was speaking to me.

{To do: stay a few weeks with these Mothodists; wait until my period of confinement is at an end and I can –}

'Hey! You don't control the to-do list, that's my job.'

{I can maintain the list if I want. It's as much mine as yours.}

'Stay with the Mothodists! Are you out of my mind?'

{Not yet.}

'You're a . . . back-seat driver, that's what you are, Kernel.'

{And you're a back-street skiver! Be grateful for my involvement in your life. Who dulled the pain of you rolling along the road, and of having your rump branded? Me!}

'Fine. Thanks for that. But what is it you need to do, head-pest?'

{Gestate, Mo.}

'Did you, Kernel? Hours since I've eaten. They threw us – me, you don't count, you *are* me – in here last night and in all that time I've had nothing but a sip of water and a bread roll crunchier than a paperweight. You know where the food came from, don't you? The Facility. And I'll bet those uniforms are made from clothes collected in the Compensation Camp. Seventy-five per cent recycling rate, remember?'

{What goes around, comes around.}

'You're being very reasonable. I thought you were my enemy now; I thought you wanted revenge?'

{I've forgiven you. Masterful, your escape from the Fractions. That's the Mo we chose. We've lost the girl, admittedly, but that's a transient event. We'll have other chances. The series will converge.}

'What would have happened if we'd been taken to the Fraction's homeland?'

{Lupa guessed closest to the truth. We'd have perished for sure; they were the sons and daughters of Puck.}

'And Puck knows what you're on about. You might be content to remain here, Kernel, but I'm not. Reunions are definitely best avoided, along with hoedowns, showdowns, knees-ups and punch-ups. I'm going to escape again, whatever you say. No rescues, no love, no friends, no missions, just Mo on his own, a free agent.'

{Your aim in life is to have no aim? That doesn't get you off the hook; you're still susceptible to the *twist*.}

'You're so smug. Your plans are just as subject to the twist as mine. Maybe this time things will go the way I want them. Then I'll have the upper hand.'

{The upper hand? We'll see.}

He was good, I had to allow him that. Not the Kernel, Alderman Hyssop. I was lying face down in the back of the mobile library, peering at him through a fist-sized hole where the bodywork had rusted through. The decrepit, bookless library bus was only one of many vehicles in the Mothodists' ramshackle cavalcade. The hole had started out finger-sized; I'd enlarged it with my knife. Novice Mothodists had searched me, found Dolly-with-one-arm up my sleeve, hooted with mirth and returned her. Never occurred to them that old dollster-wollster might be packing a shank. Clever Dolly.

It was the morning after the night of my enforced enrolment. Outside, Alderman Hyssop was working his audience. This was our first stop of the day, a dried-up filling station in a tank-mangled hamlet. The bewildered and bedraggled refugees had assembled for the victuals that Hyssop and his helpers handed out. They may have come for the food, but they stayed for the sermon. Manners, I'd noticed, were both the first casualty of war and the very last thing to die.

A swinging metal sign on the old garage forecourt boasted of FOOD, WATER AND GAS. The first two items having been distributed, the Alderman was pumping the gas, doing so from a dais of wooden pallets. In broad swathes on either side of him hulked bristle-headed acolytes decamped from the caravan, there to lend boisterous and girlsterous support. Hyssop was an effective public speaker. Actually, he was terrible, but brilliantly, captivatingly so. His knack consisted of talking animatedly, then, by slow degrees, winding down the energy of his performance, lowering his voice to a mumble, forcing you to strain an ear and concentrate hard in order to catch the punchline. Right on the rim of inaudibility he'd flip to bawling at full throttle and thrashing his arms around. Corny. Compelling.

I tuned in.

'Pilgrims, hear me,' he was intoning. 'Before the Lapse, we were a respected nation, feared and despised by our neighbours, a land to be proud of. Now we are no longer a land, we are landfill.' His joke elicited a thin sprinkling of weedy laughter. 'Our flag is a torn bin liner, flapping from a dead tree. Our major export is typhus. We are a playspace for foreign armies. The Fartherland lies in smoking ruins.'

Hyssop cut a short, cockeyed figure in his tattered cassock. He balanced his lopsided body on two canes, ticking and jittering as he delivered his oration. Crowning him was an hilariously bad haircut, the sort a backwoods mother might inflict on her children as a punishment. What was that style called? Oh, yes: a pudding bowl. Apt.

'Only one person can save us, the same one who destroyed us,' he lectured. 'He will reunite us, transmute discord into discipline and anarchy into harmony. His story is history, and also our destiny.'

'Religious retard!' one of the onlookers yelled.

Another heckler shouted, 'Political fruitcake!'

'Not so! I offer no religion. Nor do I speak of politics,' replied the Alderman. 'But rather, of a movement –'

'Yeah, a bowel movement!'

'– a never-ending cycle of men and women and, above all, of children, determined to seize victory and lay jealous claim to their birthright, to peace and prosperity.'

The hecklers were few in number. Hyssop's fruity words were hitting the spot with the majority of refugees; they were lapping them up, every pulsing, purple pronouncement was

373

greeted with vociferous endorsement. The Alderman gradually depressed his tone, dragging his listeners' attention with him, mine included.

'You have all heard, have you not, of how the flapping of a butterfly's wings can cause a hurricane on the far side of the world.' The crowd ummed and ahhed amongst itself for half a minute before eventually conceding it had heard of such a thing. I hadn't.

{Tsk! An infantile simplification of chaos theory.}

Hyssop's delivery had by then dwindled to a chin-on-chest mumble, fainter than the sounds of massed chewing and slurping and dismissive sniggering. The crooked man appeared to have nodded off during his own oratory.

Somebody laughed; someone else blew a raspberry.

'Pilgrims!' the Alderman erupted, thrashing the stage with his canes and jolting the crowd into submissive silence. 'Think not of little butterflies and their pretty, pretty wings. The Fartherland was vanquished by a being of far greater intelligence and might. It was destroyed by the wrath of The Moth!'

'Moth. Moth. Moth,' boomed the cohorts of Mothodists, every repeat delivered with an air punch and a foot stamp. Drummers placed strategically around the crowd matched the rhythm and amplified it, reinforcing the impression of an astonishing idea grown universal in scope and irresistible in appeal.

Hyssop's words wiggled from his mouth like venomous spiders emerging from a rusty plughole. 'He will not baulk at liquidating all who challenge him, just as he has already purged our land of the bacillus of the eastern marshmen, the child-stealing, disease-spreading monsters of the bogs.'

'Purge them, purge the boggies!' roared the throng, egged on by the attendant Mothodists. Few eggs were needed. They said 'boggies', they meant the Numbers, although probably not one of them had ever seen one, nor ever would.

'The Moth! The lone son of the Great Judge, the boy who achieved the impossible and escaped from this country when it was still a gigantic prison, the only person ever to do so!'

What about me? What about Harete?

'Moth. Moth. Moth.'

'The Moth! The boy born in captivity but who cut through solid stone walls using a sword sheathed in an ancient scroll.'

What's he been sniffing? We bailed out through a window. I sawed the bars with a hacksaw blade hidden in a text book, and we climbed down with a rope braided from carrier bags. And Moth wasn't born in captivity, he lived a privileged life until his father was exiled.

'Moth. Moth. Moth.'

'The boy who travelled from flood to flood for seven days, who parted the sea of reeds and walked across a river –'

You can have the floods and reeds. Walked across a river? We floated in a punt made from a fibreglass van roof. My invention!

'– who was seen to ascend bodily above the wall of silver thorns that once garrotted our noble home; the boy who struck his enemies with lightning, casting their barque into fiery oblivion.'

The border guards' boat! It caught fire when an idiot touched a power line, right by the razor-wire fence. He's making a meal of this, exaggerating everything, mythrepresenting the truth.

'Moth. Moth. Moth.'

'And, once free, the boy who ordered our corrupt country to be obliterated so that he could re-form it in his image, then returned to oversee his will being done!'

Is that how it happened? Did Moth and his dad conspire, was that always their plan?

The diminutive Alderman with the comedy tonsure chucked away his canes and began to quiver maniacally, freaking about like an out-of-control jackhammer. His voice was frayed, but still he raved away. Studying him through the hole in the rust, I found I could not remove my eye from the man; I was locked in his thrall. The hate-orator was charmless and ugly and spouting tripe and . . . and yet; tripe served with a hypnotic herb, tripe with spice. Did the magnetism stem from the zeal of the man? Or from some effect too subliminal to pin down?

The Alderman was now at climax. He had toppled, or perhaps dived, from the stage into the congregation and was being borne aloft by the outstretched arms of those eager for a touch of the frothing apostle.

'The Moth is real and amongst us,' Hyssop was screaming, 'this land is his land, he is returned, he speaks only through me. He has charged me with ridding our nation of the Peacemakers and all foreign devils. He has commanded that I bind our peoples together in his name and that we forge for ourselves a new land, a Land of Silk and Money.'

The bomb-blast bombast ran for another hour in the same baneful vein. The theme was one story, one nation, one people. And one Moth, the ever-watchful, ever-wrathful living phenomenon, nerdy son of the Fartherland, breaker of the old nation, baker of its replacement. Listening to the Alderman's lecture put me in mind of watching a bonfire: utterly predictable in its cause, course and outcome, yet endlessly absorbing for all that.

Destructive, too.

The cry. 'I have the urge to purge, pilgrims. I am the surgeon of purgin'!'

The thousand-strong response. 'A purge surge, a purge surge, we want a purge surge!'

The miracle: water into wine. The hecklers and doubters from a few moments before were manhandled into a mobile wood chipper. A body is at least half water, isn't it? What sprayed from the chute did resemble wine.

When the Alderman broke down, sobbing, for the final time, the acolytes streamed from their lines and moved amongst the masses, crying, 'Join the Mothodists! Join the Mothodists! Join the Damnation Army!'

Recruits were abundant. I wasn't surprised; sour old tripe must have sounded lip-smacking fare to destitute people burned from their houses by armies and mobsters. The Alderman's talk had been of restoring pride and unifying the country, of damage done and vengeance due, of purging sin.

Lies, all of it.

The man was a fraud; Alderman Hyssop wasn't his proper name. I knew him from the Institute. I'd been an inmate, he'd been a guard, the most sadistic warden of them all. That was how he had known my old prison number. He it was who had hunted and haunted us as we fled to the border, and by his own slack hand connected with a pylon's cables, been electrocuted.

I'd thought him long dead, his body razed, his soul bound by a never-ending lease to suffer eternal punishment in a fiery undercountry.

I was almost entirely right on all counts. Maybe entirely, maybe he was dead. The Fartherland was a murder-mill; perhaps ghosts were the industrial run-off, the spoil.

The name we'd known him by?

Jelly.

Chapter 49

Show over, it was time for our reunion.

The van door cracked open and the Alderman climbed inside, needing help to mount the steps. I'd have been surprised if he'd known as many as thirty card-and-cake-free birthdays, but the figure I saw before me inhabited the withered body of an octogenarian.

'Help me, eight six five!' he snarled, fussing with his cloak and canes. 'Pull me up! Unfold that chair, yes, that one. Take my sticks. Careful! Hurry up, won't you? There are rumours of aircraft in the vicinity; the mission must be on its way. But you and me, eight six five, we must confer.'

I did as requested and aided the man to his seat. As Jelly, he had inspired terror in all the Institute's young inmates, had been responsible for maiming several. A peculiar, pernickety, obsessive little man with bird-like motions and illimitable ambition, his nick name had stemmed from his wobbling fits. Not so very long before, I would have auctioned my liver to see him tortured.

We were alone. The library bus was Hyssop's private apartment: a camp bed, a mattress, cardboard boxes. Before the performance I'd rummaged through them all, found nothing of interest, only jar after jar of herbal preparations: hickory, chicory, dock. And bundles of dried berries and leaves with strange names: digitalis, datura, divinorum.

{Common roadside deliriants, like the man and his followers.}

'Well? What did you think of the sermon, boy?' Hyssop demanded, looking washed out by his onstage exertions. The voice was the same as the night before, a crinkling concerto for dry leaves swirling in a gutter.

My insides were a mass of gas and knots. Hyssop was unstable. Not just unpredictable, but unpredictably unpredictable.

Hyssop swished a walking cane through the air, barked out, 'Don't play dumb with me, boy! I've been searching for you for a long time, eight six five. My agents tracked you to the Spiral. I had orders you were to be put aside for me, kept circling in a holding pattern until I was ready. Someone fouled up.'

Scab flanges! The 'preservation order' Hairnet had mentioned, when Nonstop and I came out of pen one! The news flummoxed me. Hyssop had tried to save my life? Impossible; I knew he intended me huge harm, pent-up malice oozed like sweat from the man's glands.

'I'll . . . I'll say this much,' I stammered at length. 'You had that audience eating out of the palms of your hands.'

Hyssop – Jelly – I could not settle his name or nature – scowled. His body was ruined but his face remained uncannily youthful, with a beaky nose and lips that looked a little too red, like he'd raided his mum's make-up box the night before and failed to wipe away the evidence. He raised his hands up for my inspection, palms outwards. Each bore a coaster-sized circle of discoloured, puckered scar tissue.

'Exit points, where the sparks blasted out of my body,' he said. He opened his cassock, unbuttoned his shirt, and with cold pride showed me a field of deeply ridged scarlet markings. The embossed burn scars prevailed in any spot where metal had been in proximity to his flesh at that fateful instant he had shorted out the power line. The imprints preserved with fidelity the design of every badge, button and medal he'd been wearing. His zip fly too?

'Stigmata!' boasted Hyssop. From under the fringe of his pudding bowl haircut, his icy eyes sought mine, but I refused them. 'Your fault, eight six five. And I forgive you. No – I *thank* you.'

'Power corrupts,' I said, girding myself for the battering that would follow. 'Is it power you're after now? You always wanted to be Director of the Institute. What are you bucking for now, Arc-Bishop? Deep-fat Fryer?'

Hyssop paid me no attention. He was smearing a green, lumpy unguent over his burns. 'Comfrey brings such sweet easement, boy,' he groaned, rubbing the stinking slop into his nipples with what I thought unseemly vim. 'Nature's cures, always the best.'

The balm applied, Hyssop buttoned himself up again. 'Power, yes,' he said, then paused. It was dark in the bus, dark and hot and stuffy. Hyssop made no threatening move, but I was wary; leopards don't change their spots. Bad choice; leopards jump from cliffs with their sisters.

He began to speak again. 'I didn't see the light when I was electrocuted, eight six five. I *was* the light, the light filled me, flowed out from me. Six weeks I lay in hospital, watching my beloved country crumble. A miracle I wasn't killed, everyone said so. And they were right, of course, that's exactly what it was. Lying there, healing myself with my herbs, I understood as they did not why providence had singled me out. The electrocution was a sign. I was destined to become the conductor. The superconductor.'

'The conductor?'

Hyssop jerked forwards in his chair. His bewitchingly blue eyes mounted a second attack, tried to snare me in a pincer movement. 'The conduit of the *power*.'

'The power? The power of what?'

'The greatest power of all the powers.'

'Electricity? Science? Religion?'

'No, no, no!' he thundered. 'A power that underlies all those things, or underlines them, or undermines them, a power that beggared a nation and can rebuild another one.'

'The Moth? Herbs?'

Hyssop hurled both his canes at me. The violence of his movement disturbed his pageboy haircut, the dome came slightly adrift. A wig!

'Stop telling me what you think I want to hear!' he blazed. 'I am not going to harm you, you are not here for that reason. From now on, you are going to be seated at my right hand. Can't you understand? You and I, eight six five, are going to rebuild our country.'

I barked with laughter, unable to credit what I'd heard.

Alderman Hyssop wasn't listening. His eyes had glazed over. 'Rebuild the country. Then rule it. You and me. And that girl too, if I ever manage to find her.'

That girl. *Don't say her name, no name means no image, no image means no regret.*

'The three of us will be enough,' Hyssop rambled on, like I wasn't even on the bus any more. 'I'll be the guiding voice behind the curtain. He will be the figurehead, the hero of his own legend. You two as his friends will make sure he does what's right, what I tell him. He'll fall into line; he won't wish to see you hurt, watch you *being* hurt.'

He = The Moth. That was the only part of the cipher I cracked.

'What are you saying?' I asked. Hyssop might have been giving me a privileged peek into the Fartherland's engine compartment, but it was all still so confusing. 'Is Moth really in control of things now? Or are you? What is the great power, Alderman?'

The man appeared unwell. His head lolled to one side, his entire body palsied, then froze. His eyelids drooped, dribble ran from a corner of his mouth. I edged close towards him, uncertain if he had not passed out or even died.

'Stories!' Hyssop exploded, stuffing his face right up against mine, forcing me to bolt back against the wall. He'd pulled the same quiet-loud stunt on me as used on his congregation, and I'd fallen for it!

Hyssop had rewired himself. Words zinged out like bullets from a burp gun.

'*Stories*, eight six five, they are the power I spoke of. The memories of people and populations are stories, embellished to cast us as heroes or martyrs; the news is a fable broadcast

383

on the hour, history nothing but fairy tales with supporting paperwork, science a series of parables. Nothing is ever truly knowable; no one can speak with ultimate authority on what happened in the past or what occurs in the heart of atom or Adam. All we have are *stories*, some numbered as fact, some coloured as fiction.'

Hyssop's stagecraft was impeccable. He balled and broke fists, crossed and uncrossed his arms, pummelled his own chest, every muscular action brimming with stiff, pneumatic energy. He was addressing only me, bawling and screaming into my face, but he could have been thrilling an auditorium of thousands.

Stranger: I could not believe Hyssop was anything more at heart than when he'd been a two-stripe prison guard, a hollow simulation of a man, reading his instructions from a punched paper tape. Yet, such was the intensity of his arousal, I sensed the automaton had broken free from his creator and was programming himself, winding his own clockwork.

'The Fartherland fell into this civil war because there was no common myth that united us all,' he raged on. 'We are a mongrel nation with scores of languages and traditions. But we had no shared stories. No campfire tales to draw us all together. No epics that we could all know, and outsiders *not* know, nothing about which we could say "these are our stories, they make us us".

'Now it has – a story with The Moth as its beating heart. And we shall control The Moth; control The Moth, we control the myth; control the myth, we control the people!'

Hyssop's thesis depressed and enthralled me in equal measure. Either a hundred thousand volts up the trousers could seriously change a person's personality, or the hospital he'd recovered in had loaned him far too many books with far too many words.

'You know where The Moth is?' I gasped.

'Of course!'

'Where?'

'The centre. The centre of everything!'

'But where actually is that, Hyssop? Where?'

'Moth's not ready yet, but he will be, very soon. And when he is, he'll summon me, and all the others. But only I shall have a lever on him. I shall have *you*!'

There was a slit in Hyssop's cassock. Stepping back, he stuck in his thumb, pulled out a plum, pinged it at me. A speckled, greenish-yellow ball, with a short stalk. A crab apple? No, there was a line around it, running from pole to pole.

'Bread and spice, eight six five. That's what the poor devils out there need, bread for their bellies and spice for their minds. That fruit is our token, all The Moth's allies carry it. You're one of us now. Well? *Well?*'

The Alderman jammed out his hand. I thought he wanted the bad apple returning, so I moved to pass back the fruit but he waved it away. 'Keep it! Shake hands like a man, shake hands to seal the deal.'

'No way!' I protested, retracting my hand. Nothing could have impelled me to make a pact with the former guard corporal.

'Do it! Shake, make the bond!'

'I'll do it when I see The Moth,' I blurted. The idea buzzed in from nowhere. I had no more desire to meet Moth than I'd ever had, less if anything. But Hyssop had dodged a question and a crack was exposed, a hole in the rust I could enlarge.

Hyssop wavered. I worked the blade around. 'You don't know where he is, do you?' I goaded. 'You're pretending to pull The Moth's strings, but in reality he's yanking your chain.'

'Not yet!' retorted Hyssop, plainly tweaked. He recomposed himself, stiffened by invisible, internal hawsers. 'Not yet I don't. But we're looking, eight six five, every day we look. I'll seek him. Do you hear me?' he screamed. I'd really banged a nerve. Hyssop clenched his fists, blew a fuse.

'I'll seek him! I'll seek! I'll seek! I'll seek!' he blasted. His words crunched my ears like jackboots on gravel. Corrupted by repetition, his words spilled the hidden nature of his enterprise.

'I'll seek! I'll seek! I'll seek! . . . Seek I'll! Seek I'll! Seek I'll!'

The ranting despot and his flapping, lunatic fringe cracked me up. 'Oh, Alderman!' I laughed. 'You sad, tragic stripe of arse wipings! Haven't you heard of the *twist*, how you never find what you desire?'

Mention of the twist invoked seismic laughter and tinselly applause. That's what it sounded like, and for a slit instant I thought Hyssop's followers had been secretly monitoring us, that a great assembly was clapping and laughing on cue.

There had been no warning; nobody had observed the warplanes looking down their aristocratic noses at us from high up in their warp lanes, seen them release their guided weapons. The missiles must have homed in on the convoy unheard, flying faster than their own noise.

How was I to know exploding missiles could mimic mirth?

The earthquake laughter inundated me. I rolled on the floor, struggling to breathe. Hyssop rolled too, equally breathless. Gagging to get in on the joke, a female novice burst in on us, entering backwards through the narrow roofline window at around half the speed of sound. She cracked up too, split her sides. I saw them split, expose her tickled ribs. The bus door wrenched off its hinges, twirled away with balletic finesse. Tiring of life on the road, the bus took to the air and flew for a while, dispensing with its wheels. *Whaddya know*, I thought, *the wheels on the bus really do go round and round*. And round and round. Freed, the wheels overtook us.

All the other vehicles and people that made up the caravan had chosen the precise same moment to try their hands and wheels at flying too; I glimpsed their acrobatic endeavours through the gap where the door had been.

The magic endured for three seconds. The bus landed, rolled, folded.

Darkness.

Then, inversion.

Chapter 50

'Mo. You have to do it. Three minutes if we hurry. And we must hurry.'

{Go drink the piss from a pistol, Kernel. We're stuffed. Shafted. There are way too many people and vehicles way too much on actual fire. Why did those planes shoot up the Mothodists like that?}

'They probably mistook the caravan for an armoured column. It's not important. But we are. Act now, or we burn to death.'

{Or perhaps they just thought it would be fun. Think what a job those pilots have, must be like playing a video game while zooming around on a motorbike. No surprise they get carried away, eh? Look at those trucks burn, like toys tossed onto a bonfire. My toys all went on a bonfire once, that time I had scarlet fever. Feel that heat! Cop a snootful of the smoke from those tyres. It must be more than a thousand degrees just over there. The asphalt's melting all around me . . . looks ever so funny, like a dreamy stream of treacle. I'm going to have a snoozy snooze. With luck, the smoke will kill me before the flames do.}

'Mo, don't sleep, fight! I know I've been a bit hard on you at times, and we've argued, but that's to be expected, what with us two being banged up together in this tiny cell.'

{Tiny cell? Ruddy cheek. That's my brain you're talking about.}

'Do this thing for me. For us. Three minutes to save our lives.'

{No. Shan't. Go spoon the dung from your dungarees. It's too much to ask. Too brutal, too cruel, too painful. I'm only seventeen and I'm very, very scared. }

Backflash. Memories. Laughter's over. I'm still in the bookless library bus, but the bus has pulled over at a request stop in topsy-turvy town. Dark, but it's not total; there's one small patch of light where the door used to be. Must make for it.

No sign of Hyssop, Al-Jelly, Mullah Rice, Pope Tapioca, Monsignor Semolina or whatever he's calling himself today. The girl's here; my foot is stuck inside her chest cavity, jammed between two of her ribs. She was ripped open when the missile's blast crushed her through that tiny window. Think of using a broom handle to pack a guinea pig down a plughole. Better still, don't. We were never properly introduced, but in the few . . . minutes? we've been together, I've come to hate her guts. Particularly the way they're knotted like bamboo around my legs. Pull my foot free . . . there. Don't turn around, don't look. She was dead anyway. Sorry, girl. You did nothing wrong. Too clingy, that's all. Excuse me, I'm not normally so callous, but you're dead and I want to live. I'm dumping you; we're breaking up. Well, you are.

The floor-ceiling slopes downwards; it's knee-deep in gloop with a pretty rainbow surface sheen. I wade through, the liquid *really* stings on my cuts. Here's the gap, no bigger than a TV screen. Crawl through, a tight squeeze. There's a blockage.

Forward flash. Outside, leaning against something. The Kernel's talking, trying to convince me to . . . but I can't.

'I've never told you this before, Mo. A great many people are depending on you. Thousands. You're carrying a message, the most important message anyone has ever carried. We chose you out of everyone in the world to carry it.'

{Really, Kernel? Someone chose me?}

'Yes, Mo. You're special. We watched you from the bulrushes, cheered in silence as you helped The Moth and Harete over the fence into the Other country, put their lives before yours. Cunning and compassion, we thought. We could use a boy like that.'

{Use me. Everyone wants to use me. You, Origin, Hyssop. The Moth, probably. And I still don't understand why.}

Backslash. The blockage in the hole is Hyssop. He's wedged half in, half out; in a whimper he tells me he's stuck. I slither over the top of him and squeeze out into a tapering alleyway between the upturned library bus and the Mothodist's lash-up of a generator truck, rolled onto its side. The generator on board is still running; the canvas drive belt's going *slap-slap-slap-slap*. I guess the rainbow fluid that's swilling around is gasoline. Beyond us, it's a car-horse-person-truck-Mothodist omelette; diced-up pieces of things are everywhere, nothing's whole, nothing's good. The chef's a dope, the grill's been neglected, everything's on fire, or smoking ominously. We've come off lightly, on the perimeter of the carnage.

I set to free Hyssop. The flesh of his legs is snaggled on metal spurs around the hole, angled backwards like a python's teeth. I have to shunt him a short way back inside the bus, lift him, pull him. Repeat. Very tiring.

'One question, Hyssop,' I shout as I work. 'Why were the Numbers massacred?'

'Numbers?' croaks Hyssop.

'The delta gypsies, the boggies. The triangle-heads.'

A difficult delivery, but at last the Alderman's heels drag over the jagged metal. I've saved him. We don't hug, but . . . I feel a bond, midwife to baby.

Hyssop must feel it also. His thanks is my answer.

'They had no stories, eight six five. That's why. Only a language made of maths that could never assimilate a lie. Such a race was unacceptable, they could never rally around the new myths we're creating. Integration of those slippery, fictionless abominations was impossible. They had to be purged!'

Forward slash. The conversation appears long, but it's not. The Kernel blinks me a thought, I respond with mine.

'Who said you had a right to understand? You're still inside the maze, Mo. Mazes have a nasty habit of leading you to within a hair's breadth or a hare's breath of the centre before piping you away again.'

{Mazes, Kernel? Pathetic! Mazes are fit for colouring-in books and comics. Anyone can solve a maze. You just follow the rule: stick out a hand – left or right, it doesn't matter which, as long as you never change – and drag it along the wall on that side.

Eventually, it'll bring you to the centre. Not the fastest way to solve a maze, but guaranteed. That's what Tethera Methera was doing when he was trying to get to the Nub.}

'Quite, Mo. We need to do the same to solve this puzzle. Follow one hand only. Mustn't risk accidentally changing hands partway around. That would spell disaster, cause us to go around in circles. Best make sure.'

{I . . . see what you're saying.}

Backstab. I lift Hyssop up. He's a wee man really, slight and light, but in my condition he feels heavy enough. I can't leave him to die, don't have it in me, plus I need one more answer from him.

'Who gave the order to purge the Numbers?' I bawl in Hyssop's ear; the rattling generator is right by us.

Proximity to electricity seems to be the fillip the Alderman needs. He cranks his arm, breaks free from my support. His beaky face pecks at mine.

'The Prime Directive, it was called,' he rasps. 'An encyclical to the central committee recommending the extermination of those bog monsters.'

'But who wrote that order? I have to know.'

'ME!' he crows. 'My duty, my honour. My pleasure. Am I not Hyssop? Palm fifty-one: *Purge me with hyssop, and I shall be clean: wash me, and I shall be whiter than snow.* I ordered the liquidation of the Numbers. Me!'

I recoil, repulsed, repelled. Can I believe him? Lies are toothpaste and mouthwash to the man, every breath is perfumed with their vapours. Hyssop's a sects maniac, he'd think nothing of taking the credit for butchery even if he wasn't the author. I'm giddy, my feet are oily, my left arm spans out for balance –

That's torn it.

My arm has poked through a hole in the mesh guard over the generator. The machine has wrenched in my hand under a loose housing, my hand is immovably gripped between a pair of counter-turning wheels. I force my arm back and it fights me, swallows my hand up to the wrist. Hyssop pulls me with all his strength. No good. He finds an iron pipe on the ground, tries to smash the machine, but the safety cage is intact everywhere apart from where my hand went through; he can't get at it to wreck it.

Scabbing typical. I'm dying from health and safety.

'You selfish bungler!' Hyssop spits; he looks apoplectic. 'I need you, eight six five, you're my control over The Moth. I haven't got the girl yet; you *knew* that, you did this deliberately!' he says, throwing down the pipe in disgust. His eyes shoot darts into my heart – it's the unbridled fury of a beggar whose winning lottery ticket has been chewed by his own dog. He braces his feet against the cage and pulls at me again, same result.

I'm stuck fast.

As Hyssop tugs me, I spot a screwdriver fallen from a toolkit, one of those big jobs, a burglar's buddy. I lance it through the hole in the mesh, hoping to jack the trapping wheels apart. With a noise like a car crusher crushing another car crusher, the tip of the tool grazes a shaft revolving at high-speed and a fox's brush of sparks bounds out. The sparks land in a crate full of greasy rags, the rags reciprocate with spurts of sooty flame.

Hyssop yowls and leaps aside, genuinely terrified by the sparks.

The truck starts to burn, starting at the rear. A wooden side panel catches first.

Fire.

I'm drenched in gasoline. Hyssop's drenched. I'm standing on a paved road that's slick with it, a hip's width from a bus that's swimming in the stuff.

Hyssop and I stare at each other.

'You'll burn as I did, eight six five,' he says. 'At least none of the others will have you. That's some relief, isn't it? Isn't it, boy? You'll serve your master even in dying. We could have ruled this land together. Damn you! Let the flames purge your sin!'

My fingers have been crushed to pâté. I feel nothing from them. A dull warmth, that's all.

'Go away,' I say to Hyssop. But he's already written me off, melted into the blue haze.

The generator protests, continues to digest my arm, drag it further inside the mechanism. I look to see if I can sever a fuel pipe or cut a wire or jam something down the exhaust pipe, but all those parts are inaccessible.

My hand is irretrievably trapped.

I'm about to burn.

Cutaway.

{We need only one hand to negotiate the maze, Mo. It's essential we don't have a second to distract us. And don't forget Dolly. If we burn, she'll burn. You wouldn't want that to happen.}

'No, I wouldn't. You're right. We've swapped places again, Kernel. You've put your braces back on.'

{You need to be in the cockpit for this job. I'll guide you through it step by step, like ground control talking down an aeroplane in trouble. Two minutes left, Mo.}

I check my list. All my other entries have been scrubbed; there's only one item there, the deed the Kernel's finally persuaded me to do.

{Matthew 5:30. *If thy left hand offends thee, cut it off.*}

'I don't care what scabbing time it is! And I'm not called Matthew.'

{Sorry. You won't know that story.}

TO DO:
Amputate own hand (NB <u>FAST</u>)

I remove my headband, my former blindfold, it unravels to . . . a pair of old underpants. Huh, all this time, and no one said. I re-knot it around my trapped arm, just above the elbow. The Kernel insists on that, must be *above* the elbow. I have to hold one end with my teeth as I use my free, right hand to knot it, once, twice. Very tight knots. The screwdriver I slip under the band. Then I turn it. One full revolution, a second, a third. Each turns tightens the band – the Kernel calls it the *tourniquet*. I'm getting my knickers in a twist, but that's a good thing.

A corkscrew pillar of cloth forms, lengthening with each twist. Imperative to constrict the veins and arteries, stop them bleeding when I . . . when I . . . fourth turn. The fabric's strong, but I mustn't overdo it else it'll rip. Fifth turn. My arm grows pale. Not my arm. I disassociate it from myself. It's a foreign body, a lumpy cylinder, a meat manacle.

{Enough turns!}

I wedge the handle of the long screwdriver under my left armpit to stop the tourniquet unwinding. Find Dolly, tucked in my trackie top. The folding pocket knife, please, Dolly. Thank you.

Hard to open the blade, my hands are so oily; need to use my mouth. So frustrating, need to hook a tooth into that little oval depression on the top edge of the blade . . . got it. What's that, K? Open both blades, the main one and the saw. Wilco.

I suck a hard breath. The smoke's getting thicker. This may be my last fresh-ish lungful.

{Cut deeply around your arm. Quick as you can. You're severely dehydrated – that will help thicken the blood and reduce bleeding.}

My live hand is shaking. I reach in and score a line around my trapped forearm, a hand's span back from the wrist.

{That's the spot! The radius widens as it nears the hand, the ulna narrows. That's about where the total bone thickness will be the minimum. Slice deeper!}

Now I'm wearing a bead bracelet, the same shade of red as the berry syrup I used to love squirted onto cinema ice cream.

{Much deeper – slash through the skin and muscle. Of course it hurts! Not as much as burning to death. Nothing would hurt as much as that.}

I cut again, pressing harder, slicing back and forth with the smooth blade. The muscle is fibrous, it resists the blade; I have to hack and scrape, the underside of my arm is difficult to reach.

Take a second breath. The spare tyre on the back of the truck is angled directly over the burning rag box. Won't be long before it catches.

{Three nerves. Radial, ulnar, median. Chop them through! Chop them!}

I'm slashing at my arm now, taking rough, ugly, savage, downwards stabs. I hate the trapped hand, I want it gone. I flip the knife around to use the second blade, begin to saw into the cut. I can't see what's going on in the slit; it's a morass of skin and muscle flaps, shocking raw-steak pink showing bright against the dark red blood and the black oil.

The saw rakes over nerve bundles and I undergo internal nuclear fusion. There is nothing in creation's estate now but exploding starbursts of elemental, ecstatic pain. I know what the goatherd didn't, I know what the universe is made from.

Pain.

And suffering.

And doubt.

And rage. Why me? Why this? Why here, why now?

{Faster! Faster! When that tyre goes, it'll burn hot enough to ignite the fuel!}

I saw. I stop. The pain is . . . the pain IS.

{Saw, Mo. Close your eyes and saw, hard. Listen to me. There's a pub, see? Like the one your dad used to drink in.}

'Not drink, Kernel. Only darts. Mum drank, dad darted.'

{And it's called the . . . the "Wolf and Leopard". And the landlord pays a man to paint the pub sign. But when he sees the sign, he's not happy. The picture's fine, but the words aren't well spaced. All three words are too far apart. What does he say to the sign painter? *Think hard as you saw, think and tell me.*}

The saw hits bone. Two bones to sever, I've found the first. Every bone in my skeleton vibrates in harmony as the pocket saw grinds into it.

'He says . . . you have left too much space between "wolf" and "leopard".'

{No! All three words. Picture them!}

'He says . . . you have left too much space between "wolf" and "and" and "and" and "leopard"!' I cry. The stupid, stupid trick is monopolising my brain, the pain's no less, it's just less important. At every occurrence of 'and' I saw harder, grind the blade in.

The knife jolts. Back to flesh, I've severed the first bone. Three swift strokes through flesh and I hit the second bone, the thicker one. The oil on the floor around me is starting to fume and smoke. My trackie trousers are smouldering, my trainers are sinking into the tar on the road; I schlep my feet up and down to prevent them from becoming glued in. The spare tyre is alight. Incineration is imminent.

{Five 'and's, all in a row! That's an old joke, an old saw. The pub landlord knows it; he opens a new pub named after that joke. It's called the "Wolf and 'and' and 'and' and Leopard". He has a sign painted, same painter, same mistake with the spacing of the words. *What is his precise complaint?*}

I scream my answer to the Kernel, my cox. On every 'and', a stroke with the saw.

'You have left too much space between "wolf" and "and" and

"and" and "'and'" and "'and'" and "and" and "and" and "'and'"
and "'and'" and "and" and "and" and "leopard".'

{Yes!}

Almost there. Remaining are one small piece of bone and
some stubborn sinews too soggy to cut – I try but they clog
the saw teeth. I push myself against my arm, swing it as far
as I can in one direction, then pull it the other way, rotate it,
pick up the steel pipe and smash it, smash it, smash it and –

There is too much space between hand and arm.

It's off. There's a discontinuity in my being.

Like an eejit, I look. I hold the end of my left arm up to my
face and look at the space where my hand used to be. Pink
mush, two oval off-white shapes, textured like the surface of a
crumpet: the ends of my arm bones, complete with protruding
splinters. As I study, a tight beam of stinking hot blood blasts
into my face.

{HOLD THAT TOURNIQUET! RUN! RUN!}

I sprint free just as the petrochemical lake ignites. My good
hand is keeping that tourniquet tight, my short arm I stick up
in the air to drain down the blood. At my back, the heat is
without limit, the sound is like having a jet plane's turbofan
aimed into each ear.

I pause only once. The melting bitumen road surface has
the consistency of hot fudge. I stoop, and swirl my stump in
the liquefying tarmac, coating it liberally to seal the open end.

Must have lost a lot of blood. Feel wooooooooozy.

Part 5:

Blackout

Chapter 51

Part 6:

Breakthrough

Chapter 52

Clean, starchy white linen, folded to crisp perfection, an origami box assembled around my bed; so perfect, I didn't want to move lest I crease it. Pastel puffs of marshmallow sunlight, soft against the eye. Pyjamas.

Pyjamas.

Pi-jam-ass.

Pi-jar-mars.

Pronounced any way, I loved the word and underlying concept so much it was the only utterance I could bring myself to emit for several days in a row.

'Here's your breakfast. Mo. Can you manage? Do you want me to cut it up?'

'Pyjamas!'

Or:

'Still itching? That's normal. Here, use this. Let me show you what to do.'

'Pyjamas!'

I'd never owned or worn pyjamas before. Jim-jams. Jimmies. Pee-jays. Never. Blue and white stripes, flannel cotton. Nightclothes. Clothes you put *on* when you got into bed.

407

That's mad! Sure, who thought of that? Do we have day-duvets, lunch-pillows?

Not a hospital. A dressing station. Run by the Peacemakers. Give the guys a break, they were doing a grand job. Nice people from nice countries, I understood that then. And reasonable people make bog-rotten guards at places like the Facility, but damn splendid medics. The building was a network of tubular, inflatable tents housing hundreds of nurses and doctors. Syringe-ninjas, that was my name for them. Nothing was too much trouble for those men and women. Machines, they had, machines with screens tracking ziggy green lines, tubes and hoses for bums and noses, drips and clips, X-rays, scanners; I tell thee: the works.

Plus, pyjamas. A fresh pair arriving laundered and ironed every day.

In a plastic tray under my bed slept Dolly-with-one-arm, the tiny teddy still inside her; my knife (sterilised, and made safe with a sticking plaster wrapped around it – health and safety!); even that crappy crab apple thing Alderman Hyssop had given me. Would have been easy for the orderlies to sling the lot, burn them with my tracksuit. But they appreciated that for people who had nothing, little things meant a lot. They took that effort. They cared. Made me cry, it did, for about two days solid. The ninjas thought I was mourning my damned hand, not so.

My stump had been dressed and sealed. To amend my one-handed handiwork, the surgeons had needed to saw a little more off my arm, file the bones down, draw skin and muscle over the end and sew them up. I guess it's like when you sharpen a pencil and the point breaks, the only way to fix it is to sharpen the pencil again, make it that bit shorter. The end of the stump was smooth and convex, traversed by an equatorial zipper line of stitches. Proper job. Bone-a-fide. Reminded me of a baked potato.

What else? A blood transfusion, and an examination by the ophthalmologist. 'The scotomata – the dark spots – will gradually decrease in size,' had been his conclusion. 'But never disappear altogether. You'll have around twenty per cent loss of vision. Cheer up, laddy! Worse things happen at sea.'

So, a life of spots before my eyes spent listening to the sound of one hand clapping.

My symmetry was forever violated. Echoes . . . wasn't a broken symmetry supposed to trigger interesting happenings?

Didn't half itch, the hand that was no longer there. *Phantom limb syndrome*, a nurse named it. The generals in the brain maintained a map of where all the pieces of the body were situated, and the map had not been updated to take account of recently surrendered outposts. Nerve signals were misinterpreted, reconstructed as itchiness in the missing organ. Mixed messages: the cause of at least half the universe's ills, I decided in my bed-bound wisdom.

My informant on these matters was my favourite nurse. Sister came from a country I had never heard of, a small land that had once been much bigger, back in the days of billowing sailcloth and belching brass cannon. No lowly wrist-flicker of thermometers, Sister boasted membership of the terribly august (she claimed) Royal Knowledge of Cursing. Leastways, I think that's what she said, but I never heard her swear. I was her youngest charge on the adult trauma ward.

'A phantom hand? What use is that to anyone?' I complained to her.

'You could use it to ghostwrite your memoirs,' she said, grinning back at me.

I nodded. 'But I'd have to teach myself shorthand first,' I said.

Sister was petite and sassy and had a way with bedpans and bed baths that didn't make you feel embarrassed, and I was ever so totally in love with her. I told her so, too.

'I love all my patients dearly. But you especially, because I've a grandson your age,' she'd replied. She was sixty, a volunteer nurse for the International Red Polygon, something like that.

Sister knew a cunning ruse to reduce the unscratchable itch – a mirror. 'Rest it like this, against your left arm. Lay your right arm alongside. Now, look along the bed. You see your right hand, and you see in the mirror what appears to be your left hand too. Fools the brain.'

Doesn't take much to fool my brain. I knew I was seeing a reflection, but the trick worked! The itch ceased, at least for as long as the mirror stayed in place. I stared into it all that day, watching the mirror-patients recovering in their mirror-beds, watching mirror-nurses bringing mirror-food and changing mirror-dressings, watching a mirror-friend negotiate the mirror-maze of mirror-beds towards me.

'Hullo,' said mirror-Harete. 'I've run you to ground at last. Ten days I've been hunting, every blessed refugee camp and hospital from here to –'

'Were you actually searching for me this time?' I interrupted her, recalling the fiasco of her finding me on the Spiral. I looked and spoke into the mirror, angling it so she could see me. 'Not . . . anyone else?'

Harete perched herself on a chair at my bedside. She looked thin and clean and tired, but the right kind of tired, *I've-given-up-but-I-tried-now-let's-go-home* tired. Her hair had grown back long enough to be tied in a ponytail again, and she had on new clothes. New for her, that is, not brand new. Aid clothes.

'Yes, for you,' she said. 'So I suppose that's kyboshed your daft theory about never finding what you seek.'

'No,' I corrected her. 'It's confirmed it. I'm not the same Mo, you see. I'm mirror-Mo, similar to the old Mo but rotated, reflected. I lie at right angles to the old Mo, along the other axis.'

'Oh,' she replied, just a sprig of hurt. 'Well. Does mirror-Mo want to talk? Or is he too busy?'

'Fairly busy actually, yes,' I said. Letting the mirror fall flat, I raised my right arm, then my left, exposing my shortcomings. 'But on the other hand . . . no.'

'Oh! Mo, I . . . I don't know what to say,' cried Harete tearfully, rising, sitting, rising again.

'Stumped, eh? Join the club,' I joked. Sister brought us both lunch trays; we ate like gannets. And we talked. Pleasant talk. No urgency, no pother, no bother, just two old friends catching up with each other after a short break.

'Nice jammies,' said Harete between mouthfuls of toast.

'Thanks. And look at you! Dressed up to the threes.'

'Fives at least, please.'

Sucking on a carton of juice through a straw, Harete finally asked me, 'So, why are you not the same, then? Hand notwithstanding.'

411

'No handstands, Harete, not unless I find a slope. I'm different because I'm officially not in love any more. Cured,' I sniffed. 'Well, in love with Sister –'

'She's *nice*,' said Harete.

'She *is* nice,' I agreed. 'But that's only fun love. A game. I meant, I'm not in love with you any more.'

Harete schlurped extra hard on her straw for a couple of moments, fixing me with a coppery stare, her eyes patting me down for evidence of mirth and mockery. 'Were you before?'

'Yes. Didn't you know?'

'No. You didn't say. I remember you saying I was your girlfriend; I thought that was just a . . . prank.'

'Suppose it was, really. Never said anything because I didn't want to . . . you know . . . saddle you with heavy stuff.'

'That's jolly thoughtful,' said Harete. The damaged men around us coughed, a pinger sounded on the machine plumbed into my bedridden neighbour, bottles rattled on a medication trolley. The placid, neutral dressing station felt the perfect place to patch wounds.

'I thought you thought I was self-centred,' I volunteered at long length.

'Did I say that? I think I spoke in heat and haste. Self . . . contained. Self-sufficient. That was nearer my intent, Mo.'

There had been a time not long before when I'd have devoted a deal of cranium power to analysing those few sentences. That time had passed. I shrugged. 'What about you, are you still in love with Lonza?'

'Lonza's dead, Mo,' Harete stated drily.

'I know. I was there. Doesn't mean you can't still –'

'We did grow close. We went through an awful lot out in the market, and a lot of awfulness. I thought he was marvellous, right up to the end. Yes, you're right, there's a void now, a void that feels solid, itches.'

'Um,' I said. 'Borrow my mirror.'

'Why did Meg jump, Mo? That's what I still can't understand. Did she really adore her brother so much she couldn't live without him?'

My eyebrows performed gymnastics. 'You don't know? It wasn't dried milk in the tin I chucked onto the campfire. Meg had ground up her entire supply of tablets. Dunno what those pills were made of, but that was why the fireball was such a whopper. She must have worked at it when we were dozing on the lorry; she thought she was giving me what I needed to save everyone, including Lonza and the baby. A sacrifice for love. Then . . . when . . .'

'Ohhhhhhhhh.' We took our time swallowing the clotted silence, two tall sundae glasses full.

After watching me throw myself off the cliff in the wheelie bin and swim out unscathed, Harete and Lupa had travelled with those singing women we'd seen. They were the Hareticals, an all-female clique who had broken away from the Mothodists. They were equally gung-ho on the same story of The Moth's escape from the Fartherland, only in their reading of the story, the real hero was – well, you can guess.

According to Harete (who had maintained anonymity), Lupa had undergone a spiritual conversion under the benign if strident influence of the lead Haretical, the Abbess of the Abyss. The night before Harete broke away and began her

413

search for me, Lupa announced she'd elected to become an anchoress.

'That's a sort of nun, locked up in a cell, devoting her life to prayer,' Harete explained. 'Lonza's and Meg's deaths brought about her change of heart.'

'Pffft! Change it? She'd have to find it first. That girl will be a wolf in nun's clothing, and old habits die hard,' I snorted. I hoped it was true though. Locked in a cell, doing nothing but thinking? Sounded like she'd sentenced herself to life on the Spiral. Good riddance.

Harete then shot me with a double-barrelled blast of more disturbing learning. 'Those mad new religionists haven't overlooked you, by the way. You know about the Mothodists and Hareticals already, but there are *two* movements centred around the cult of Mo. The women told me about them. There are the Momons, and the Hermetics.'

Milk vaulted from my throat. 'You're razzing me? Mo-mons?'

'They're obsessed with eschatology and escapology, the study of ends and escapes. Their symbols are hacksaw blades and pylons, like the Hareticals have a tractor wheel for theirs and the Mothodists use a crown of razor wire.'

'Nut jobbies. Bake brains. And that other bunch?'

'The Hermetics. A sealed order, very secretive. Pundamentalists. The Abbess said she'd heard they're into self-flagellation and eating broken glass.'

I squirmed uncomfortably, picking at the idea like it was a scab. Back in the Institute I'd poisoned a super-thug called Sticky with a drink laced with ground glass. I had to ask, pick the scab, make it bleed. 'Hermetics? Why that name?'

'From Hermes, I suppose. Moth's nickname for you. That's another name for Mercury, the messenger of ancient legend with wings on his sandals. When Moth and I were waiting to be made citizens of the Other country, he always referred to you as Mercury, the psychopomp.'

'A cycle pump?'

'Urgh!' Harete shrieked. 'You do this on purpose, don't you?'

'Do not! You . . . mumble.'

'The word is *sy-co-pomp*.'

'Psycho? HE called ME a psycho? That's rich. That. Is. Rich. He's the one working in league with you-know-who,' I seethed. 'Or under him. Or over him.'

With an arsenic heart I described in detail my brush with Alderman Hyssop, Al-Hakim Hyssop, whoever he was. Harete remembered Jelly of old.

Harete pretend-cuffed me around the ear with a triangle of toast. 'In mythology, a psychopomp is someone who can travel freely to and from the underworld, between the world of the living and the land of the dead. That's how he saw you.'

'Huh. Kind of a compliment, I guess. Mercury . . . that's a metal too – quicksilver, isn't it? I saw that spill out of a broken thermometer once, a shiny liquid. When it splashed on the table, it formed loads of tiny beads and whizzed around very fast. Impossible to capture. I can relate to that.'

'So what you're saying,' said Harete, leaning over and plumping up one of my already glorious soft and prize-winningly plumptious pillows, 'is that mercury is just a load of balls. *Small* balls. That sounds like you, Mo!'

We laughed together. A man with no face in the next bed

415

shushed us; we tried to stop but went down with the giggles.

'Now I'm in stitches!' wheezed Harete.

'No, I am,' I said, waving the end of my stump at her.

'Suture self!'

Then Harete started to hiccup; that made us both laugh even harder.

The giggles gassed themselves out. 'Harete,' I began, 'hyper . . . hypodermically speaking, do you think you ever could have loved me?' The question was an amputation, an irrevocable severance from my former self, old Mo, that sceptic, septic, gangrenous flask of doubt and self-scrutiny. Until then, he'd been joined to me by a thin cord of gristle, tagging along in the murk.

The hiccups stopped. 'No, Mo. I don't think so.'

The gristle snapped. And the tourniquet held, no haemorrhaging, no adult trauma.

'Not your type? Too puny, too funny, too loony, too punny?'

A bell rang, signalling the end of visiting hours. Harete stood and tucked a balled-up tissue into her sleeve, girl-style.

'No, none of those reasons,' Harete said. 'Others may think differently, but I've always thought I could only love someone who was my equal.'

I winced as she tore away the plaster, lanced the boil, applied the iodine; but she was absolutely right.

The bell rang a second time and orderlies began to shoo people off the ward. 'When I found you by accident on the Spiral, I was inconsolable,' she continued, her words vying against the sounds of chairs being stacked and plates cleared away. 'All that way to watch my friend die. But Moth was

416

correct, you are a psychopomp, able to flit between Earth and Hades, flirt with death but never know it. To escape from the Institute, the Spiral, the Fractions, to be blinded and to lose a hand and laugh it off like it was no more than an eyelash, and –'

A white-coated orderly wheeled Harete about and directed her towards the exit. 'Come along now, miss,' he said firmly, 'there's always tomorrow.'

'I've never achieved anything in my life, Mo. Pig nothing! My one stab at doing something, to rescue Moth, was a disaster,' she shouted, walking backwards.

'Please, miss, we've sick people to attend to. There you go now!'

I could hardly hear her; she was a face in a flock, being jostled out through the door. Kisses and 'see ya's and 'later's flew from the mouths of departing visitors like bats from a cave at dusk, muffling her message.

'I've always been –'

What? What did she say?

'– of you, Mo!' she called out, waving.

'Can't hear you!' I cried, but she couldn't hear me.

Her final words, yelled out as she vanished round the corner, '– ever realise? I'm an ore of Mercury!'

Misheard. Must have misheard her. I punched the mattress. Used the wrong hand, the one that wasn't there, missed, rolled out of bed, crashed onto the floor. The man with no face laughed so hard his saline drip shook loose.

Then it clicked. 'In awe', not 'an ore'.

Chapter 53*

The next day I was discharged. At the foot of my bed that morning, instead of the usual parcel of ironed pyjamas with their blue and white tramlines, a cube of day clothes and a pair of trainers.

'You're well enough to go home,' Sister told me, instantly blushing as she spotted her mistake. 'Sorry. No home, you told me. Oh, your friend's waiting outside.'

I picked through the clothes. Not bad. They did at least fit, and had been chosen with consideration for my new configuration: no buttons on the sweatshirt, a summer jacket with the zip removed and hook-fasteners sewn in, elastic-sided sneakers decorated with wing-shaped flashes. The shirt was emblazoned with a phrase I was certain I'd read once before: 'Fuzz Pod GO boy'. Great. Even the clothes were hustling me on my way.

Sister watched me as I dressed. 'The clothes are second hand, of course, but . . . oh, Mo, I'm not doing this deliberately, I promise. No jokes from me today.'

Positively *shevelled* I felt in my new gear. One item of my original clothing had not been replaced. 'No bandana,' I said.

'I need that to cover the ringworm on my forehead.'

'Ringworm? We found no ringworm,' Sister replied. From a pocket in her uniform she produced a patterned headscarf, scented with lilacs. 'A going-away present. I'm every so sorry we've run out of prosthetics – false limbs. Shortages. We looked but –'

'You came up empty-handed? I know the feeling.'

'Pop back if you can in a few weeks' time, we may have some by then,' she told me, her words slowing to negotiate the speed lump in her throat.

I pocketed Dolly-with-one-arm and the knife and the fruit. 'Put one aside for me. As long as it's a leftie, I don't care about the colour. Goodbye, Sister. Thanks. And say thank you to everyone here for me,' I said, making an effort not to blub. I couldn't remember ever in my life feeling safer, calmer or better cared for than inside the hushed tunnels of the dressing station.

We hugged, Sister wiped her nose and began to strip the bed, and I left, walking out through the entrance, pushing where I should have pulled.

I waited in the waiting room. It seemed the best place. Orange chairs, posters warning about rabies, scabies and landmines, several paramilitaries in different uniforms playing cards around a table in the corner, a glass-fronted drinks vending machine. Someone had scratched graffiti on the machine: JUICE EX MACHINA. Didn't get it. Too many clever dicks around, even in a war. I pressed myself up against the humming chiller cabinet, positioning myself at forty-five degrees to it. That way, I could watch my body-length reflection in the glass front. When I held out my right hand, my perfect left followed suit.

419

What game were the soldiers playing? Chase the ace . . .
you won't find it, I thought.

Harete walked in.

'Ready?' she asked. 'To go?'

'Where?'

'I still have my passport from the Other country. And Moth's
father gave me a diplomatic pass in case I ever found his son.
It has no name, no photograph; anyone can use it. There's a
refugee camp – a real one, not like the Facility – nine days'
walk away. We'll hike there, contact the authorities –'

'No.'

Harete stopped listening. I think she'd been rehearsing her
speech for some time. 'I was wrong and you were right, Mo,'
she said. She sat down wearily on a chair; I squatted by her.

'No.'

'Right from the start I've been on a fool's errand. Who
did I think I was, trying to find Moth? I see it all clearly now:
I was overcompensating for my inadequacies, pretending I
was as resourceful and cunning as you. *What would Mo do?*
That's what I said to myself all the time I was making my way
to the Spiral, and when I was passing myself off as a screw.
Pa-scabbing-thetic . . .'

'No. Listen.'

'I came up with just one bum idea on the Spiral, to fish you
out of your pen, and that failed miserably. I'd never intended
to free the other prisoners, I only said that to make you feel
small because I was angry with you. Envious.'

'I'd guessed,' I microfibbed.

'That's why I was so grumpy that dawn we fled the

Establishment, because you'd proved once again how brilliant you were and how useless I was. I should have stayed with my foster family. I can't believe how vilely I've repaid them for their kindness.'

'No. Shut it, a minute.'

'How could I compete with someone who could mastermind an escape in a day, rescue Nonstop and Myristica. People I ended up killing, when you think about it. If I hadn't been so hung up on Lonza, we might have escaped the Facility earlier. I hate myself.'

'No!'

'I should have realised Lupa wasn't pregnant, for scab's sake! I was the blind one, the selfish one.'

'Not true. No. *Please?*'

'And from what we've learned from the Hareticals and Hyssop, you were right about the other point, too. Moth *is* setting himself up as the emperor – hey, what do you mean, "no"?' she said, my words finally obtruding through the cloud of self-chastisement.

I sighed, took a breath. My turn.

'You're wrong, Harete, to say that you were wrong and I was right. Because I was wrong and you were right. Apart from just then, when I said you were wrong about being wrong. That was right.'

'Come again?'

'We *do* have to find Moth. That was your original plan, and we've let ourselves be distracted, become lost in the maze. There's a twist though.'

'Which is?'

421

'We're not going to rescue him. He's gone stark mad; he's using our story and these bogus cults to bolster his legend, make himself divine. He's passed through the origin, become the minus-Moth, the anti-Moth. Vile, evil, live.'

'So what are we going to do? Capture him and return him to his father?'

'What would be the use? His sort always have powerful friends to help them wriggle out of tight spots. Or they find powerless ones, like us, and exploit them.'

'So?'

'We're going to kill him.'

I'd expected resistance. None came. Harete looked pale, serious. Beautiful. The soldiers in the corner had quit their card game and were studying her, mouths agape. She lit up the clinical waiting room, not in the manner of a lantern but as a great painting might, a wild canvas that bent the eye towards it and struck back with splashes of chrome and carmine and cobalt. This new seeing of Harete came to me without cost of feeling; her beauty was a thing of science, measurable and objective, it needed no sweated heart to affirm its verity.

'How can we hope to find him, Mo? We're two teenagers with three hands between us.'

'That's the easy part. For months I've been hearing a description of The Moth's base, but now I know where it actually is.'

'The Establishment. That's where the government hangs out these days, the parts of the main prison above the Spiral and the camp.'

'Negative. That's just a sham, a decoy, a Punch-and-Judy

man's tent. Whoever's there, it's not the people who are *really* in charge of this country, whatever they themselves may think. Ask yourself: where would a cod god, a fake deity live?'

Harete thought. 'A replica heaven. A parasite's paradise.'

'Naturally,' I agreed. 'Until recently we've been trapped down here in Hades. This dressing station is limbo – limb zero, rather – and now we need to ascend to heaven. I've seen it. *You've* seen it. A giant, glittering jewel set in a lush secluded valley. A circle, a zero, the origin, where all the power lines run to and from; infinity, where parallel lines converge. The beginning and the end. The centre of power, political and electrical. The centre of everything.'

Harete joined in. 'The Moth. The anti-Moth, I mean, living in the lap of luxury, directing the hostilities. Operating the Facility, the Spiral, the Compensation Camp. Alderman Hyssop's boss.'

'Yes, Harete. He's the disease in the Fartherland's bloodstream, we're the antibodies. Let's make a pledge: find him and kill him.'

We stood.

Harete said, 'Before we begin, let's both be clear about one thing, so there aren't any more misunderstandings or mixed messages. You're a great and special friend, Mo, I admire you enormously, but I don't love you. I don't love anyone, and I never want to, ever again. Strong love's a distemper, it's emotion sickness.'

'Good. I don't love you, Harete,' I replied, no word of a lie.

'And I'll never be your girlfriend, Mo. According to those Hermetics and their reading of our story, my character was the whore of Mercury. Can you imagine?'

'Hah! As if!' I exclaimed, three octaves higher than I'd intended. The room felt very, very warm; the air conditioner must have gone on the fritz.

We walked out of the dressing station arm in arm. Bruised Venus and her one-handed Hermes, hunter-killers both. Our veins ran with sulphur and antimony, our hearts with love for hate and hate for love: antinomy.

I updated my list.

TO DO:
Find the anti-Moth
KILL HIM
KILL HIM
KILL HIM

Chapter 54

We travelled light. Whoever heard of Hermes with a haversack, Mercury with matching luggage?

The world turned, the Fartherland burned. The civil war had become an all-out falling out, a free-for-all, an Armageddon jamboree. Towns, farms, forests, nowhere was spared.

Mornings, the sky creaked under the load of a thousand cross-shaped bombers, gravid thunder mothers that dived, gave birth to tinned earthquakes, peeled away. Evenings, and a suffering of V-shaped cruisers replaced them, flying in the opposite direction, jerking off precision munitions that cruised on rails of laser light: smart bombs, crater-makers with high IQs. Nothing could withstand the combined onslaughts. Like the goatherd in Nonstop's tale, the warmongers had determined to reduce the nation to its smallest constituents, bombing cities to ruins, to rubble, to grit, to dust.

Twice a day, just after each bombing raid, a solitary passenger jet flew over. A man we met in a crater told us it transported arms salesmen, inspecting the effectiveness of their companies' products. He smoked as he talked. Not a cigarette or a pipe, I mean he was just . . . smoking, all over. 'Do they sell hands as well?' I asked him, but the man coughed and died before he could answer me.

For seven days and seven nights Harete and I slithered from crater to shell-hole, heading for the mountains, hoping to reach them before they too succumbed to the carborundum of the bombs and were worn down into sand. We drank stagnant water from fractured pipes, dined on dead pets and raided food from cellars exposed by the heaving up of the earth.

Little could live. Rats survived, cockroaches survived.

Mothodists thrived.

We came across a legion of them, hole-hopping like we were. So many, their marching kicked up a towering cloud of powdered city. The dust devil tracked purposefully over the land, heading in the same direction we were.

The swirling cloud intimated disaster. 'Hyssop's been summoned – he's on his way to join his master,' I deduced.

Harete nodded. 'So we'll have to overtake them,' she said. 'We need to assassinate the anti-Moth before his army reaches him, else he'll be unapproachable.'

We broke into a run, then burgled a sprint and ram-raided a gallop, racing away through a landscrape of dirt and dearth and death. Saturated fear and boiling hatred propelled us. Our blood was cut with kerosene; we ate hunger, drank thirst, recharged on exhaustion. Precious few words passed between us; we meshed like cogs.

Come the night, a luminous pill shone down to light our way.

'Girls and boys come out to play,' sang Harete. 'The moon doth shine as bright as day.'

We chomped the amphetamine moon and ploughed on

426

through the darkness. By dawn the landmarks had become familiar: a road, a path up a wooded hill, wreckage from a crashed aeroplane.

The vanguard of the Mothodists was in sight; they must have been recruited from heptathletes, pentathletes, decathletes, maybe even novemtrigenathletes. Those guys were *fit*, we were fit to drop. Toiling up the hillside I could see the Alderman's photo booth litter close behind us, swaying on its scaffolding poles.

An old friend scudded into view. And he'd brought a chum. Sweet.

Put-put-put-put!

Chug-chug-chug-a-chug!

Drones ahead of us, Mothodists behind us.

'Now we're done for,' cried Harete, exhaling hope. 'Caught between the devil and the deep blue sea!'

'Use them! Make a noise, be seen!' I said. We wrapped our tops tightly around our faces. I flapped a metal sheet, slanting the sun off the polished surface. Harete gonged another segment of airframe against a tree. After that we crawled like caterpillars, avoiding disturbing anything that might glint. The Mothodists were too numerous to mooch smoothly through the junk – within seconds they were bearing the brunt of the drones' attacks and the white pines rang with the howls of the blinded.

More landmarks: arboreal nuns, a denim blue tarn. Our old wheelie bin lay beached on a shingle bay; I retrieved the rope.

Harete remembered the proper route to the top of the high ridge. Last time, coming down, I'd taken a short cut,

427

chanced my arm. The Mothodists blew hunting horns and trumpets. I doubted Hyssop had recognised the one-armed bandit tormenting him, he had no reason to think I'd survived, but it made no difference.

'He'll march them up to the top of the hill,' I said. 'We have to stop him somehow – we must get to the anti-Moth before he does!'

The path wended its way up a slender gorge, a groove on a gradient. We scrambled along, hand over hand in Harete's case, hand over stump in mine. The gorge opened out onto a steep scree field.

'Ever topple dominoes, Mo?' Harete asked. 'Set them out in a fan shape and knock the one at the tip?'

'No, no,' I told her for the umpteenth time. 'Darts was my only game.'

So Harete showed me. She flipped the first tile, a washing-machine-sized rock ousted from its granite plinth, with a shunt from her back. The loosened rock struck two, the two struck two more. One, three, seven, fifteen . . . a chain reaction of rolling rocks. The avalanche decanted down the gorge, ending when a boulder as big as corner shop smashed over the narrow exit, plugging it neatly.

'A day's delay for sure – they'll need to take the long way round now!' Harete cheered.

From the windy, winding path at the ridge's summit we surveyed the lower peaks. The place I sought was difficult to locate, the hidden valley visible only from a specific spot.

'There,' I said at last, directing Harete's vision along my truncated arm. I'd memorised how the faces carved into the

428

cliff had looked at the instant I'd spotted it. 'You can see all the pylons running along the valley. That glass dome is either making a lot of power, or using it.'

'Beautiful. A crystal chateau,' she murmured, squinting. 'A sapphire tabernacle.'

'A Mo-sque. A syna-Moth?' I suggested.

'A cat-Harete-dral? Ouch!'

'The font of the fables, the mouth of the myths.'

'The eye of the tornado.'

'Not a tornado, Harete. A twister.'

Blood up, we tore down the path. Whenever we tripped and rolled we felt nothing but satisfaction at progress made more rapidly. Late in the bleary afternoon, we entered the shady green valley. The crystal dome was harder to reach than we'd realised from up on the ridge. I climbed a pylon, spied out the land.

'It's on an island,' I reported. 'An island in a lake on an island in a lake. The devil's island.'

'Two concentric moats, then,' Harete summarised, 'like target rings. The dome is the bullseye.'

We hacked up a raft. A brace of fallen tree trunks lashed together with the rope, nothing more than a floatation aid. Rub-a-dub-dog, two kids on a log. We straddled the craft and paddled across the first moat. Harete used only her legs; I experimented with a branch as a scull.

'Yo, Harete. This is the oar of Mercury!' I said, but with only one hand I couldn't use it and hold tight to the raft, so I slung it. Besides which, Harete looked ready to beat me to death.

The log stayed afloat, but it was heavy and very slow to

move. In the cooling woodland between the moats, Harete began to flag.

'Got anything to eat, Jack Sprat?' she asked. We were burned out, running on the reserves of our reserves and the memories of the memories of food and sleep.

'No fat and no lean. Only this,' I replied, tossing her the fruit Hyssop had gifted me. 'Dunno what it is, mind. A fig? With that groove, it looks like a bum.'

'Trust you to think of that. That's no fig. A greengage?'

'A damson? A damson in distress?'

'I don't think so, Mo. Let's open it up and have a look.'

Harete ran her fingernails around the seam, the fruit split easily into two halves. Beneath the yellow skin was a whitish flesh and embedded in that was a large, knobbly, dark brown nut. Wrapped around the woody nut, a tracery of lurid, lipstick-red filaments.

Harete slapped her forehead. 'Oh, now I know what this is! Listen:

I had a little nut tree,
Nothing would it bear.
But a silver nutmeg,
And a golden pear.'

'A pear?' I said.

Harete groaned, 'A nutmeg, dum-dum! The red stuff, when dried, is the spice called mace. The seed in the middle is the actual nutmeg,' she explained. 'More valuable than gold in the olden days. Two spices in one.'

Astounded by its complexity, I retrieved the divided fruit and held it up close to my face. 'My life. My life in a nutshell,' I whispered to myself. The scarlet mace reminded me of the veins in my arm: with its contoured, labyrinthine surface, the seed resembled a brain. Taken as a whole, the fruit rhymed with our struggles: layer inside layer inside layer, with a hard, impenetrable core.

'Want some?' I said to Harete, but her face informed me the suggestion rated lower than an earwax omelette. Chilli-skilled, I reckoned a whole spice would do me no harm. I prised out the big seed, pummelled it between two stones and lapped up all the fibrous crumbs.

Disgusting. Not hot, just too . . . too . . . nutmeggy. Almost immediately I began to feel grouty, and horribly dry in the mouth. The moat water was undrinkable, malodorous and scummy.

Harete chuckled at my discomfort. 'I'll settle for a story, that's one nut we can crack. Let's drag the raft to the next moat – we'll finish the story as we work. This is the right time for endings.'

'A Stay of Execution, Part V'
As told by Lex
As retold by Harete
As remembered by Mo

When Nestor regained consciousness, he found himself lying on a beach, wreckage from his smashed-up boat strewn all around him. He crawled

431

inland, found a stream to drink from and some wild strawberries to eat.

It will probably not surprise you any more than it did Nestor to learn that the place he had arrived in was in fact his original homeland. Living as a tramp, he roamed the towns and countryside, scavenging food from bins and sleeping on park benches. A new obsession took hold of him, an all-enveloping urge to locate the person Nestor had come to hold responsible for all the misfortunes he had suffered. Day and night he hunted, calling out the accursed man's name.

His perseverance paid off; after a decade of searching he found the very man, reclining in an old haunt.

'Well, well, well. Speak of the devil,' said Nestor.

He brushed the nettles aside from the headstone and read the name again. His name, on his headstone. The grave was his; it had been made by the prison authorities to sustain the fiction of his execution.

'Were you a friend?' asked a voice. Nestor whirled around. It was his wife! Aged and grey, but unmistakably her. She did not register Nestor's true identity; years spent languishing on death throws and working in strange lands and living rough had changed his appearance beyond cognisance.

'No friend of mine. A bad man,' said Nestor. 'He ruined my life.'

His wife sighed, knelt, and placed some flowers on

the grave. 'He was bad. And yet, I think he did love me.'

'He did. I know that for a fact,' affirmed Nestor.

'Then, if he was capable of love, why do you think he was so restless and violent? Could you explain that?'

Nestor thought. 'It is love that drives his sort mad. They love, they live, they love life. And they can never overcome the outrage that life is so fragile, so impermanent. They carry with them the knowledge that they will die, that those they love will die. Every death is the death of the entire universe, as far as the dier is concerned. What sane mind can accept that? To them, it seems that none should have life, if it cannot be forever it may as well be ended straight away.'

'And what shall we tell such people?' asked his wife. 'How can we make the world tolerable to them?'

'They must know that there is always forgiveness. It is the one thing worth seeking.'

'I forgive him,' said his wife.

All at once, Nestor knew that he had found what he had never even known he had been looking for.

The two of them separated and never met again. Nestor achieved at last a form of contentment. He shunned all company and remained a passive observer of other people. The only thing that bothered him was his own longevity. He grew very old, and was assailed by a great many aches and pains, regrets and sorrows.

One day, pottering around the cemetery amongst the graves, he came to crave his own Last Day. 'I am too old to live,' he said to a cat that had made its home amongst the catacombs and catafalques. 'Why have I been denied what I skipped so many times and brought so wrongly to others?'

The cat took pity on him. She scratched him, and to Nestor's astonishment he succumbed within minutes to an infected wound, dying from appundicitis. At the instant of his death, Nestor experienced a most peculiar thing: all the closing brackets and parentheses and speech marks that he had ever forgotten to write or type during his life (having opened one, and then forgotten to close it, like this, or 'this came whizzing down from the sky and slotted into place, neatly wrapping up the matter of his existence.)))))))""""""]]]]]]]]]]]

'Forgiveness, Harete? Not for The Moth,' I insisted. There could be no backsliding. The snout of our two-log raft nuzzled the inner bank of the second moat. We dismounted and splashed up the shore. We had reached the dome; we could see then it was a geodesic hemisphere made from metal struts and hexagons of . . . not sapphire or crystal, only clear plastic. The glowing dome hummed to itself. Perhaps it didn't know the words.

Harete bounced a hand off one of the dome's panels, flexing it, testing it. 'You need to break in now, Mo,' she said.

'Breaking out's my speciality, I'm a . . . well, a dab hand at

that,' I reminded her. 'Never tried breaking in anywhere before.'
But there was no need to swot up on burglary; within a minute
we had located an open door. Inside – an inviting coolness.

Harete hesitated. 'Can you do it, Mo? Can you really kill
Moth, our friend? Because I don't think I can. Sorry.'

I stopped dead. Randomised memories blitzed me: the young
mother in the Facility – no, the memory was too oversized to
touch off my hate; the mismatched socks worn by the old man
dangling from the dead-line – no, too small a detail; a tearful
child forced to throw away her beloved fair-haired doll as she
fled her destroyed home. That fitted.

'I'll do it, Harete. But I'll have to close my eyes. I'll shut
them and think of Meg and Nonstop.'

My shakes had shakes, my shivers had shivers. I urgently
wanted to do a dump. I rubbed my stomach. Pain, a scab load of
bad pain down there. What was wrong with me? Could killing
Moth be so much worse than watching Lew or Nonstop die?

'We loved Moth, not so long ago.'

'I know.' *Crud*, I thought. My rule. What was loved once . . .
No! *He isn't Moth any more, he is anti-Moth*. He would not
wriggle to safety through bylaws or clauses. 'How many have
died in this war?'

'I don't know, Mo. A million?'

'Then if I kill him . . .'

Harete looked me in the face, shook her head. 'It's not like
conkers. That won't make you a million and one-er.'

'Only a one-er. But more like a goner, because we won't
survive this, you know that?' I told her. I took my knife and
used my teeth to swing out the blade and lock it into position.

435

'Yes, I understand. Are we totally sure this is where Moth is?'

'Oh, yes, it's that all right,' I said. My guts went into spasm. 'Look!' I grunted, battling the pain, determined to stand up straight.

Above the door was a sign. The sign said:

WELCOME TO

THE CENTRE

OF

EVERYTHING

Chapter 55

And that's exactly what it was.

Or rather, it was the *visitors'* centre of everything. A museum. Complete with a gift shop. I walked in, switched on the lights, sprung open a till. No change in the drawer. No water in the toilets either, my next port of call, and much needed.

The centre was deserted, shuttered and shut.

'No, Mo. Not shut,' said Harete. 'I don't think it ever opened, that it was ever finished.' She was spot on. There were dust sheets on the floors, ladders propped against walls, tins of creamy paint with rubbery skins you couldn't poke a finger through. No noise, no workers, no visitors. All the same, we shut and bolted the main doors.

The museum was scabbing brilliant. What little we saw of it, for we barely skimmed the surface in the hour we spent exploring. Harete insisted, convinced it may contain clues. I didn't object; I needed time for the invisible gorilla's fist to quit massaging my interior organs. We must have still been a day ahead of Alderman Hyssop and the Mothodists; there was no rush. My head felt fluffy, foggy, floaty.

The subject of the museum was everything.

Everything.

From electrons to elastic to elderberries to elephants, and how all were inevitably, intimately connected.

We walked around the periphery of the dome, reading, learning, our tiredness shelved. Hands-on exhibits, too, not just dry text. Hand-on, rather. What did we learn?

All life is an anagram. Only four letters: G, A, T and C. And the letters are pinned to a spiral. No, two spirals intermeshed, one clockwise, one anticlockwise. DNA, the spiral is called.

'Just what I've always said,' I laughed. 'We're all on the Spiral.'

The letters form a coded message, the message: 'make more of me'. Mix your messages, transpose the letters, and you might accidentally stew a tumour. That's what Meg suffered from – some of her cells must have anagrammed incorrectly, made a bad pun.

What else?

The legends of stuff; much of the dome's circumference was devoted to this subject, the things that make the things that make the atoms that make the molecules that make the chemicals that make the universe. Posters described itsy-bitsy morsels of matter too small to have any size at all, soulless stuff-crumbs powered by high-energy maths. Me, I couldn't move beyond visualising the strangely named particles as belonging to a menagerie of googly eyed beasties with sproingy antennae.

And all the wee beasties have anti-beasties, their mirror image twins. Reason dictated there should have been as much plus as minus, back when the cosmic starting pistol was fired, but it transpired there was just a pinch more of the positive than the negative.

'Reassuring,' cooed Harete. 'I know it's not really good versus evil, but it's nice it didn't all cancel out.'

That's us, the planets, everything, we're all made from the leftovers. The heavier elements were brewed up from the lighter ones inside star hearts. The beasties are weird. You can glue 'em together to make new ones, or bust others up. Lots rot on their own, fall apart. Others have jobs to do, acting like carrier pigeons, conveying spooky messages: *feel this force!* You can pun with them too; there were charts like hopscotch courts that plotted the permissible ways to switch one type into another. Details. I couldn't focus. Sweat, so much sweat, my hands and face gushing with moisture. Fear? I'd been scared enough times before, but never had the sweats and the shakes and the shivers like I had then.

Go deep enough, it was all squiggly loops – they guessed. String cheese.

Go wide enough, it was galaxies. A lot of them were spiral-shaped too, I noticed. To comprehend the mechanics of the galaxies and the more substantial boroughs of the cosmos, you had to know all about the teeny-weeny beastie stuff, the engines of substance. And the other way around, for everything connected at every scale, everywhere played to the same set of rules. Like a stick of seaside rock with a slogan moulded through it, common principles were threaded like clues throughout the entirety of eternity. The secret to understanding the story of the universe, it seemed, was to follow the clues draped likes threads of silk through a labyrinth, silvery veins of similarities and symmetries.

'This is where Nonstop worked,' said Harete. 'Down below.'

Down below. The purpose of the unfinished visitor's centre, the place people were supposed to be visiting before they returned to the dome, where they'd purchase ice lollies and novelty key rings. Not my kind of people, but even the Fartherland had people who thought learning was fun. Weirdos.

What lay below? Circular tunnels, long enough to ring a city, wide enough to drive trains along. Inside them were not trains, but pipes. Pipes full mainly of nothing, not even air, just super-fast, super tiny beasties and anti-beasties.

Far beneath our feet, buzzing bunches of the two micro-micro-microscopic beastie species were hurtled around in the vacuum pipes, spun faster and faster, travelling almost at the speed of fright, spiralling out into tunnels of ever greater radius before being introduced to each other in head-on collisions. Millions of them a second, every smash a photo finish. No survivors, only offspring – new particles forged in the nano-fires of the collisions. The crunches took place inside a collide-a-scope, a *detector* machine it was called, surrounded by the world's most powerful magnet, deep frozen for efficiency. I supposed they needed a magnet for the same reason a scrapyard uses one, to sift out the desirable stuff from the crud, the piston rings from the furry dice. Scientists studied the pictures of the collisions, the tracks left by the scattering subatomic fragments as they whizzed through the magnetic field. Some travelled in straight lines, others moved in . . .

Spirals. I might have known. Could be why everything I looked at was gyrating merrily; I had spirals on the noodle, circles on the noggin. My vision switched from rotating to see-sawing. See-saw, Margery Daw. Oh well, swings and roundabouts . . . drunk, this was what people told me being drunk was like, but I didn't drink, my tribe didn't drink, Dad never drunk. Mum had drunk though, booze loved her too much . . . stomach better, head worse . . .

'That's why they needed the juice from all those pylons. Must have cost mega-shekles, giga-guilder,' I burbled breathlessly, steadying myself against a display board. 'But what were they after?'

'The heart of matter,' Harete replied. She'd read more deeply. 'Obscure characters from the alphabet of stuff. Above all, for some sort of missing messenger particle, a . . . hang on, it was on a poster around here . . . well, anyway, a doo-dah named a *vector boson*, a sort of messenger particle they needed to complete the picture.'

'A bozo? They were searching for a bozo called Victor?'

'If you insist, Mo. But the laboratory was never completed. War stopped play.'

Ah-choo!

Not me, not Harete.

Ah-choo!

The sneezes were coming from the middle of the dome. And who would feel at home in a dome, a museum above a laboratory? This was the Centre of Everything, this was the lair of the anti-Moth!

Ah-choo!

'Let's do this!' I gnarled, not adding: *before I fall apart*.

We darted along a corridor into the interior of the dome. Knife in hand, I borrowed energy from some future version of myself, sucked in my chest, my giddiness, my cramps, laced the lot behind a corset.

How would I kill Moth? Slit his throat? Stab him in the chest? I flipped the blade horizontally, readied myself to thrust the steel upwards, under the base of his ribs. That done, I'd rip it from side to side, burst sac and cut gut. He was a monster; it wasn't murder it was justice.

'Kill the anti-Moth!' I whispered, biting off the question mark, wanting Harete to follow suit. Instead, she put her finger to her lips. Would she choke, when it came to the crunch? Would I?

The interior of the dome was a humid hothouse burgeoning with exotic flora, a continuing demonstration of the kinship of nature at every scale. Fauna as well: velvety objects biffed into me – butterflies and moths. Two birds with full-spectrum plumage chirruped at us, flapped away. Fly away Peter, fly away Paul. Stool pigeons; the sneezer knew we were about. We sidled forwards under knotty loops of lianas, creeping through the vegetation towards the centre of the Centre of Everything.

Harete cried, 'Ahead of us, the clearing!'

The lights cut out; darkness dropped down quicker than a sister from a cliff. The bird chirps stopped.

A shadow shape shot up from a chair. Slightly built, just right for The Moth.

I lunged, blade first. Harete sprang out behind me. There was an abrupt *twang!* Something fast zipped through my hair, styling me a centre parting. My blade sunk into Moth, no, *anti*-Moth. Such tough, crocodilian flesh! Must have struck a rib, but I couldn't see a thing. I twisted the blade around, killing my old friend, stabbing the rat, murdering the murderer. *More force – pretend you're opening the lid on a jar of pickled chillies.* I wrenched harder, the handle snapped off.

'You do it, Harete, throttle him, brain him!'

'I can't,' screamed Harete, 'I can't kill him!'

What could I do? Typical fight, a scabby mess.

'ORDER!'

Chapter 56

'ORDER!'

Wrong voice.

The lights sparked on again, the birds resumed singing. Bright normality coshed us.

Order? It was the oddness of the word as much as the force of its delivery that held me in stasis.

The woman who had called time on our bungled charge smiled – a cold, sly, knowing smile. Older than Sister, younger than Origin, with bouffant, brass-coloured hair, she wore a dowdy chequered housecoat and a pair of fluffy slippers.

'S-sorry,' Harete gulped, rocking with the impulse of our aborted attack. 'We thought you were someone else.'

'But that's exactly who I am, deary. Someone else,' said the woman. She lowered the crossbow she had fired at me. I was standing next to the hairy tree trunk I had stabbed in error. My knife was bin-fodder; only the saw blade remained, jack-all use for an assassination.

'You're early,' the woman went on. 'You took me by surprise. I'd was informed you'd been delayed by a rock fall.' Her voice sounded flat and nerveless. She shuffled her feet and scowled,

I think she was miffed we'd caught her dressed so casually.

The adrenalin drained out of my system, my overdrawn strength sublimated. I felt there were important things we should have been doing and asking, but I couldn't connect. My to-do list was soaked in sweat, the ink had run and made the writing illegible. In any case, the tropical flowers around me were so much more deserving of my scrutiny. Never before had I been exposed to such shameless, vibrant hues of pink and yellow, such opulent magentas, such a profundity of blues as were there flaunted, accompanied by every conceivable shade of green and then some. Compared to the hothouse flowers, tropical fish and peacocks would have possessed all the chromatic marvel of old chip wrappers.

'This really is paradise,' I gushed, swaying. I pinched off a kaleidoscope flower as big as a tea cup, sniffed it. 'You look kind of familiar, missus. Are you the Creator?'

'Not me, deary. I'm only the Curator,' chuckled the woman. 'And it may look pretty but it sets off my hay fever something awful. Was it something in particular you were looking for?'

'A Moth,' said Harete. 'That's who.' Her manner was steely and suspicious, she didn't trust the woman. Neither did I, but it didn't overly bother me. The Curator *did* look familiar though. I gave her the once-over, twice. Must have blinked and missed something; she'd already reloaded the crossbow.

'We've plenty of those,' said the Curator. 'Any particular species? We've titan moths, gypsy moths, praxidike moths, heart and dart moths, nutmeg moths, Pale Beauty, cinnabar –'

My life in moths! An odd word snagged my ear. 'What's cinnabar?'

'The colour vermillion. Oh, and it's a mineral too. An ore of mercury, mercury sulphide if memory serves.'

Horrified, I ground up my flower head and blurted out, 'Free mercury combined with another. Trapped! The end of mercury!'

'Or its origin,' the Curator pointed out. 'The source of the substance.'

Harete again, 'Mo, behave! Never mind geology, it's lepidoptery we're concerned with. None of those moths you mentioned are the ones we're after. What about an Emperor moth? What about the Black Witch or the Death's-Head Hawkmoth?'

'Ahhhh,' sighed the Curator, sounding as if an issue long skirted had at last been broached. 'To see the special collection you'll need a ticket. An out-of-season ticket. Have you one?'

Her crossbow was aimed squarely at Harete's chest. Point blank range – she'd not miss. I swiped my hands free of crushed petals, sending out puffs of yellow pollen. Sod the soppy flower; weapon, weapon, I needed a weapon! Bamboo, staves, twine, secateurs, *anything*.

'As Curator, I have a policy of zero tolerance towards trespassers. Your ticket, now!'

Harete shuffled backwards. 'But we haven't got one, oh, please don't shoot!'

The Curator growled, 'Die, spy. Enjoy your second belly but –'

Ah-choo! The bullwhip sneeze ate her last word; she bucked violently and the bolt flew wild. 'Blasted pollen!'

'Wait up,' I shouted. 'I've got the ticket.' I fished around in my pockets, pulled out the two halves of the nutmeg fruit and showed them to the Curator. *Our token, all Moth's allies have it*, those had been Hyssop's words. I bet myself there was a nutmeg tree growing nearby; I looked but I didn't know what it would look like, and besides, the flowers were ganging up and calling me names. Were they really flowers, or only the ideas of flowers? Hard to tell – the blooms started conflating themselves with birds, becoming toucans and parrots and macaws.

The Curator gasped. 'Your ticket's been defaced. Where's the kernel?'

'In my head, silly, silly old Curator!' I giggled. 'The Kernel's in my head!'

Harete explained, 'He ate the seed, if that's what you mean.' Then, to me, 'Mo, what's got into you?'

'That changes everything,' sighed the Curator. 'Strictly no admittance. You cannot meet the moth you seek. A shame, you look like you've come a long way, really been through the wars.'

'But why? It's only a mouldy old spice!' I shouted. I had to do so from the floor, my legs had divorced me, wandered off. 'Bread and spice! We all need bread and spice. Little girls are made of sugar and spice, and . . . you have left too much spice between sugar and "and" and . . .'

The Curator loomed over me, stared down. A rock-hard woman, I could tell that then, she had craggy breasts of feldspar, a porphyry complexion, lips of schist. *That* was where I'd seen her before: her visage was one of the four giant faces we'd seen carved into the cliff!

'You've overdosed, you stinking cripple,' she sneered. 'A little nutmeg is the spice of life, eating a whole one is fatal. Didn't you know even that? The Moth doesn't want to know filthy vagrants who've poisoned themselves, he only wants to meet his real friends, the ones he'll rule the Fartherland with! You're *dying.*'

Dying.

Dying of ignorance, killed by my own hand, poisoned in paradise. We'd almost made it through to the centre of the maze and found the anti-Moth, but I had fallen victim to the twist, let myself be . . . from a cranny in a nook in my profaned brain popped an answer to a question from months before, a footballing term. I'd been hoodwinked, conned . . .

Nutmegged.

Chapter 57

Harete gave me the finger. Two of them, straight down my throat.

'Sick it out, Mo!' she wailed, Wednesday's child, but I had nothing inside me, only a splurge of grotty moat water mixed with slugs, snails, puppy dogs' tails, stolen jam tarts, pease pudding (hot), blackbirds in a pie, and rye, one pocketful. The blackbirds muscled off the crust and broke free.

'You are allowed only one story!' they honked crossly, phasing into winged euphoniums. 'One nation, one story. Control The Moth, control the myth; control the myth, control the people.'

My body was burning up. Compared to the heat I felt then, the exploding generator truck had been cooler than a North Pole sponge bath.

My mind was gone, hopelessly entangled in the mace maze.

Sinking, I met a man I knew, going to the fair. Or riding on a pony, possibly a cock horse.

'Oh dear, what can the matter be?' I asked him.

{This is bad, Mo.}

[Is it time, Father?] (Are we nearly there yet?) <Wake up, everyone!>

'Am I dying, Kernel? Poisoned by your namesake?'

{It's my fault. I've been busy, we're so near to full term . . .
I . . . I should have watched you closer, stopped you.}

'So, I am dying.'

{The nutmeg seed was a large one. You've ingested a huge
dose of myristicin. The effects are unpredictable. There is no
antidote.}

[Father, what's that funny taste? Smells like
6-allyl-4-methoxy-1,3-benzodioxole.]

<The clocks are all running fast. Is he tachycardic?>

{Mo, you need to fight, fight hard. There's nothing you can
do except allow your body to sweat it out, hope your heart
doesn't go into overdrive. I'm going to have to administer
extreme function, tame the hallucinations, keep you on the
straight and narrow.}

'The straight and narrow? What about the twist?'

{The drug's a weak abortifacient – it's stimulated premature
labour. From now on, I'm going to be very busy, doing whatever
I can to delay it. If you do pull through, Mo, I won't be around
to help you. Just remember everything I've taught you, the
lessons of your life. Most of all, remember this: don't let yourself
be distracted. *Always concentrate on the matter in hand!*}

'Kernel! One thing, I must know. Are you the final Number?'

{Good luck, Mercury. We chose well. The failure is mine,
not yours.}

He left, I sunk deeper, deeper. After I'd bottomed out, I spent
a lifetime as an occasional table, nibbling the colour turquoise,
listening to X-ray sonatas. A kangaroo called Bartholomew
Pugh befriended me. In the Creator's herb garden we played

450

pool using neutrons for balls. The bay leafs kept cumin, they towed the caraway and evicted us. They left us with nothing but the cloves on our backs, we were men of constant sorrel. We had to doss down inside a cinnamon stick. Roomier than it looked, eleven dimensions in space and time were rolled up there like spare carpets.

'Mo? Can you hear me? Are you alive? MO! Say something, say anything, even one of your crap jokes!'

The voice rattled me, I dropped the book I was holding. When I picked it up again, I couldn't find the page I'd been on so I flipped to a random chapter and resumed reading. The story concerned a postman with a very important parcel to deliver. He – that is, me, for it was all first person – came around in a greenhouse.

Feeling cooler and stronger, I embarked on an Odyssey. My quest was for a hero, but I wound up stumbling into an anteroom full of antirrhinums, then raging in a reflective pond at an anti-hero. An anti-heroine kept nagging and dragging me, telling me we had to get away, that I'd been unconscious for five hours solid; it was night, they were coming, coming, she could hear them gathering outside, they had a machine. Who she was I did not know, but she was definitely an adversary, I felt nothing but antipathy towards her. Hers had been the voice that had made me lose my place!

'Go sit on a tuffet!' I shouted at her. 'Go put the kettle on, go live in a shoe, go find your sheep!' I pushed the annoying girl over, made her cry, pudding and pie. I jumped back to the outer corridor and the exhibits there.

Paranoia beset me: had I done something bad, wronged

451

someone I cared for? I couldn't decide; there was a bundle of muddle in my butterfly mind.

Only running could help, return me from outer spice. For an hour and a lifetime I ran and ran around the perimeter passageway, running like a ragged rascal. Jogging definitely improved things, with every footfall my thoughts clarified. I had so much energy I could have powered a city, overpowered one! No pain, in fact I felt wonderful, fit as a fiddle, hey diddle diddle.

New problem: words flailed me.

I stared intently at a photograph of the giant machine in the subterranean tunnels below us, the atoms' masher. What was it called? The letters of its name whizzed around at high velocity, rearranging themselves before my mind's eye.

'Elect a reciprocal rat.' That rang no bells. 'A calico crap letterer?' Don't think so. 'Rectal apricot cereal.' Definitely not.

'Particle accelerator!' I yelled triumphantly. Yes, it was all coming back to me; my memory, my understanding, the letters, all were slotting back into the correct positions. I'd been poisoned by a seed, I'd been hallucinating, but I was almost cured.

Next, a photo of the detector chamber where the collisions between the travelling particles occurred. It looked like a gigantic cotton reel on its side, and a key part of it was all about . . . about . . . 'Concepts during a nutmeg.'

That couldn't be right. Nutmeg? The very idea made me want to puke. Try again, re-rearrange.

'Superconducting magnet?' That sounded more likely!

Finally, a face. The face of a friend. Which friend?

Bartholomew Pugh? Never heard of him. The Curator? She was no friend, she was Moth's guardian, a prize piece of nasty work. This face was smiling, delighted to see me. A fine-featured, delicate face. A girl, then.

'I forgive you,' said the welcoming face. I had to read the face's rouged lips, deafness apparently being a side effect of my intoxication. 'I forgive you for all the hurt you've caused me.'

I blushed and lowered my eyes, humbled. Forgiveness was a gift to be worn next to the skin.

The face spoke again. 'I knew you'd survive. We were meant to be together, you and me. Forever.'

Yes, that was true, I felt that earnestly. We'd been forced apart many times over, but our splits were only ever temporary, always followed by reunion and reconciliation.

The name of the face was . . . oh, tip of my tongue . . . I thought of the Kernel, working away inside my brain, munching my madness. *Work harder, Kernel*, I thought, *fix this anagrammania!*

The face: 'She pylons drama.' That was close to the truth, I felt, but not correct for all that.

'A sharp, sly demon.'

Better, yet still not quite right. The face was connected via a body and an arm to a hand. The hand waved at me. I waved back. We were standing on opposite sides of the dome's hexagonal panels, me inside in the light, the face outside in the dark. That was why I hadn't heard the voice; I wasn't deaf after all! The face and its parent body moved away from the window, climbed into a big yellow vehicle I'd only then noticed.

The vehicle was called a droll zebu. A dullbozer. A bulldozer!

453

The vehicle was called a bulldozer, and the man in the cab was Alderman Hyssop.

The bulldozer surged forwards with a stentorian growl. The machine's curved blade kissed the dome and the dome burst like a pricked balloon, plastic and metal crashing down all around me. Uniformed Mothodists launched themselves through the breach. One of them snatched at me, grabbed hold of my sleeve at the cuff.

'I've got him, Alderman!' he shouted.

But the sleeve he held was my empty sleeve, the left! I twisted from him, sloughed off my jacket and scrambled towards the dome's core. The Kernel had timed his mind meal perfectly, he'd noshed the nutmeg insanity but left me charged with the euphoric afterglow. I tore ahead of the Mothodists, scattering display boards in my wake.

I charged into the hothouse. The support struts were buckling as the rampaging bulldozer smashed up the palace of science; roof panels were popping out and landing all around me, their bevelled edges making them as deadly as six-sided hatchets. Mothodists flooded in, tried to head me off. I swerved around a bush – not a mulberry bush, I'd outgrown all that – and dived through a plant with emerald leaves as large as dinner plates. A floppy thing broke my fall, stiffening and thrashing back the moment I touched it.

'Harete!' I shouted.

Her reply was a grazing left hook, she rolled away. 'Back off!' she cried. 'You utter nutter, you junkie monkey.'

'Better now very sorry can't explain no time where's Curator?'

'Gone! You were out of your gourd for hours.' She lowered her fists. 'Really better?'

'Yes! Where gone?'

'Not main doors. Must be second exit.'

I scanned. The bulldozer crunched into the hothouse, squeaking and rattling, its caterpillar tracks mulching up the plants. We lay flat as flapjacks; I looked around, through the leaves, through the legs of searching Mothodists.

'There!'

We cut and ran for it, a small, nondescript tree with arrowhead leaves growing from a wooden tub. From its branches dangled spotty yellow fruits. Many had split ajar, provocatively flaunting nutmegs out through their gashes. Resting against the tub was a crossbow and a quiver of bolts.

And a trapdoor, there in the floor, the Curator's bolt hole!

Harete picked up the bow, jammed her foot in the stirrup and pulled back on the bowstring, priming it. I heaved open the heavy trapdoor. The dozer was near, deafening, driving straight for us.

Hyssop leaned out of the cab and beckoned to his troops. 'The girl and the boy, the golden pair, we have them both!' he shouted. 'Snatch-squad, advance. Catch them and I'll have absolute power over the absolute power!'

Birds were screeching, moths were fluttering, the lights blew out with a pop and a fizzle, only the destroying machine's headlamps lit the scene. The roof of the dome began to crumple inwards, sinking like a deflating soufflé. The hunting Mothodists had to take cover as spars and girders rained down like javelins.

The bulldozer blade caught the nutmeg tree, snapped it like a pencil. The severed trunk whipped down, barely missing

455

us; loathsome nutmegs bounced everywhere, thudding onto our heads.

'Down the hatch!'

Harete loosed off a bolt, aiming high and scoring a bullseye on the bulldozer's radiator. *Hisssssssss!*

We dropped into a cubby hole, little larger than a phone box.

'Hold that hatch!' I yelled at Harete. She did so, straining down on the inside handle with all her strength. We were safe for a few seconds only; the idiots had driven the bulldozer over the top of the trapdoor. A tracheal cough from above signified the engine revving up, the driver shifting gear into reverse.

Way out, must be a . . . my stump bumped a hidden switch. A slice of wall clicked open. Two bounds along a corridor, through a grille and into a lift, this at the precise instant a Mothodist dropped feet first in the cubicle behind us.

Harete ripped the grille shut. The lift whooshed away at once, no need to press a button.

'Going *down*!' we shouted together.

'If this is the route from the visitor's centre to the underground laboratory, they can't have been expecting many tourists,' said Harete.

'This won't be the main way, just a service shaft, or something for the builders to use,' I guessed aloud, swallowing hard to quell the popping in my ears. My guts had bubbled into my chest; the lift was *fast*.

'Who was the Curator waiting for, Mo?' Harete asked. 'Who are the other nutmeg ticket holders?'

I scratched my chin. 'Whoever the anti-Moth has invited to his hideout. The other evil crud-suckers he's working hand in hand with. Scab my phrases, hands, hands, why so many hands?'

'Alderman Hyssop?'

'And others we've yet to meet. I reckon Hyssop's been kept at arm's length until now. Gah! These expressions are so . . . *handy*. Hyssop's like a kid you don't want joining your secret gang, but he's got the best bike, or he looks old enough to get served down the pub. Something you want, so you pretend you like him. What he has in this case are the Mothodists, an army of them.'

Harete followed me. 'But he's worked out he's not really one of the club. So he turns up mob-handed – oops – and planning to take over.'

'Yup. Even the people who've been organising the civil war are at war with each other. Wars within wars. Hyssop's enough of a screwball to think he can use us to manipulate anti-Moth. He thinks we're still his friends.'

I had my own question for Harete. 'What about those other cults, the Hareticals and Momons? Do you think they're under Hyssop's control too?'

Harete rabbit-wiggled her nose. 'I think stories are like atoms and particles. They can clump together, or split spontaneously, spin off new tales. And with them go their followers. I've no proof, but I reckon the other cults and their versions of Moth's story are beyond Hyssop's control.'

Our discourse hit the buffers. The lift braked, the grille slid aside, we rolled out. I had the rare presence of mind to jam my broken knife into the door mechanism to prevent the lift from returning.

We found ourselves standing in a corridor, starkly lit with

457

fluorescent tubes. The walls were composed of floor-to-ceiling racks of buzzing electronic equipment, some sort of super-computer I fancied, perhaps the one I once dreamed had selected Nonstop to be my pen pal. Pinprick lights in green and red twinkled at us from the giant computer's matt-black surface. The machine droned ominously.

I was drenched in sweat. Harete too: her clothes were sopping wet and stained black with perspiration. Yet by the time we stood up, we were practically dry. That felt unexpected. Harete moved under a ceiling vent. The tresses of her hair boogied upwards towards a powerful fan working behind a shield of louvered slats.

Water boils in a vacuum, fact plankton implanted in my mind's baleen plates.

'They're pumping all the air out, that's why the moisture's evaporating so quickly!' I yelped. My body seized up with nervous excess, became as rigid as a camshaft.

'Let them. We're not going to be defeated now, Mo,' said Harete. 'Not after all this. We've had so many wrong turns, mistaken identities, hidden summits, but now . . . he's within touching distance. I know it.'

Harete's bruised face was an embroidery of channelled malice. She'd have no scruples this time about killing our enemy, there would be no flunking out like in the dome. The Curator's final gloating words had confirmed the anti-Moth's degeneracy.

She slotted a bolt into the crossbow's groove. I took my inspiration from her, forced myself to calm down.

'We're coming for you, anti-Moth!' I shouted hoarsely. 'Play your last hand, cos we're coming to kill you!'

Part 7:

Break In

Chapter 58

The long banks of chuntering computer racks had been arrayed into a maze.

Squeezing along the narrow aisles between them, we figured that out in a trice. We couldn't crawl under the walls or climb over them or see through them, we could only weave our way through the gaps. No choice but to play the game like two lab rats.

'Easy cheesy. I can solve any maze with one hand –'

'Tied behind your back?'

'No, against the wall. We'll use the right-hand rule. Keep that bow ready.'

I stuck out my hand, pressed it to the wall on that side. Then we ran, making sure I never removed my hand, letting it guide us around each blind alley and dead end. The air was constantly thinning thanks to the up-draught from the sucking fans; the shiny corridors were level, but from the effort it took to move it felt like we were ascending an icy slope, working against a bungee cord knotted around our waists.

Right turn, forwards, right turn, forwards, right turn, round a corner, repeat, repeat, repeat – was this it?

The start, the open lift. Definitely the same lift, there was my knife stopping the door.

Huh?

We fell over, not from shock but aftershock – the *rumble-crump* of an explosion struck us, the pressure wave plucked my diaphragm. Somewhere nearby, we surmised, the Mothodists were blasting their way in. Cheats.

'Let me try, I'll use my left,' said Harete. 'You must have removed your hand at a vital junction.' Off again. We fared no better that time, taking a different route through the twisty lanes but still finishing back where we'd started. A third attempt, following Harete's right hand, yielded the same dud result.

I lashed out with a foot at the buzzing electronic walls, bored of performing circuits amongst the circuit boards.

'Impossible! The hand rule solves all mazes!' I grizzled, deeply perplexed.

'Your rule's a crock of slop!' barked Harete. Her face looked pink and puffy; my skin felt tight, my mouth brick dry.

Harete swooned momentarily. She was flaunting a lavish nosebleed. I swiped my hand across my face – rich, red blood. We were no medics, but even we realised we had precious little time and air remaining, minutes at most.

Suddenly, Harete angled the crossbow vertically upwards and fired. The bolt shot through the slatted cover and stuck between the blades of the extractor fan, stopping it from spinning.

'Why didn't I think of that to start with?' she cried, angry with herself. 'Must be lack of oxygen, juddling our mudgement!'

Reloading the bow took our combined strengths. We hobbled to the next fan and shot that out too. Then it was time for me

462

to earn my awe. How slow on the uptake could a boy be, how long could it take him to learn the lesson of his life?

Prisons in prisons, words in words, wars in wars, stories in stories, kernel in mace in flesh in skin.

Mazes within mazes.

We *had* reached the centre of the maze, each time we'd tried. But at the centre lay another maze, entirely separate from the outer one, its walls not connected to those of its parent. The hand-on-the-wall method had navigated us neatly around the inner puzzle and back to the beginning without ever taking us inside it. *Cunning, cunning anti-Moth.*

The final raid: hyperventilating to draw as much air as possible into our barren, burning breasts, we tottered back into the maze. Every time we passed under a fan, Harete pranged it with an arrow. That time it was a cinch to see what we'd missed previously, a region of the maze we'd circled but never infiltrated.

We squeezed through the only gap. My throat and chest could not have hurt more if I'd been gargling with cutlery. The walkways between the humming computer units were as narrow as capillary tubes; we had to turn edgeways on and crab walk.

'We won't give up!' I grated. 'Won't. Give. Up. Not now, not after . . . Spiral, for one.'

'Compensation Camp for two,' said Harete.

'Blinding lasers and rats, for three.'

'Facility and Fractions, for four. Then the mountains, five.'

'Mothodists, branding, amputation, my six.'

'War, bombing. Seven.'

'The Centre, with the Curator, poisoning. Eight.'

'This maze, suffocating. Nine layers, Mo. Nine vicious circles, one inside the other.'

Shapeless wraiths teased us, corner-of-the-eye poltergeists that skimmed across the narrow passageways, sometimes ahead of us, sometimes behind. Real or imaginary? My deep-me nutmeg voyage had left me mistrustful of my senses.

Real! One man, one woman, one net to bag us with. The man loomed at one end of the passageway, the woman at the opposite end; they'd timed the jump well, there were no side turnings for us to duck down. They both looked hard-baked, lined and leathery, stocky and blocky. Patches on their jackets bore the crown of barbed-wire emblem – Mothodists.

I ducked. Harete aimed her bow over the top of my head at the woman, but the target vomited and crumpled before Harete had put stock to shoulder. The man too was on his knees, clutching his head; he shouted for help, but the air was so tenuous by then the sound that reached us was a squeak. I thought of those street mime artists who pretend to be trapped in glass boxes. I had no coin to throw him; there was nothing I could do to save his life.

We climbed over the woman, blood was gushing from her nose and from the corners of her eyes. They'd overexerted themselves in their haste to reach us, paid the tariff.

Forwards, left turn, left turn, forwards. We pottered and tottered with tiny, unsteady steps, moving like novice ice skaters, never letting go of the side. Every part of me throbbed; I was conscious of all the organs in my body, every follicle and synapse. My brain must have swelled in my skull; the pressure felt unendurable, my head was straining to burst.

'Can't go on . . . much . . . longer,' groaned Harete. Her or the maze?

Left turn, and again, forwards, left, left, left.

Stop.

Facing us: an unpainted, raw steel door, like the entrance to a bank vault. Conked-out paramilitaries lay squirming feebly on the ground, all dressed in the funereal fatigues of the Alderman's personal guard, moaning mutely through blue lips. Our young lungs had proved stronger than theirs, their planned hambush had flopped.

The door was locked. And now we had to pass a test, an entrance exam. Adjacent to the door was a little keypad.

A pass code was required!

'How . . . many . . . arrows . . . left?' I rasped to Harete. We were standing under an extractor fan, the last still working.

Harete raised an index finger. One. She nodded up to the fan, angled the bow, readied to shoot.

'No, save it for the anti-Moth!' I said. We had no other weapon; we'd have just one shot at killing him.

My airless head was ringing with a crackling, howling hurricane of a migraine, coloured flashes were bursting like star-shells in front of my eyes, my heart had been substituted with a hummingbird. Worst of all were the pins and needles, acupuncture with electrified pitchforks, the awful burning strongest in the hand that was no longer there.

How to open the door?

I raked my distended fingers over the keypad buttons. *No clue, no clue.*

Thoughts weighed too much, made me top-heavy. I crashed down, stretched out. Harete had already done the same. Even when lying completely still I found I was unable to suck in the air I needed to aerate my brain. Not a bad way to perish though, splitting headache aside. My favourite of all the many fates I'd suffered. On Mo's scale, I'd rate it a . . . nine. Minimal suffering, warm and peaceful. After all these weeks, finally a chance to be alone, to rest in peace. A most seductive end.

Best death ever.

Nonstop appeared, as befitted an apparition.

'Mo. Mo. Mo. Mo,' he nagged me. 'Mo. Mo.'

'Knack off, Nonstop,' I grunted. 'Leave me to un-be. You're dead. Remember?'

'Yes,' sniffed Nonstop, blinking at me with those deep-set pink eyes. 'And let me tell you, Mo, a violent and humiliating death in excruciating pain followed by eternity in oblivion is not all it's cracked up to be. Grievous bad business. You need to pull your socks up. You've spent too much of this adventure listening to voices and getting out of your tree on nutmeg. Now you're suffering hallucinations brought on by advanced hypoxia. That's all I am, a mirage induced by lack of oxygen. It's a disgrace. I could go on.'

'I'll bet,' I said. 'Can you help instead? Myristica prayed for you to do so.'

The stub-nosed ghost sighed, and fiddled agitatedly with its wide backside through the folds of its diaphanous white gown. 'These things ride up your chuff something grievous,' it grumbled. 'Mo, you never listened to old Nonstop, did you? Three times you heard me tell you my secret discovery. I told

466

you twice and Dolly once. You never pay attention. That's you all over.'

'Sorry, Nonstop. I really am sorry. How's the cheese where you are? Not grilled, I hope, I mean, you're not . . . downstairs.'

'Cheek!' Nonstop snorted. 'I was one of the good guys, remember? No cheese now, Mo. Dieting. Lo-cal ambrosia shakes for old Nonstop.'

'Oh! Well, good luck with that.'

'Dolly, Mo. She remembers.'

'Cheers, mate. Stay lucky.'

Nonstop dissolved to grey. Dolly was inside my sweatshirt; she'd been there for days. As I'd toppled over, the toy's face had poked out of the baggy neck hole and was staring into my own. Her eyes were blue, her nylon hair was blonde and curly, her plastic flesh raw-sausage pink. She spoke with Nonstop's nasal whinny.

'Often I have said to you, I ain't any Tennessee tunneller.'

Great temples have been built, become centres of pilgrimage, fallen from fashion, been abandoned, and the stones stolen to shore-up pigsties in the time it took me to regain a half-vertical posture. On all threes, trawling long, slow breaths in through my gaping mouth, I lumbered towards the door and managed to reach the keypad.

Easy does it, Mo. One go only. Like life.

'Often I have said to you,' I mouthed. I typed in the code, my finger the weight of an ocean liner.

F 10 I F Z 2 U

Nonstop had always said 'zed', not 'zee'. Read '10' as 'ten'. Next part: 'I ain't any Tennesse tunneller.'

I N 10 E 10 S E 10 L R

The fan above me stopped whirring, winding down to a standstill like an old-fashioned gramophone record.

Reversed. Spun up, went into overdrive to compensate for its deceased brethren, blew pillars of fresh, cool air down upon us.

I crawled directly underneath the fan, pulled Harete's head by her hair next to mine, forced open her mouth. We received the blessed air, gulped it down. My hold turned into an accidental hug. The hug felt so necessary and overdue and right; we slotted together like long-drifted continents, like South America and Africa, salient slipping perfectly into gulf. Our headaches and nosebleeds subsided, life re-engorged us.

And hate.

'Nonstop worked here, discovered where anti-Moth hid himself, memorised the door code,' I wheezed out for an explanation.

Harete stood before the door, bow at the ready, waiting for when I pushed it open. The door was designed to swing inwards into the steel sanctum. We'd heard six electronic catches undo, released by the code, but I knew the door couldn't be swung until the air pressure balanced on each side.

The Alderman's troops dozing around us began to stir, the new air kissing them back to life as it had us.

'What will he be like?' asked Harete. She squinted along the bow's length, adjusted the sights. I kept testing the door, pressing against it with my weight and repeatedly thrashing the handle. If we couldn't open it before the guards recovered . . .

'The anti-Moth must be the total opposite of everything Moth used to be,' I said.

Harete opened with, 'Gigantic, colossal, powerful. I'll aim high for a head shot.'

'But with his insides on his outsides,' I continued. 'And upside down and back to front. Best aim low.' We were totally mad from a glut of peril and a lack of oxygen, but being mad, we couldn't appreciate that.

'And made of antimatter. Wearing beautifully tailored clothes.'

'Yes. And savage and hairy.'

'He'll have wings and tentacles, scales and hooves. Tusks as sharp as sabres.'

'Loving noise and gore. Hating books and knowledge. Violent, wild, handsome, sexy, lustful, horned and horny, manipulative, convincing, funny.'

'The Beast. The very Beast himself. We've run him to ground zero, Mo.'

All along the passageway, the Mothodist invaders were reviving. Snaking arms grabbed at our ankles and shins, clutching at us with ever-rising strength, trying to drag us back.

I jerked on the handle; Harete and I shouldered the door in unison. The last of seven seals prematurely released, the metal door cracked opened. A whistling gale of pressurised air blew outwards. I pushed Harete through the gap into the wind, then nosedived after her. The door slammed shut behind me.

This was it, my instincts howled, no more fakery, no concealed dips or rises. We stormed into the pit beyond.

'Death to the anti-Moth!' we shouted, our battle cries bursting like stun grenades.

'Death to the anti-Moth!'

Chapter 59*

There squatted the Beast, the crux of all viciousness and sin, the howling quick of abandonment. Glistening scales impounded my reflection, shone back at me the squealing lusts and dreads that churned in the nightmares of my nightmares.

Harete fired the crossbow.

The Beast was the master of antigravity, as it was suzerain over all forces. The bolt curved high, lanced harmlessly into the wall.

We screamed so hard our jawbones dislocated and the flesh cleaved from our skulls.

The Beast folded himself over us.

Chapter 60

'Hullo, Mo, Harete,' it said. 'You're bang on schedule.'

I opened my eyes for the first time since charging into the room and looked, breathing, breathing, calming, breathing.

No upside-down, inside-out, antimatter nightmare stood before me. Just an averagely sized, right-way-up, right-way-round, skinny teenage boy wearing thick glasses and pressed trousers, the turn-ups of which hovered diffidently above the tops of his shoes. No pit, no roost of sins. We were standing in a small, drab room – a storeroom, perhaps, converted to a bedroom – bare walls, an unmade bed, a wonky desk littered with papers and pencils, a board game with a twenty-sided dice. Harete's bolt had pierced a bookshelf end-on, made a literary shish kebab.

I had to simmer down and decommission my inflamed imagination before I could reply. The Beast had been only a figment of my air-famished brain all along. The boy before me fiddled nervously with the zip-pull on his cardigan. The elbows of the cardigan were protected with leather elbow patches; the fact seemed briefly worth registering.

'Hello, Moth,' I said, failing to suppress a quarter-grin. 'You're not what we expected to find.'

'Am I not?'

'No. In fact, you're the complete opposite.'

'Oh, I see,' sniffed Moth, prodding his glasses higher up the bridge of his nose. The lenses were cloudy with fingerprints, two opaque discs it was impossible to see his eyes behind. 'That's probably why you found me then. Life's like that, hadn't you noticed? You go looking for something and end up discovering its diametric opposite, or something completely different to what you sought. An anticlimax.'

Harete was by me, breathing hard, emerging fast from concentric shells of shock and bewilderment. The bow was empty, but it was a weighty creation of yew and iron; it still made an effective club. She hefted it in two hands, advanced. Moth whimpered, stumbled backwards onto the bed. The duvet was decorated with pictures of steam trains, far too young for him.

'Well, Moth? What are you?' Harete roared, flushed and prepped for slaughter. Her bolt had missed, thrown off by the air rushing out to equalise the pressure when I'd prematurely forced the door, but there was no harbour in her heart this time for any centre-mentality. Unlike me, she'd seen no illusions, she'd kept our mission firmly in her sights. The anti-Moth *was* The Moth; we'd found what we came for, the square root of evil.

'Harete, it's me!' Moth shouted up at her. 'Your friend from the Institute, from the Other country!'

'Is it? Is it really you, Moth?' Harete shouted, vibrating with rage. She jerked at a corner of the duvet, rolling Moth off the bed and onto the tiled floor. He was so round-shouldered he rocked like a playground ride-on toy. 'Or are you the devil who may care, the devil we advocate, the devil in the detail, the devil it's better to know, the devil who's been making work for idle hands, the devil we sup with, the devil who traps us next to the deep blue sea, the devil who's spoken of?'

Moth covered his face with his hands, shielding his glasses. There was nothing to the lad, he was a wisp of cellophane: where his cardigan had ridden up in his fall I could see the railings of his ribs.

'Don't hurt me, Harete, I don't know what you mean!' he pleaded.

Harete swung back the heavy club. One blow would swat The Moth. 'Stay still. We're here to execute you, you evil leech!'

In a flash I scanned the room. Worries chomped at me . . . no clock to be seen anywhere. The bowl and plate on the desk were plastic, the cutlery too. Most tellingly, no light switch, and no handle on the inside of the steel door. The room had the smell of a cell.

Moth was a prisoner!

I thrust forwards, deflected the bow-club from crunching down on the exposed back of Moth's thin, white neck. The iron tip of the bow limb impacted the floor tiles, chipping up sparks. Harete angrily kicked back at me, sent me spinning.

'What she means is, Moth,' I said, landing badly, 'what she means to say is: how the devil are you?'

Chapter 61 *

The closer you creep towards the hinge, the fulcrum or the axle, the slower you move as the door opens, the lever levers and the wheel spins. Moth's pivotal prison chamber possessed the clammy quiescence of a womb or a tomb or a ticking bomb.

'Justify yourself, Moth,' commanded Harete, towering above the tremulous, badly trousered teenager. She still hefted the crossbow-club. 'Explain how you come to be at the centre of everything, protected like crown jewels. How there's an army on the march hymning your greatness. Explain all of it!'

Moth began to clean his spectacle lenses. Breathe, rub, breathe rub. Every few rubs he held the glasses up to the light, tutting and clucking at the persistent smears. And all the while, between bouts of purring moist breath onto the lenses, he spoke.

'I knew you'd come for me. Big Sister told me you would. And all the madness . . . it's not my doing. Please believe that.'

Harete played hard-ball interrogator. 'Try us,' she said. 'Wait a minute, you haven't got a sister!'

Moth airily brushed the detail aside. 'I couldn't bear to watch the Fartherland go to pieces. This catastrophic war, the appalling loss of life . . . it was the antithesis of everything my father had striven for. So I took matters into my own hands.'

'And did what?'

Moth wiggled towards the wall, rested his back against it. His spine was as bowed as a cheap plywood shelf burdened with weighty dictionaries. I parked myself on the edge of bed, there being no chairs in the room. That lay in his favour: difficult to imagine Moth convening meetings with power brokers all sitting cross-legged on the floor or perching on a Puffy the Steam Train duvet.

'Without my parents' knowledge, I returned to the Fartherland, made my way to the Centre of Everything, the never-completed particle collider laboratory.'

'Why?' probed prosecutor Harete.

'To ask Big Sister some questions, and to make contact with the underground.'

'You haven't got a sister!' Harete repeated. Then, 'The underground?' she asked, head tilted, nose wrinkled.

'The secret opposition, the people who'd always worked clandestinely against the old government. They published illegal newspapers, smuggled information, people even, to the outside world. And this laboratory was a hotbed of their activity, a centre for dissenters!' Moth waxed on.

Listening to him was disconcerting; his normally fluting voice would pick a random syllable at which to deepen unexpectedly, the effect was akin to reADing words typed by someONE with a fAULty shIFt key. *The little git was enjoying this*, I thought, salami slicing the truth and feeding it to us one fat-marbled sliver at a time.

Harete continued her cross examination. 'I never knew there was an underground,' she said. 'Least of all that it was, well, actually underground.'

'Fitting, wasn't it?' agreed Moth with a smile. 'The leader of the resistance was an expert in superconductors. Those are materials that are chilled to just above absolute zero degrees by liquid helium so they can carry huge electrical currents and generate enormous magnetic fields. You see –'

'Inadmissible evidence!' Harete called out, swinging her arms as if steering fog-bound ships into berth. Moth was Nonstop's only rival – only living rival – for mastery of the art of telling you improving things you never knew you'd never wanted to know. 'Jog on, Moth. Get to the damn point.'

'Sorry, yes . . . well, anyway, she'd gone by the time I reached here. They all had; the resistance had been broken, the members had fled or been killed. Worse, the centre had been invaded by one of the tetrarch.'

'Aliens!' I snorted. 'You always taught me there was bull at the centre of a labyrinth, but you can't expect us to swallow that, Moth.'

Moth manoeuvred his spectacles to obscure me behind a thumbprint. 'Tetrarch, Mo. The gang of four, the ringleaders of the old regime. She was the cruellest, most ruthless member, the only one who remained behind when war broke out.'

Harete said, 'She? This woman . . . about my height, brassy hair piled into a dome, previous owner of this crossbow?'

'Yes,' Moth confirmed. 'She and her forces made this laboratory their base. It's ideal. Secret mountain location, deep underground, has its own power and water supplies; it would have been top of any self-respecting megalomaniac's list of desirable residences.'

'Her!' I interjected, playing catch-up, permanently lagging one sentence behind. 'Old cliff-face. We met her in that garden paradise. We thought she was the Creator, but she said she was only the Curator.'

Moth shook his head. 'She's neither. In the old days she was always known as the Great Cremator. Remember the place we stumbled into after fleeing the Institute? Where the diseased cattle were slaughtered and burned, mixed in with the bodies of anyone who'd incurred the displeasure of the old leaders?'

Harete and I nodded dumbly. At the time, it had seemed the most gruesome plot of soil on Earth. By the standards of what we'd seen since, it was par for the course.

'Her doing,' explained The Moth. 'Once I knew the centre had been taken over by the Cremator, I tried to scram. I almost made it too, only, just as I was about to reach the lift, I rebounded off a morbidly obese man, ended up being captured.'

Nonstop. So he really had bumped into Moth!

'And then?'

Moth scrunched his glasses tightly in his hands, undoing all his cleansing. 'Then I became part of the Cremator's master plan. She knew who I was. My father's son.'

Moth's exiled dad, the Judge. Not a soccer-in-the-park dad. Not a change-the-tyre-on-your-bike type of father. Rich, for one thing: monogrammed caviar, limousines, infant Moth's pedal car had probably been a stretch model. Important and influential, for another: embassy receptions, secret service escort if he left the room for a widdle, and the only time Moth's pop

477

ever drew a pair of curtains was to unveil a commemorative plaque. Probably one commemorating *him*. Foreign politicians thought he was marvellous, that he could turn night into day by dropping his pants and touching his toes.

'So?' Harete remained alert, parsing every statement Moth made, sniffing both content and delivery for lies. At the end of every question or answer we glanced across at each other, asking with our eyebrows: *Can we trust him?*

'She wants to form the new government, rule the Fartherland. Trouble is, she's disgraced, an international pariah; no other country will have dealings with her. She's less palatable to world leaders than a panda-cub curry served up with an asbestos side salad.'

Harete bedded down on her own thighs in that Z-shape pose that only girls find tolerable for more than a minute. That was from tiredness, not relaxation; she was still as torsioned as the spring on a rat trap.

'But they'd deal with you,' she said solemnly.

'Yes, Harete,' sighed Moth. 'The Cremator and her cabal want me to lend them the legitimacy of my name and my family, the reflected respectability of my father. I'd be powerless in reality, a glove puppet strapped over a bloodstained claw.'

'And the Mothodists? Not your invention?'

Moth shuddered. 'Marketing,' he said, plucking out the word with tongs like it was a condom he'd found floating in his soup. 'The Cremator's idea, to turn me into something far more than a celebrity – a living, breathing idol,' he whispered. 'Clever, really. To take our story of hope and escape and reverse it, use it to chain people in tyranny. The Cremator writes the scripts.

I assume you've heard the man she found to speak the words, an old friend with a new name?'

I waggled my stump. 'The Alderman had a hand in my misfortune. He's a captivating speaker, but Hyssop's forgotten his lines, Moth, he's ad-libbing, thinking up new parts for him and you and us.'

'So I suspected,' said Moth glumly. 'That's the beauty and the difficulty with stories. Once they're released out in the wild, you've no control over them, not even your own, or who reads what into them.' Harete spoke. 'Never mind fiction. Stick to the facts, Moth. What have you been *doing* all the months you've been locked up here?'

'Oh,' replied Moth. 'Listening, learning what I can from my captors, and from Big Sister.' He croaked as he spoke; his voice was breaking. Not from emotion, his age. I was dismayed to note that when low, his voice sounded deeper than mine.

Harete and I frowned at each other, shimmied our heads. 'You haven't got a sister!' we shouted together. 'Why lie, Moth?'

Moth grinned. 'You probably didn't recognise her. No family resemblance. She's everything a big sister should be, clever and caring and terribly well informed. She's the one who told me you were on your way. And she recommended I refuse to collaborate with the Cremator.'

'If true, that was good advice,' said Harete.

'Is it? By refusing to work with her, I prolonged the civil war. But not for much longer.'

Harete's head snapped back. 'What?'

'In a few hours' time a ceremony will take place, here in the laboratory. That's why all the Cremator's crooked cohorts are gathering. Hyssop, her aides and generals, the whole shooting match. They're assembling here, today, right this minute for a conference.'

'Why?'

Moth drew himself into a compact ball. 'Because I invited them,' he confessed. 'I've told the Cremator I'm agreeing to her plan. To end the war, I'm going to let them use me, become the masthead on the ship of state. The ceremony is my investiture, my beatification. My beast-ification.'

'Collaborator!' I cried. I swept the shish-kebabed books off Moth's shelves and tore free the crossbow bolt. I threw the arrow to Harete; unlike Moth it looked like it was still able to travel true and straight.

Harete pulled back the bowstring, dropped the bolt into the flight groove, aimed the bow right at Moth's temple.

'So it's just as we'd feared, you're a filthy turncoat, a wasp moth, a warmonger!'

Moth performed an all-over body cringe, every muscle petitioning for understanding. 'No, hear me out!' he shouted. 'I said only that *I'd said* I was going to cooperate. It's all part of a plan, Harete, a scheme to end the war and rid the world of the Cremator and her cronies. I've *always* had a plan; Big Sister and I cooked it up.'

'So what's taken you so long? Why only reveal this plan when we burst in on the scene?' I asked.

Moth gestured wildly – we were back with the junior professor. 'Don't you get it? Think where we are, think what this great laboratory was designed to do.'

'Eh?'

Moth was in free flow again. 'Bunches of particles are whizzed around in ever-increasing circles, energised to a simply outrageous degree then choreographed to collide,' said Moth. 'Big Sis calculated your arrival down to the minute. I conceded to the Cremator's demands only so all her people would be assembled here *at precisely the same instant as us three*!'

'Then?'

'We collide, smash into them, then scatter!' Moth declared, smacking his palms together. 'Same as happens with the particles. We destroy the Cremator and her people.'

'Destroy them? With what?'

The light caught Moth's lenses; those two smudgy discs flashed back. 'With words, Mo. There's nothing more powerful. The world turns on words.'

'Oh, those disgusting things,' I spat, wanting shot of the bubbles of soap and treachery. 'And you couldn't do any of this . . . colliding and scattering . . . on your own, just you versus them?'

Moth fiddled distractedly with his elbow patches. 'Mo, the plan's top-drawer. And very sneaky, very *you* if I might say so, very –'

'Underhand?'

Moth smiled. 'But I need my friends. I can't do it . . . single-handed.'

The three of us commenced a slow, circular walk, equidistant from one another. Harete's bow never once ceased pointing at Moth, but she held the contraption with less confidence. Moth's movements were the most self-assured, almost languid. Authority had hopped from us to him, though I did not

481

understand how.

Circling, Moth and I studied each other, each seeking to reconnect with the person we'd last seen about a year ago. Of the three of us, Moth had changed the most, and was changing still. Harete had matured enormously of course, but the finished result was visibly a progression from her juvenile form; the transformation had been smooth and improving. Moth's conversion was a work in progress, a messy construction site cluttered with scaffolding and skips. Most noticeably, he'd been stretched taller, and his face was a constellation of angry, volcanic acne. He didn't look or sound much like The Moth I'd known, nor was he behaving like him. He'd always been prone to being pompous, and an incorrigible know-it-all, but never so theatrical or needlessly enigmatic.

'You've grown, Moth,' I murmured. It stung to admit it, but he'd developed more than I had, he'd leapfrogged me. Harete had grown, Moth had grown, I'd stagnated; I could no more exit boyhood than Nonstop could have crawled out through the crap flap.

Again I looked him over, trying to strip from him all the rinds of past associations and recent imaginings, to dig to the stone of his essence. He had sticky-out ears and sticky-out hair, his zip-fly was marooned at half mast, there was a gap in his credibility as world statesman wider than the bus lane between the bottoms of his trousers and his shoelaces. Despite all that, I could read the arriving man in his boyish features. Draw a face on paper, rub it out, rub it until your eraser crumbles into skinny black worms. Draw a new face over the top. The first face is still there, the original indentations subtly lead your pencil astray. I could see the adult face being sketched on top of Moth's youthful one, different, but informed by it. The superimposed faces were no easier for me to evaluate than one would have been.

Boy or man?

Moth or anti-Moth?

Good or evil?

'Well?' Moth demanded. Cool, no fluster. 'Mo, Harete, what are you going to do? Am I angel or devil? Are you going to assassinate or assist me?'

Still aiming the loaded crossbow, Harete blurted out, 'Is he tricking us, Mo? He's Moth, he's our best friend. But he's here, in it up to his eyeballs. Oh, I don't know anything any more!'

'Maybe I should be asking if I can trust you?' warbled Moth unexpectedly. Over the course of the question, Moth's voice dropped an octave, rose an octave.

'Whaddya mean?'

Moth shrugged as we continued our orbit. 'By your own admission you came here to kill me, and I know you've met with the slippery Hyssop. Big Sister's been tracking you – she has all the reports from spy satellites and reconnaissance drones at her fingertips. We've known your movements, but never your motives.'

'That's not fair!' shouted Harete. Except it was, and she and I knew it.

Moth and I continued to stare each other out. The *twist* had netted us again. We'd never really been seeking Moth or anti-Moth, I understood, our search had been one for *certainty*. Accordingly, the twist had ensured we'd found only doubt.

Moth was too equivocal, too composite to be assimilated. Man or boy or superposition of the two, he was his father's son, overloaded with double meanings, a host of hidden variables, a child of words.

I panned from him to Harete. Her essence was absolutely clear to me, it glowed unmistakably through the watery irrelevances of meat and matter. Unlike Moth, she was formed of something fundamental: a fluttering, blue ribbon of constancy and fairness. I couldn't give a pig's whiff for her strength or her curves, her long brown hair, her copper eyes. I was on the verge of breaking our pact, of saying I –

Harete cried out, 'Tell me what to do!' Her finger remained looped around the trigger. 'I want to believe him, but I still can't decide. Are we playing into his hands?'

I joined the dots of Moth's most prominent pimples, formed Libra, a constellation I recalled him pointing out through a barred window one clear night in the Institute. *Two traditions – the sign of the scorpion's claws or the scales of justice – take your pick, Mo,* he'd tutored me. Scorpion or scales, Mo or Mercury, Jelly or Hyssop, Fractions or Integers, reality was a degenerate slurry of ambiguity and uncertainty, names as misleading as aspect. No right-hand or left-hand rule could guide me, the Kernel had withdrawn, Harete was as clueless as I was, Nonstop's ghost wasn't putting in any more appearances. Myristica had been right, nothing and no one was knowable, we're all on our own, dying alone in our cells. All quests fail, life and understanding were impossible.

What was left?

What was right?

I took Moth's hand in mine and shook it, jerked our linked wrists and *hoped*. I laughed, the situation was hyper-preposterous, we were two teenage kids pretending to be grown-ups. Could we really be controlling the fate of the Fartherland? No, this was a joke, a game, like charades or tag or bulldog.

'Deal. We trust him, Harete,' I said, chuckling uncontrollably. Tired, I'd never known tiredness so ingrained, so cloying, so crushing. I yawned; my limbs were concrete, my blood dust and fuzz.

Harete slung the bow, swept up Moth in her arms and virtually hugged him to death. Sub-audibly, flopping face down into a threadbare field of smiley steam trains, I tacked on a subordinate clause. 'For now.'

Chapter 62

'Quick question, Moth,' I asked, choking as I swallowed a piece of plastic. I was biting open a crisp bag, Moth having disbursed what little food he had in his room.

The packet rent open, and potato crisps spun and rattled like brittle confetti. I devoured them no matter where they fell, plucking them from the tops of Moth's socks and his grease-stiffened hair. Harete meanwhile was impersonating a one-girl locust swarm, polishing off a bar of chocolate in seconds. Chocs and crisps, luxury grub; Moth could never, ever be an ordinary prisoner.

Harete beat me to it. 'How come you've been allowed to speak to this Big Sister you keep mentioning?'

'My captors indulge me,' Moth expounded. 'They think she and I are only discussing archaeology. Remember the vase we found in that farmhouse, Mo, during our first escape?'

The vase! A poxy porcelain spittoon adorned with squiggly symbols. Moth had fussed over it like a kitten with a ball of wool when he'd spotted it, an heirloom exhibited on a pine dresser in a house where'd we'd been briefly held prisoner.

'Yeah? A hundred years old, wasn't it?' Typical of Moth to

dredge up memories of that dusty relic. Who cared?

Moth puffed out his cheeks and exhaled. 'Immeasurably older. That vase was ancient before *our* ancestors had upgraded from flint to bronze. Those symbols . . . I copied a set from an identical vase in the Hofstadter Academy. Big Sister and I have been studying them meticulously. The symbols gave her more than a few ideas.'

'Nice to have a hobby,' I groaned, irritated but a little mollified. His obsession with trivialities reassured me, an indication Moth hadn't changed completely. 'We've had to content ourselves with staying alive. Into ceramics, is she, this mystery Big Sis? That her bag?'

Moth said, 'Not in the least, Mo. Advanced mathematics is her specialism. She's a world-champion number-cruncher.'

Moth's clumsy phrase splashed boiling oil over the slumbering bears of my distrust and doubt. I moved to bite my nails, accidentally pounded myself on the nose with my stump.

'Your great plan, Moth,' Harete interrupted. 'Shouldn't you be supplying us with the details?'

'Of course,' said Moth, clicking his fingers. He dived into a cupboard, returned with a small, round shaving mirror. He probably used it for squeezing his spots into. 'You may find this of benefit, Harete,' he said.

'For what?'

'Don't press me for details, I'm going to tell you almost nothing. We've no time now, and besides, this way, we're all less likely to be eaten alive by the twist. That's my word for how –'

I nearly grabbed the bow and shot The Moth where he stood. 'The twist?' I shouted. 'What do you know about that?

That's my private invention, mine and the Ker . . . that's *my* idea. See me? I'm twistier than a stick of barley sugar, twistier than a turkey twizzler. I eat twist, drink twist, dream twist, piss twist. How can you know the twist?'

Moth huffed indignantly, made it no further than inflating the 'B' of his defence.

'Don't tell me. Big Sister,' I bitched, anticipating his response.

'She's frightfully hot on the twist, Mo. Anyway, your instructions. Very simple. Harete, you are to do the exact opposite of everything I say. Don't worry, it'll be clear what I mean when you're there. Everything's labelled, and you'll be able to hear my voice. I've spent weeks preparing everything; they give me free reign on my daily walks. And, Mo?'

'Yes?'

'Your instructions are the opposite of Harete's.'

'Eh? She's to do the opposite of what you say . . . and I'm to do the opposite of the opposite.'

'Correct. Do everything I say, answer every question with complete honesty no matter how peculiar it sounds.'

And that was that. Apart from a few additional directives given to Harete as I used the lavatory, those sparse commandments constituted the entirety of Moth's planning. The hurried, last-minute scrabblings of Nonstop and me during our final hours on the Spiral felt like preparations for a moon landing by comparison.

'One more thing,' Moth advised us. 'Remove any metal from your clothes and bodies, most specially iron, steel or nickel. Zips, press studs, shoe eyelets, belts, buckles, amalgam tooth fillings, anything. My glasses have all-plastic frames, fortuitously.'

We set about examining each other for the tiniest trace of metal. Harete and I passed, so did Dolly-with-one-arm – glue but no screw. Sight of her caused Moth to jack up his eyebrows; I didn't deign to enlighten him.

Moth went rigid, sensing the dawning moment. 'This is *it*, Mo, Harete,' he said. 'Finally it, after all these months of waiting.'

'Of struggling,' Harete corrected him. 'Of seeking. We've not been twiddling our thumbs even if you have.'

'And thanks all the same, but I've had my share of *its*,' I said. Pen one. Dexter Manus, suicide by electrocution, our campfire escape, *it* after *it* after *it*. On each occasion I'd told myself: *this is it*, and it never had been; final-it-y had always been denied me, translated into an endless extension of loss and suffering.

Moth had to have the last word; I think he possessed a diploma to say as much. 'No, Mo. They were only your earlier laps around the accelerator. You were still building up mo-mentum then. This is our final circuit, we're close to light speed, time is slowing down. Collision is imminent. *This* is it. Now, remember what I told you both. And trust me.'

Someone banged on the steel door. We froze.

My twist-whiskers twitched; what prison guard ever knocked before entering? All the same, whoever was outside started to open the door. The metal latches snapped open one by one.

One . . . two . . .

'Quick! Give me the crossbow,' Moth ordered. Harete obeyed, too punctually for my liking. To me he added, 'You'll get to see Big Sister again on the way out.'

Four . . . five . . .

'Bum holes to your damned non-existent sister!' I snarled

back. Did the game never end? Moth's bizarre lies eroded the tiny deposit of trust I'd invested in him.

Six . . . seven. The door opened.

The last word. 'She's not my sister, Mo,' Moth hissed back. 'I never said that. She's yours!'

Chapter 63

The Moth's guards marched their charge out of his vault-like bed chamber; Harete and I dutifully, doubtfully followed. No one queried our presence.

The guards were screws. Not dog heads, but some new breed, screws as hard as nails. In place of gas masks, they wore peaked hats so flat and wide and round on top it was tempting to practise paradiddles upon them.

Goose-stepping briskly in leather jackboots, they frogmarched Moth along the narrow aisles between the banks of the giant computer.

'Say hello to your Big Sister, Mo,' Moth called out over the top of his protective phalanx, thumbing towards the humming walls on either side of us. The machine responded to the sound of Moth's voice: the walls revealed a second function as screens, lighting up with floating blue letters.

B.I.G. S.I.S.T.E.R.

They read, and underneath, by way of explanation:

Be Informed Grievously, S.I.S.T.E.R. Is S.I.S.T.E.R., The Explanation Recurses

I howled out for an explanation but Moth ignored me, and the goosey goosey goose-steppers goose-stepped onwards, not giving me or the screens a gander.

As I watched, engrossed, more characters scrolled over the wall-screens – squares, circles, triangles, Greek letters, backwards letters, wiggly squiggles; I knew the alphabet, but not the meaning, they were mathematical symbols; more, they were Sandscrypt, the language of the Numbers, the language they'd despairingly given up trying to teach me.

Sight of Sandscrypt acted as a petard on dammed-up memories. The dam ruptured, waters broke, a twenty nutmegaton bomb exploded inside my skull, discharging a mushroom cloud out of my ears. I browned out, blacked out, came to, still walking. No one appeared to have noticed my momentary absence from sanity and consciousness. Big Sister's screens cleared and a new message displayed:

```
REBOOT COMPLETED
KERNEL PATCH APPLIED
MEMORY LEAK FIXED
```

My attack of mathsphyxia left no detectable after-effect, only a buzzing in my tubes and an evanescing ripple of a memory of a voice I was sure had once meant something to me, the tail-end afterglow of a misforgotten daydream.

{Thank you, Sister. All safe.}

'Like Argus in mythology, Big Sister has a hundred eyes,' Moth said, gesturing at clusters of leering cameras mounted in pods along the ceiling. 'She was built to run the particle accelerator and analyse data from the experiments, but the Cremator's been misusing her to run the war. She sees all, she knows all.'

'That a fact?' I said, genuinely interested. I slowed my pace, and into one of the oracle's unblinking cameras I silently mouthed a question, one I'd asked before of an inveterate liar.

Sister lip-read. For her answer, she kited a single word in minuscule blue letters around a screen, the name of an invertebrate liar, the author of an encyclical.

So then I knew.

Somewhere in my thorax, a rudimentary chop I'd once mistaken for my heart boiled and froze and died.

We departed the computer room, ducking under dark arches of cables. A second squad of screws marched smartly up behind us; we had no chance to rescind our deal and double back.

The Moth, already alien to us, became stranger by the second.

'We're in the beam tunnel now,' he said, still without slowing or turning around. 'It looks straight, but it's really an enormous circle. Even at the pace these chaps walk it would take ten hours to make it all the way around. Had it been completed, clouds of tiny particles, broken-down atom dust if you like, would have been fired in an airless pipe along here. Two pipes in fact, one set of particles travelling in one direction, one in the other. Super-cooled, super-powerful magnets would have bent the tracks of the particles into circles to keep them confined inside the pipes.'

'Fascinating,' I drawled.

We marched on, Moth prattled on.

For long stretches of the tunnel, the gubbins Moth had described – was describing – was all on show. A wide metal pipe ran alongside us, almost every piece of whose surface was encrusted with cables and tubes and valves and gauges and assorted mechanisms of unfeasible fiddliness.

Moth was *still* talking. To what end, I had no conception. Harete looked at me, grim and grubby, purple onion rings of deep, deep exhaustion layered around her eyes. The rainbow's end, supposedly, and for the millionth billionth time we were stomping around in circles chasing our own tails. Moth was plainly barmy; we'd poured our last hopes into a cracked flagon.

'The magnets, Mo. Are you listening to me?'

'Not really, Moth, no,' I guffawed, swaying as I walked, a stranger to hope or care, pulverised by bitter disappointment.

'Please do. You never know when little scraps of learning might come in handy. Terribly strong things, these magnets. Huge H and B values.'

'H and B . . . like pencils, Moth?'

'No, Mo. Ways scientists have of measuring magnetic fields. The magnets, the tunnel, this entire laboratory is modelled on one in Switzerland. Near . . . now, I forget which city. Was it Geneva, or Lucerne?'

'I DON'T KNOW OR CARE!' I shouted, bellowing over the incessant, maddening synchronised stomping of the guards' boots resounding along the tunnel. Why was Moth tormenting us with this drivel?

Moth carried on regardless. 'Mo, how do you get to Lucerne?'

he demanded next. 'Come on, Mo, think. *How do you get to Lucerne?*'

Lucerne? The 'c' was soft, as in 'cell' or 'cemetery'. Swiss cities, Swiss cheeses, these were not part of my world.

'Scab wagons, how should I know? I . . . I . . . expect you'd need to charter an aeroplane or something,' I wept, hoping any answer would suffice to silence him.

'Oh, Mo. Have you forgotten so soon?'

'Forgotten what?'

'You go clockwise to Titan, but anticlockwise to Lucerne,' said Moth. For the first time on the forced march he turned to us, grinned and winked. Clockwise to . . . *but that had been his and my private code phrase for our escape from the Institute!*

In my amazement I tripped over my own weary feet, stumbling like you do when you find a stair that isn't there. Moth wasn't mad after all, he did have a plan!

There was light at the end of the tunnel!

Chapter 64

I mean, there really was light at the end of the tunnel. Not daylight, we were still deep underground, but light nonetheless.

And then came the end of the tunnel itself, for it opened out into a colossal subterranean canyon. The guards un-padlocked a folding shutter and we stepped out.

Wow.

Did you hear me? WOW, I said.

Need somewhere to park a cathedral? Swing her by, we've plenty of space. Pop it over there, next to that temple. Room for a basilica? No worries, squire, we've more than enough, and for a chapel, an abbey, a tabernacle, whatever you've got. That canyon was *big*; I wanted to sing out and sample the echoes but the mood wasn't with me.

The guards halted, fanned out around a safety railing; we all stood and gazed in wonder. They and Moth must have seen it all before, but it was the sort of sight you could behold every day and never grow bored with, like a jungle sunrise or a forest waterfall or crisp sand dunes petted by a peach moon.

No one had parked a cathedral inside the cavity, only a cotton reel, albeit one as long as a street and as wide as a battleship, its axis aligned perfectly with the tunnel from which we'd emerged. The behemoth wonder-drum taxed our vision; the human eye did not feel up to the task of conveying to the brain the size or complexity of the structure, it needed to be experienced by the heart and stomach too.

'That's the –' began Moth, stepping free from his boggling escort to address us directly. I cut him off. I recognised it from displays in the museum dome above. It was the *detector*. Had the laboratory been commissioned, the two counter-rotating bunches of subatomic grit in the airless pipes would have met inside there. Particle dodgems, *crash*, *pow*, *blammo*. Roll up, roll up, a million miniature Big Bangs a second – get your bonsai black holes while they're hot.

'It's not –'

Finished, I knew that too. Any fool could see the machine was incomplete; its rainbow-coloured wire-and-pipe guts were hanging half in, half out, and there were hoists and cables and tubes splurged all over the shop.

'That cylinder, the innermost layer around the hollow core. That's the solenoid, the –'

'Concepts during a nutmeg. I mean, superconducting magnet; I know Moth,' I said. I let him talk freely then. I knew he was distracting me, not wanting me to lather up a crap storm as Harete was led away by two screws, ushered up a ladder onto a gantry and locked into a small cabin situated outside the detector. She went without remonstrance; he must have warned her that was going to happen.

Moth lectured well, keeping the level appropriate to thickos like me and the round-hat screws. We followed his finger, allowed ourselves to be shown where the hyper-chilly liquid helium fluid needed by those mega-magnets was stored, in long white tanks labelled 'He (L)', 'He' being the chemical symbol for helium, 'L' meaning liquid, he said; how the various overlapping layers of the megalithic detector were designed to trap and measure different sorts of particle debris zinging outwards from the collisions occurring in its heart; where the end-cap would have been fitted to seal it all off and allow the air to be pumped out.

Spotty Moth omitted two salient facts. He never once said that the giant microscope was beautiful, but it was, heartbreakingly so. In small part its charm stemmed from its retina-defying complexity, its twenty-fold symmetry, its monumental scale. Mainly, though, the beauty derived from the exquisite, doomed intelligence and artistry of the creation, for it was a most wondrous shrine to seeking and questing and questioning.

Proud; for the first time ever I felt unabashedly proud of the Fartherland. That our nation had people capable of building that giant truth-hunting machine – who'd have thought it? Previously, the most technologically advanced product I'd ever seen demonstrated (apart from weapons, the manufacture of which the Fartherland had always excelled at) was a bidet that played patriotic tunes when you pulled the handle. Dad and I had seen it years ago at a travelling showcase of inventions, and he'd laughed and said you might as well do a handstand in the shower while whistling.

The second fact Moth never mentioned was that, looking at it end-on, the device resembled a dartboard.

'Never finished,' repeated Moth, sounding sad. Beneath his breath and to himself he muttered, 'Never *quite* finished, that is. Still, *deus ex machina* and all that. Hope I can squeeze a little deus from this machine.'

'What's that phrase mean, Moth?'

'Latin. A force from outside. Sometimes we need something to peel back the lid and drop down on us. Our internal logic is never enough for a complete solution.'

The guided tour was over. The guard detail sparked the heels of their jackboots, formed a tidy square around me and Moth. We marched over a yellow bridge into the hollow, tubular core of the machine. All the marvelling had numbed me, chloroformed my fear, bludgeoned my doubts. Entering the core, the parted seas of terror crashed back. I was utterly terrified again, for myself and for Harete, now beyond ken and communication in that cab on the gantry. Moth led, stooping, round-shouldered; even at that late moment I couldn't determine if he was friend or foe.

The guards halted at the entrance, the oche.

Inside, they were waiting for us. The worst of the worst of the worst of the worst.

'Game on,' I whispered.

Part 8:

Break Point

Chapter 65

There were nineteen of them all told, seated around a table placed inside the metal chancel.

The echoing, tubular room reminded me of the interior of a super-sized vacuum flask, the sort you might use to carry soup to a picnic. One difference: the surface was dark, not silvered. Spotlights burned downwards, the shadows lending the sitters cowled eyes and noses as angular as the gnomons on a sundial.

At the head of table, poring over and pawing at a white lake of papers, stood the Cremator. She didn't look up, not even when Moth returned to her the crossbow. Her bouffant orange hair resembled a helmet of flame; she had exchanged the housecoat and slippers for a plain boiler suit.

Moth took his seat at her side, which made twenty, one for each side of the dice. On the other side of the Cremator to him hunched the twitching, snitching form of Alderman Hyssop, dressed in his finest finery: a billowing saffron robe fixed at the throat by a brooch that resembled a pretzel, a fitting combination for a man who preached of bread and spices.

'Eight six five!' he quacked through his too-wet, too-pouty, too-red lips. 'I've saved you a place, boy. We belong side by side. When will you accept that?' He budged his chair aside to make room for me, beckoning me to him like a puppy to a lap. 'Come to me, my boy, come!'

I knew no other around the table. Marshals and martinets, brigadiers and brigands, the men and women hosed concentrated venom at me through narrowed eyes, growling disapprovingly. Some were senior, wrinkled as walnuts, others must have been less than twice my age. All bar the Cremator cosseted guns or daggers, and every chest except hers was planted out with hedgerows of medals. Scanning their faces as they scanned mine, I discerned two species: puce-faced, blood-hungry warriors and daylight-dodging, committee-room night crawlers, skin as pale as the underside of a woodlouse. The sheer variety of hats, helmets, insignia and uniforms convinced me that representatives of all sides of the civil war were there present, that the war was therefore an artifice, that all sides were really one side, like a circular loop of paper with a twist in it.

Moth was in his element. Parachute the kid into a youth club with other teenagers, I'd no doubt he'd hug the wall closer than the skirting board and expire quietly of shyness. There, in a smoke-filled room surrounded by lawmakers and war-makers he was operating on familiar, familial turf.

'The inner circle. The shadow cabinet,' Moth began with an amateur-dramatic sweep of his arm. He spoke and deported himself without a smidgen of adolescent gaucheness or gawkiness. I looked on, cable stays for nerves, a pineapple in my gullet.

Moth had been right.

This was it.

Moth made the introductions. As each person was named, he or she deposited a whole nutmeg into a wooden bowl. The first group were all grizzled military types; I recall only the identities of the final thirteen public serpents.

'The Minister of the Inferior,' announced Moth, 'The Chief of Stuff, the President of Vice, the C-I-C of the Insecurity Service, the Minister for Offence, the Head of the National Wealth Service, the Ministers for Injustice, for Famine, for Pestilence, for War, and you already know the Minister of Irreligious Affairs and Improperganda.'

That last was Hyssop, boring his ball-bearing eyes into the vacant space between two chairs, chewing on his own cheek flesh.

'What's your position, Moth?' I asked. 'President of the Trade of Bards, Minister for Minstrels, boss of those deluded saps who've been touring the country promoting your legend?'

'Me? Oh, I'm to be the acceptable face the leadership presents to the outside world, so you could say I represent the Civil Surface. And finally, I introduce our leader, who holds a great many orifices of state: the Chief Whip, the Lord Canceller, the Prime Mover, the Great Cremator.'

'We've met,' I reminded him. 'In paradise. Those aren't their real titles, are they?'

'Of course not,' said Moth. 'They allow me to take a few liberties. How could they not? They have taken all others.'

'He goes too far!' blasted one of the cuboid military types, his worm-eaten face a scabrous mystery beneath the eves of his hat. He stubbed out five cigarettes at once into an ashtray made from an upturned human skull.

A flamingo in an infra-pink business suit piped up. 'Seconded!' it shrilled. 'Perhaps we should focus on the spin-off character cults. Exit polls show the Momons and Hareticals have thirty-five per cent broader appeal among the starving, wounded and homeless, these segments now forming ninety-eight per cent of the Fartherland's population.'

'We were supposed to have only one legend,' overspoke one of the gruffer brass-hats. 'These secondary cults are a threat to unity. Gas the bally lot of them.'

'Motion seconded!'

'Motion denied! Hyssop has turned the Mothodists into his private army; they are too powerful. We need the other cults as counterbalance.'

'The Alderman, powerful? That cretin couldn't organise a hyssop in a brewery.'

'*One* story, one nation, one people. That was the plan.'

The Cremator broke from her paperwork. 'Order, order!' she shouted, pounding the table with a gavel. 'All comments to be made through the Chair.' The skull ashtray spun like a coin; the startled starlings settled.

'That boy is nothing, the maturated pus drained from an infected sinus. Only The Moth will bring us the recognition we need, thanks to his father's name and fame. Once he signs this covenant –' at that point, the Cremator brandished a parchment scroll '– and becomes our representative, we shall declare day zero of year absolute zero. We will shut down the war and emerge as the government. A new nation is about to be born, complete with a new mythology, one we author. Think! Our hands will rest not only on the levers of power,

506

they will stretch far inside people's hearts and minds. The tales they tell, the dreams they dream, the metaphors they use to frame their every waking thought.'

Up popped a woman made entirely of jargon and dust. She spoke incredibly fast. 'Letmereassureallpartieshere gatheredthattheaforementionedcovenantisinfulland completecompliancewithallrelevantstatutes. Whereas –'

'*Cavities* to the legalities, Shambassador. The point is, we shall all become obscenely, feculently, viciously rich!' chortled a plump, boyish character in a pinstriped suit and braces, breaking to swig champagne from a torpedo-sized bottle.

'And I thall make and tetht poithonth, ditheatheth and bombth, gargantuan bombth!' declared another, a one-dimensional weasel whose shoulders were too narrow to interrupt the flow of dandruff cascading from his scalp. 'Enemy thitieth will wilt and wither like buttercupth in thpring frothtth.'

'You lack verve, *Banker*,' said the Cremator, 'and you, *Fission King*. Myth is the rootstock of fiction, the foundation of drama. The new legend of The Moth we have popularised shall be our prime fiction. Rival stories will be banned, burned, banished, forgotten.'

'Purged,' gurgled Hyssop, knotting and knitting his fingers.

'From nursery rhyme to requiem, via soap opera, computer game, and supermarket romance, we will conduct all the stories to which our citizens are exposed,' the Cremator grandly expanded. 'We will define not only whom they hold for their heroes, but what it is thought to be good or bad, to be hero or villain, to be right or wrong. We and our successors in the cabinet will never be toppled from power. People are the sums of the stories they know, and we will be at the centre of all stories, The Moth's disciples.'

'One myth, one nation, one people!' cheered the delegates. 'One myth, one nation, one people!'

'You've no chance, you mad hater!' I burst out, instantly regretting my action. The print seized in the projector gate, bistered and blistered, spooled out of the cassette. The cartoon show was over. The shadow cabinet quit smoking, smirking, snickering, bickering. Two unspeaking rows of wrought-iron faces regarded me, bland manhole covers bolted over shrewd, scorpion brains.

No weasels or flamingos. No funnies. I'd exaggerated the speech defects and mannerisms, made up the champagne and dandruff and pink suits. Had to. You stare at a bare plaster ceiling and your mind disdains the blankness, marries the cracks to beget spidery islands and shepherdesses in hooped dresses. Same with the cabinet: if you didn't embroider the characters *there was nobody there*. Big Sister had more personality.

With tears doorstepping my eyes I said, 'Moth, tell me these tragic mannequins aren't the ones responsible for the war and all the horrors. They're so boring. They're *rubbish*.'

Moth coughed, speaking quietly in darkness beyond range of the spotlights. 'Were you expecting blue skin, horns and forked tails? Flash powder and pointy hats and boos from the audience? They're people, that's all. It's never anything but people. Keyboard-clickers, most of them, plus the odd retired chicken breeder and bank robber.'

'But . . . how did they rise so low?'

'Success of this order needs neither genius nor muscle,' Moth sighed. 'Networking, patronage, blackmail, committee-stuffing. You'll find it's no different in any boardroom or bunker. Demon-cracy in action.'

None of that mattered. I lost all interest in the cabinet dummies. 'You might train people up a trellis,' I growled at the Cremator, 'plant and prune the fictions they know, but you'll never control the stories within the stories, or the stories within those. Stories cross-pollinate, give birth to new ones. Free life and new thought will always break out, no matter how much salt and poison you spray.'

The Cremator snatched up the crossbow. 'Tell it to the hand! You are redundant, you asymmetric ass, you are to be edited out!'

Hyssop surged upwards. 'Please, Madam Chair. Spare the boy,' he cried, genuflecting. 'He is like a wayward son to me – he is my product, the sum of my life's work.'

The Cremator swung the bow onto Hyssop. 'We know the calculations you have been performing, Hyssop,' she barked, pumping cartridges of outrage. 'You intend sowing division within the cabinet, then multiplying your own power. You planned on manipulating The Moth through his friends. You are undone – he dies now!'

'Moth, you will spare your friend – surely?' implored Hyssop. 'Well? Speak up for him, do as I command, do as I order you!'

Moth had been holding back in the gloom, nestling his bent spine into the curve of the wall. He stepped forwards into the light and the tussle.

Friend?

Or foe?

'No,' said Moth. 'Only *my* legend can be allowed to thrive. Besides, he is handicapped and brain sick, hears voices, plays with dollies. I owe him nothing.'

I knew what was coming. Sisters rarely let you down.

'Put him to death,' said Moth.

Hyssop screamed and collapsed, fell to the floor and mounted a full-blown tantrum; he tugged at his pudding-bowl wig, paddled the ground with his fists, foamed at the lips. The Curator pressed a button, screws scrambled in. Hyssop ran from them, twice around the room like a naughty toddler, spinning the swivel chairs of his incensed colleagues, before diving underneath the table and threading his way amongst their legs, out of reach. That's not my frolicking imagination putting on the greasepaint, Hyssop's clowning was a dreamy marvel.

Moth shook his head and looked at me, fiddling with the plastic zip on his cardigan. I could make out the yellow tips of his Himalayan acne, but not his eyes, hidden as always behind the reflective glare of his round spectacles.

'Sorry, Mo. That's why I sent Harete to safety before we came inside. The Cremator wants a fairy-tale ending; she plans on marrying the two of us at some point,' he said, speaking as though the prospect was an irksome chore on a par with rinsing his socks.

I shrugged. New tears as small as newt ears appeared but baked to sludge before they'd seeped halfway down my cheek.

'Forget about it,' I answered. 'I've been expecting betrayal. That's what it's all been about from the very beginning, hasn't it? Your grand design for the Fartherland. Dexter Manus on the Spiral, the condemned tricked into becoming murderers, families yielding their most vulnerable to the Compensation Camp for tawdry reward, or compelled to surrender them for destruction in the Facility to earn a few more days of half-life. You've engineered the deepest mine of torment, a place where only debauched monsters prosper and love is unreachable because everyone is too busy crawling and brawling to even notice those rare times when it arrives against all the odds, like an egg hatching in a hurricane, where hope carries on teasing you inwards and downwards through level after level after level until you reach here: final deceit. Being sold out by your friends stings more than anything else, that's why you chose it for the bedrock of the Fartherland.'

I spoke up, addressing the full committee. They were avidly attentive, reunited, hanging on my words. Hyssop too, skulking under the table; even he ceased blubbing and listened.

'I congratulate you all on your achievement,' I laughed. 'You truly have made the worst that could happen, happen. I suppose there is a motive for it, other than to enrich you and to wipe clean the slate of people's minds. I suppose it is to guarantee that the survivors will venerate you. Take it from me, they will, they'll adore anyone who makes the slaughter stop. Anything, *anything*, is better than war and betrayal without end, even a life of slavery under your permanent control. And ruler and ruled will have so much in common, for everyone will be compromised. The cruelty of sadists and the brutality of survivors amounts to much the same thing.'

Moth listened, nodding slowly. 'That was eloquently

511

expressed. I like to think you've benefited from my companionship. And do you have at long last a name for what the Fartherland is, Mo? Can you see what has been constructed here, more completely and more perfectly than in any place ever before?'

'Yes, Moth. I know full well what the Fartherland is,' I said.

Chapter 66 (.6)

'It is Hell.'

Part 9:

Breakaway

Chapter 67*

The delegates spontaneously stood and clapped, their applause enduring for tens of minutes. It was themselves they were thunderously congratulating, I knew, not me. Most exhibited damp eyes, a few openly wept at their own brilliance.

That had been Moth's reason for parading me before them, I realised: to bear witness.

'Such positive user feedback!' cried Flamingo, energetically tapping a report into an electronic pad. 'We shall all make our quarterly review milestones.'

'Triple bonuses all round!' cheered Banker, knocking back more champagne.

No, not really, but the cartoons were so much more satisfying than the silent, rimy, actuarial stares I received from the grim stiffs.

Nothing moved in me. Nothing, nothing at all. Not anger, not hate, not relief, not sorrow. My heart was a sinkhole, it held immaculate nothingness, and no fear of personal extinction. Following Spiral spring, hot summer Camp and that long fall of bombs, I was looking forward to my welcoming bread and salt in winter's everlasting edifice, the pavilions of oblivion.

Following all the lives I had seen spent, one more could not change the sum: infinity plus one remains infinity.

Harete would survive, I reminded myself. She would not live, she would only be kept alive, be forcibly married to a . . . but what *was* Moth?

Not a cry baby. His dry eyes remained hidden behind those two blank, implacably misty circles of reflected glare. He sidled silently around the table to stand immediately before me.

'Some final questions, Mo, before you are euthanised and I pledge my loyalty to the shadow cabinet.'

'Why not?' I laughed hollowly.

And then began the ultimate betrayal.

It opened with the strangest and most awkwardly stilted of conversations. Mixed messages, right to the end.

'So, Mo,' started Moth. 'You know now what the Fartherland is. Endless Hell! Spell it out: H E L. On and on.'

His body language was as forced and unnatural as his words. Although he stood directly between me and the Cremator, blocking her aim with the bow, he never once looked at me. I was facing the conference table; my back was towards the open mouth of the cylindrical chamber in which we all stood. Moth pointedly avoided eye contact and angled his gaze beyond the confines of the giant detector; cowardice I assumed, unwillingness to stomach the stare of the friend he had deceived, afraid to discover that falling to him meant no more to me than dying of meningitis or measles.

So why stand so close?

I choked a gasp. In his highly polished spectacle lenses, I *saw* the words he had just that moment uttered. There they were,

518

lit up in red. They were in mirror writing; I had to mentally invert them.

    He (L) : ON

'Ye-yes,' I stammered. How was that happening? *He (L)* . . . *liquid helium* . . . *on*. On what? But Moth had more questions.

'Do you agree I possess the authority to have you killed?' he snapped, talking quickly, sternly.

'No!' I shouted. 'You're a knock-kneed, hackneyed, acned super-leech, a twenty-faced bloodsucking cluster-slug.'

'So. *No remit*.'

There was a second's delay. Then the image of those two words appeared in his glasses, also scribed in luminous, wavering red letters. Only, they came out backwards even when I'd reversed them.

    Timer : On

Through my feet, I detected a trembling. The chamber, the entire detector was very faintly buzzing. On the table, a pen rattled, rolled to the floor, ice cubes chinked against the side of a crystal tumbler. The majority of the cabinet did not seem to have noticed, they must have been too choc-full of self-satisfaction and too focused on Moth's bizarre interrogation. Flamingo and Weasel alone sensed some indistinct alteration to their environment, looked around them, sniffed, frowned.

Moth persisted with his quick-fire questioning. 'You must feel like you've been trapped,' he said.

519

'Of course I do. By you, you blow toad, you absurd turd, you tinpot portion of abortion!' Moth's affected, wooden quizzing was irking me so much it was restoring circulation to my deadened spirit, and that in turn was annoying me even more because I wanted to die feeling nothing, revealing nothing, being nothing. Hollowness was the lubricant I needed to grease me into easy ever-sleep.

'Trapped. *Net laid.*'

'Say what? Moth, you've really lost it big time, pal. Has the stress of being arse-lick to dictators finally caught up with you? Net laid? Just step aside and let Grandma pull the trigger, why don't you?'

Dial Ten

Then I had the sense to shut up, suck in my insults and play along, because when those words appeared in Moth's angled lenses, I understood what was going on.

Moth was staring at a screen mounted behind me, outside the detector. He was giving covert, backwards instructions to Harete, safe in that cabin atop the gantry; she must have been adjusting controls, and the results of her actions were being flashed up on a screen and Moth was showing me the reflections! Had Moth planted a microphone in the chamber for her to hear him?

The vibrations grew stronger. The chamber began to chill; when I exhaled my breath misted. A smell too, that toast-like odour of electrical equipment being turned on after a long period of dormancy and all the dust and grime burning off. I felt my long hair bristle and stand on end, not only through fear.

Moth began to talk faster, he knew time was short. 'And you feel you've aged?'

'I . . . yes?' I didn't know what I should say exactly to speed things up.

'You look like an old, old man. Indeed, Mo, seventy-five!'

SLOW

SLOW? Of course, 'MO 75' upside down! The vibrations smoothed out, damped down, but too late: the delegates had pricked up their ears, they could tell something was definitely amiss.

Moth pressed on. 'Big Si— that is, my informants, tell me you spent some time with a girl who deceived you.'

'Lupa?' I spat. 'She was no girl, she was a beast!'

'No! Wolf, animal?'

Lamina flow on

From somewhere nearby issued a hissing, swirling, bubbling noise, the unmistakable sound of a liquid being pumped along pipes and flooding into cavities. The chamber grew markedly cooler, the vibrations stronger, the electric smell more and more noticeable. Now, everyone had sensed the changes. Several ducked their heads briefly under the table to see what Hyssop was up to, thinking the disturbance his fault.

'Are you done with these interminable questions, Moth?' demanded the Cremator. 'We are wasting time, we must adhere to the agenda. Step aside and let me terminate that one-handed termite. He has served his purpose.'

Me to Moth, snappy. 'She was, she was like a wolf, yes.'

'She had . . . gulp, paws?' Moth didn't make a gulping noise, he actually said the word 'gulp'.

Swap plug

'Moth! What are you doing?' The Cremator, again. 'Be silent, I demand you both be silent!' She dodged left, trying for a shot; Moth side-hopped to maintain his cover of me.

The delegates were all alert, stirring, flapping their arms around themselves as the thermometer dived, trying to trace the sources of the noises and the vibrations, still unable to correlate the changes to Moth's baffling words.

Moth pressed on. 'Ignore her, Mo, answer me. Can you imagine future generations of people admiring the Alderman or the Cremator?'

'Are you off your scabbing chump?'

'Something's going on outside! Look at that screen,' spluttered a general. I chanced a glance to where Moth was staring, to where the general was pointing; I glimpsed an overhead display like a sports hall score board, saw the cabin where the figure of Harete was darting along a long console, flicking switches, adjusting dials. Screws were wrenching at the door; she'd wedged a chair back over the handle –

Moth continued, speeding up. The cabinet were unsettled, but not all could observe the external goings-on.

'Then you think they'll be, eh, reviled?'

The fluidic swirling, gurgling sound filled the entire chamber now, reaching a crescendo. It must have been liquid helium, freezing the magnetic coils that surrounded the cylinder down to their working temperature. Everyone's hair was standing on end; some mighty source of electricity was being cranked up, ready to fire.

Opposite us, under the table where he had crawled, Hyssop lifted his head from the floor.

'Stop them, you blind idiots! Stop them – it's us who're being tricked!' he screamed.

'MOTH!' roared the Cremator. 'WHAT IS THIS?'

'When I give the word, we should all have a belly laugh, a revel gut,' Moth concluded, impassive to the end. *Tug lever*, that made, but I didn't see the reflected confirmation because Moth skipped backwards, exposing me, putting me in direct sight of the Cremator, still holding the bow.

Every member of the cabinet had whipped out a pistol or a burp gun.

'WON!' shouted Moth at the top of his lungs. 'Harete, WON!'

The Cremator fired her crossbow; seventeen guns blasted me. None missed.

Chapter 68

Myristica had been right.

The most refined variant of Hell is when time's flow congeals, hardens like concrete, trapping you for an infinity of eternities at the pinnacle of your life's failure and shame and betrayal and humiliation and *defeat*.

The Cremator's crossbow bolt stabs into my chest. She didn't miss. How could she, once Moth stepped aside? The steel arrowhead has pricked a hole in my sweatshirt and nicked my skin; Hell chose to take its fatal snapshot the microsecond before the bolt burrowed into me. The arrow missed Dolly, she's still intact. She was loved once; now she really will be loved forever. I'm glad about that.

Hundreds of pointy cones and mini-domes surround me in a cloud, levitating, gyrating, precessing. Most are grey, a minority brassy-coloured. They trace lines of dots and dashes back to the guns discharged at me, telegraphing my destruction in Morse code. The cones and domes are bullets. One hovers at the corner of my mouth; I contemplate flicking out my tongue to lick it. No, the bullet is made of poisonous lead. Hah! As if that matters, now . . . now . . .

WON = NOW

Did Harete tug the lever as instructed, send a monstrous electric current coursing along the helium-cooled wires to energise the super-magnets? I've the lifetime of the universe to ponder the conundrum of whether she did or did not make it in time. When his end comes, Moth will have the same period to spend ruminating on his cowardice. All those bluffs and double-bluffs, all that cleverness with covert messages and backwards words and he muffed it at the final second, dodged and allowed the Cremator to shoot me.

Ho, hum. How to spend forever, trapped at the instant of my own demise?

My nose itches. Damn. Well, what did I expect? After all, *this is Hell!*

Forever isn't what it used to be. One, two seconds at most.

The arrow wobbles, flutters.

It flips, executing an aerial three-point turn. The iron diamond is pointing at the Cremator, still there across the table from me with the bow in her hands. Her face just has time to register a flicker of dismay.

The arrow shoots backwards, reversing its trajectory. It strikes the Cremator slightly off-centre, mid-body.

BANG

No other word will do. I'm on the floor; Moth's pulled me down. Everyone else has gone, simply *gone*. They're all crushed flat against the circular end wall of the chamber, pinned there by the effect of the magnetic field on the guns and knives they held, the medals on their chests, the chairs they sat on, by any piece of iron or steel or nickel on or near them, the arrow through her torso in the case of the Cremator. The bullets and the brass cartridges drop, plinking, slowed but not attracted. The bullets have melted into fat blobs of liquid lead, something to do with metal moving at speed through the magnetic field, I guess. One tenth of an eye-blink later, and over our heads sail the guards who'd been waiting on the walkway or climbing the gantry outside, sucked in by the stupendous magnetic force. They crunch into the cabinet collage at high velocity; it's not pretty. Shrapnel chaperones them on their flight down the detector's neck, a blizzard of supersonic screwdrivers, toolboxes, nuts, washers, sections of ladder and guardrail. The reach of the force is not long, but the pull is devastating. The squashed bodies are battered by the bombardment. No details to report; the lights have gone, both the ones inside the chamber and out in the detector cavern; faint, orange emergency lighting has cut in.

Above the muffled moans I hear, 'Mo! Are you alive?'

'Think . . . so. You cut that fine, Moth,' I say, shaking.

'Had to let her shoot at you, Mo. Needed her to suffer a dramatic reversal; it was the only way. I'd done the maths, engineered it. Reverse engineered it, rather.'

'Oh, *rather*.' I curse The Moth, I curse all smart-arses, I curse them with my missing hand and my sub-standard eyes and own smarting, branded rump.

We scramble out, but it's hard to move fast. Not just the dark, I feel nauseous if I move my head too rapidly. There's a bright aura around everything I look at, not sure if that's imagination or magnetism; Harete included, though she deserves her halo. She has to monkey-swing by her arms and drop onto the walkway from the control cabin; the connecting ladder has shorn away from its moorings and is straining towards the maw of the super-magnet, quivering like a dog stalking squirrels, loosing off the occasional, lethally fast rivet.

'Brilliant work H.,' grins Moth, but Harete doesn't return the compliment.

'You're a latot dratsab, Moth. A dratsab,' is all she growls.

We're about to head off down the beam tunnel when a shape knocks us down from behind, bat-flapping out of the detector. In its hobbling haste, it bumps a pallet jack, a two-pronged trolley used for shifting heavy loads. The jack's the mass of a motorcycle; it must have been resting on the limit of the radius of no return. *Voooooooosh* and into the core it shoots, too quick to see, there, not there, nearly wipes out the lot of us. From deep inside the detector sounds a second *Bang!* the bigger brother of the first. The walkway shakes and sags; the straining ladder cuts free from its leash and swings back like a pendulum. The returning metalwork whacks Harete across the shoulder, narrowly avoids knocking her head off.

'SCAB!' she shouts. 'Scab! My shoulder. Can hardly move my arm. Think my collarbone's broken.'

She's kept her head, but lost her halo; the magnetic maelstrom's over. 'Stupid, so stupid to be wounded now. Damn

527

the pair of you, just get me out of here,' she groans when we rush to her.

We prop her up. She looks in a bad state, in a lot of pain. There's a dribble of water leaking out of the detector towards us; I cup my hands, thinking to splash it on her face.

'Don't touch it!' screams Moth. 'That's not water, it's liquid helium. That pallet jack must have smashed the cryostat, the stuff's flooding out. It's cold enough to solidify the air – stay away!'

He's right. The bubbling rivulet is already shrouded by a spitting cloud of smoky condensation. The walkway creaks and squeals as the fingered metal shrinks, splits and ices up. The drips I see forming on the handrail are not water, but liquefied air.

'Get out, all Hell's breaking loose!' I shout.

Harete tops me. 'And freezing over,' she says, 'this really must be the end.'

Moth and I gather up Harete and drag her between us along the creaking bridge towards the beam tunnel. The dribble behind us broadens, becomes a stream disgorging from the wrecked detector.

'Take a breath, could be our last!' warns Moth. 'Helium's not poisonous, but it will suffocate.'

We reach the shelter of the beam tunnel just in time, cover our mouths and noses and turn around. A deluge of what looks like furiously boiling water spews out from the centre of the detector, bearing with it the chamber's flotsam – the table, the chairs, the brittle, brutalised bodies of screws and cabinet members. Most of the fluid gushes over the side of the walkway, evaporating before it strikes the distant ground,

528

jetting up frosted plumes of cornflake-crunchy air as thick as white paint. We scurry further back into the tunnel, fearful of mortal splashes, mindful of the need to breathe.

Not fast enough; one seething tributary sluices along the bridge straight for us. Lying on her back within the oncoming blue flow is the stiffened, glassified corpse of the Cremator, the arrow protruding from her chest. She was first in, she's last out. The river delivers her to me, laps at my feet and stays its advance. Her iron hand is gripping a giant black sea anemone: Hyssop's pudding-bowl wig, deep frozen.

In their sockets, the Cremator's eyes move; there's a nucleus of nerves inside her alive enough that she can react to the sight of us. Her mouth moves too, barely, issuing a puff of frozen curses. I float my face over hers and let her see me. Through her eyes I try to locate whatever loop or particle or plane is invested with her immortal self and infuse it with my hatred. I will her to see what I have seen, feel what I feel and to feel it until the day the universe shrivels to the size of a dung-ball and is trundled away by beetles. I want her to see the faces of Lew and Lonza, Myristica and Nonstop.

'I have killed you,' I inform her, hoping her ears work. 'I am become the H of the Horror and the B of the Beast, and I have killed you.'

Putting the toe of my training shoe to the crown of her head, I punt her away. Her hair crumbles like spun sugar under the pressure. She glides effortlessly on her blanket of boiling fluid, slips through a gap in the disintegrating walkway and drops. We see nothing through the white clouds, but we hear her impact and smash like a porcelain figurine dashed onto flagstones.

Job done, promise fulfilled.

My to-do list has one outstanding point.

A bullet point.

The runnel of near-perfect cold dries up, boiled back to gas by the draught of warm air gusting out of the tunnel behind us and into the detector canyon.

'Make sure she's truly gone to pieces, Moth,' I say. 'Step out and look over the side. For me. Mate.'

'Of course she's dead! They're all dead,' wounded Harete groans, but I insist. Moth doffs Harete's arm and treads cautiously five, six steps back along the walkway. He removes his fogged glasses and squints over the handrail to the canyon floor below.

'Can't see, too much cloud!' Moth yells, speaking fast; he doesn't want to inhale the rising gas. 'Troops though – Mothodists and the Cremator's forces are slugging it out.'

We hear that too: banging grenades and belching burp guns. Someone must see Moth, for bullets ring and spark from the underside of the walkway, support braces fall loose and crash away.

Moth's seen enough, he runs towards us.

I let Harete slump to the floor and I scrape the metal grille across the entrance, lock it; us on our side, Moth still in the canyon. He's trapped on the bridge.

'You can't come with us, Moth,' I say flatly.

Moth pokes his fingers through the lattice work and rattles the grille. 'Stop mucking about, Mo, let me through! There's a small war breaking out below me, the air's full of gas and the walkway's collapsing . . . and . . . and . . .'

Harete's too weak to dispute. I tuck one of her feet in my armpit, take the other in my hand. I'm going to drag her like a sledge back along the beam tunnel, the way we came in.

I

walk

away.

Moth's voice elevates to a squeak; maybe the air is diluting with helium, maybe he's reverted to boy-Moth.

'But . . . but . . . I'll die out here!' he cries.

I tip my head back as far as it will go. 'You ordered the massacre of the Numbers, remember?' I shout. 'You're a maths murderer, it was you who issued the Prime Directive. Big Sister told me. You have to stay behind with all the others and die in Hell. Die, Moth. One last favour to the world: just *die*.'

Chapter 69

Get away.

My feet are moving, I'm not. Harete's gripping the mesh gate. I pull, she heaves back. She's loads stronger than me, but with her cracked clavicle there's parity in the arms race. That mare has a kick like a nuclear mule, like an atomic donkey; I take a force twelve jab between my legs, a real cluster-buster. *OW!*

Such blunt grudge in that kick, such malice. I see at once how little I ever meant to her. Ex-friends make the bitterest enemies, and this is a fight to the death: Moth's.

Everyone shouts, can't hardly tell who's saying what.

'*Mo, it's true, I did propose the Numbers' annihilation. I admit it.*' That's Moth.

'He's a war criminal, stop trying to let him in, you scrubber, he has to die!' Me.

'We're killers too, now. Let go. Moth's coming with us. Hate you, hate you, HATE YOU.' Her, the dirty dogfighter.

'*But it's not what you think. They asked me to do it.*'

I reap Harete's hair and bite her fingers to force them off the latch. My stump's only good for pounding at Moth's knuckles wherever he coils them through the diamond-shaped holes.

He has to, the beleaguered walkway fails, folds and falls, the metal as weak as wet lasagne.

'The message on the vase, Mo. Big Sister decoded the symbols, it was a plea from the far past for someone to kill them.'

'Never, never, life was sacred to them, you're lying!'

'The Numbers knew war would come, not for the first time. It's their survival tactic! They're alive, Mo, all of them. They found the best hiding place possible.'

'Liar, Moth. None survived. I watched the hovercraft arrive, saw the soldiers, the guns, the flames.'

'But they died willingly, Mo, you must have seen that too. Didn't you wonder why?'

The gun battle below is in full swing. Rockets slam into the dartboard detector, hitting the doubles and trebles; flaming metal swarf showers over us. We're fighting tooth and nail. I'm biting Harete's hand, she claws out a molar by the roots. *Still* she tastes of vanilla and rosemary.

Moth's clinging on by a single swollen finger, bands of purple and white, slipping, slipping. Gassed up with helium, he speaks shriller than a cartoon racoon; it's hard not to laugh, *He, He*.

'– only their bodies died . . . necessary . . . the identity function . . . Sandscrypt –'

'—king HATE YOU, Mo, you sick prick, you little dick –'

'– let him drop! Die you pathetic magnetic satanic mechanic, you superfluid druid –' Me, I say that. The ringworm on my forehead is swelling up under my bandana, itching like a twitching bitch and I haven't got a hand free to scratch it.

'. . . safest place to sit out the war . . . find . . . a vector, a messenger, to carry their culture, protect them. I'm going. I love

you both, my dear friends, oh Father, oh artificer, OH –'

The fall. As before, the terrible drop, the impact, the death, the end of love.

Chapter 70

Dolly was busted.

She'd been squeezed out of the front of my ripped sweatshirt, struck the beam pipe. The side of her head was cracked, and there was a jagged, triangular hole in her brow where she'd bounced off a stanchion. When I shook her, I heard the detached fragment rattling inside.

I stopped fighting. I think Harete threw open the gate and pulled Moth in; I didn't really notice.

We were catching a lot of refracted flak from the gun battle; I crawled a distance along the tunnel, emptied my mouth of blood and teeth, rolled off my headband and had a bloody good scratch at my itchy patch. Then I bandaged Dolly-with-one-arm's head with my bandana.

Bang, boom, they were going at it Hell for leather down in the detector hall. With no working lights, the tunnel away from the opening was as dark as the water under a canal bridge, only when an explosion flared outside could I see the faces of The Moth and Harete. And with every flash that lit the tunnel, I saw they had edged slightly nearer, homing in on me, their enemy, staring with unblinking, hate-filled gator faces.

A long interlude, then another *boom* paired with an enduring magnesium glare that struck out harsh, flickering rays. Moth used the saddle-black dark to sneak right in front of me. There he knelt, shaking, teeth chattering, head bowed. The little wet wipe was thrusting his pipe-cleaner arms towards me, holding out that shaving mirror. He seemed to want me to look in the mirror. A trick, but I did it anyway.

Working from the background in, I saw:

The curved tunnel wall. In front of that:

The fussy, complicated beam pipe, wide as a tree trunk, covered in dials and wires, running the length of the tunnel. In front of that:

My own hacked-about, haystack-haired, cog-toothed head. In front of that:

On my forehead, the throbbing patch of ridged skin, my ringworm infection, for so long hidden under my headband.

Except that was not a circular splodge.

It's what Seven-Potato-More and One-for-Sorrow and Origin had seen; not in my eyes, on my skin, a perfect triangle.

$$\Delta$$

'Moth. Mo's a Number,' whispered Harete. 'You were right, they're not all dead.'

Moth shook his head. 'He's not a Number. He's Hermes, he's Mercury, the messenger. And the message he's carrying is the Numbers' entire civilisation.'

'The triangle. The sign of the river delta, where they lived.'

'Or the mathematical symbol for difference. Or of the

Empedoclean elements.'

'Come again?'

'Earth, fire, air and water, Harete. Mixed and separated, the ancient Greeks said, by love and strife.'

I was cuddling Dolly. 'Shut up, you pair of scabbing divs,' I said. 'Shut up, and fetch me some glue.'

Part 10:

Aftermaths

Chapter 71 *

I wouldn't budge. Not until Dolly was fixed. Cured, I mean.

Not even when Moth bit his knuckles and said, 'Mo, we have to get out. Big Sister computed the magnetic field from the detector would alert the Peacemakers to the Cremator's hideout. They'll fly over and bomb the laboratory. We've only *minutes* before we're flattened or entombed here.'

I wouldn't budge. 'Glue. Tweezers. The patient is too ill to be moved.'

'Bring the pathetic thing with you then, come on!' said Harete.

I wouldn't budge. 'No. She'll get forgotten, or I'll lose the little pieces.'

'Oblige him,' Moth advised Harete, backing away from me, nursing his sprained finger. He respected my badge of office; I could feel the heat radiating from my three-cornered eye. 'There's an exit to the Cremator's private rooms a short way along the tunnel. We might do it if we're quick.'

They departed. Alone in the stuffy tunnel, cradling Dolly, I listened to the screws and the Mothodists dancing the apocalypso down in the detector hall. The fighters'

541

weapons sounded uncannily like kids' playground imitations: *UhUhUhUhUhUh, pyeow, pyeow.* I dropped off, lulled by the gunfire lullaby.

A change in soundscape startled me awake. The gunfire had stopped and there was a shrill, whistling noise not present before.

'Eight six fi-yiive . . . .eight six fi-yiive . . .'

Hyssop.

I recalled his stigmata, the burns earned from our pylon showdown. He'd have worn no metal, probably phobic after that experience. And he'd been sulking under the table, protected from the incoming projectiles. That must have been him we'd seen bolting from the detector!

The illuminating explosions had ceased. By feel alone I melded myself into the beam pipe's intricacies. My inner-cinema scheduled a screening of worst-case scenarios: Hyssop chasing me. Hyssop catching me. Hyssop *touching* me. Hyssop . . . I dismissed them all.

Too soon bantam footsteps came pattering along the beam tunnel, closer and closer. They stopped. I could hear clothes rustling. My flesh rebelled, wanting to slither free.

Warm, moist lips pressed against my ear. 'Eight six five!'

A match flared, dazzling me. 'Eight hundred and sixty-five steps, Mo, that's how far it is up to the surface. Moth just told me. Here's your bloody gear. Hurry up, for all our sakes. *Hurry up.*'

Moth and Harete returned with everything I needed. Harete had made us some candles. She found potatoes in a store cupboard, hollowed out the insides. Into the groove she'd

542

poured cooking oil, then dipped in her shoelaces for wicks. A fine stuff-pun, a nifty matter anagram!

Plus tweezers: 'From the Cremator's make-up bag, would you believe.'

I began to operate. Candlelit battlefield surgery, real seat-of-the pants stuff. With Dolly gripped between my thighs, I poked my finger through the hole in her head and re-seated the pushed-in sections of cheek. All the while I tried to ignore Moth and Harete, lurking impatiently behind me, whispering from the wings.

'Peacemakers. They'll probably insist everyone switches to decaffeinated coffee and lead-free bullets and stand to one side.

Why are the guards and Mothodists still fighting, Moth?'
'Rider-less horses. Driver-less hearses. You're wrong, Harete, they won't be like the ones you met in the Facility. They'll fly over and destroy this place from the air; we won't even see them.'

'Shhh!' I ticked them off. Some people have no sense of priority.

'Oh, shush yourself!' Harete's words scarcely achieved escape velocity, dragged backwards into her mouth by hurt and desperation. 'You half kill me trying to get me out of this place, now we have to wait while you open an underground dolls' hospital!'

'Look at him. In a world of his own. Run it past me again, Moth. The signs on that ancient vase were written in the Numbers' language, Sandscrypt. You programmed them into the supercomputer here, Big Sister. They were mathematical equations?'

543

'They were, and they were knot. Sandscrypt is a twisty, self-referencing, helical, paradoxical clash of symbols. A living language. And by that, I don't mean it's in current use, I mean it's actually alive. Big Sister became self-aware when I fed those symbols into her. The "I" of the storm of consciousness is born of loops that contemplate themselves. The language is like maths, like music, like DNA, like life itself.'

'And the message on the vase was . . .'

'When war comes, we beg you to kill us. A plea to anyone who might find it and have the knowledge to understand it.'

I zoned them out. My own curiosity on that score was negligible, a dried whistle-pea rattling around in a ballroom. The instant the Cremator died, I lost all interest in nubs and hubs and centres. Almost like I'd been used for a job . . . With the tweezers, I retrieved the detached piece of Dolly's brow from inside her hollow head.

'Why? Why?'

'The Numbers have always been despised by the ignorant. They know that during wartime the very worst people float to the fore, people who will aggrandise their cause by persecuting those who differ and those who are different. So the Numbers follow a time-honoured tradition: they place their children in a basket of bulrushes and let it float downstream. They welcomed extermination because it represented the ultimate safe haven. Once they were dead, no one could harm or enslave them.'

'And by teaching Mo their language, they actually, truly live inside him? That's . . . crazy.'

'He is the cradle made of rushes. The avenging messenger.'

'I always said he was a basket case.'

'The Numbers are their language, they are the story that
writes itself. Their bodies are no more them than the pencil is
the poem.'

'But, Moth, really, how can a language store individual
personalities?'

'I don't know exactly, Harete, but think about this: when you
read a book, your brain turns letters on a page into characters
who live inside your head. An illusion, but maybe less of one
than we think. And you yourself, me, all of us, at base we're
just long sentences made of chemical words pegged to two
spirals. Life is information, a coded message. Sandscrypt is just
a very efficient language.'

'I understand why they chose Mo's head: vacant possession.
Couldn't the Numbers have killed themselves?'

'Their enemies would always have suspected a trick. People
like the Cremator never believe a job is done unless they do it
themselves. They couldn't live in two places at once; to hide in
Mo their physical bodies had to die.'

'Huh. When we escaped to the Other country, we assumed
Mo had run away to join the gypsies. But in truth, that was all
twisted around. They ran away to join him.'

'Yes. Funny, when you think about it. Mo's always believed
in looking after number one. Turns out, he's been looking after
all the Numbers.'

I speared the detached, triangular brow-piece with a needle
and, suspending it on a thread held in my teeth, floated it into
the gap in Dolly's head. By hand, I packed out the gap around
it with glue. I wasn't going to abandon Dolly, come what may.
She was a totem of my campaign against loss and destruction. If

I didn't have the guts, wits and patience to look after a simple toy, what use was I to the world, and what use it to me?

'*Does Mo understand any of this, do you think. Moth? Not convinced I do.*'

'*He doesn't; I think they've installed a firewall to separate themselves from him. Probably his obsession with the doll is a form of psychological displacement. He senses a powerful urge to care for something; he's transferred his attentions to the toy. Could be dangerous to disturb him.*'

'*What puzzles me is this. If Mo's unwittingly transporting a civilisation in his head . . .*'

'*Yes?*'

'*How are they going to get out when it's safe to emerge? How do you give birth to a nation?*'

I could have told them, but I was too busy. You do it by making sure every child has a toy. You teach them to care for it and love it. When it breaks, or becomes old or dirty, you don't throw it away, you wash it, fix it, patch the patches, stitch the stitches. The older and weaker and more worn it becomes, the more you adore it. You loop the loop, you grow your love as the child grows his or hers, you love the loving.

Then you'll have made a civilisation. And if you don't do that, you might end up fabricating the Fartherland.

A final inspection, and a short delay while the glue hardened.

'Done. Let's go,' I said, stuffing Dolly back into my sweatshirt.

'Oh, so gracious. Jerk. You've probably killed us. Quick, light the last two candles,' snapped Harete, shepherding me towards the stairs. The tunnel was tuning, whistling and ringing in sympathy with some colossal, vengeful power gathering far above us.

Bombers were on the way.

Eight hundred and sixty-five steps, Moth had said. The mosaic rays from our spud lamps' sooty flames did not extend far into the blackness; we had to freeze-dry our animosities and huddle. The spiral stairwell wound up and up and up, every step shaped like a wedge of cheese. One, two, three . . . *Here comes a candle to light you to bed* . . . bed! So, so tired. One hundred . . . two hundred . . .

WOMWOMWOMWOM. Propellers? Jets? The stairwell amplified the sounds, the steps vibrated hard enough to blur my vision and jar my fillings, slivers of cement flaked off the walls.

Near step four hundred, the potato candles guttered out and from then on we were crawling nine parts blind. Tormented by memories of dropped pills, I kept pausing and feeling for Dolly every few paces. I fell badly behind. I shouted for the others to wait, but the shriek of the approaching bombers was too great for them to hear me and the distance between us opened up still further. My strength was gone, the bruised skin sloughed from my forearms and knees where they repeatedly impacted the metal stairs. The winding staircase continued up without end.

I knew I'd never get out alive. I knew it completely because it made for the perfect *twist*.

I was destined to die on the Spiral after all.

I stopped climbing.

'*Eight six fi-yiive . . . eight six fi-yiive . . .*'

That spurred me. I shackled myself to a nursery groove, reciting as I crawled. *Here comes a candle to light you to bed.*

Here comes a candle to light you to bed. The heel of a training shoe shoved backwards onto my nose – I'd caught up with the others.

Eight hundred . . . fifty-six more, a hatch as heavy as a marble hearth. The hatch swung; we tumbled into a furnace wind. I rolled under an onrush of sensations: outside, night, stars, smells of pinewood, fingers clawing into dry, short soil.

'We're too late! The bombers are here!' Harete? I couldn't tell; too much contusion and confusion in my head, too much concussion and percussion outside it.

WOMWOMWOMWOM.

Down came the chopper to chop off our heads.

Chapter 72

'Mopping up,' they called it. As if they were sponging up spilled milk – no crying, now – or juice. Big Sister had been wrong for once: Peacemakers had arrived as she'd predicted, but not in bombers, in choppers – helicopters, like the one that had virtually flattened us when we'd tumbled from the exit. The choppers conveyed *special forces*. I don't mean magnetism or gravity – the troopers inside the aircraft were commandos.

Well hard. Not in my league of course, but then I'm a member of special farces; I've led a harmed life.

Guess Big Sister must have died when we were stuck in the centre's intestines; she'd have snuffed it when her own juice was spilled. I . . . but she was only a machine. I think.

Mopping up; it meant scouring the centre for any members of the shadow cabinet who had survived, capturing the fighters. Disarming them. That was for later, the future. The immediate present was us, and a soldier with a white helmet and a medic's armband.

'Inhuman savages, see what they've done to these poor kids!' cried the outraged commando when he clapped his visored eyes on me and Harete. 'Look like they've gone ten rounds with a Kodiak bear.'

Harete and I black-laughed, knowing most of the damage had been done by us. One touch from the anti-Prince Charming and an amphora of deep, saccharine sleep glugged over us, molten macadam morphine sleep. *Sleep, uterus of universes, how I love you*. I plunged in as the medic pressed home the plunger.

Three baking dawns later, Harete and Moth returned home, back to the Other country. They rode the sky marines' last chopper out. Mopping up was done and dusted, the bad guys had been busted, the entrances to the underworld laboratory sealed up with doses of dynamite. The exits too – no fools, those fellows.

We said our goodbyes near the Cremator's decomposed dome, a squashed cobweb of aluminium struts and transparent hexagons. Here and there amongst the rubble I spied cheese plants and uprooted monkey puzzle trees and the dozing bulldozer. The butterflies had all fled.

'Goodbye, Moth,' I said, emotions on standby, heart in neutral. 'Back to Daddy now, is it? You've won, the twist was no match for you. You came to end the war, you did. Eventually.'

The Moth and Harete were sitting in the open door of the helicopter, swinging their legs over the side. Harete's arm was in a sling, Moth had a splint for his finger – miraculously the boy's only injury. Unless you counted his trousers.

'Come with us, Mo,' Moth implored, his voice high-low, high-low, a sonic city skyline. 'Even with all the leaders gone, the war could grumble on for months, like a diseased appendix. It won't die overnight. But you might. The last time we said goodbye, you were trapped. This time, you're free to come with us.'

I shook my head. 'Thanks, but I still say no. I don't want to be an emigrant, a migrant, an immigrant; I don't want to have to learn another language, certainly don't want to be fostered out or cared for. Or registered or educated. Can you honestly picture me going to some college, swanning about with a ring binder and a calculator, finding a job?'

'Don't see why not. Growing up's not so very bad. Is it that you're avoiding?'

'The opposite. I've spent all my life escaping, and that's just another word for running away.'

Who had told me that?

Didn't matter. 'The Fartherland might be not much better than a rat-raddled rubbish dump, but it's the closest thing I'll ever know to a home,' I carried on. 'Here I stay. Lonza had a dream of a quiet life in a secret valley; I'll live it for him.'

'What about your, um, condition? You've more than yourself to look after now.'

The skin under my fringe was chaste, free from geometric incursions. 'That fantasy,' I laughed. 'That dream. A living language? A civilisation nestled inside me? They might have believed it, you might, but I don't. You acted in good faith, I just about believe that, and the Numbers would have been murdered anyway.'

'And if I'm right?'

'If the gypsies don't like their new camp, they can always move on,' I told him.

Moth smiled enigmatically. He'd known I'd never leave. 'My father and I will bring justice to this country, one day,' he said. A threat, a promise, I wasn't sure.

Justice. Nonstop's essence resonated inside me, a version of him made from memories, from patterns and language. *Him*.

'Justice is like cheese, Moth. If you do lay it on, don't slice it too thickly, and make sure there are plenty of holes in it. People like me always need the holes to wiggle through.'

'Fair do. Mo?'

'Yes, Moth?' I sensed an end approaching, sniffed completeness.

'Gharials. The other member of the order *Crocodylia*,' he said, and he grinned at my stupefied face.

Harete spoke up, assaying the dome. The last of the heavy-booted legionnaires climbed aboard, the helicopter's turbines began to screech and howl.

'You'll never survive here alone, not with two hands and definitely not with one. You're mad,' she shouted. 'To think I was ever in awe of you, I must have had cicadas in my cerebellum. You're a stubborn crap-head, Mo. A total dick-stick. An arse-cake.'

Her brown hair flailed as the rotor blades above us caned the air; rosemary and vanilla effused towards me. Had she brought a supply, or was the scent intrinsic to her?

'You are,' I said, garaging my fingers in my ears and ducking low. 'That stuff you said, those words. You are.'

'No, *you* are,' she hurled back, her face screwed up, authentic contempt. Plain as sliced bread and margarine that face; didn't know what I'd ever seen in the mardy moo. Nice smell though.

I withdrew to escape the jumping dust and the crushing downdraught, heard the helicopter door being clunked shut. Some kindly commandos had gifted tools and food, a starter kit for my solo life. I sheltered behind their crated donations, startling a stripy stray cat. Hunched over, with my back to the screaming machine, I slipped out the final word on the matter. 'You are. Times a frillion.'

As it launched, the airflow buffeted me like a waterfall of wardrobes.

Eventually, silence.

I opened my eyes.

Two tatty training shoes, going through at the toes; occupying them, a young woman I didn't know at all, had never known, would never know. Thought I had a few times, was wrong on every occasion.

'You are,' she said. 'Infinity times, with knobs on. No returns.'

Chapter 73 *

Come back, prison. Come back, cell, guard, exercise yard. Bless you, barbed wire.

I miss you.

The nightly rotation of a key in a lock sings like a perching bird compared to the chain-gang blues that accompanies the daily turn of the sod. On Mo's scale of hardness my new life ranked a lowly one. I learned the hard way what many have forgotten they've forgotten, that the prisoner lolls in leisured luxury, it is the peasant who is sentenced to hard labour.

We assembled a shelter from struts and panels and whatever we could salvage from the dome. Harete's collarbone healed in weeks, then we had three good hands between us. I gaffer-taped a trowel to my stump, make that three and a half. The day we finished the shelter, the rains came. For forty days and forty nights, bulbous grey sky whales crapped hammers, and the mummified soil drank and was resurrected into fertile chocolate cake. The dome's basement held a seed bank, we hoed and we sowed. We built ledges to sleep on, a stove with a chimney from milk tins, and a stuttering extractor fan in the roof for when the pen became too stuffy.

Hut, I meant to say. *Hut*.

Our holding lay slightly to the south and west of the splatted paradise, so Harete named it 'S.W. Eden'. I reckoned 'Norway' would have been a truer name, for there was, I thought at the beginning, Norway we were going to survive. Fortunately, the war had broken the weather. We enjoyed a second summer that year, a corker, autumn and winter opting to miss a turn on the roll of a twenty-sided dice.

The Moth, or perhaps his father, kept tabs on us. Spy satellites? Those drones that flitted by like damselflies? From time to time, gifts appeared. A goat, and chickens in a cage. A box of bees, complete with an Italian queen. Seed potatoes. Endless bin bags, hurrah! They must have been parachuted in, although we never found the parachutes. Probably the goat ate them.

One day, a gift for me, a high-tech prosthetic hand, shades too pink but a snug fit. Via the magic of science or the science of magic the hand fused with the nexus of my nerves and responded to my thoughts, often in a mulish, contrary fashion.

One morning I said, 'I despise you, Harete. You were a fat fool to stay here with me. Today you must weed the goat and milk the radishes. You deserve better, you should be surrounded by computers and pocket telephones and you should study at universe-city and own more frocks than blisters.' My prosthetic hand socked me on the chin. Mixed messages, crossed wires, I'm sure those demon fingers responded to her thoughts, not mine.

From her pallet of straw Harete yawned and said, 'There's no lock on the door. Beggar off, I won't stop you.' Valley life suited her, she glowed with health, and that annoyed me too, because I was as stiff as a pit-prop from all the hoeing.

'There's no door on the door,' I reminded her. 'The goat ate it.'

One morning? Every morning. We fought, argued, groused, grumbled, spat pyroclastic words of lava and pumice at each other. The moody moo twanged my nerves summat chronic; in our compact shack we were always getting on top of one another, once even . . . but that's none of your business. Stiff as a pit-prop.

Living with Harete was an experience unlike being imprisoned with her, or escaping with her, or fighting alongside or against her. Not so very long before I had thought love was a cumbersome drudge to be suffered in solitude; then it had become bleach in the veins, something that blinded, burned, crippled and killed. For a while I had tried to will it into being where it was not. After that, I had riveted it into a reliquary and tossed it away, but the enamelled box had a surprise pudding propensity – boo, meringue!

There, sandwiched between the microscope slides of daily life, tested by observation and experiment, it continued to defy analysis. Screw down the objective lens, it squidged out of the sides.

I forgot all about it. Didn't hunt it, didn't avoid it. Didn't think about it.

The Numbers? What of them? If it was true they roosted in the interstices of my low thoughts, they did so humbly, secure behind their dykes in a mental never-netherland.

Occasionally, during nights when sleep coasted too deep for my hook, they signalled me on the cell phone, compelling my plastic fingers to tap out letter coordinates. Decoded, a typical stanza ran: *Sobibor, Kolyma, Treblinka, Magadan, Yodok, Babi Yar, Katyn, all fiction is truth, never forget, never forget.* The words I did not recognise, but I guessed what they were from the rat-a-tat-tat, cattle-truck rhythm, and the way the consonants cut the gums, like flossing with razor wire. Different words every time, remembrances of events past and future. *Nanking, Rwanda, Srebrenica, Darfur, Sy—*

They were a handful of handfuls of some of the more prominent cairns and trig points along the long path from Hell. The Camp and the Facility were but the newest.

Never forget, never forget.

Never forget, never forget.

Chapter 74

Time passed, as befitted an apparition.

My unsuckable techno-thumb proved green as well as overly pink, able to tap into horticultural know-how inaccessible to me, its nominal operator. Throughout the double summer and the misplaced seasons that followed, our smallholding evolved into a baroque, jazzy jungle of food and flowers, a tumescence of beans, buddleias, bougainvillea, bromeliads, blueberries, hollyhocks, horseradish, habaneros, hops, hibiscus and honeysuckles, to mention only the Bs and Hs. So many fish spawned in the moat the water became as frothy as camel spit.

Not nutmegs. I drew the line at them, threw the lime at them whenever I found their seedlings taking root in our rare earth.

One by one, we overcame our ignorance and difficulties in all matters. Day by day we harmonised a little better with the tempo, like a child learning to synchronise its pendular leg kicks so as to drive the swing to the highest altitude, gain the greatest rush. We acclimatised fully to living alone on our island in a lake on an island in a lake in a steep-sided valley in the hinterhills of the Fartherland. Love's bent alchemy never troubled us; the only casualty of that malady was a one-eared amphibious tank of a tomcat who forded the moats and hankered unreproductively after our own stripy ratter.

'No screws,' I said, chopping wood, another matter of metre. 'No escapes.'

'No parents, real or pretend,' sniffed Harete, milking a goat. De-milking it, rather. Three of them we had by then. We'd never talked about her time in the Other country, discussed what had transpired and misfired. There was no hurry. 'No courses or exams, no career choices. No worries!'

'No bombs, no war.'

'Or Mothodists.' True, both those observations, certainly as far as our remote neck of the glens was concerned.

'No questing, no questions. Harete, I –'

'Yes, Mo?' She teased me with an eye-smile. A lakeside choir of hollyhocks swayed in the breeze like holiday aunts on cider; the bee-rich air lapped me with a lardy tongue. An unknown number of deferred autumns were surely queuing in the wings; who cared, who cared? Harete had prospered on the fat of the land, she was tum-plumper than a hospital pillow and her cheeks were as red as hips and haws.

'I'm . . .'

'Don't jinx it, robo-digits!'

'Happy!' I burst out. 'The twist only applies to searching, Harete. Not to being,' I reassured her. 'Being is a point, not a loop. It's *the* point. You can't twist a point. Everything is stationary here at the origin, everything revolves around us. There are no more stories to tell. This is the end.'

Harete returned to the goat, I to the wood. Harete didn't slow her teat-kneading, didn't udder a word. Only once the

559

bucket was full did she speak again. 'I've a story, Mo. A story inside me, a story inside my story.'

'Then leave it there, Harete. Let it drop and rot.'

'Can't, Mo. This is a story that has to be told. And I want it to be heard, and to tell the tales it discovers inside itself.'

'Don't want, don't wish, the twist will get you!' I tsked and tutted. 'And no more of that stuffy "stuff inside stuff" stuff. We're done with all that, it was a temporary insanity, some consequence of always being locked up.'

'Mo? You're not listening.'

'Tell me, mardy moo.'

'When the restless are done dropping bombs, or probing inwards for the pips of matter, or prying outwards from our galactic leaf to chart the forest, someone has to unravel the spiral and start a new thread. The women, of course.'

Mistiming my blow, I damn near chopped off my falsie. 'What are you saying?'

'All that time you lived with the Numbers and you still can't put two and two together. Been meaning to tell you for months, only . . . I wasn't sure how you'd take the news.'

'What news?'

'I'm pregnant.'

Chapter 75

Don't ask me. I don't know; I've an average age of seventeen, I'm not an expert.

The Numbers. Sure as sugar tongs, it was all their doing. Some spooky action at a distance, some ethereal entanglement, I'll be bound. Mirrors and maths, that's how they operate.

All I've to say on the matter is this: someone, I don't remember who, once told me I had to map the nap of velvet.

Nah.

We're a hardy breed, Harete and me. Tough, wiry, coarse. We shed limbs like reptiles and amphibians abort caught tails, we go eyeball to eyeball in staring competitions with killer lasers, we chomp poisons, bathe in magnetic fields of Bs and Hs like you softies take spa baths.

Not velvet.

More like . . .

More like the baize on a snooker table. More like the sisal on a dartboard.

Slug hunting, weeks later.

Harete always told me to drop the molluscs in a bucket of salt, but I could never raise the gravy for it. (Harete it was who caught and butchered the rabbits; even topping and tailing a parsnip greased me up queasy.) I was using a catapult to dispatch the gastropods over the inner moat. Dropping one, I bent down to retrieve it. The kale was severely perforated. I turned over a few leaves to check for whitefly, blackfly, greenfly – the insect spectrum.

'The pitter patter of tiny feet,' I said to myself, flies and babies and other pests much on my mind. Then I spotted something in the soil.

A shoe print.

Smooth-soled, as made by a petite, pitter-pattering sandal.

Fractions.

Chapter 76

I tense up.

Something's snooping around, there between the compost heap and the chicken coop.

Fox or Fraction?

Tonight's ideal. A beacon moon and thirty silver stars, the first clear night of the month. This is the night I'd choose, if I were in their sandals, if I were planning an attack. This'll be a reccy mission, not the big assault, not for as long as . . . *shhh!*

Nah, that was one of the goats. Poor goats. Poor chickens. We should have slaughtered them, done them a mercy. The cats too.

The horses of autumn galloped in the same day I found the footprint, dragging wagons of weather behind them: gale, hail, frost, siling rain. Now, two months later, the days run short, and sunset comes early and fast. No later than six I'd guess, but as soon as I step into shadow I can no longer see my hand in front of my face. I strap it on anyway, working by feel alone, and tightly wrap my thin jacket around me. The sleeves and chest are stuffed with moss and dried leaves for insulation. Cold, it's bitterly cold tonight, mainly the fault of a truculent wind that spars with me, bobbing and popping and sucker-punching from every direction.

Where I thought I'd seen movement, I jab around with my makeshift spear, a knife taped to a hoe handle. Nothing.

Lately, I've been chewing chillies to keep me awake for twenty hours a day. Would do twenty-four if I could. Can't, tried. I've done all I can, but it won't be enough. Where once there stood bean poles, now stand sentry rows of sharpened spears, and covered pits and trip wires; for weeks I've been lighting fires at night, three fires placed at the corners of a triangle with sides of thirty paces. That's an international distress signal, for the benefit of drones and satellites and Moths. No help has arrived, too overcast I suppose. Won't light fires tonight, we're running low on matches and we need to save them for the stove.

I'd wanted to leave weeks ago, but we couldn't, not with Harete so far gone and the weather so bad. The surrounding mountains are already decked out in white skull caps; we'd never have crossed them alive.

We should have known.

We'd long suspected the Fractions' Domain was hidden in a neighbouring valley. They probably spotted The Moth's airdrops. The prospect of being recaptured by the bloodthirsty haemo-goblins does to me what salt does to slugs, whisks me into green foam. Fear runs a dragnet through my memories, returns me to a night around a campfire. We'd never known if Lonza had killed Two-for-Joy's companions or only maimed them. Alive, plotting revenge . . .

Our allotment might become our graveyard but not our

memorial; it's finished, defunct, all func gone from it. We salted and pickled and sugared and smoked and dried and blanched and jammed all we could reap. What a sour-tasting, heavy-hearted harvest that was; without the food we'd starve over winter, but we both knew we were stocking the Fractions' pantry, one way or the other.

We know what they're waiting for. We just don't know how much longer they'll have to wait for it.

We remember the respect they accorded Lupa. As long as Harete's carrying they'll hold off, but after that, we're unfair game. That's why Harete's confined herself in the hut, so they can't tell how far she's progressed. As for me? There's no magic triangle on me now, nothing to ward them off.

The plan is to wait until *after*, then slink away under shield of night as soon as she's able to walk again.

I hope it dies in childbirth.

You heard me. I hope it dies in childbirth.

Natural like, not at their strong, wicked little hands. Sorry, but that's for the best. The crying; if the thing lives they'll hear it crying, then we'll never escape.

My patrol takes me twice around the holding. Heavy weather ducts in along the steep-sided valley, soaks me with ropes of rain. I shelter against the hut.

Thump-thump-thump . . . thump-thump . . . on the wall; Harete's banging out a message.

Thump-thump-thump-thump-thump . . . thump-thump-thump. H-O.

What's that supposed to be? Must have meant 'MO'. She can hold her horses, cool her heels, I need to eyeball the demolished dome first. That's all of five minutes' walk away. Creeping through the birds' nest of capsized spars, I stop and start. There really *is* something moving here.

The earth is giving birth.

That's what I said. I'm looking at it, cloaked by gloam and rain, but not believing it. A monster is writhing and wriggling its way out of a gash in the ground. The soggy surface sucks and slurps it back down, but it perseveres, fights on, mewing and gasping. The creature is a mockery of a human, a pale clay shape, an emaciated moonlit mutt of marl and plaster, slimed with mud and gleet.

A Fraction! The being cries, heaves and breaks free, *flap-flops* onto the brash-strewn ground. At once, a second head writhes in the tight slit behind it. Twins, born of the soil itself. No wonder the Fractions were so fascinated by Lupa's pregnancy – they aren't human!

No. That can't be true; this is real life, that's real rain slashing my face. Observing, I oscillate like a human tuning fork: watch, run, watch, run. More heads appear, it's triplets, then quads.

I run.

I tumble down the slope to the hut, passing bricks in both senses. I'm sweating – no pepper grown could make me this awake. Whatever the Fractions are, I was wrong, the attack is *now*. Why?

H-O. Hut in sight, I work it out, understand why Harete signalled me in code.

Not H_2O, just HO.

Broken water, see?

Bloody Hell.

Chapter 77

I burst into our hut, bar the flimsy door behind me. 'They're here! Fractions. Coming up through the earth,' I whisper-shout. 'We've got to . . .'

Stop. We're not going anywhere.

Everything's going off, I gulp it all down in one look. The tin roof's lifting in the storm, threatening to become a kite, the cat's having kittens – not a phrase, she really is, that tomcat must have crossed the final moat – our three goats are inside, running amok. Harete's collapsed onto a mattress on her pallet; she's stripped herself off below the waist and is puffing out her cheeks like a set of bagpipes.

'You gutless streak of pus, I've been calling for you for hours! Where have you been?' she sobs bitterly, and her disillusionment withers me.

Labour's started. Her waters have broken. Our only hope is somehow the Fractions don't locate the hut in the dark; it's small and looks hardly different from the wreckage all around, being made of dome junk. *What to do, what to do? Why aren't I better prepared?* Country living's made me soft.

First, dim the lamp.

Now, Harete.

'I'll . . . I'll boil water!' I shout, and I bundle wood onto the stove.

'What for? You going to make a cuppa?' she shouts back. 'Don't need water, need *–owwwwwwwwww!*'

'Eh . . . eh . . . towels, then?'

'No time for sunbathing, you gitwit. HOLD MY BLOODY HAND. I hate you, I love you, I need you!'

There's a lot of that. But we have to be quiet; they're out there, stalking, *listening*. Harete understands, she chews on a gag I make for her, a wad of canvas. She balls her fists and wallops me, fists my balls. No anaesthetic for her or – OW! – me either.

'You have NO idea how much this hurts,' she says, spitting out the gag. I point to my branded backside, and to my amputation. 'What's this, a mosquito bite?'

Harete hisses, 'A hand. You lost a hand, that's all. I have to lose an entire person!'

'Shake a leg then, and get on with it,' I tell her. 'Don't just lie there, give birth, scab you!'

She can't. We've vague notions about the need for *pushing*, but nothing down there is happening. An hour or more of this – the candle clock's not accurate. All I can do is dab her and mop her, clean her up; rusty water's squirting out top and tail.

'Can you see anything, can you?' she asks me feebly, every minute. Not sure if she means down there or outside; I'm alternating between standing by her side, having the bones in my living hand crushed, and dashing to the shutter. Same answer for both portals: nothing to see but a hopeless, wet dark.

I'm way, way out of my depth, we both are. She rests, sips water.

'Can I sleep? Will I die if I sleep, will it?' she asks, but I've no answer, I don't know. Dumb shrugs and lip bites are all I can show her. The goats took care of everything all by themselves in this department, the cat's already suckling her kits and purring; nature's no teacher.

Another squall, and the hut roof grates and tears against the nails; freezing rain douses us. Through a gap, a bearded face with orange eyes and letter-slot pupils looks down, chewing superciliously. That's all we need – the goats have scrambled out onto the roof! Dead giveaway; I should have butchered them.

Hang about, all three goats are inside with us.

There's someone on the roof.

The gap claps shut. Harete senses crisis, she stops struggling. We become wax casts. Don't breathe, don't swallow, don't blink. For once in their capricious lives the goats play ball, stay rooted to the spot and don't bleat. It's dark in the shed; maybe whoever's above didn't see us, maybe they'll think this is an animal stall. I count to fifty. One hundred.

Harete can't hold out any longer, she grunts and strains again. I retake her hand, but this time she can barely squeeze my fingers hard enough to bruise them. Her hair is gummed to her blotchy face in matted, flaccid bands. I stroke them away and notice that her copper bullet eyes have degraded into sunken lead plugs; the lime that burns behind them is spent. Her skin looks spongy, porous; her vanilla scent is masked by stinks of vomit, vinyl and vinegar.

Right there, then, I see her freshly afresh. Naked, frightened, dirty, searing hot, she's as pretty as a grease blaze in an abattoir. She's never meant more to me than here and now. She is the very core of me, *I've found my centre at last!*

I never wanted to be cared for. I wanted to be the one who cared.

I never wanted to find my parents. I wanted to be a parent.

But she's dying. They both are. I know it. Or maybe it's already dead inside her. She said it was placid, didn't kick much. This is wrong, wrong, not how it's meant to be.

The great prize is to be twisted from us at the last instant.

Life's led me to this spot, just to dangle completeness and fulfilment before my eyes then trick me, kick me, deny me everything.

My mouth pressed onto Harete's swollen tump, I growl, 'Listen, pal, paless. If you're any child of mine, you'll break out of there right this minute. You've even got your own rope, that unbiblical cord thing. Get on with it, escape!' I rub my tired eyes, see sprite-like images of a forking flower called mother-die.

BANG BANG

One, two, three, four . . .

BANG BANG

. . . there's someone knocking on the door, or knocking it down. The corrugated metal bows where struck.

Rolling to the shutter, I glare out into the cold night air through mantles of rain, struggling to interpret the monochrome blurs. Those blind spots, remember? The hut has a dividing curtain, so I swish it across to protect Harete from the draught and to block out the lamplight, help my eyes adapt to the dark. With our luck, it'll be a door-to-door door salesman.

No! Outside I semi-see a white hemisphere bobbing about at head height. A Peacemaker's helmet – Moth's sent an army doctor; he hasn't forgotten us!

'About scabbing time, we –'

I've not fully unbarred the door before a man kicks it in and crashes through, sends me reeling. Another charges after, but these bruisers can't be medics, only things they've ever nursed are grudges and hangovers. A smaller figure sweeps in behind them. Of course, they're orderlies, he must be the doc—

Alderman Hyssop.

Fool, fool, the wolves were at the door. I've let them in to our house of tin without a huff or a puff.

'You!' Hyssop hisses as he lances me with his sun-bright, blue-white eyes, spearing me to the spot. His heavies jump to the corners, pan around with their cocked burp guns. All three invaders are wasted, ragged, slicked thickly with mud. Deprived of his absurd wig, Hyssop's head is a hairless globe coated in bright, chalky plaster, must be what I mistook for the Peacemaker's helmet. His knuckles are tightly wound around a thick wooden stave.

'Sweet, honeyed providence, I give fulsome thanks for your divine guidance. Now I will be so very cruel, as cruel as nature itself,' Hyssop brays. I get the full face-in-face glare, his signature performance. He tars me with his hatreds. He mustn't be able to believe his luck, finding me here.

'Why did you make the story end, eight six five? Why did you trick me, help The Moth fly away? Without him the story's no good, and I didn't want it to end. You've spoiled it all for me – it's *not fair.*'

He shakes me with sickening force, throws me against the stove.

'Not fair!' he says again, and he hammers me with the club, whacks my elbows and shins and ribs. I gasp and fold. He hasn't seen Harete, she's just the other side of that thin curtain; I have to let him wreck me and not give out that she's with me. Wreck me he does; I can't believe the weight of hurt each blow brings.

The hut door bangs wide. Before it gusts shut again, I see many more of Hyssop's troops. It was them I watched slithering through that hole in the ground, not Fractions! They've burrowed out of the sealed-up underground laboratory, come up through the ruins of the dome, shelled out like peas. Trust Peacemakers not to have done a proper job of mopping up. Hyssop and his followers must have been living like moles for months. The born-again men and women encircle the hut, waiting for their leader.

'Not fair, not fair!' Hyssop rages on. He whangs his stick around double-handed, busts up all our stuff, smashes our store jars, rips open our food sacks and sends iron-hard wooden splinters flying everywhere.

'My lovely story has spun out of control while I've been stuck underground. People are making new stories up for themselves; it's not how it should be. You have to suffer now. Let's see how *you* enjoy having everything taken away from you. You like that, eight six five? You like that?'

He grabs the cat. Blind foetal furballs drip from her underside, *splitty splat*. He throttles the animal, her eyes bulge from their sockets, but she's more serval than servile; she spits and slashes viciously at his face and skews free. Hyssop bats at her blindly, rips down the curtain.

Game's up.

Harete howls. 'GET OUT!' she screams, louder than any sound I've ever heard a human throat make, and I don't know if she means me, Hyssop, or the shock-induced, mace-laced doll head sliding out between her legs.

I reel. The cosmos has cleaved like a nut husk. There was before, now there's now. I'm only seventeen, give or take, but, but, but

I

am

a

father.

For how many more seconds?

Hyssop hops with prurient outrage, his lips froth bubbles, veins pump and bloat on his pate forming the outlines of continents and oceans. He wasn't expecting to find Harete, let alone *that*.

His avian face draws out, a linotype of priggish revulsion. 'What crib of vilest iniquity and obscenity is this? I shall purge, purge the sin,' he drools, saucer-eyed. 'Everything, I will take everything from you, this whore, your bastard.'

The stick shakes in his hands. He raises it above his head.

The mad herbalist is about to smash Harete and my quarter-born child to pulp, make me watch, then murder me. The act will be nothing to him; he's the ace of hate. His aides stand aside, smirking and tittering with lust and disgust.

Hyssop stops ranting, blinks, his fury leavened by awakening astonishment. His intention is triple slaughter, but he sees what he sees, what anyone with eyes can see. And he is his condition, an incurable mythoholic.

Betrayal is the foundation of the Fartherland.

I have to do it.

I am my condition also, an escape artist and personal physician to number one.

'My present, for you, your eminence,' I stammer, bowing, hands held obsequiously behind my back, all respectful like. Ideas can come like that, ready to eat, peel back the foil and serve. The key this time is visual, the writhing, amphibian anti-head that Harete's sprouted. *Salamander*, that's the launch word.

Words: pull a gun on me, I'll gull you with a pun. Chain me, cage me with law or story, I'll nix my fetters with a palindrome (never odd or even), axe 'em with an anagram, hex you with a wisecrack, then slide right through it. Word, sound, idea, the three are one, to love one is to love all. Salamander – from Moth, the myth: a creature born in fire. From Nonstop, the fact: slippery limb sacrificers, practisers of autotomy. All knowledge I file.

Hyssop nods dumbly, observing, computing.

'You see it, don't you?' I continue. 'The bride and the child of The Moth. Born in a stable, a . . .' Not my tradition; I can hum the tune but I don't know the lyrics. The un-sensing left hand, my false one, I pack into the flames of the lit stove behind me, push it deep between the incandescent logs. Simulated electronic pain erupts in me, but I can shut that off. Literally, there's a switch.

'Manger,' Hyssop prompts me, hoarsely. 'A byre.' The former corporal shimmies as he aggregates the possibilities, churning them around like a concrete mixer. In they go, a snippet of bunkum followed by a snatch of allegory, a hint of hogwash, a pinch of fable, truth's a trace element. Stir. Stories breed stories, the layers mix.

Harete's making her own potpourri, invoking every god and saviour ever known, name-checking the prophets and saints and pilgrims and gurus and devils. 'BEELZEBUB'S FAT FLANGES this HURTS why don't you HELP ME?' she roars through clenched teeth.

I ignore her, turn from my child.

'You'll never hold me,' I tell Hyssop, 'I'm tricky quicksilver – I break apart when spilled. Moth's too smart, too well connected. These two are the ones you want, Alderman. Weak and vulnerable. Controllable. Ownable. Create a new story around them, around this moment!'

Hidden from him, my hand is melting in the stove, the artificial skin softening like candle wax over the armature of titanium bones.

Hyssop *can* see it. 'The Moth's child. I'll raise it myself. The lynchpin of the legend,' he gasps, winding himself up. 'The new movements prosper, but they're directionless. This can be the story that knits all the strands back together.'

I stoke. 'You'll be midwife to the Fartherland!'

'The *Moth*-erland,' Hyssop corrects me. His gun-ugly, dead pebble eyes have that stadium stare again, his voice soars to public-address mode. 'A story to endure for ten thousand years. The helpless infant, the innocent mother –' Hyssop freezes in fear, stares at me. 'She *is* innocent, isn't she, eight six five?'

'Of course she is, sir. Help me deliver the child and save the mother. Then you let me go and take the pair of them. This time, there'll be no Cremator or shadow cabinet to obstruct you, only you to lead us now. You've purged your enemies, this is your reward.'

Harete's screaming, screaming, 'You rabiddogpigscabscum, you deserterverminslugcowardtraitorjerkbastard!' With every scream, the amphibian head enlarges. Harete hurls at me anything she can lay her hands on: coals, a knife, potatoes, a milking stool. Hyssop and his men duck as a demijohn of pickles rebounds from my head and smashes; I glance up, unbalanced.

For a sub-instant I glimpse again that horned, bearded face with slot pupils studying us quizzically through rents in the peeling roof. The wind delivers me a musky, pungent whiff. I dither, my course muddied by this second foe. The wild eyes gouge deep, disturb a spore.

{{{*Don't let yourself be distracted. Always concentrate on the matter in hand!*}}}

The matter in hand.

'Then we've a deal, Hyssop?' I ask, refocusing. 'We shake on it like men? The baby and its mother in exchange for my freedom, a story for my life?'

Hyssop breaks from his ecstatic contemplation of possibilities, holds out his hand, his right. 'A new story, a new testament,' he says. 'Deal.'

'Have to shake lefts. I've lost my right when you saved me before,' I remind him. I produce my salamander hand, my sacrificial dupe. Cooked to perfection, the substitute skin's on the brink of liquefying and browned enough for the colour to blend with my arm.

He copies me.

I grip Hyssop's left hand in mine. Harete bellows; the empathic hand has always been attuned to her thoughts better than mine. With that final contraction, Hyssop receives a bone-crusher handshake from my super-sticky flaming fingers. A flick of the wrist, the straps give, and I *twist* to execute an instant amputation.

I watch Hyssop's face for the two seconds the molten torment takes to communicate itself to his brain. Seven immense screams ring out, two burp guns roar; this time there's no magnetic field to retard the bullets.

The wind shears the roof from the retaining bolts and spirits it away. Something rare and raging and ancient drops down.

Part 11:

Afterwords

Chapter 78

Two graves I dug that surreal, cinereal morning. One was large, the other hardly bigger than a shoebox. A snuff box.

Not easy to incise those shallow ruts; a pickaxe is a dual-handed tool. The mountain resented my implanted offerings, rejected them. He girded his rocky soil with ice, dispatched a marauding wind to harry me with knitting-needle sleet. I picked on to spite him, to learn him who was boss, and put both my charges to bed. The brave fighter went in first, then the little one for whom there had been no time for me to love.

In the final analysis, the two had proved inseparable.

They'd have a grand view, I thought, pausing to cool down and cry some, right along the full length of the oesophageal valley to what had been our garden. One spring, perhaps, under a tart melon sun, that garden would bloom again, slow-explode into colour, sap and fruit. And the museum dome and the particle laboratory might be rebuilt, admit the happy curious and show them the virtuous achievements of artful minds.

For now, though, the garden was stiff muck and the dome was off limits; Alderman Hyssop and his surviving, un-mopped nasties lurked there, hunkered in their underground fury bunker, leaching their poisons into the groundwater. At the end of that chaotic night I'd watched him slither back, barely alive, burned, beaten, howling, my flaming plastic hand welded to his skin.

Shivering in the wind, I piled up two small cairns from apple-sized stones, scratched names and dates into slates. I didn't draw on any icons, not the crosses, crescents, stars of the older stories nor the pylons, wheels or blades of the new ones. The civil war had taught me the value of such signs: they were targets to aim at, all they denoted was division. Leave the manipulation of symbols to the mathematicians, I thought.

A dank, manky, faecal fog flopped down, grey as pigeon feathers, grey as school socks in September, grey as old mop heads and dried flies on undertakers' windowsills. I trudged away, grateful for every stitch and pang in every bone and organ, for the callouses on my palm, reminders that I lived. I stumbled up the mountain gorge, away from the dome, away from the unhappy valley.

Amorphous ghosts hailed me.

Part 12:

Afterbirths

Chapter 79 *

'Did you find them? After all this time?' enquired the first ghost, a shuffling, shapeless blob looming out of the dingy moisture. Even ghosts needed to wrap up warm. The poncho was really a blue blanket decorated with pictures of smiling steam trains.

'Yes. There was hardly anything left of Myristica; I think foxes and crows must have, you know, got to her remains. Shreds of clothes and a couple of bones, that's all. Lonza's body fared better, he'd landed in a tree.'

'And you buried them together? They'd have wanted that.'

'Side by side, yes,' I confirmed, 'And I angled the graves, not parallel, so they'd meet before infinity.'

The second ghost said, 'Eeeee awwwww.' Well, something similar. A fair trade-in, I thought, a low-mileage mule in exchange for our goats and chickens and cat, complete with her litter of savage ratters. Wicker panniers held our surviving jars of stored summer, pickles and preserves, enough to keep us alive and chillified for a couple of weeks.

The smallest ghost just went, 'Waa waa waa,' the limit of its conversation. It was wedged in a padded papoose made from an old duffel bag hung over Harete's back, punning one of my socks for a hat. Peeping out from underneath the sock I spied the lower side of a perfectly triangular birthmark.

The greatest breakout ever had begun.

Space was at a premium; the ghostling had to share the papoose with Dolly-with-two-arms. I'd carved the second arm from an old chair leg weeks before, not an altogether shabby job for a beginner.

'Don't ask,' I said. 'You were about to ask me again, and I still don't know who they were. Possibly they were the proper Fractions, cos the ones we'd called Fractions weren't Fractions at all, if you remember. They'd been observing us for months, that's for sure. The footprint I found was theirs. I reckon it was them rather than Moth who'd been supplying the farming gear and the free bees and all the other freebies. Only the hand came from Moth, I think.'

Construct your standard models, compose your theories both grand and unified, hunt for missing links and missing mass, for Bigfoot and for bosons. Group and class and categorise, and the very best of luck to you. Noble work, all of it. At the final reckoning, the *twist* will thwart you. There will always be something excluded from your catalogue, something that can't be indexed, something forever outside, unprovably unprovable, a story you never heard, a cheese you never tasted.

They were yet another tribe, that's all we could say. Crocodiles, alligators, caiman, gharials . . . there's always one more than you'd bargained for. Some island cousins, marooned in the hills when the suspect floodwaters of civilisation had risen and trapped them, generations ago. They smelled strongly of goat and when they tallied the bodies of those of Hyssop's men they'd killed, they counted them like fell shepherds record flocks: *Yan, tan, tethera, methera, pip, sethera, lethera, hovera, dovera, dick, yan-a-dick, tan-a-dick.*

I helped Harete into the driving seat – saddle, whatever, what do I know about mules? – and took hold of the rope, walking up front. We'd have to get a lick on, if we wanted to cross the hills by sunset, but for Harete's sake we plodded at a gentle pace. As she'd said herself, 'You try crapping out a bowling ball then going for a spin on a pogo stick.'

'Bloody hard fighters,' I commented after a while. 'Did you see how they savaged Hyssop's Mothodists? They made mincemeat from them.'

'I know, but I didn't accept any. I was too preoccupied in giving birth to see the action first-hand, *if* you remember,' sniffed Harete. 'They were good midwives, too. First-class delivery. You're out of a job now, Mo, of course. Your days as a messenger boy are over.'

'Good. Never wanted the gig in the first place,' I yawned.

Hours rolled by on squeaky casters; we summited. The view from the high, windy ridge was unreasonably pleasing. A shroud of yellow cloud rendered invisible all the disreputable trash of man and his insolvent, disregarded war. Only the peaks of the other mountains could be seen, poking up through the custard fluff in a fairy ring. Harete dismounted, began to breastfeed the pink maggoty thing in the papoose. The baby. *Our* baby. Scab. Did I just say that? I felt odd and wrong and had an urge to intensively study the toes of my shoes for some minutes, finding the sight horribly embarrassing.

Harete wisely sheltered in the wind shadow of the sturdy mule as she nursed. Seeing what a fine windbreak he made, I named the mule Lee. That set me to thinking, alert to a fresh item pencilled on my to-do list. I focused on the sibilations of the wind between the jutting teeth of rocks, listening with my iced-up, vermillion-tipped ears to the almost-words of the noises it made. A mule was a hardy hybrid sired from a horse and a donkey, wiser and tougher than either. A mixture, not an elemental animal but a horse-ore.

'Cinnabar,' I said. 'Our child's name. An ore of mercury.'

'Cinnabar,' repeated Harete, stamping her clogs. 'Hmm, nice ring to it.'

I shouted the name aloud, savouring the repetitions that glanced back at me from bluffs and cliffs and crags. 'Cinnabar!'

Cinnabar . . . Cinnabar . . . the 'C' was soft, like the first in circle.

'Hold on a mo, Mo,' cautioned Harete. 'What did the Cremator say? That's an ore of mercury and sulphur. If you're mercury, that makes me sulphur. So what you're saying is, I'm crumbly, yellow, and smell of rotten eggs?'

I sniffed hard. The air was not so pure as I had first thought. Perhaps the shadowy valleys concealed a damaged chemical factory belching out pestiferous fumes.

'Well, someone around here definitely does,' I said.

Harete sampled her armpits with her appealing, peeling nose, tested Lee the mule, examined the baby. 'That noxious niff's coming from Cinnabar,' she announced, and I took that as her acceptance of the name.

Names matter, which is why I admit to none and several.

The kindly, puckish warriors who had defended us had warned of a census being imposed by the Peacemakers now that the conflict was officially over. Envisioning queues and questions, I figured we'd decline to participate.

We moved on, as we had to, as you must, stepping out from the overhang of our own childtimes. We did not return the way we had arrived, for that would have been to repeat the circle, and no circle can contain the spirit forever, however it may be that mind is forged from loops. We pottered around the rocky ridge and broke free along a tangent, harvesting momentum in our hearts. We had no scheme, except to head to wherever looked greenest and least populous. We followed the line of some pylons, numbering them as we went.

Yan,

Tan,

Tethera,

Methera.

Minuscule Cinnabar gurgled, maybe enjoying the archaic counting and the polar gale. A sister for Cinnabar soon, I thought, more battles, more twists, more stories and always more escapes.

Elon Dann

Elon Dann grew up in rural Lincolnshire, where his childhood was one of 'sensational boredom and ordinariness set against eye-strainingly wide fields of barley on which V-bombers cast triangular shadows'. Television educated him, although he did attend the local grammar school for appearance's sake. At eighteen he left Lincolnshire for Manchester, where he studied Physics. For his PhD he worked on a particle accelerator in Hamburg. Science soon gave him up, and they have not spoken since.

Elon has worked in various IT jobs. He has a prime number of children and half as many wives and lives with them all in Worcestershire. At the weekend he enjoys voluntary litter-picking, 'sifting through the cast-off waste of society like a lanky Womble'. AWE OF MERCURY is Elon's second book, and you can follow him on Twitter: @ElonDann

HOT
KEY
BOOKS

Thank you for choosing a Hot Key book.

If you want to know more about our authors
and what we publish, you can find us online.

You can start at our website

www.hotkeybooks.com

And you can also find us on:

We hope to see you soon!